HEART OF A PAGAN

HEART OF A PAGAN

THE STORY OF SWOOP

A Novel by
Andrew Bernstein

Published by:
The Paper Tiger, Inc.
335 Jefferson Avenue
Cresskill, NJ 07626
(201) 567-5620
www.papertig.com

Cover illustration by Simon Federman
Book layout by Mark Van Horne

ISBN: 1-889439-29-0

The highest thing in a man is not his god. It's that in him which knows the reverence due a god.
—Ayn Rand, *We the Living*

Table of Contents

PROLOGUE

Some say there are no gods; that all we have are fables and empty cant. Some say there was a god once but he perished, leaving true believers to wonder why the spirit of consecration had fled, emptying their lives. A few sneer at deity and celebrate its demise. Some desecrate their temple; some abandon it, let it run down and go to seed.

Some devote themselves to god, but conceive him beyond their reach, a pure being on high, with a swarm of followers on their knees, a horde polluted by the transgression of another.

Some say there are no heroes any more; some say there never were. Some say that dwarves deserve more consideration than giants. Some say that cripples should be coddled. Some are cynics, holding human nature unworthy of reverence.

But not all live their lives in such darkness, devoid of light.

THE PRE-DAYS

In the beginning, a shadow lay over the valley. Ignorance and superstition afflicted the good burghers; they elevated false deities and darkness was on the land.

Structures had been erected throughout the valley, by denominations professing devotion to god. The buildings were crowned with steeples and ornamented with crosses. The denominations proclaimed meekness an ideal, mercy a virtue and man a sinner; they urged penance, suffering, service.

In the long night, many honest residents lost their way; they thought this creed their path to the sublime, and followed it. They knelt to pray, bowed their heads and begged forgiveness. Many accepted in-born guilt and banded faithfully into flocks. They sought a shepherd to obey and a savior to cleanse them. In their homes, on the walls overhead, loomed the black symbol of suffering.

The spines of the townsmen had bowed with their burden, their spirits lacked the bright fervor of the saints. Bold plans to assail the gates of heaven were no longer broached, and honor was ascribed not to daring but to disease. At the State Hospital, many gathered to comfort the sickly. It was not that the townsmen razed the shrines; they did not build any. A mere handful even conceived of one.

A restless few wondered what had become of the pioneer spirit that had once, long ago, settled the valley. But now, a spirit of enervation ruled; robustness and vitality were not prized; the last glow appeared to ebb in the western sky.

But one day, from the east, came the dawn.

CHAPTER ONE
THE SPIRIT . . . AND THE FLESH

It started like any other day.

I got up at six, two-and-a-half hours before the start of classes. The library wasn't open at that hour, so I spread out my books on the desk and immediately pored over their pages. It was the first day of classes in early September, but it was the beginning of my junior year, and one of the country's top graduate programs would be my next step.

I knew the texts that would be used for this semester's philosophy courses. I didn't need to buy them, because they were already in my library—Descartes' *Meditations,* Aristotle's *Metaphysics,* Plato's *Republic* and Locke's *Treatises on Civil Government.* Such books had been my only friends for a long time.

I looked up when the campus started stirring after seven. From my third floor dorm window I could see students walking slowly across the quad towards the cafeteria. You could tell the freshman by their halting steps, uncertain of the direction, their heads swiveling to take in the sights. Hoppo Valley State College was a small school in a town of the same name, a community of 30,000 tucked away in the southwest corner of rural Iowa—but with its respected programs in biology, music and religious studies/philosophy, it was the largest school, and town, that many of our farm kids had seen.

Morning classes were cake. Though they were 400-level courses, I had long since read the material and was already, in my head, writing critical essays. The professors knew what they had. They looked at me throughout the silent moments when they desired student participation, looked for input, insight and dialogue. But I kept my mouth shut. I hadn't forgotten high school.

The afternoon routine was the same as it had been for the last two years. I got to the gym at two, an hour before the players. Even though basketball practice wouldn't officially begin for another month, Coach encouraged his players to scrimmage regularly, to work at their weaknesses and to familiarize themselves with their teammates' style. Since the Hoppo Valley Crusaders had gone 3–21 the previous year, and were the perennial doormat of the Iowa Valley Conference, the practice was needed.

I was in my little cubby—the trainer's office—off of the locker room, unloading boxes of tape and inventorying medical supplies, when Freddie Zender entered.

"Duggan," the captain said. "How was your summer?"

"Good. I worked in my father's office and read philosophy. How about you?"

He shrugged his broad shoulders.

"Worked in the freight yards near home and tried to make time for my medical texts. Saw Kathy as much as possible."

I turned away and tried to read the label on a carton of knee and ankle supports.

"Made enough money to pay my tuition this year," he said.

"Great."

Freddie's family was poor, but he compensated by working harder than anybody else. Pre-med classes in the morning and early afternoon, basketball practice after class, Bible study following dinner, late nights studying with his fiancée—this was his day. If his work ethic knew any bounds, no one had yet discovered them. He was only six-three-and-a-half—small for the center position he played—but he was powerful across the chest and his legs were tree trunks. The heart and hustle with which he battled bigger men to a draw every night won him respect. The uncomplaining tirelessness with which he worked for the handicapped and weak made him loved.

"Prayer meeting tonight if you care to join us." His voice, though earnest, sounded subdued, abashed, a diffidence based no doubt on the two years of contempt I had returned to his proselytizing. I turned to face him.

"Kathy going to be there?" I tried for an impish glitter in my eyes, but wasn't sure I pulled it off.

He smiled sadly but respectfully.

"You know she won't. Kathy's God is different from everyone else's."

The players were coming in, and I could hear their raucous greetings after the months apart.

"Hey, you sorry lump," one voice said. "How the bleep are

you?" "Sorry lump?" came the retort. "Look who's talking. You're the one with a rear end so big, you can't drag it down the court."

I listened silently to the back-slapping greetings and good-natured raillery from which I was barred. Then I nodded at Freddie.

"I see your problem. A religious freethinker doesn't fit in with a bunch of Bible-thumpers like your crowd."

I didn't wait for a response, but turned to a newly-delivered crate of medical supplies. Though I got a good grip, my right leg, weak since birth, gave out when I hefted it—and I staggered under the load. Freddie was on me in a heartbeat.

"Duggan, are you OK? Here, give me that."

"No—" I started, fighting to keep my balance and my hold, but he didn't listen, just planted his sequoia thighs and lifted it from me like a toy.

"Where do you want it?" He turned to me, his eyes warm and solicitous, brimming with good will.

"How about planted on top of your groin?" I almost blurted, but bit it off.

"The top shelf," I said sullenly.

When he left, I wrapped my hands around the shelves' metal frame and shook it, wanting to feel as if my muscles, like his, could rip it from the wall. But before I could ask for the thousandth time the question of why a philosopher would be trainer to a team of muscle-bound ignoramuses, the locker room door flew open and a brash voice announced the dawn of a new day.

CHAPTER TWO
THE COMING

Hoppo to the heights now!" Swoop roared that afternoon when he walked into our locker room for the first time.

He swaggered through the door and slung his purple gym bag to the floor. All eyes followed as it skidded to a halt, then his laughter echoed through the lockers.

"Going to take this squad to the top!"

In the quiet that followed, the only sound was the sharp intake of someone's breath. Nobody spoke—it's possible that for several seconds nobody even breathed.

I couldn't see. I stood in the rear of the trainer's room, behind the table, away from the door opening onto the lockers. I stood transfixed, because of his proud boast unable to move nearer, but because of his brash vitality unwilling to turn away. Though I couldn't see, I could hear, and my mind somehow held a clearer picture than it ever had before.

He punctuated his words by thrusting his finger at the team, and several players backed off. He ignored it. He advanced upon them until he had several pinned against the lockers, then he swiveled to face the team. There was no laughter now and his voice sounded like he pronounced the elemental truths of arithmetic.

"I will change your lives," he said.

Nobody moved and everybody, even Coach, was speechless. I shifted uncomfortably behind the trainer's table. When I moved, the congenital ailment that afflicted my right leg since birth caused a sharp jolt of pain. It seemed stronger than usual. But the players neither knew nor cared what occurred in the trainer's room, because for now they all stood gaping at Swoop. After the ensuing scrimmage, such gaping became habitual.

Because of the team's long string of losing seasons, it was the butt of endless jokes in hoops-mad Iowa. Everybody—the players, the town, people throughout the Valley—hungered to see Swoop play, to see if this hotshot New York import could live up to his advance PR. He'd been the country's high school player of the year several years ago but, despite heavy recruiting from the major programs, had refused all offers and dropped out of sight. Rumor had it that he'd been playing invitation-only private games against pros. Nobody knew why he'd finally chosen a nowhere school barely on the map—but people's ignorance only fueled their imagination. One of the school janitors, not known for his sobriety, told me that Swoop had been incarcerated and, in a prison league season, had averaged 100 points per game. Speculation in bars downtown was that he'd been rejected from Duke and Kentucky for testing positive for performance-enhancing drugs—and a passing stranger swore Swoop barn-stormed the east coast, playing high-stakes pick-up games and never losing. In the days leading to his arrival, the stories whispered grew taller and the town's mood more feverish.

The players themselves were divided. Some expected to find a washed-up loser who had squandered his talent. But others had followed his high school career and remembered the state championships he had won. Nobody knew what to expect and the buzz was undeniable.

Coach didn't disappoint, playing him with the scrubs to see what he could do against the starters. The reserves had never beaten the starters, though they practiced against them daily, and Swoop grinned when Bobby Stenaker told him so.

"The last are about to become first!" he boomed, then added modestly. "Under Swoop's tutelage, of course."

On the game's first possession, he stole the entry pass to Freddie Zender and then rocketed upcourt. When defenders swarmed at him, he zipped a no-look, one-hop dart to Raif Lockett for a lay-up. On the next play, he swatted E.J.'s jumper off the glass, grabbed the carom while still airborne and hit the deck with both feet moving. He found Bobby Stenaker racing upcourt and fired a court-length strike like a quarterback to a streaking receiver. On play after play he sliced to the rim, breaking down defenders with breath-catching quickness, then skying over them for slams or dishing off for easy lay-ups. When he took point guard Drew Doherty incessantly off the dribble, Doherty—a barbell-hefting, beer-swilling safety on the football team—cursed in his face. When Swoop stated, his voice earnest, that "The gods prize deeds, not vulgar words," Doherty—certain now to lose his starting spot—fired a whistling elbow at his face. As the games wore on, and Doherty and the other defenders backed off, leery of Swoop's slashing thrusts, Swoop drilled jumper after jumper, singing "Make it rain!" as his high-arcing shot dropped softly from the sky. After two hours, a glassy-eyed Coach called a halt: the scrubs had whacked the starters five straight, spanking them worse with each game. Players on both sides just stared, and fans who had shown up for Swoop's debut scurried from the gym to report what they had seen.

In the locker room after, Swoop held court.

"No way this team's going to have a losing record again. Three-and twenty-four? That's bulls—t! Twenty-four-and-three this year—at least!"

He paced the room as he spoke. It was a small room befitting a low-budget team from a bush-league conference. It held only three rows of lockers, the small trainer's room and shower stalls in the rear. As its only adornment, a large wooden cross had been hung by Coach and Freddie Zender on the front wall next to the door.

He turned at the room's far end and strutted back, pointing at his teammates as he moved. Some of our farmboys were built like tractors—their girth should have dwarfed Swoop—but the room suddenly seemed smaller than it ever had before. He was lean, barely over six foot, with a litheness of motion that more resembled ballet than athletics. His hair was not quite blond, but a light brown, worn wavy and long in a style that contrasted with the buzz cuts of his new teammates. He had green eyes that, when he spoke, cut into his listeners more sharply than his words. He spat words like commands—this stranger and mere player assuming authority like a conquering general—and yet, what mesmerized me, holding my focus like a trap, was the gliding flow of his movement. But I woke in time to hear his final prediction.

"Next year," Swoop concluded, his voice low. "We're going to win the national championship."

Coach wrapped one of his paws around his shoulder and introduced him to each team member individually. I was last.

"Swoop, this is our trainer, Duggan Claveen."

He grabbed my hand and jerked me to him, so that our chests were inches apart. I was too startled to move and his eyes held me even more than his grip.

"Digs," he said, "I like you. I'm going to let you carry my bags."

I was aware in the abnormal silence that followed that his teammates stared with eyes too big for their faces. Freddie Zender's look was more a scowl than a stare. He frowned, this strong man who made time for hours of charity work in the midst of his duties as medical student and team captain—frowned at an overbearing creep who would treat as a porter a man suffering from a crippling birth defect.

But it wasn't clear in that first instant Swoop grinned at me—with current pouring from his hand and eyes like conduits—whether I wanted to swing at him or stand transfixed and bathe in the energy. I did neither. I stared at him—at the supple hips and ease of motion—and felt a hard resentment pulse somewhere in my gut. Who the hell was he to have so much when I struggled to heft up a flight of stairs an armful of hardcover texts? I jerked away, bristling at his arrogance, and sensed the soft glance of Freddie Zender on me, solicitous now as he turned from Swoop. After all, it was for me that they carried equipment, for me that they opened doors even when my hands were empty. Freddie's eyes told the story: I was the scrawny crip to be bullied by the cruel and coddled by the kind. Brusquely, I turned from him and returned to my work.

Although Swoop said nothing else, neither to me nor the team, his promise regarding the national title seemed a good bet in those first months following his arrival.

He dominated our daily intra-squad pick-up games, treating every practice like a playoff game. He rose hours before dawn to run, lift weights and shoot thousands of jump shots. When the pre-season games started, he single-handedly buried opposing teams, then bristled when Coach pulled him out, though we led by thirty.

The reaction, in this basketball-crazed state, was predictable. When we routed tough Bethel College at their gym, getting them down twenty before half and not letting up, the townspeople welcomed us home, meeting the team bus on Main Street, waving the school colors and pictures of Swoop. When Bobby Stenaker approached him seeking help, Swoop coached him regarding both conditioning and specific basketball skills. When several of the other reserves, weeks later, noticing Bobby's improvement, asked for the same, he formed them into a unit, dubbed it "The Swoop Troop" and demanded of its members the same exhausting regimen as his own. When townspeople saw them running in the pre-dawn darkness, some smiled, some waved, some called "National champs!"

They ran through the heart of town at the crack of dawn, Swoop leading some of the time, but more often dropping back, insisting that one of the others set the pace. But whoever led, they ran the same five mile course every day, Swoop pushing them along the town's busiest and most affluent streets.

The town of Hoppo Valley, though rural, did not lack for cultural life, for the state college on its western outskirts had an enrollment of 4,000 with several accomplished faculty members, especially in music and religious studies/philosophy. Music faculty members regularly gave recitals on campus and a small art museum had recently been established in one wing of the Humanities Building. The town itself, lying near the center of the valley, had the largest population for over one hundred square miles, and the rural hamlets surrounding it added a thousand more. The community was able to support a major newspaper and a small radio station.

The Troop ran the half-mile along Highway 40 to the business district, a well-maintained four-block stretch of Main Street lined with thriving shops on both sides. They continued past the stores, then made a left up Broadway and ran the "Salvation Mile," the roughly one-mile distance between Main and Walnut that was home to the Catholic and several major Protestant churches. At Walnut Street they turned right and ran the block to Douglas Avenue, the exclusive, tree-lined, north-south boulevard where resided the Valley's wealthiest citizens in a series of stately homes. At the corner of Walnut and Douglas stood the imposing stone structure of the First Episcopal Church, a sentinel guarding the elite's cherished values. Its extensive lawn curved gracefully down to the street on both Walnut and Douglas.

Although they conceded the benefits of such training, The Troop members still indulged extra-curricular activities that Swoop insisted hampered their development. Raif Lockett, the six-seven Nebraska plow-boy, a reserve forward, had a taste for a wide range of alcoholic beverages. Ricky Crockett, a willowy eighteen-year old freshman, immediately dubbed "Davy" by Swoop, idled hours in the rec room, hustling pool and pin-ball. Where others saw only that Davy was a skinny six-three, too small for the forward position he played, Swoop saw his smooth moves and soft medium-range jumper, and did everything he could to encourage his development. Dandy Halliday, Freddie's back-up at center, a self-styled homeboy from Lenox Avenue in Harlem, had cultivated, despite his strict Baptist upbringing, a refined fondness for certain illicit, though non-toxic substances. Bobby Stenaker, the lithe, sandy-haired Montana cowboy, a five-eleven shooting guard, characteristically kept late hours—and with a variety of female companions. Swoop didn't preach to them; he merely lived clean and dragged their rumps through the streets at five A.M. Slowly, imperceptibly, and not without back-sliding, their hedonic tendencies began to wane. Coach, who fully agreed with his friend College President Robert MacPherson's frequent denunciations of vice-filled campus life, smiled warmly when Swoop was near, and gave him, without prompting, a key to the gym.

One Saturday morning in late October, Raif was severely hung over, and Swoop struggled to wake him up. When several minutes of lusty pounding at his door succeeded in waking half the floor but not Raif, Swoop added a song to his onslaught. I lived near the end of the third-floor hall that housed many team members, six doors down and across the corridor from Raif. I'd been up till three A.M. reading, and had fallen asleep with the Ross translation of Aristotle's *Metaphysics* on my chest. When Swoop's clamor woke me, the reading lamp by my bed still burned. Swoop's voice sang jauntily, though off-key, as the wood of Raif's door vibrated under his attack.

"Oh, it's great to get up in the morning when the sun begins begin to shine! Four and five and—"

"Shut the hell up, you sick bastard!" croaked a surprisingly firm voice from next door to Raif's room, giving vent to a generally negative evaluation of Swoop's serenade. But Swoop ignored the catcalls and continued his concert.

"—six o'clock in the good old summertime! Even when the day is rainy—"

I groaned and rolled over, wrapping the pillow around my head. But it couldn't deaden the harsh sound of a door banging open at the other end of the hall near the stairs.

"I got a shotgun in the truck, boy!" shouted a voice with a distinct redneck twang. "Just for assholes like you!"

By the time Raif finally opened the door, Swoop had half the floor threatening his future and the other half cursing his genesis. Raif didn't sound pleased either.

"Damn, Swoop," he groaned. Bystanders said he was white as he clapped his hand to his head. "Run five miles now? I think I'd die."

Swoop paused, and his words were so soft that I couldn't hear them, and was told only later.

"You just might, Raif," he said.

But the groans were louder and more widespread when Swoop turned to admonish the on-lookers.

"You should be striving for achievement," he said. "Not sleeping your lives away."

While Raif staggered back inside to get dressed, Swoop shooed away the crowd, ignoring their complaints about being awakened before six. Several minutes later, they set out from the dorm's side entrance for their five mile run. Raif, unable to keep up, limped along painfully in the rear. I, as I often did, sat at my desk by the window and watched.

Word soon got around that, rain or shine, in sickness or in health, The Troop worked out every day. Dozens of locals started attending team practices, some even watched the extra-curricular workouts of The Swoop Troop, and the sports editor of the local paper predicted in his pre-season preview that we'd climb from the cellar to the penthouse of the Iowa Valley Conference. Several merchants downtown displayed the team's picture in their windows, conversation in the local bars centered on basketball, and pre-season ticket sales were the strongest in school history. Local interest in Hoppo Valley basketball, high even when we lost, was rising.

The Dean of Student Life, J.T. Pearsall, caught the scent in the wind. He had long sought recognition for Hoppo Valley among the member schools of the Iowa state university system, and he immediately paid more attention to the basketball program. He had his picture taken with Swoop and Troop members, attended all exhibition games, traveled to road games on a school bus decked out with "Hoppo to the heights" banners, and increased funding for advertisement of team games. The result was that school administrators, leading merchants and even town council members began attending all home games.

But the ascent was not without struggle.

It was in the pre-season, during a pick-up game one Saturday afternoon, that Swoop challenged the starters. They still refused to work out with The Troop, and I had heard them criticize the newcomer's arrogance on more than one occasion. After soaring over the much taller E.J. and pinning his lay-up from behind, Swoop jerked down the rebound, darted up the far sideline and smashed home the game winner. He turned to his beaten foes.

"You got to go stronger around the rim, guys, go up and slam it. Work out tonight with The Swoop Troop and I'll show you."

"Listen, Hotshot—" E.J. began, but Freddie cut him off.

"We've got a prayer meeting tonight," he said.

Swoop's patience was limited.

"Forget the prayer meeting!" he exploded. "We'll make our own miracles."

E.J.'s face turned red and he glared. The others watched calmly, silent, looking to Freddie for their cue.

"We'll pray for you, Swoop," the captain said.

He motioned the others to leave, and when they turned and walked away we all thought that was the end.

But when Swoop strode that night into the First Commandment Missionary Church—Judas Bittner's home base—he found them on their knees.

"On your feet!" he roared.

He strutted down the aisle in long, gliding strides, clutching a basketball in his left hand. There were four of them, not just Freddie and E.J., but the core of the team. They rose as Swoop approached, the same question in eight eyes, but Swoop answered it before any of them could speak.

"You're searching for God," he said. "But He's not here."

When one of them retorted, "How would you know?" Swoop replied, "Because I know God better than you do." When they stared blankly, he pointed out the door, which he had left open.

"He's in the gym," he said. "It's where we're going. Now."

He didn't wait for a reply. He turned on his heel and started down the aisle.

"Maybe we don't want to practice with you," one of them protested.

"Good," Swoop said, whirling to face them. "Because this isn't practice."

"No? What is it?"

"Worship," he said, then resumed his march to the door.

He stopped at the last pew at the rear of the chapel, where a lone figure sat, observing, taking notes, doing field research for his Comparative Religion class.

"Big Brain," he said to me. "Philosophy major, student extraordinaire, IQ near genius." He paused. "But a sad, pathetic little wannabe."

I put down my pen and carefully laid my notebook on the empty pew next to me. I looked into the green eyes staring at me.

"What do you know about me?"

Swoop laughed. But he didn't smile.

"You're not the only one who does research. You, too. To the gym now."

I sat in my pew, feeling the way a raccoon must after being flattened by a car. But the guys, though bewildered, didn't hesitate. They knelt again, re-opened their Bibles, and led by Freddie, read: "'Beware of false prophets which come to you in sheep's clothing, but inwardly they are ravening wolves. Ye shall know them by their fruits. Do men gather grapes of thorns, or figs of thistles? Even so every good tree bringeth forth good fruit; but a corrupt tree—'" outside the noise of the dribbling basketball exploded through the clapboard chapel like tremors of the earth rather than sound waves.

The four worshippers stared as Swoop surrounded the chapel like a marauder, chanting his battle cry, "Hoppo to the heights!" But when they confronted him outside—four giants towering over his slender frame—they didn't get the resolution for which they hoped.

"God doesn't favor insolent boasters who strut into the chapel," they said.

"They're the only ones He favors," he replied.

"You shouldn't disrupt a man's worship."

"You shouldn't worship false gods."

"You speak blasphemy."

"Or gospel."

They had no answer, only three blank stares and a scowl, and when E.J. started for him, Freddie wrapped his arms around his teammate and jerked him back.

"That's an end," the captain said.

"It's a beginning," Swoop said. "The end is when your souls are saved."

He took one look at me standing in the door, then walked away. The five of us stood in silence and watched his back.

But though his sauntering gait took him out of sight in moments, it was not that easy to forget him. His departing glance had lingered on me. But why? I was not one of the players. I couldn't work out with him and contribute to his grandiose quest. It made no sense that he had asked me to follow. I told myself that it also made no difference, that I desired no part of either him or his pretensions, but for several days I couldn't shake images of him from my mind. Though I bridled at his insult, it was neither his words nor his final glance that stuck in my mind. It was only the gliding motion of his departure.

Although the starters refused to work out with The Troop—then or ever—the story of Swoop breaking up the prayer meeting was soon all over town. What the town didn't know, what its residents had no way of knowing, was the meaning behind his departing words that day.

Two days later, when the players walked into the locker room after their last classes, they found the wooden cross gone, taken down and replaced by a huge poster of Hermes, the wing-footed lord of the wind, depicted in soaring flight, sword drawn, head high. "The patron god of athletes," Swoop said. "He'll stand by us throughout our championship run."

When he held workouts at Healey Park—replete with appeals to Athena for wisdom and to Zeus for strength, alternated with the pounding practice sessions of The Swoop Troop—dozens of townspeople showed up to watch.

And when he spoke before hundreds of thronging fans at Homecoming, a crowd including several Religion majors and a pair of ministers, proclaiming that "the gods demand of champions the two 'Ps,' Prowess and Pride," he got several raised eyebrows but more than a little applause.

Any objections on campus were referred directly to Dean Pearsall's office, whose trained staff smiled and told protesters to set aside their convictions in the interest of solidarity of spirit. There were mutterings of dissatisfaction expressed during Religion classes and, especially, at the Bible study sessions led by Freddie Zender. But nobody directly confronted Swoop until an evening in late November just before the season started.

I left the library that night after three hours of research for a paper on the contrasting evaluations of pride held by the Greeks and the Christians. When I saw Swoop coming up the stairs, I realized that this was the one place I had not seen him—and had not expected to. I started to hurry as best I could down the steps, but when several of the students talking outside the door pointedly raised their voices I slowed down.

In the dark I couldn't make out faces, but when the light glinted off of several metal crosses worn outside their sweaters I guessed they were members of the Campus March for Redemption.

"Guess there's no prayer meeting tonight to break up, huh?" one voice said loud enough to be heard.

"Maybe he got Dean Pearsall's office to do it for him."

"Hide your crosses, gents," said a third student, grabbing his in mock alarm. "I hear he sacrifices Christians in the Coliseum."

Swoop had been angling toward me, cutting off my escape, but turned away, veering straight toward the dissidents at the first sound of protest. As they snickered, he sauntered up to them.

"This must be the inaugural meeting of the Swoop fan club," he said mildly. "Why don't we meet indoors, where it's warmer? The gym's a good place." As I peered closely, I noticed that his smile had never been friendlier.

They stood silently staring at him, and as I inched closer I could make out their faces. I knew a few by sight, but having scrupulously avoided such groups that combined sanctimonious proselytizing with turn-the-other-cheek humility, none by name. Though I counted five of them, nobody spoke and a few shifted their weight uneasily as Swoop calmly watched. Finally, someone said in a heavy tone, "Nobody's talking to you."

Swoop's reply was immediate. "Talking about me's talking to me. You got complaints, let's hear them."

"Wait a—" somebody started, but was waved to silence. A tall boy in a sweater that bore the navy and white school colors stepped forward. He looked no more than sixteen, but his expression and tone were earnest.

"It's wrong to talk about someone," he acknowledged, speaking more to his friends. But turning to Swoop, he added, "God doesn't make complaints. And He doesn't make out personalized warnings to those who sin."

"No?" Swoop responded, with a perplexed look. "Does He at least make house calls?"

Involuntarily, I suppressed a laugh. If Swoop heard me, he didn't turn, but when they stirred angrily at what must to them have seemed mockery, he quickly moved into their midst. "Because I do," he said, swiveling to face each individual in turn. "And we will go to places never dreamed of in your Bible."

Though the words "he's mad," flashed through my mind, I couldn't hold them because the racing of my heart made thinking difficult. The raptness of his tone was unmistakable to anyone searching for religious fulfillment, but his audience couldn't correlate his tone with his content.

"Someone please pray for him," one of them pleaded in honest pain. "Because I don't think I can."

Slowly, with newfound dignity and without another word, they walked down the steps and away from the library. Nobody else was present.

When I started away, my motion must have awakened Swoop from his reverie, for he turned quickly to me. Though it took me a while to get down the stairs, I felt his eyes on me the entire time, watching the difficulty with which I navigated the steps. He said nothing, and he didn't laugh, but it was only hours later, after a long bout with Aristotle's *Nicomachean Ethics,* that I was able to shake the feeling that his glance was like a line with a hook at the end—and I was a fish with it fastened in my gills.

But real dissent didn't start until the season got under way.

We won our first two games at home, no-contests before screaming thousands in which Swoop averaged fifty and shut off the opponents' leading scorers like turning a faucet. Our first challenge came on the road against Jabez College.

Jabez was fifty miles south of us in a rural, redneck community, a fierce little place full of liquored-up hellraisers. They had a decrepit rathole of a gym with dim lighting and a narrow court; they sardined twenty-five hundred sweating farm boys into their bandbox stands, raising the air temperature to a sweltering level; and their gym's low ceiling pounded that hooting mob's cacophony into the skulls of opposing teams. Typically, their xenophobic mentality welcomed visitors like outland invaders come to rape their women.

The Jabez fans howled as soon as our players—with their names stitched across the back of their jerseys—came onto the floor. The second they saw number 12 with the bold red letters proclaiming S W O O P, they became a jeering mob, starting a chanting drone that lasted all night.

"S-W-O-O-P! D-O-O-P!" they screamed.

The player introductions began, and when Swoop's name was announced the crash of the loudspeaker was drowned by that frenetic howling.

"Doop! Doop!" washed down from the stands. A rubber bone bounced onto the floor, the universal symbol of a "choke."

"Hey Swoop," I hollered from the sidelines. "Your fan club's here!"

He smiled a face-splitting smile, laughing purely, gaily at the

din. He looked up at the teeming stands, childlike fervor lighting
his face, and with both hands to his mouth blew kisses to the crowd.
He was in his element now, charging lines of energy held back,
poised on the brink of explosion.

It didn't take long. The opposing center outjumped E.J. for
the tip, but Swoop anticipated like a jungle huntress. He cut in
front of their guard and swiped the ball like a carnival pickpocket.
But when he whipped it behind his back to Freddie streaking down
the lane, the captain's lay-up attempt was snuffed in a tangle of
hands and arms belonging to Jabez's hulking swat team, setting
off a fresh roar from the crowd.

"Little pukes," they sneered at our players, and later, after their
brontosaurus-sized center established low-post dominance, they
screamed "Snack time!" holding gum drops to their mouths and
raining jelly beans on our heads.

Their front line averaged six-feet-ten—a trio of plodding Cly-
desdales—and their grazing ground was under the basket, where
they banged the boards all night. They muscled aside our smaller
guys and played volleyball off the offensive glass.

On one possession right before half, Swoop dropped low and
soared, swatting their center's shot from behind. The ball rico-
cheted off the rim and was snatched by their six-nine power forward
on the other side. Leaning in, his bulk drove E.J. back, and for
one instant he had an open look. But Swoop sprang from the other
side of the rim, hovering high over the basket, and smashed the
shot downward. It crashed off the shooter's head, bouncing high,
and when several of our fans shouted "Eat it!" they were silenced
by menacing looks from the crowd. Their other forward, six-ten
with the wingspan of a South American condor, grabbed the ball
in the lane and went right up over our guys for two.

"Box him out!" Swoop cried, but his words could barely be
heard above the hellish screaming.

The place was overflowing, and the fans spilled out of their seats,
milling onto the sidelines, screaming, hooting derision, gesticulating at our players. Their big guys fed on the frenzy and charged
the glass like bellicose dinosaurs, grabbing rebound after rebound,
tossing aside smaller men like stuffed dolls. At one point, after the
brontosaurus jammed home an offensive rebound, three of their
fans raced onto the court to mouth obscenities and jab their fingers in the faces of our players. Swoop opened his arms for a hug,

but our other guys backed away before security hustled the fans off.

Coach called time-out three times trying to bolster morale, but it was hopeless. Our guys' heads were down under the barrage and the crowd was getting to them. They feared for their safety— it was in their eyes as they clung together—and they were getting whipped at both ends of the floor.

But not Swoop. He rose above the fracas like a flying artist on the trapeze. On fire now, he threw in shots from every spot on the floor—or rather, from every spot six feet above the floor, from every angle imaginable. He broke the Jabez press single-handedly, racing the ball upcourt, a whirlwind of motion that shed defenders like storm-tossed debris. He ignored their jump shooters and dropped into the paint, swatting shots and clutching precious rebounds. He clapped backs, pumped his fist, roared encouragement. He leaped into the passing lanes, stole the ball repeatedly and slashed upcourt for bone-jarring slams. He didn't sit the entire game. At half, he had twenty-nine and we only trailed by three.

In the locker room at half, Coach bawled them out. Swoop sat by himself in back, eating oranges and shooting the peels into the trash. He leaned way back, his legs hanging easily over the bench in front, and looked at me. He smacked his lips in satisfaction, though he didn't smile.

"Ambrosia," he said.

For one second I ignored Coach to glance at this sneaker-clad Caesar. I almost went to him then. After the second half, nobody could refuse to.

Coach pulled him aside right before start of play.

"Get them involved. Everyone's got to get involved!"

On our first possession, Swoop brought it up the middle of the floor, then cut for the right sideline. The Jabez defenders had given up trying to trap him, so when he beat his man with a whistling spin, he was wide open at the line. But instead of drilling the shot, he flashed down the lane, drawing defenders like rats to cheese. Bobby was open on the wing, and Swoop zipped a no-look strike through traffic that hit him in the chest.

"Shoot!"

But Bobby was nervous. He hesitated and his shot, when it came, hit the back iron and arced outward toward the hungry carnivores below. Swoop set his jaw, took one stride down the lane

and exploded into the air. He soared cleanly over the carnivores'
backs, got his fingertips on the ball but, instead of tapping it rimward, flicked it toward Bobby on the wing.

"Again!"

This time Bobby went straight up and drilled it clean.

Swoop whacked his butt and chattered at him all the way downcourt. At the other end, the ball squirted free from their two-guard,
was scooped by Bobby, who whipped it to Swoop. Swoop knifed
to the hoop, eyes seeing only rim but, with the all-court command of a field general, left it for a trailing E.J., who crammed it.

"Great pass!" the scrubs on our bench sang, but Swoop was
back across halfcourt, exhorting his teammates to play defense.

Swoop slashed to the basket from every spot on the floor—
from the baseline, from the wing, from the key—on the break,
against the press, in the half-court sets—from the opening seconds of the half to the buzz of the horn at game's end. Nobody
was quick enough to stop him. They could only gang-guard him,
leaving guys open, teammates found unerringly by Swoop's passes,
which flashed through the melee to their targets as if laser-guided.

Nobody had seen such a display of point-guard play, not even
in professional games on television. As the game wore towards its
climax people forgot the score, the clock, the rivalry and other
irrelevancies, all they could do was watch Swoop play. With no will
and no choice they sat on their hands and stared, silent, motionless, all derision forgotten, and when the buzzer sounded they
sighed audibly, not because they'd lost, but because their glimpse
into something sublime was ended and they had to go home and
exist in its absence.

We surrounded him in the locker room. Nobody spoke, but all
gathered at his locker as he undressed. When he had stripped off
his sweaty clothes and stood naked before us, he looked up. All he
wore was a gold basketball and chain around his neck.

"Converts?" he asked simply.

Though I looked around, noticing that many turned away and
only Coach, standing alone in the doorway of the visiting staff's
office, stared with eyes gleaming, I couldn't escape the realization
that he looked at me. He was still looking as I moved to the trainer's
table.

We received a hero's welcome when the school's bus returned
to Hoppo Valley. The small Hoppo Valley radio station had always

broadcast the school's games, but now virtually the entire population, not just a sizable segment, was listening. Close to one hundred met us on our arrival. Within a week, after two more convincing wins, Swoop and Coach had been interviewed on local radio, and the town's newspaper, *The Daily Independent*, had run a feature story on the team. In Iowa, where every basketball success is news, the former sad-sack team in Hoppo Valley was becoming closely watched. The high water mark of media attention was Swoop's interview on KBUZ, "The Buzz," the area's most powerful station, located an hour-and-a-half away in Des Moines.

Ron Zatechka had an aggressive, in-your-face talk show on weekday mornings. His style was simple and non-sectarian: he insulted everybody. "Get up, farm boys, and milk the damn cows!" he boomed before dawn. He condemned Hollywood, Washington, Moscow and the Vatican. He hated politicians, journalists and Presbyterians. He brought ministers on only to abuse religion. He scorned all causes but one—Zatechka—and knew only one god: more volume. He was short and hard and spent hours pumping iron. He chain-smoked cigarettes, talked through the smoke and blew it in environmentalists' faces. He hated bankers and clergymen. He lived alone, had no friends and called his fans "imbeciles." He denounced liberals, Christianity and Wall Street with equal zeal. He refused the governor an interview and berated the mayor daily. He hated movie stars and professors. He called local militias "fascists." He swore, told sexually offensive stories and insulted homosexuals. He was damned at cocktail parties, charity functions, Sunday services and Republican fund raisers.

He had the most popular radio show in the state.

"What you going to do, kid!" he roared. "Turn the town on its ear?"

"Or stand it upright."

"Take these pig-farming clods to the top and be a hero?"

"When they get to the top they won't be clods."

"Yeah, touché. Pretty sharp for a dumb jock." He fired a butt from the stub in his mouth and leaned forward, breathing smoke.

"How long?" he asked.

Experienced listeners followed his sharp transitions, novices floundered. Swoop didn't bat an eye.

"Next season," he said.

"And the year after that?"

"We win the title again."

"You're a cocky bastard. How you going to take these Iowa sod-humpers to the top?"

"Practice. Every day. Weekends too."

"Yeah?"

"Uh huh. Got the gym reserved. Saturday and Sunday mornings. Some weekdays too. We scrimmage and play teams from town. The public's invited."

Zatechka snorted. "Think these hen-house yo-yos want to see you? They're in church on Sunday morning."

Swoop's voice came soft next to Zatechka's.

, "So are we."

Zatechka was silent for the first moment of his radio life.

"God help you," he said.

The following Sunday thirty people showed up at the gym. The next week, after two more Hoppo Valley wins, the number surpassed fifty. After a month we were eight and zero, held first place in the Iowa Valley Conference and the gym was crammed with a hundred lunatics waving banners and action shots of Swoop.

But not all the attention was positive. Until this point, the town's clergymen had ignored the growing hoopla, but with church attendance starting to dwindle, some began to notice. Though none yet openly denounced the Swoopmania growing in the Valley, the talk around town was that more than a few had expressed misgivings privately to parishioners. Beyond that, the pastors of the established churches did nothing at first.

But when Swoop held a "Celebrate Self" party several days before Christmas, they regarded it as a declaration of war.

He announced it to teammates, fans, students and townspeople at Sunday morning practice three days before the event. Though I avoided Swoop's practice sessions, and was at the library at the time, dozens of students were there, and their description of Swoop's words was soon all over campus.

"It's the Saturnalia," he told them. "The Roman festival of the sun, the triumph of light over darkness, of Spring over Winter, and of fertility."

He walked the length of the gym as he spoke, dripping sweat from more than an hour of hard practice. Troop members lay sprawled in the middle of the floor, sucking huge draughts of air during the break, and fans crowded both sidelines and the baseline nearest the door, standing two and three deep against the walls.

There must have been a hundred of them and Swoop monitored their faces as he spoke.

When they stared blankly, he was among them, laying hands on their shoulders, swatting their butts, working the crowd like some politician demented on earnestness. "In your lives," he stressed. "Not just in your team. It's a quest for excellence."

They didn't understand what he was getting at, it was in their eyes, they had only the vaguest inkling what they were in for. But Swoop had his gym bag with him on the stage beyond the baseline farthest from the door. In a heartbeat he grabbed it, rummaging among spare sweatsocks, a clean tee shirt and a towel until he found what he was looking for. Brandishing a paperback copy of *The Iliad*, thrusting it like Achilles might a dagger, he stalked the center of the gym floor.

"Hector," he said. "Odysseus, Diomedes, Achilles—heroes. We can be like them in our lives—not warriors, but brave enough to go full bore after what we want." Though he swung around 360 degrees to face them all, his eyes urging them as much as his words, he still received as many perplexed glances as excited ones. But by this time there were some who'd follow him on a second Crusade to wrest back the Holy Land. And a few understood. They contributed money and they came.

He held it at the Sacred Assembly of the Father Evangelical Church, a poor denomination on the edge of town from whom he'd rented space. He approached me that day before practice.

"It begins for you tonight."

I'd ignored his cryptic comments and hints for months, but now I had a scissors in my hands, tape in my mouth, half a dozen behemoths lined up at the trainer's table and no need of a religious crank trying to save my soul. I spat tape and whirled on him.

"I'm at the library tonight—studying! I'm not going to some sacred shrine."

I turned back but there was no escaping his words.

"Aren't you?"

It was several seconds before I caught his meaning and then it was too late to face him, for though I'd heard no sound I knew he was no longer there.

The party began at eight. I skipped dinner and arrived at the library before six. I pored over Aristotle's *Posterior Analytics*, taking careful notes, immersed in my world, in the essence of what was me and when, at seven-forty, I glanced at my watch, observing the antsy feeling starting to sprout within, watching it with the clinical detachment of a trained logician, there was one element of the bastard's character that couldn't be dispelled. Not the arrogance, the prodding words, the cocky laugh, not even the athletic gifts or unquenchable drive that could not be denied. These could be, if not scorned, at least set aside, held in abeyance, viewed as part of another man's world. But the eyes, the eyes that never laughed, never smiled, but only burned, even as his raucous laughter rang across a room, the eyes that saw nothing but what he wanted out of the world and a path that cut through obstacles—those damn eyes could haunt a man. But only if he shared the same soul.

I didn't shut my books but left them open on the table, to be there when I returned, tonight or tomorrow, left them open because what had to be done now was not a halt or even an interruption but only the smooth continuity of an unbroken life-flow.

The church was at the other end of town. Like its rivals it was a small white building made of cheap plasterboard. Swoop had removed all of its religious ornaments and had, in their place, a single adornment hanging above the altar: an artist's rendition of Odysseus before the mast, driving towards Ithaka despite ten years of struggle against gods and men.

There were close to one hundred people there, students, townspeople, fans from across the area jamming the chapel's narrow confines. Most didn't know each other, but many did. People talked in animated clusters, their voices rising with the excitement of the moment. An expectant air filled the room, and many people smiled at strangers, but I stood by myself in the rear and spoke to no one. The crowd hushed when Swoop mounted the pulpit.

He wore jeans, sneakers and a black rugby shirt. His hair was even longer now, reaching almost to his shoulders, its light brown shade contrasting with the shirt. Many of the men wore jackets and most of the women dresses, but tonight there were no thoughts of dress code, hair style or other matters of convention. One hundred pairs of eyes were fixed on Swoop, waiting.

"My life," he said, "is dedicated to being the best."

The room was hushed as he spoke, the fans rapt as they stared up at him. Most of those in attendance had seen him play, so they had no difficulty following his meaning.

"We're done losing," he stated flatly. "We'll win now—the conference, the district, the nationals. To carry a losing team to the top—it's the secondary reason I came here."

The quiet way he spoke, his eyes alight but not smiling, made the claim a realistic statement of fact, not an outrageous boast. The listeners were with him, so caught up in his drive toward the title that I'm not sure it occurred to them to inquire regarding his primary reason.

"We will learn to expect notable deeds from ourselves—like those of Theseus and Aeneas, like Alexander and Hannibal and Caesar, like all of the mighty heroes, real or fictitious, that I've spent my life studying. From them, we'll draw inspiration—but it is to ourselves that we will dedicate our triumphs. In basketball and in every aspect of our lives."

He paused, his glance sweeping the room, his voice quiet but clearly audible.

"You see, the purpose tonight is a celebration. We have no music, no food, no drink—but we are here to celebrate. Admission to this party isn't free, either, even though we've charged no money." He leaned forward, pointing at individuals, sweeping the crowd, and people didn't back away. Safe in the rear, near the door, I still felt an urge to turn and exit. More shocking was the simultaneous urge to walk to the front and join him. "The price," Swoop continued, "is to stand—in public but alone in the cathedral of your own soul—and venerate the goals and drives that are the essence of each of you."

He spoke briefly for several minutes more—of his achievements to come in the pros, and of Literature, of how he had weaned himself on the poems and epics of the great heroes of the past. But his voice broke when he spoke of one person, a girl he had known once in New York, though he mentioned no names. When he concluded, there was no applause, not even a whisper, only the silence of men existing for once with no barrier between them and the sacred truths of their lives.

Slowly, haltingly, one-by-one, they followed his lead, ascending to the altar to stand before the crowd, alone with their dreams, faced by a multitude for once not hostile, but glowing with the spirit of the first speaker and the man in the painting above; liberated for this evening from the shackles of convention, and in this one moment of hushed observance they held forth and whispered their aspirations, speaking of hopes in education, career and love, some weeping, some shaking, but for at least this one instant of their lives all willing to stand revealed. And when it was my turn, I neither backed off nor fled out the door, but walked unhesitatingly to the front where—feeling his eyes on me—I bragged shamelessly of the knowledge I had gained, of earning the straight "A's" I received, of the interest shown in me by the Princeton and Yale graduate programs, of my future career as philosophy professor and Aristotle scholar, and of the erudite books on the *Metaphysics* and the *De Anima* I would write. For five inebriating minutes I spilled my guts and bared my soul. But there was still one aspiration I omitted.

We were at it for hours. And when we were done, nobody left, though it was the wee hours on a work day; we milled around speaking to former strangers who were now intimates, even those who had been shy beaming now amidst the crowd. Nobody was tired, nobody wanted to leave, we only desired to cling to the intoxicating, elusive feeling of freedom to love ourselves.

But not everybody responded in the same way.

One hundred enthusiastic voices quickly spread the word through town—and a number of throats opened to reply with something less than enthusiasm. "He removed the cross from the chapel. Can you imagine?" said one minister appearing as a guest on Ron Zatechka's show. "Thinking of only yourself on Christmas—and in a church?" asked my Religion professor in class. "Is this an attack on everything held as holy in the heartland?" queried a letter to the editor of the town newspaper.

Swoop's supporters fired back on all fronts. Fredric Westegaard, editor and publisher of the local paper, *The Daily Independent*, wrote on the editorial page a fervent defense of the right of every free man to seek passionately after his own personal happiness. Westegaard was a fervent defender of the First Amendment and, more broadly, of an individual's Constitutional right to pursue his own fulfillment. He was regarded as a pariah, even an apostate by the Valley's more fanatical residents, because he embraced any cause upholding a man's right to live as he chose. He made clear in his editorial that he saw in Swoop's "Celebrate Self" party a means to advance his own cause. Judging by the increasing crowds at The Troop's practice sessions, a significant segment of the Valley's population agreed with him.

I personally felt no compulsion to answer my professor's criticisms, but Kathryn Gately did not agree.

"Where better to think of yourself?" she asked, her question a challenge to the teacher and the class in general.

Kathy was a Religion major whose red hair flamed only slightly less brightly than her passion for the sublime. Despite her family's allegiance to the Church, her zeal for God was more catholic than Catholic. She believed that God rewarded only a personal quest for spiritual insight and improvement that questioned every rule mandated by religious authority. More than once I had told her that in the Middle Ages she would have been burned as a heretic—and her impudent smile never sparkled as brightly as when she responded: "But you would have joined me—right?—so I wouldn't have suffered alone." Now, I missed the professor's scholarly response, because my ears still heard only her words, and my eyes saw only the mouth that uttered them.

Swoop ignored all criticism. On Sunday morning he told two hundred championship-crazed fans jammed into the gym that "we are the vanguard of a new faith, the creed worshipping an individual's own loves," and that "after we win the title, the members of other churches will see the light." He proclaimed: "We must recognize that for each of us to embark on a championship crusade in our own lives is to follow the only true religion." The crowd stamped and whooped throughout The Troop's ensuing workout.

Others, too, stamped and whooped when *The Daily Independent* printed Swoop's words on page two. These included some fellow students on the Hoppo Valley campus. Members of the Campus March for Redemption advertised their Wednesday night meeting, usually reserved for Bible Study, as a response to the threat of what they termed a manic presence in our otherwise Christian community.

I was torn. I wanted to hear what the Bible-thumpers said—wanted to study it as part of my on-going research and because it represented a counterattack against Swoop's thrust into the Valley. But what did I care about Swoop's goal to transform the community? I had enough in my life to keep me busy. Sure, I had attended his "Celebrate Self" party—and yes, I had even been temporarily moved—but every time I saw that swaggering creep glance at me with his knowing look—half pitying, half projecting himself as my redeemer—I wasn't sure if I wanted to kick him in the stomach myself or root for the Bible brigade to sweep him out of town. Or, perhaps, to root for a turn of events very different.

I didn't go. I stayed in the stacks of the library basement, immersed safely in my studies, determined to ignore the ruckus that his activities had kicked up. But when I overheard Freddie Zender describing it the next day to two of his friends at lunch, I immediately sat down and swamped everybody else out of the conversation with my questions. I realized only later that the creep's influence extended to me as well.

Freddie's description was vivid. The meeting was not held in the CMR's small office in the Student Life Building. Rather, they had received permission to hold it in Marian Auditorium, anticipating a large turnout. In fact, they drew thirty-three students in addition to their fifteen full-time members. The lights were dim in the auditorium, to underscore the somber mood, and the first person to speak was the young leader—whose name turned out to be Rodger Huntford—that had confronted Swoop earlier on the steps of the library.

Huntford was as young as he looked—sixteen to be exact—and had graduated with honors from Christian Calvary Prep in Des Moines. Tall and slender, with light brown hair worn short and close to the ear, he looked like Swoop except for the haircut. Like so many in this burg, he suffered from a severe case of earnestness.

"It's Christmas," he said, reaching out past his comrades to the other students who had joined them. "A time to be thinking about love of God and our fellow man, not about ourselves. An all-night reveling in self-indulgence, and in a church, at precisely this time of year is a deliberate and decadent mockery of every principle held dear in our community. We cannot let it go unopposed."

Huntford's quiet words were echoed by the message of the other CMR members. Most of the students agreed, and they decided to draft a written statement for College President MacPherson, urging him to look into those extracurricular activities of students that blasphemed against Christian teaching. The school authorities, the group believed, must be a vigilant watchdog regarding the moral character of its student body.

Early Tuesday morning, when dozens of fans lined up outside the gym to attend The Swoop Troop's extracurricular workouts, they found themselves joined by a silent group of picketers, who filed past them solemnly, hoisting placards that read, "Lost Sheep: Return to the Fold" and "Sin is not an Achievement." When Swoop approached the gym entrance, they called to him, "The Savior loves you." He stopped and looked sadly. "But does He love you?"

I tried to ignore the religious hubbub. As a man dedicated to logic, I had no use for the bizarre beliefs and zealous holy wars of those committed to faith. Although I had been raised in rural Iowa, the son of a small-town doctor, I had been frightened by people who talked seriously of burning bushes that spoke and virgins who gave birth. All of the biology, chemistry and physics courses I had excelled in as my high school's valedictorian, and as a pre-med major my first year at Hoppo Valley, only confirmed my commitment to observation and science, and my rejection of unthinking unbelief. Now the guardians of conventional faith were beginning to stir up the flocks against this brash interloper who preached his own brand of resurrection. I tried to turn away from it, to immerse myself in schoolwork and forget the religious agitation. I succeeded, anyway, in filling my life with the study of secular philosophy.

The turmoil accelerated after the college paper printed a story about the protest, including a photo of the picketers circling the gym. *The Daily Independent*, which treated Swoop's attempt to win national gold as the biggest story in recent Hoppo Valley history, picked up the story and ran it in its news section. Dean Pearsall, who had issued a national press release regarding Hoppo Valley's hold on the conference leadership and its design on the national title, could not be described as happy. His office informed campus groups that picketing would result in the revocation of funding and in their decertification as recognized university organizations.

A pair of irate parents called the Dean's office, the campus paper printed several letters of protest, and a DJ on college radio labeled the Dean's act an un-American suppression of free speech. When Pastor Buttle of the First Episcopal Church called for student groups to picket not the basketball team but the Dean of Student Life, an *Independent* columnist seconded the idea, Zatechka drove to Hoppo Valley to interview both and Pearsall began moving toward the center of the storm swirling into Hoppo Valley.

Then Judas Bittner addressed the faithful. He was a student at Hoppo, though older than most, having spent years as a missionary in Brazil. As the star preacher for the First Commandment Missionary Church, he lived for and by only one thing—the Bible.

Some regarded him a saint and others a lunatic, but I avoided him
altogether. For several months he had lain low, saying nothing about
the heathen presence taking root in his home territory, awaiting
the propitious moment. He spoke now, though he still said nothing about Swoop. But then, according to some, he did.

It was at Bible study, in a midweek sermon delivered before
twenty-five members of the flock at the First Commandment Missionary Church. Freddie Zender, E.J. Speed and several of the
team's other starters were there, though none of the reserves. Bittner, a lay preacher and a Religious Studies major at the college,
extemporized on his favorite passage in Judges. He was short and
slight, though possessed of a powerful voice that often boomed
through the narrow confines of the ramshackle church. When he
spoke of divine justice, he pulled up to his full height and, with
the unconscious pride of a devoted man of God, seemed to speak
down to his audience from on high. He spoke of Samson now.

"What this nugget of God's word shows us," he said, his voice
modulated, barely above a whisper, "is that any weapon, so long
as it is employed against an onslaught of the Philistine, is sanctified by that alone." Witnesses said that a hush fell over the church,
as it often did when Judas wrestled with the profundities of revealed truth. An air of expectation filled the room, as if the listeners
sensed that an insight of great moment would imminently be un-
veiled. Judas lowered his voice further, making his listeners work
to earn the wisdom he bestowed. "Even so prosaic an instrument
as the jawbone of an ass, in the right hands and wielded against
the true foe, becomes an instrument of retribution. Jawbones and
slingshots," he concluded, "can fell even the most vainglorious of
the heathen."

Most parishioners remained calm, but several members of the
Hoppo Valley basketball team started to rise, shouting "Amen!"
Freddie Zender was able to restrain all except E.J. Speed.

But Swoop had unlikely supporters, as well as detractors. One
day after practice, as I left the gym, I saw him standing on the
stairs leading down to the lawn and the walkway to the cafeteria,
engrossed in conversation with a slender woman in a full-length
camel's hair coat. Swoop listened as the woman did most of the
talking, emphasizing her points with an occasional touch on his
arm. Though uninvited, I approached them with no hesitation.

Janet McMenamin held a Ph.D. in Psychology and was the
Valley's only psychotherapist. She was a member of the university's

adjunct faculty, and regularly taught an upper division class in Clinical Psychology, which I had taken two years previously, though I was only a freshman at the time. She was also outspoken, challenging many of the community's beliefs and, predictably, had made enemies. In her quiet way, she stood up to them all. She smiled warmly at my approach.

"Hello, Duggan," she said. "How's the star student?"

"Good, Dr. McMenamin. How are you?"

Though not tall, she was an athletic woman in her late thirties with a rich head of hair that flowed gracefully to her shoulders. She spent most of her spare time outdoors, gardening and biking, so that her face and arms were brown from exposure, contrasting with her blue eyes and red hair. Her private sorrow, she often said, was her lack of height. "But then," she added, "brains and beauty are not bad compensations—are they?" She had a quick smile and was slow to anger, but could be merciless towards those who made the mistake of provoking her. The past year, in an auditorium full of hecklers, she had given a talk on abortion rights. When several of Bittner's followers accused her of supporting the practice of baby butchering, she responded unhesitatingly that it was unfortunate abortion had not been a legal option in their mothers' day.

She half-turned so that her glance and conversation included us both.

"Remember what I said," she stated, reiterating her point to Swoop and filling me in at the same time. "People know what they love. Even those whose lives are floundering. If they're directionless, it's not because they lack knowledge of what they want. It's because they lack the courage to acknowledge that they want it. I see it in my practice all the time. Events like the "Celebrate Self Party" can give them the inspiration they need." Her hand took Swoop's arm in a gentle grip, and she smiled self-deprecatingly. "I'm no guru to tell people what to do, but I hope you'll continue."

Swoop stood motionless as she held his arm, and if he looked toward town, not at her, it was because the understanding they had established seemed at some level deeper than a glance required.

"Inspiration is what I do," he said in a tone so devoid of guile or self-consciousness that for one second I wanted to hug him and, shocked, I turned quickly and faced the psychotherapist.

For several moments she was silent, then she released her grip on his arm to wipe her eye.

"Great things are ahead for this town," she said softly. She shook her head, as if to get back from some vision of her own to the present moment. "Though, to be as honest as you, I must warn you that I will use you to push my own agenda."

"I'll trust your agenda, Dr. McMenamin," Swoop responded immediately. "Anytime."

"But you just met—" she began, then stopped. "Yes, I suppose you would." She smiled wryly. "You also know full well that now I have to live up to that."

She turned and walked away.

In the midst of the town's upheaval came our conference showdown against Huntington State.

Their only loss had come against us at their gym, a game in which Swoop poured in twenty-five in the first half and we blew them out. They remembered, and came stomping into Hoppo Valley like gunslingers in a two-horse town.

"We'll deck him, he gets hot on us," Tetzel, their power forward, had said in a radio interview. The editors of *The Independent* plastered that promise all over the paper's sports pages. Local fans spoke of assaulting the Huntington bus just outside the town line and hundreds arrived at the gym early, drinking beer in the parking lot and waving banners with drawings of Swoop.

But some residents wished secretly for Tetzel's threat to come true, and others came to the game to cheer Huntington. A dozen picketers ignored Dean Pearsall's warning and circled the gym, hefting posters that read, "Bittner and the Bible" and "Swoop, Pearsall, Satan: Hoppo Valley's New Trinity." A fight broke out with local fans, one shattered a beer bottle on a picketer's skull, and the Hoppo Valley police sent every available man. Several belligerents were dragged off by the cops, the injured picketer rushed to the hospital, and the Huntington team escorted to the locker room. Campus Security insisted that our players also receive an escort.

"Since when do our guys need protection at home?" a fan asked as the players ducked through the mob. "Since God's gift got here," E.J. shot over his shoulder and walked on. Freddie said nothing but walked by his side, eyes staring ahead, the veins of his neck straining like wires.

The day before the game Swoop had approached me in the library. I had an hour between lunch and my three hour intensive in Ancient Greek and I was at my usual table, barricaded behind rows of texts, poring over a volume of Aeschylus, engrossed in translating *Prometheus Bound*, when a shadow on the page caused me to look up.

"Why don't you make some noise when you approach people?" I snapped, the sight of him immediately engendering rudeness in me. He was unruffled.

"Would you hear it if I did?"

"I'm not deaf."

"No, not deaf," he said.

He stared at me with a solemn look befitting the enterprise in which I engaged, but trespassing, boring holes in some private part of me.

"Why do you badger me? You see I'm busy. What do you want?" He waited patiently until I finished.

"You know what I want."

"Tell me."

"Your soul."

He could have been asking to borrow my watch, he spoke so simply, and it was his very openness that demanded a depth of authenticity to match it.

"You can't have..." I started, but knew suddenly that I could achieve greater honesty with this man than with any other, and started over, finishing in a whisper, "You have it already."

He let those words hang in the air, silence as his acknowledgment and tribute, and as he waited—staring at me like we stood in a temple—something cracked inside of me, some wall erected to keep him at a distance, and tears welled in my eyes.

"You're moving toward a bad end," I said.

He took that in too, but for him warnings were only open declarations of alliance that represented further opportunities.

"Men on a sacred quest are disparaged by non-believers," he said. "You belong with The Swoop Troop."

"I know," I said, helpless to deny it.

"We work out every morning at five. Weekends too. You're the trainer."

He didn't wait for a nod or even a grunt, but turned and started away. Then he stopped and turned back to me. "No one else will do."

"Thank you," I said, so softly that he couldn't hear it.

As I watched him stroll away, my eyes went to his hands, the hands that surprisingly were too small to palm a basketball but which I had seen many times efficiently tape the ankles of his comrades. Some half-formed thought stirred within, questioning whether The Swoop Troop required a trainer. But when the logic asserted that I needed his ministrations far more than he needed mine, I pushed the thought away before it spawned an anger that threatened the fragile bond just formed. The bastard knows it, a hard voice within me said. True, answered an equally-implacable voice, but he's not the only one who knows it—is he?

But that evening, when a fellow student in my Comparative Religion class repeated Judas Bittner's words, several in the class nodded and I looked up from the text to see Kathryn Gately pin the culprit with her eyes.

"Yes," she said. "Jawbones and slingshots can be sanctified weapons. And Mr. Bittner is right. Samson is a religious hero—a mighty man showing us God's will." She paused, and the insolent derision of her voice was directed at neither the Biblical hero nor her classmates. "Can you think of anybody like that in the community today?"

And though her question silenced them, some quality in the room made me want to cry out.

"Where does Swoop live?" I blurted to her in the hall after class.

"Swoop? I'm not sure." She laughed, a glittering sound so full of vitality I almost forgot my fears. Standing next to her, the fragrance of her hair filled my nostrils, as her tall, slender shape filled my eyes. Whenever I looked at her, I saw far more than a brilliant student and tireless activist for religious freethinking. I saw her paintings—the sales of which financed her way through the Religious Studies Department—of the most robust, intensely-alive scenes imaginable; especially those depicting Freddie Zender in action, straining, battling, reaching heavenward against taller foes. I looked away, unable to forget those scenes of her fiancé in action.

"I only see him running at the crack of dawn," she said. "Try the top floor of the highest dorm." She paused, and when I looked back her eyes as well as her words mocked me. "After all, it's closest to Olympus."

I asked around and found that her guess was accurate. Making only a quick stop in my room I went, for the first time, to visit Swoop at home. I rejected the elevator of his ten story dorm and opted instead to hobble to the top floor. In my right hand I carried a copy of *The Iliad* in its original.

CHAPTER THREE
THE PILGRIMAGE

B eware of Greeks bearing gifts," he said when he saw what I held in my hand.

"It's not a gift," I said. "And I'm not Greek."

"And I've nothing to fear from you."

"No, not from me."

I looked around his room and though, seconds before, I would have professed ignorance regarding what I expected to find, on seeing it I knew better. This was exactly what I expected to find: not a basketball, a pair of sneakers or an athletic poster in sight; but a desk littered with books—copies of *The Love Songs* of Sappho, hard-bound volumes of Homer, a copy of *Ovid*, one of Virgil's *Aeneid* and myriad editions of mythology. Piled by themselves as in a place of honor under the lamp rested several beat-up and well-used biographies of Alexander by modern writers familiar to Greek scholars—editions of Droysen, Tarn and Wilcken. The room was softly lit, the overhead light was off, only a reading lamp burned on the desk and another on a nightstand by the bed. The walls were bare except for a lone painting: hanging in a frame facing the bed was a print of Turner's *Ulysses Deriding Polyphemos*. In the semi-darkness, Ulysses's torch flared more brightly, mocking his disabled foe.

Swoop stood in front of me, wearing only a tank top and gym shorts. The gold chain and basketball medallion he wore around his neck had slipped outside his shirt and lay still across his chest. I pointed to it.

"What's the meaning of that?"

"It's a religious symbol." His eyes sparkled mischievously as he spoke, but there was a firmness in his tone that showed he was serious.

I just nodded.

He lay back down to resume his reading, and I noticed the battered, heavy textbooks next to him on the bed. Shamelessly, I stuck my nose into his business, picking up one of his books. The way my eyes bugged was a philosopher's equivalent of a whistle.

"Kinesiology?"

I was familiar with the subject. My father was a small-town doctor and—for years, until my freshman Humanities courses shifted my interest to Philosophy—I had sought to emulate him. Many hours I had spent poring over the texts in his library at home and asking him questions.

Swoop said nothing. He just watched as I leafed through his texts, as I observed the underlinings, the margin notes, the dog-eared pages, as I read his comments on this study of anatomy in relation to human motion. "Work the latissimus dorsi with one-arm dumbbell rows," he'd scrawled. "Support the back by developing the rectus abdominus, the transversus abdominus and especially the external and internal obliques." I looked up.

"You exercise based on this?"

"Every day. For hours. Working on all muscle groups—for flexibility, for suppleness, for power."

I was at his desk, reading snippets of sentences, questions spinning so rapidly through my mind that I could barely comprehend what I read, and only my years of medical background keeping me from utter confusion. Then I found the inscription at the front. "For Swoop, the greatest ever, only the top will do—Jonathan Lefkowitz."

I looked up.

"You know Jonathan Lefkowitz?"

He said nothing. But the faint smile that turned up the corners of his mouth was an answer.

"You study kinesiology with the greatest authority in the history of sports medicine." It wasn't a question, there was no rising inflection at the end of my statement, for despite the blurring before my eyes it all made the most exquisite sense. When I looked back at the text, I noticed what Swoop used for a bookmark—a white business card with plain black lettering that read simply: Jonathan Lefkowitz, Sports Medicine. The phone number had a New York City area code.

I clutched one thick medical text in my hand and had the other one opened in front of me. My eyes scanned ceaselessly the literary titles strewn across his desk and I leaned way back in his leather easy chair, taking off my shoes, placing my feet on his desk as if I owned the place, though careful not to disturb the books. He watched me, the quiet acceptance in his eyes underscoring my right to this ownership, of him, his books, his soul. My eyes focused on Tarn's two-volume, *Alexander the Great.*

"I've read Tarn's biography, you know."

"And?"

"Scholars find it too idealistic. No 4th century Macedonian thought of uniting all races into one brotherhood of man. They say it's too noble and grand-scale. Especially for one twenty-two years old."

Swoop's eyes gleamed at me.

"What do you think?"

"It's pretty far-fetched."

"And conquering the mighty Persian empire?"

I looked away.

"That's far-fetched, too."

Swoop let those defeatist words hang in the air.

"We'll see," he said quietly.

We said nothing after that. I leafed through his volumes of mythology and examined his kinesiology texts. The stories of Theseus and Heracles recalled my high-school literature courses, and Swoop's anatomy books my first year pre-med major before classes in Greek Civilization shifted my interest to philosophy. Minutes went by before I disturbed the silence.

"What's the plan?"

"We work out every morning. Coach gave me the keys to the gym. We meet there."

I nodded. For a long time I didn't move, but rested quietly in my chair, caressing my book, until I heard Swoop's voice from what seemed a distance.

"What?"

"I said it's a lot of time. Will it take you from your studies?"

"Nothing will take me from my studies. Ever."

"You'll get it done after?"

"After, before, during. In the dead of night, if necessary. It will get done."

He nodded, satisfied, and we said nothing else.

As I sat, surrounded by kinesiology texts, works of classical literature and a print of Ulysses celebrating his triumph over a merciless foe, I began to slip into a mode of association unlike those I'd seen, experienced or discussed; not something deeper or more than, for those involved mere addition to what was already known, not into a mode that was familiar but one familial, in the only proper sense of that term; not family by genetic inheritance or accident of birth, not by blood but by some tie infinitely more ineffable, yet infinitely more binding.

Time passed unobserved, perceptual reality slipped into a state of secondary consequence, worries receded into a glowing oblivion and eventually, when it was past midnight, I realized that neither Swoop nor I had done any work. I didn't care. In the selfishness of quiet joy I didn't give a damn. With my eyes half-shut, I let my mind wander from the likeness of Ulysses on the wall to the image of Swoop stretched on the bed to the possibilities that existed in the world of such men—and suddenly, there was a yearning to evacuate my former surroundings and move into Swoop's domain. I knew then the longing that drove men to emigrate, to depart their squalid homes and seek refuge in a shining land—and when I finally got up and left him, it seemed that I carried that new realm with me.

What I didn't take into account were the forces arrayed against the fulfillment of such aspirations. The next day we played arch-rival Huntington, and other dreams than Swoop's would also be thrust into harm's way.

CHAPTER FOUR
THE CRUCIFIXION

Swoop's crusade, by its nature, had made enemies, and not all of them wore the uniforms of opposing teams.

"Move the ball!" Swoop roared at E.J. Speed when the Huntington triple team engulfed him.

There was a purple welt under E.J.'s left eye and drops of red trickling down his shoulder. He swung his elbows, trying to clear space amongst the arms and hands clawing at him, but his pass was deflected by Tetzel, Huntington's bruising forward, and scooped off the floor by their two-guard, igniting their fast break.

"Snap your passes!" Swoop flung the words over his shoulder as he raced downcourt, one against three.

Their guard faked left, then dished right, but Swoop let the play develop, then soared over their forward's left shoulder. He swatted the shot off glass and grabbed the carom in midair. He hit the floor with both feet moving and darted upcourt while the three attackers still moved in the opposite direction.

He snapped the ball from mid-court, hitting E.J. right in the numbers, then cut wide-open down the lane.

"Ball! Ball!" he cried.

But E.J. saw only Tetzel and a chance for payback. Putting the ball on the floor, he slashed to his right, but Tetzel shoved his knee and barrel chest in his path and the ensuing collision knocked E.J.'s wiry frame backward.

"Call the fouls!" Coach raged from our bench, but the rough contact accompanied every play and he knew it.

Tetzel banged E.J. with his hip on the shot, knocking him to the deck, and still no call came. The ball floated straight into the air as Huntington's reinforcements arrived from downcourt. Swoop went up among three defenders, skying above their big men, grabbing the ball in one hand and ripping it down. Landing, he spun to the hoop and hurtled again into the air; he absorbed a whistling elbow to the solar plexus from their six-ten mastodon at center and, as the whistle finally blew, slammed it in their faces.

He doubled over momentarily, then slowly straightened, the color gradually returning to his face. Stepping to the line, he sidled momentarily against his foes' Cro-Magnon frames. His eyes were alight with an unholy glow.

"Go stronger!" he sang joyously, then ducked quickly away.

Turning to his teammates, he cried, "Give me the ball!" punctuating his words by swinging his right arm down in repetition of his slam. Then he strode to the foul line.

It was hard to say who looked with more venom, his foes or several of his teammates.

Players on both sides were bent at the waist, gasping for breath. Sweat streamed on their flanks, several grimaced against the pain and more than one of our guys bled.

Swoop stood at the line, apart not merely by spatial positioning but by virtue that he alone neither scowled nor bled. He had already shaken off the pain of the hard foul, as he had the earlier ones, and now he barely panted. He gazed at the rim as at the first rays of a spring sun, and spoke so softly that I couldn't hear him over the roar of the crowd. But, as he took the ball from the ref, his words were audible to the players lined up on both sides of the lane.

"Athena, goddess of wisdom," he said. "Grant enlightenment to these troubled mortals."

What they didn't know was whether he referred exclusively to the Huntington goons or not. But either way, Freddie and E.J. turned away, frowning, looking as if they'd plug their ears with their fingers if only they didn't need their hands for a possible rebound. They crouched, leaning forward, revealing under their jerseys the plain, stainless steel crosses they wore around their necks.

We had seen those same frowns in the locker room scant minutes before the contest began. Swoop had swept through the beefed-up security force as if it were his personal entourage, entering the room with the expectant look of a child on his birthday. Changing into his uniform, he took off a tee-shirt bearing the striking figure of Nike, goddess of victory.

When the team gathered with Coach, huddling together in prayer, Swoop joined them, but stood in the rear, apart from the others. As Coach opened his Holy Bible and chose from Psalms, Swoop's teammates lowered their heads, and he raised his.

"Blessed is he whose transgression is forgiven, whose sin is covered. Blessed is the man unto whom the Lord imputeth not iniquity..." The conviction in Coach's voice resonated through the room.

He continued while the players' chins rested on their chests, their eyes closed. But when he read: "I acknowledged my sin unto thee—" Swoop's voice cut in, "Unlike them, o god, some of us have not sinned." Several heads jerked up, but Coach continued calmly and they slowly lowered again. "...and mine iniquity have I not hid. I said I will confess my transgressions unto the Lord; and thou forgavest the iniquity of my sin—" but Swoop interjected again. "I commend my soul," he said, "and those of the noblest heroes unto the Lord. And thou rewardest the sanctity of our virtue." For one moment, Coach's eyes flickered with tired interest at Swoop's words and upturned gaze, but then he turned his attention back to the book in his hand. He appeared tired, encumbered by the weight of the book he carried, or by some equivalent burden in his life that prevented him from sharing in Swoop's vision. He forged ahead, completing the psalm, and though Swoop interrupted no further, the conclusion of the prayer brought several angry retorts.

"Psalm 32 is about the humility of a sinful being toward his Creator," E.J. said, glaring at Swoop.

"It's sacrilege to countermand the Bible," Freddie stated, with more sadness than anger.

When several stared angrily at the offender, Coach interceded. With a motion of his hand, he waved his players to silence and his eyes seemed, for a moment, more alive. "Perhaps God makes some of us purer than others," he conceded. He stood at his full height, his wasted frame even now capable of filling a room. He did not look at Swoop, but allowed his glance to rest briefly on E.J., the Bible still clutched in his fist. Then he turned and strode away. Though E.J. said nothing else, he glared at Swoop for a long time. By this time, it had become habitual.

E.J. Speed was a six-six Neanderthal from Texas, a lean, big-boned one-ninety-five, with long arms and red knuckles that scraped the floor. He was a hard-driving Baptist who approached a college game as if it were a revival meeting, with the glare of one warring in the back alleys of sin. He had the hands of a ditch digger, the shoulders of a dock worker, the face of a 12th century Crusader.

Coach had unquestioned control of his team, but when I looked at E.J. I felt something constrict the back of my throat, and for one second it was difficult to breathe. I couldn't tell whether it was fear or anger—or both. I glared at E.J. as he glared at Swoop, and I continued to even after he turned away. But nobody paid attention to me.

On the foul line now, as Swoop let the free throw fly, E.J. stepped in and Tetzel shoved an elbow below his heart, forcing the air out with a rush. Swoop drained the shot, then raced downcourt to play defense.

"Get back!" he hollered at the doubled-up E.J. Gamely, Speed took a deep breath and hobbled downcourt to play defense.

This was how the game continued well into the first half, elbows and shoves on virtually every play. On Huntington's next possession, Tetzel whacked Dandy across the chops with a forearm as they battled for position under the boards, and the two had to be pulled apart. Time and again, the mastodon beat on anyone within range, bloodying Freddie's nose and raising a knot on Raif's forehead. There were cheap shots and jolts to the back throughout—but in the general roughness the refs had to let it go, and I could see E.J.'s face redden as the game wore on.

But it was against Swoop that most of the violence was directed. They handchecked and pushed him as he brought the ball upcourt against their swarming press, banged and undercut him as he swooped to the basket. It was dangerous. Coach was off the bench, raging at the referees. The fans were spitting their fury. The refs were doing their best, but the roughness was all-pervasive. They could only call the more blatant stuff and warn the players involved. It wasn't enough. Well before half-time, it was obvious that the game was out of hand.

Swoop was under the gun. He had put three players on the bench with fouls, and was murdering them from the line. He stood there calmly, eyes seeing only rim, his flowing hair pasted to his face, and drilled one free throw after another. Every foul shot he hit sunk Huntington deeper behind. They were desperate as the game slipped away.

With five minutes remaining in the first half, Swoop slashed to the middle with a blurring between-the-legs dribble, passed the ball to Dandy, then cut to the hoop. Dandy grabbed the pass and fired it back in one movement, a textbook give-and-go, and Swoop took the return pass, sprang for the sky and slammed it home. But while he was coming down, one of Huntington's forwards cut under his legs and catapulted him topsy-turvy through the air. He landed on his back with a ringing thump and just lay there, still, for a moment. I leaped to my feet, stretching my neck to see over the crowd. Swoop got up slowly and stood under the basket, stretching gingerly. The referee had called a technical foul and issued a warning to the Huntington bench. The basket was good, and Swoop had two foul shots coming.

The fans were like gorillas in a cage, stamping, screaming, banging. They wanted retaliation. They wanted blood. A few hated Swoop, and would cross to the other side of the street if they saw him coming—but at this moment they hated Huntington more. They thirsted for vengeance.

Swoop glided to the foul line and looked up at the score. We led by eighteen. Tetzel, taking inside rebounding position, bumped him with his shoulder as he passed. Swoop smiled in delight. Moving quickly, he got on his tip-toes and kissed Tetzel's cheek.

"Good, clean play," he said. "Congratulations."

He easily dodged Tetzel's elbow and his laughter, as the big man was restrained by the refs, reverberated throughout the narrow confines of the gym. The crowd stood and hooted at Tetzel's chagrin.

Swoop swished both free throws, then charged forward to play the ball.

He deflected the in-bounds pass, but their two-guard out-raced Bobby Stenaker to the ball. He fired it ahead to their forward on the wing, but Swoop hustled upcourt in time to tip the entry pass into the low post. Freddie leaped, getting a hand on it, but the mastodon gave him a shove that sent him tumbling. Freddie sprawled, scraping elbows and knees on the hardwood floor. The refs didn't see the push and the ball squirted along the sideline as our fans screamed for retaliation. Their point guard got to it first but Swoop slapped it away. He raced it down at mid-court, then sprinted into the offensive end.

Defenders swarmed around him desperately, abandoning their men, trying to stop Swoop. They surrounded him in the lane and Swoop laughed in their faces before elevating over them. As the defenders rose to challenge the shot, he drilled it to E.J. open on the baseline. But E.J. passed up the free jumper and tried to force a pass through traffic to Freddie cutting into the lane. Huntington's small forward got his hand on the ball, deflecting it off Freddie's leg out of bounds.

Swoop reacted instantly.

"Take the open shot, big guy! Take the shot!"

E.J. bled from cuts on both knees and an elbow. There was a knot on his forehead where the mastodon had drilled him with an elbow. Sweat streamed on his neck and flanks. He turned to Swoop, face red. His mouth opened to reply, but Swoop cut him off.

"Play the D!" he urged and raced to the point.

The ball came in to one of their guards. Swoop cut off his dribbling lane upcourt on the right sideline, and when their guard tried to spin back to the middle, he was trapped. He fired a whistling elbow to Swoop's midsection, but Swoop was so concentrated on the action that he didn't feel it. He reached in with his left hand and knocked the dribble away, then pounced on it like a starving man on food and rocketed towards the rim. He came left along the baseline with one man to beat; threw his body into the air, twisted himself to the right and shot a soft lay-up around the defender. The ball kissed off glass as Tetzel and the mastodon flew at him. E.J. leaped into the melee, going for a possible rebound— but he looked neither at the ball nor the rim, he looked at Swoop. Then all three of them hurtled into Swoop, and as the ball dropped through the net the four bodies crashed to the deck with Swoop on the bottom. I saw his right leg twisted at a disjointed angle as he went down under six hundred pounds of heaving beef, then I heard the savage crack of bone and ligament snapping, a long tearing sound that grated across the gym and above the crowd's roar.

I didn't rise from my seat to see the body stretched on the floor. I sat on the bench as others rushed to him, sat alone and stared at the ground. I looked up as Freddie Zender approached the pile. E.J. and the Huntington players slowly rose, leaving Swoop stretched motionless on the floor. Freddie looked down at Swoop's inert body and for an instant I could have sworn he smiled, a fleeting "I-told-you-so" look that spoke silent volumes. But it was only an instant. Then he got to his knees—the captain, the leader, the man of charity—to minister to Swoop as he did to sick orphans.

He could be loved now, I realized, because he had been torn down. He was smaller, diminished, so they needn't fear him any longer. In sudden insight, I realized that I was no different, that I hated them, and did so for the same reason—not because they loathed Swoop, but because they had so much that I didn't. But even as that realization flooded me with self-loathing, another thought—the memory of the Celebrate Self Party—entered my mind. I had attended, I thought solemnly. I had most definitely attended.

It was only then, when it was clear that Swoop's career was over, when it was obvious that he was as crippled as I, that I rose from the bench and went to him. I hobbled to where he lay because now, for the first time, it was I who had something to teach him. Anybody could see that now he needed me.

But even now, in the depth of my concern, I could not escape the realization that this event was not solely about who needed whom. It was also about who didn't need whom; about those who felt no need for either Swoop or his faith. This was about those who would rather him scorned, even crippled, than embrace that faith as their salvation.

CHAPTER FIVE
THE TWILIGHT OF THE GODS

He just lay there. His face was drained of color, leaving him pasty white, almost lifeless. Under a blanket, the outline of his right leg was clear, twisted and misshapen. He was conscious, his eyes glazed with pain, and blood spurted from where his teeth bit through his lips.

"It's over now," somebody in the crowd said quietly.

Swoop said nothing as they loaded him on a stretcher and began carrying him out. His eyes roved the crowd, searching. Then he spotted me as I moved toward him.

"Digs," he croaked. "It's only beginning."

His face was soaked in sweat and his hands were knotted into fists. He was delirious. I started to speak, but no words came, and the EMTs continued carting him past. They stopped when he seized my wrist.

"Digs," he hissed. "Don't let them touch me. No doctor touches my body but Lefkowitz. Get Lefkowitz!"

He passed out.

They carried him through the door to the ambulance waiting outside. I stood and watched, though I didn't see, then I felt Freddie Zender towering over me. He took my arm.

"He'll survive, he'll overcome. He's strong. You'll see."

When I turned, my vision refocused and his stolid face was inches from mine. There was a sincere look of concern in his eyes, and the soft glance of solicitous support was directed predominantly, though not exclusively, at Swoop.

"Visit him in the hospital," I said. "You'll like that."

I tore my arm away and struggled through the crowd to Coach's side. The fans were hushed, sensing something fateful had happened, no longer sure how to evaluate it. Coach's huge, wasted frame hunched more than usual and his face rested on his chest. He looked up as I approached.

"Duggan," he said, clinging to the quaint notion that a man's name was given him by his parents, not by Swoop. "It's the worst damn thing I ever saw."

His voice had a pleading quality, as if he were searching for help with something that he left unnamed but whose presence in the gym was undeniable. I nodded but said nothing.

"What a kid," he said, shaking his head, looking at the Huntington bench. "What a great kid."

"Sure," I said, looking at the fans and Swoop's teammates. "Universally beloved."

He looked hard at me, a question forming in his eyes, and I took advantage of his confusion.

"I need your calling card, Coach."

The game was about to resume. He had no time for questions.

Standing in the unheated lobby of the Auditorium, shivering, I made call after call to New York. It was almost eleven on the East Coast, but I didn't care. I disturbed people at home, got some out of bed, pleaded with them, threatened, and used my father's name.

"This is Dr. Jarrett Claveen calling from Hutchinson, Iowa," I said. "It's an emergency. I *must* speak to Dr. Lefkowitz."

I finally reached him at home and woke him from a sound sleep.

"Hello!"

"Dr. Lefkowitz," I said. "Swoop is hurt. He needs you."

All grogginess dropped from his voice and he sounded instantly alert.

"Where?"

"Hoppo Valley, Iowa. On our home court."

"The details?"

"It's his right leg. It's badly broken. And I think his knee practically burst."

Silence on the other end. No sense of anger or panic, just silent appraisal. I leaped in.

"He said no other doctor could touch—"

"Shut up, kid. I get the picture."

I waited.

"I have surgery in the morning and an NFL quarterback flying in from Dallas. That's all."

"Then you'll come?"

"Of course I'll come! Are you brain dead? Where's he now?"

"The hospital. He passed out."

"All right. Tell the doctors to keep his leg iced, but not to touch him. They're dealing with the greatest athletic body in the world and they're not to touch him, do you hear? Tell the morons it's not just their careers, it's their asses. I'm on my way."

I caught my breath, afraid that if I pushed it any further, he'd change his mind.

"You're coming on the first flight?"

"I'm coming on my private jet. Hopscotch Valley have an airport?"

"Hoppo. Yes, it does."

"Good. I'm on my way."

He hung up. He hadn't asked who I was.

I walked slowly to the parking lot on campus and got my car. By the time I reached the hospital, they had already received a call from Lefkowitz's staff, giving exact orders regarding treatment. Swoop was sleeping under heavy sedation, his entire leg immersed in ice.

They wouldn't let me up to see him. His room was guarded by security, and I waited for word in the lobby, pacing the floor like a young father with his first child. Coach and several members of The Troop got there immediately following the game, and we waited together in silence for hours.

Lefkowitz arrived just before four A.M. with one assistant and his own nurse. He was average height and built like a hockey puck. He wore tailored slacks, a silk shirt and Italian loafers, but no jacket or tie. The sleeves were rolled above the elbows, revealing the bulging forearms of a body builder and the dark, scorched numbers of an Auschwitz survivor. His hair was cut short, carefully combed, dark as night. His eyes were darker still. He had to be sixty-five but looked no more than fifty. He didn't walk, he strutted, as if he looked for a fight.

Dr. Jensen, the town's leading orthopedist, rushed to meet him in the lobby.

"Dr. Lefkowitz, it will be a great honor to watch you work."

"Shut up," said Lefkowitz. "Where's the patient?"

Lefkowitz operated immediately. We all knew that Swoop was in the best hands possible, and that the surgery would take hours. I left the hospital and walked into the bitter night. It was December, and the streets of Hoppo Valley were lined with walls of snow. The temperature hovered near zero and the roads were slick with a film of ice. Driving, walking even, was treacherous. A guy in a Buick skidded making the turn onto Broadway, although he took the corner at a crawl. I watched, thinking that with many things in life danger lurked in the innocuous occurrences, the seemingly benign individuals, and even the most carefully-wrought plan could meet with disaster.

Swoop had arrived in Hoppo Valley with such a dream. Just a few months before, he had initiated a plan to transfigure this rural backwater, to re-create it in his own image and thrust it into national prominence. He and his heathen creed had stormed into Hoppo Valley with the velocity of a twister. The impact and devastation had been, in hindsight, predictable. Now the destruction was complete—the healthy had been crippled and the crippled left to wallow. Unanswered questions hung over the valley—critical queries regarding its past and its present—but the one uppermost to those dissatisfied few yearning for change involved its immediate future: quo vadis Hoppo Valley now?

CHAPTER SIX
THE CONVERSION

There was a hint of light in the eastern sky when I returned to the hospital.

Swoop had gotten out of surgery, but wasn't allowed visitors yet. Coach had sent The Troop members home to rest, but he had remained and was dozing, his head lying sideways on his shoulder. His navy suit was rumpled and fit now like a tent. His red face looked peaceful, as if sleep were a fore-taste of the deeper rest that would eventually place him beyond care. He awoke with a start as I sat across from him.

"Duggan," he said. "Never have children."

The motion of his shoulder as he straightened made him wince slightly, and his hand went to his left side.

"It wouldn't make any difference," I said. "You got to have a wife or lover or friend."

He took that in, then nodded.

"You're right."

Peter Betorsky had been a hulking figure, big-boned and sagging, who towered over people like a two-family home over milk boxes. He'd come out of western Illinois, and for years after Korea had been a football and basketball coach in high schools across Illinois and Iowa before getting his first college job at Hoppo. He'd married late, and his family had been the farm boys who, though undersized and slow, had always competed for him, though they'd never won—the boys whom, despite the losing, his quiet discipline and gentle strength had helped mold into men. But now, he was wasting away. I, and many others who knew him, remembered clearly the cause—the dark November afternoon of my freshman year, just two years ago; the rain slanting down and the highways slick; the shattering accident that crushed the family station wagon, snuffing the lives of his wife and six-year-old daughter; and then the paralyzing grief that never abated, turning gradually to apathy and slow starvation.

I heard the whispers around town growing louder, acknowledging a truth that neither I nor others wanted to face—that he would never recover, and would, before long, be joining the ones he loved. His old clothes hung on him now and he shuffled rather than walked, but the administration didn't seek to can him. They knew it would be replacing an institution—and the old Marine could still be a commanding presence. But I felt it palpably whenever I was with him—the looks he drew these days were filled as much with pity as with respect.

We waited a long time in shared silence until they let us up to Swoop's room.

He was awake, though drugged with pain killers, his right leg encased by a cylinder cast from hip to ankle. He lay propped on pillows, his body motionless, his hands limp at his sides, a book open on his lap. But he wasn't reading. His eyes were closed, and he paid no attention as Coach heaved his bulk to the far side of the bed and I settled at the other. We leaned over him. The book was Pope's translation of *The Iliad*.

"The wrath of Peleus' son," I said softly, as if he were asleep. "The direful spring of all the Grecian woes."

He opened his eyes. He glanced at us silently, one at a time, and his eyes, glazed from pain killers, looked as if all he wanted was to sleep.

"That wrath which hurled to Pluto's gloomy reign the souls of mighty chiefs untimely slain," he said. The croak of his voice was just one more shock driving us to silence. "Know anybody like that?"

I started to say "no" but I couldn't choke out the lie, so Coach finally answered.

"Basketball's not all there is."

"No?" Swoop said.

The silence that followed was not of companionable ease, and when the door opened, and Lefkowitz walked in with his assistant, it was a relief.

He stood in the room's center and stared. As he glanced around the room, taking in the curtained hospital bed, the non-descript furniture and the full-length cast on Swoop's leg, the cruel truth in his eyes made him look more than ever like a Chicago leg-breaker.

He walked to the bedside and I gave him room.

"Swoop," he said. "It's no good mincing words. You'll never play basketball again."

Swoop didn't respond.

"The bone was snapped in three places. One of the most terrible breaks I've ever seen. It'll knit back OK, but never be as strong. Too much stress could damage it." He paused. "Do you understand?"

Swoop's eyes flickered.

"But that's not the worst, it's nothing compared to the knee. The anterior cruciate ligament was torn. It's the band of tissue, as you know, that connects the articular extremities of bones at the front of the knee. It will never be strong enough again to take the pounding. But the medial collateral ligament was also torn. As was the posterior capsule, if you want the full accounting. You know enough to realize that such a combination of damage is devastating. You'll be able to walk, but that's it. Anything more will be excruciating...and dangerous. You have to see this. The sooner the better. Do you understand?"

Swoop said nothing. He stared at Lefkowitz.

The surgeon looked back for a long time, and the will to do what had to be done mixed now in his eyes with something else.

"I'd give half my practice for it to be otherwise," he whispered.

When Swoop still remained silent, Lefkowitz nodded. "Call me," he said. "Anytime. Day or night." He started for the door.

"Dr. Lefkowitz," Swoop said.

The orthopedist turned back.

"I'll be back. Next year. Greater than ever."

Lefkowitz didn't sigh or shake his head. There was stillness in his posture, and he didn't blink.

"Nobody's ever done it. Not from this."

"I'll do it."

"If anybody could do it, it's you."

"Count on it."

"I would if it were humanly possible. I'm not sure it is."

"I'll do it."

"Swoop!" It was Lefkowitz's assistant. "Didn't you hear what Dr. Lefkowitz said? You'll never play again. Not at your level. Give up the fantasy or the frustration will—"

"Easy," Lefkowitz said. He turned to Swoop and walked back to the bed, slowly, breathing deeply, as if preparing to ladle out meaning with a teaspoon.

"We're talking miracle," he said. "Long shot beyond any odds. You've studied kinesiology for seven years, this is not news." He let his preliminary words hang, a prelude to the main event, and when he finished he had four pairs of ears straining for a possible death verdict. "It happens, but any doctor worth a damn knows that the 'miracle' is a function of the patient's will. So it's possible. *Miracles are will.*" He paused and shook his head, and his final words, though distinct, were barely audible. "But it's five million to one against. If you're going to try, you must know."

Swoop's eyes had never left the surgeon's face.

"Dr. Lefkowitz," he said. "Maybe you don't hear so good. I said I'll be back."

Lefkowitz's eyes locked with his as if, for one moment, he construed Swoop not as a patient but as a foe. Then he relaxed.

"Hannibal got his army over the Alps," he said. "The Spartans held off Persia at Thermopylae."

Swoop said nothing else.

Lefkowitz turned and left, his assistant trailing.

"And some spartans survived Auschwitz," Swoop whispered after him.

Coach got up and walked to the door.

"Got a few questions. I'll be back." He shut the door quietly.

We were alone. Coach's bulk was gone from the chair by Swoop's bed. I counted the ticks of the clock. Nobody moved.

I looked around. The room's wallpaper was a pale yellow. A humidifier made the air damp, heavy, and my shirt stuck to my armpits. Swoop stared straight ahead, motionless. I couldn't bear the silence.

"Swoop, I—"

He stopped me with a brusque wave and looked straight at me. "In six months I'll dunk the ball. Next year I'll be All-American."

"But Swoop, Lefkowitz said—"

"Is Lefkowitz a heart specialist?"

"What? No, he's the world's greatest orthopedist. You know that. But what—"

"Then he doesn't know."

"Wait a minute, Swoop—"

"No, you wait!" He started to rise, to stand on a shattered leg that had just had surgery. I reached for the crutches by his bed.

"Here, don't put any weight—"

He knocked one crutch from my hand, sending it spinning; he grabbed the other and smashed it against the bed post. He stood on one leg and jerked my shirt down my back, pinning my arms.

"He doesn't know me! He knows bones, not me! He knows my bones! That's all!"

He shook me by my shirt until my bones rattled and I had no breath. He pushed me into a chair, and stood over me like a big cat with only three good legs—limping but still a lion.

"Can't you see?"

Yeah, I could see. Oh yeah, I could see that he was a goddamn lunatic, that he was completely out of his mind. I couldn't look at him, couldn't bear to look at him now. Not now, not any more, looking at him meant something to me, something unbearable, something that I had spent a lifetime trying not to look at. So I looked at the floor and said nothing. Swoop sat down, panting.

I tore myself away then, to the window.

It was raining outside. I stood looking, watching the near-Arctic temperature freeze the cold rain to pellets of ice. They stormed and rattled at the window, trying to pry themselves inside where they could melt their lives out on the warm sick-house floor. The sick-house floor. I looked around. How many people had died in this room? How many suffered and gasped and breathed their last wheezing breath? How many dreams perished here too soon?

I whirled on him then, flinging my rage and pain and fear at him, at his stupid, senseless, impossible dream.

"You're through, Swoop! Can't you see that? Can't you see? You're just another broken-down cripple, another of yesterday's heroes! Just another sorry crip like me!"

He watched me rage, silent as I squeezed out bitter drops of loathing from some reservoir within. The fury had passed from his face, and the quiet set of his jaw looked like a man ready to climb Everest—unbacked, unaccompanied, yet equipped and undaunted. His confidence just goaded me further.

"Don't you know when to quit? Lefkowitz's assistant, Lefkowitz himself, the top man in sports medicine—they both say you've had it. Isn't that enough for you? Whose authority would be enough?"

"God's," said a quiet voice at the door, and I whirled to look. Standing in the doorway, alone, hatless and coatless, was Judas Bittner.

His hair dripped from the rain, and his robe clung to his chest, but he advanced slowly into Swoop's room like a Pope entering the Sistine Chapel. He ignored me, seeing only Swoop. He approached the bedside and stopped. When he spoke his words came softly but with great clarity.

"Mr. Claveen and I don't often agree, but this time he's right. You are through. You will never play basketball again. No, I'm not a doctor or a physical therapist, only a man of God. But the fact is clear. He has laid His hand upon you."

Swoop looked silently, neither pained nor puzzled, just curious. I was too taken aback to be angry.

"If there is a God," I said. "He laid His hand upon Swoop long ago."

"Comforting thought," he sneered. "Let it reassure him as he watches games from a wheelchair."

"You'd like that?"

"I prayed for it," he insisted.

Seeing the look on my face, he laughed, the sound harsh, guttural, but not malignant.

"Not as an end," he said almost kindly, as to a comrade, turning to me for the first time. "I prayed for his downfall as a beginning."

I was going to ask a question but no words came. I stared dumbly. He turned back to Swoop.

"Your spiritual rebirth," he said. "Let it begin today."

Swoop ignored him and turned away.

"There are gods," he said to me. "They're the most extraordinary beings on earth. Never doubt it."

"Earth," Bittner said. "Is a refuge of vermin."

Judas Bittner was the star preacher for The First Commandment Missionary Church. They believed there was only one Commandment that mattered—the First. They opened all services on their knees, the minister too, speaking reverently the words of Exodus: "I am the Lord thy God...Thou shalt have no other gods before me." They followed no liturgy and allowed no authority but one—the Bible. They believed that a man either worshipped God or he worshipped false gods; there was no middle ground: one's life was ruled by God or by Satan, by good or by evil. For those who chose evil, they had violent contempt—and burning desire to convert. They were missionaries—at home and abroad—and strove tirelessly to reach the un-Godly.

His goal as a student was to take a degree, then devote his years to the global mission. "The meaning of life," he said, "is simple: Christ died for our vice, we must live for His virtue...even if it kills us." He studied Religion because he had to know God; he studied anything else because he had to graduate. He stood several inches over five foot and weighed one hundred pounds. He had the arms and shoulders of a dainty girl, and though part Indian, his complexion was white, almost never in the sun. His hair was dark, long, parted in the middle and swept back in braids like an Indian brave. He wore a brown and white deer leather head-band—and no other adornment.

His voice had a gravel rasp that slashed like a razor; it pen-etrated—"goes right through you," one campus girl said. But when he spoke of the Lord, his voice hit like an axe and his slight frame swelled, filling with a force he said "came not from within but above." He hammered the Word at the sinful—and they knew they'd been hit. He saved souls, but savaged them first. He spent no time on the sick and no effort on the needy: he was not to be found in hospitals or nursing homes, but in bars and pool halls—never crying for the needs of the weak, but battling for the souls of the strong.

He was a fighting man, a soldier of Christ, who'd take a beat-ing for his faith. The story of one of his encounters with the unGodly had grown into local folklore, and I'd heard it told many times. But unlike other tales of legendary proportion, this one was told the same way every time. It had happened the summer before my arrival in Hoppo Valley. The local biker gang had long been notorious for its wild, often violent revels, and when Bittner sought and found them one night at the lake they were drunk and, with their female companions, in various stages of undress. He'd thrust into their midst. Alone, dressed in a white monk's robe and san-dals, he lashed them like St. Paul: "Wine is a mocker, strong drink is raging, and whosoever is deceived thereby is not wise!"

The bikers beat him with crow bars. They snapped his legs, gashed his skull and left his body in the woods. But over a period of tortuous hours, he dragged himself half a mile uphill to a coun-try road, where he flagged down a passer-by. He went to the cops, not the hospital. They rounded up the thugs, Judas identified them, and only then did he go for medical treatment. Four months later his testimony sent three of the bikers to the state pen for five years.

But every night in the chapel he prayed to the Savior to redeem their souls.

And every day thereafter he wore the torn and bloodied monk's robe, wore it unwashed and reeking—as a uniform...and as a badge of honor.

He valued no company except God's—and permitted only a handful to assist his work. To those who felt a need to follow him, he was cold—"Jesus is who you need, not Judas." But to those who felt no need to follow his creed, he was blazing hot—"The Father casts thee in the Pit!" People meant nothing to him, but souls meant all; life held no value, but the afterlife did. Man was sinful, only God was pure.

He preached this way in towns around Iowa—and envisioned the day when he would do so in towns around the world. When others said he was mad, he glared; when they said he was vicious, he snarled; when they said he was fearless, he smiled; but when they said he was Godly, he bowed his head. There were many phrases uttered by men—some he fought, some he accepted, some he ignored; but only one he revered: "Thy will be done."

He stood by Swoop's bed now, his face solemn, as befitting a funeral, but tinged with a hint of expectation, as if the hope of great things could be imminently kindled.

"Man has told you it's the end," he said. "God tells you it's the beginning."

Swoop was beginning to revive from the pain killers. It was in his eyes. No medication was a match for the stream of vitality that could be summoned on command from some vast interior sea. He was alert and looked at Bittner with sad interest, as he might look at the eight-hundred pound woman in a sideshow.

Bittner noticed only the interest.

"There was Pharaoh," he said quietly, "who believed himself a god. There were the deluded visionaries of Babel who believed Heaven attainable on Earth. There were Philistine idolaters taunting the blinded prophet of Yahweh. A lesson here, gentlemen?" He swiveled at the waist to include me in his query, but quickly returned his gaze to Swoop, as if he could not bear to look away for longer than a second. "Must I draw the obvious conclusion? Must I connect it to the story of the Hoppo Valley Adonis whose charismatic career came to a sudden and tragic end? Or is the hand of the irrevocable unmistakably present?"

The air in the room seemed chilled. I looked around. Had someone lowered the heat? I reached over but the radiator was hot. Still I shivered. I grabbed for my coat. Bittner ignored me.

"A sinful creature does not aspire to heights occupied by the deity. Ignore His warning and die. But heed it—take it to heart—and live eternally. This is the choice given to men. Your time is now."

Sincerity of conviction rang in his tone. He struck a blow for his god. His body quivered under his robe like a cat on its haunches before an unsuspecting squirrel. I couldn't look at the cast on Swoop's leg or at his body lying on a hospital bed. I concentrated on his eyes, his face was all that existed now and I looked to it as a sailor to a lighthouse from a raging sea.

He was calm, his eyes untroubled, as if all decisions had been made and all contradictory admonishments rendered irrelevant. He gazed at Bittner, his brow furrowed with puzzled concentration as if, to him, Bittner were denying the most elementary truths. "Two plus two equals five?" Swoop's face asked. He was silent.

I was in a dream, caught between two conflicting forces, each certain to itself, both fantasy to me. I spoke doubtfully to Bittner with a skepticism which, minutes earlier, had been directed at Swoop.

"He doesn't respond because you don't speak his language." My voice sounded firm—at least to me.

"Then he better learn mine."

"Or else—what?"

"God's punishment will not be limited to his body ultimately." His eyes glittered as he took in my weakened right leg and the glazed expression of my eyes. "Or yours."

I said nothing and just looked at the floor. I sat huddled in my coat, frozen for the winter, like a reptile waiting for the rays of Spring to warm me. Swoop was across the room, but he was incapacitated. He might have been across interstellar space.

Bittner looked at the two of us and smiled bitterly.

"Two cripples," he jeered. "Bigger than God's law. Look at them now."

His eyes focused on me.

"Where's your atheism now? All your logical arguments that omnipotence and omniscience are self-contradictions—that the existence of evil proves there is no God—that the onus of proof principle can never be addressed by men of faith—where did your Aristotelian philosophy lead you?"

When he met no resistance, his voice softened—and though I didn't look I could feel his hard eyes taking me in, calculating, pitiless.

"You, Claveen," he said.

I didn't answer.

He stood over me, staring, and I felt rather than saw his glance turn to pity.

"You look like you suffer from terminal cancer," he said not roughly. "Not a deformed leg."

The air in the room stagnated. Despite its fetid quality, I was still cold and sat wrapped in my coat. The ticks of the clock were loud between his sentences.

"But the soul is God's treasure. Leave the puerile concerns of the body to juveniles."

When I continued as if paralyzed he lost his patience.

"Claveen, God's hope is not lost! There is yet time! Save your soul and assist your vainglorious friend!"

"He doesn't need you," Swoop said, speaking to Bittner for the first time. "His soul is saved already."

He threw the covers off and, for a second time, began to rise on a shattered leg. This time I made no move to help.

"Self-glorification is a path to the Pit," Bittner said, hissing the words like some prophetic reptile.

Swoop hopped past him, holding his injured leg stiffly to the side, keeping it off the floor. He grabbed the handle of the door, hopped backwards and thrust it wide.

"No," he said. "Swoop saves."

He jerked his head at the door, indicating the audience was over.

Bittner looked at him quietly, then he nodded. Without a backward glance he walked to the door, moving with slow dignity, befitting a man who has delivered a momentous message. He paused at the threshold.

"Pride goeth before a fall," he said. He stared at Swoop's face.

"Or before an ascension," Swoop stared upward at the ceiling and the sky beyond.

Bittner waited for Swoop's eyes to return to earth and he held Swoop's gaze.

"God has patience," he said.

When he had gone, Swoop shut the door and limped to where I sat.

I stared out the window. The freezing rain had changed to snow. It fell in a sloppy gray sprawl, not blanketing the ground in white but making the street slick with ice. The few pedestrians who had ventured out were wrapped in hoods and even the healthiest walked scrunched over, their weight shifted forward. When the wind rattled the window, I pulled my coat tighter around me.

"What were you saying?"

I looked up. "When?"

"Before we were interrupted. What were you saying?"

I shook my head. "Nothing."

"Oh, yeah, you were saying something. Something about being through. Something about a couple of lame guys, two 'broken-down cripples.' You have any idea who they are?"

"Swoop, I—"

"Shut up. You are through. Through talking and whining and bellyaching. You're going to start doing." He looked down at my own crippled leg and spoke in a whisper. "We'll work out together. I'll dunk the goddamned ball again in six months—and so will you. No injury or birth defect can stop us. We'll work like Spartan warriors. You're going to be a specimen—and a better student than ever." He spat the words like a cornered cat, fired them like a machine gun. He was a man obsessed, and knew only one reaction to tragedy. I laughed involuntarily.

"It's not possible to be a better student than I already am."

"Goddamn right. But half a man won't do. We want the total package."

I looked at him and wasn't sure if I wanted to shake his hand or kick his ass. I got up and stood in his face. Part of me wanted to grab two fistfuls of his hospital blouse and push his crippled self backward onto the bed. But my mind held unforgettable pictures of him soaring over every form of opposition against Jabez and Huntington.

"Do you ever lose?" I whispered.

"Would you like me to?"

I reached out to brush back a strand of hair over his eye.

"No."

"All right," he said, sitting down. "Now you've got a week's vacation for Christmas. Go home and enjoy the hell out of it. Because when you get back, I'm going to work you like a slave. So go on, beat it. And here..." He grabbed the crutches off the floor and tossed them to me. "Take these goddamn things with you. We won't need them."

As I caught the two pieces, the door opened and Coach came

in. He looked ready for a funeral, but he walked without hesitation to Swoop's side.

"How do you feel?"

"I'll be fine, Coach."

"Need anything?"

Swoop looked at me.

"I got what I need."

Coach nodded and fidgeted with his hands.

"Son, I'm not good at making talk, so I'll only say this once. No matter what else you've done or failed to do, for one season you've made us winners. I can't overlook that. So I'd be honored if you'd live with me. While you're recuperating and for as long as you like."

"Thank you," Swoop said. He didn't lower his head, though drops of moisture appeared suddenly in the corner of each eye.

Coach shook his hand firmly and joined me at the door. I never looked back, but heard his chanting vow: "In six months, Digs, six months."

I floated through the week at home, drifting in a private euphoria that speeded up the process of time while creating a flowing sense of timelessness in me. I was living in Swoop's spring-garden world while everybody else was in December. Before I could look at a calendar, it was time to get back to school. Our schedule resumed in early January, and floating or not, I was expected to be there. It was like time had rushed past me at quickened pace, refusing to disturb this dreaming child. But that wasn't it: the motion of other things hadn't accelerated. Rather, it was that I had slowed down in some sense, serenely strolling through my own inner garden while the rushing world tore past outside. I finally woke up on the long drive back to school and wondered why there was so much ice on the road. I skidded twice before I realized that it was January and the ice was supposed to be there. I clenched my fists on the wheel then and concentrated on winter driving.

He was still in the hospital when I got back. Immediately I went to see him. I expected to find him bouncing with vigor, ready to tear off his cast and step onto the courts. Instead, I found his hospital room filled with cards whose covers bore representations in various forms of an infant with his virgin mother. Swoop himself lay pale and still in bed. But he was surrounded by copies of his books, and open on his lap was a verse translation of *The Aeneid*.

"What's this?" I asked, pointing at the cards.

Swoop looked dazed. "I don't know. People been sending me this stuff every day."

"Why?"

He handed me a copy of *The Independent*, dated several days after his injury. It was open to the Letters to the Editor page. The first letter was entitled "Succor the Afflicted."

I read it aloud:

> The shattering injury that so tragically ended Swoop's basketball career last night is known now throughout town. What is also known is that Swoop himself, with his brash, vociferous manner, has led many brethren to reject him as a vain braggart. Some of the faithful have even gone so far as to suggest that his crippling injury is an act of divine justice.
>
> This interpretation is profoundly anti-Christian.
>
> It is crucial to remember that it is our first duty to love Christ. Our Lord does not distinguish between "those who are with sin" and "those who are without"; there are none without sin. The Savior loves us all. It is our duty, in our limited human way, to emulate His example.
>
> Swoop's affliction must be ministered to, not because he is great or sinless—he isn't—but because he is miserable. *Christ would not be stopped by his swaggering, heathen manner.* Neither should we. His relief is paramount, and if done with the proper sincerity, may melt his proud heart with Christian love. As for us, we must never forget the words of the Apostle Paul: "Though I speak with the tongues of men and of angels, and have not charity, I am become as sounding brass, or a tinkling cymbal."
>
> (signed) Freddie Zender, Captain
> Hoppo Valley State College
> Basketball Team

Swoop had looked away while I read, his hands squeezing *The Aeneid*. When I finished, he turned to me.

"Why do they think I'm a cripple?" he asked in a voice so hoarse I could barely hear him.

"You mean, why do some want..." I started but couldn't finish.

Swoop seemed not to have heard. He sat in reverie, staring at his leg. Then he turned to me.

"I'm not a Christian, you know."

"Oh, really? I'm shocked."

"But my parents are—they're Catholic."

"So what happened?"

He looked down at Virgil's epic, the great tale of the founding of classical Rome, and his words came softly.

"I wasn't born with Original Sin."

"I was," I whispered.

He let those words rest on the air currents of the room, then he looked at me.

"We're going to wash that away."

I didn't answer. I just looked back.

"Proximal femoral focal deficiency is not untreatable, you know."

I stared.

"How did you know…" I started, but my question trailed off when I noticed Swoop grinning.

"You think I study kinesiology with Jonathan Lefkowitz for nothing?"

I remained silent, for the discussion was straying too near a topic I had avoided for a long time.

"The top part of the femur is missing—why didn't you wear braces when you were a kid?"

"Swoop, I don't want to discuss—"

"Come on! Why didn't you? That's the treatment. And your father's a doctor."

I kept my voice low, but even I could hear something in it straining to reach the surface.

"Because my parents made me. They coddled and hovered and fussed over me. So I ripped it off—that's why."

Swoop stopped and took that in.

"Are your parents still involved?"

I shook my head.

"Then we get started today—now. We're going to build the gluteal muscles—all three, the maximus, medius and minimus—like they've never been built before. You're going to work your ass off—literally. But first, go to the nurse's station and get a garbage bag."

I did as I was told. When I came back, Swoop pointed to the cards.

"No coddling—throw them out."

Swoop said nothing as I filled the bag and carried it from his room. But when I got back, he said, "There's one thing more."

"What?"

"Go to my room. Here's the key. Get the barbells I stash under the desk. It's a hundred pounds. Think you can handle it?"

I grabbed the key. "I'll handle it."

Swoop didn't speak, but looked at me as if I were a member of the basketball team. That look stayed with me as I staggered with the weights up and down stairs, in and out of my car. Sweating on my return, I dumped them beside Swoop's bed.

"Let's get started," I said.

"Easy, tiger. We'll lift tomorrow. Sit down."

I sat in the chair next to his bed, placing my feet on the steel bar of the weights, rolling them gently back and forth, feeling the sensuous movement run upwards from the soles of my feet through my legs.

"I sing of arms and of two men," I said.

He didn't answer, but looked at me as Aeneas might at one of his captains.

For the first time, I didn't squirm, but accepted it and stared back.

I stayed that night until the staff threw me out. We talked no more about ourselves and the future, only about basketball, girls, movies, days at the beach—Swoop read to me from Virgil—and despite the late hour, when they finally booted me out, I wasn't tired. I left my old Ford in the lot and walked back to the dorm. I wanted time to think, to feel, to experience new sensations. I was standing at the end of an era—and anticipating the start of a better one. Standing at the crossroads of pity and something else, I had made my decision to hobble into a new, unknown direction. And, perhaps, to hobble no more. The new direction was terrifying. But I had implicit trust in my guide.

CHAPTER SEVEN
THE RESURRECTION

Swoop was in the hospital for more than a month. Although classes didn't begin until early February, we were leaving soon for an extended road trip through the western part of the state. It was the toughest segment of our season, containing nine games, including a concluding tournament at Winota. I spent every minute that I could with Swoop.

His room contained dozens of cards and letters from his family, who, though not well-off, had flown in and spent a week with him while I was on vacation. On the desk next to his bed stood several cards from a girl in New York; their covers held pictures of skyscrapers or mountain peaks; in all, the backgrounds were stark blue and the sun shined on the summits. Coach came to see him every morning and The Troop members were frequent visitors. But still, most of the time he was alone. He was now.

I found him lying in bed, the covers thrown off, pen and paper in his hands, a heavy text book open at his side.

"Comments on Virgil?" I asked.

"No," he grimaced. "Working out."

"How? Exercising your fingers?" But I looked at the paper filled with his calculations, the numbers running into the tens of thousands. "What's this?"

"Leg raises," he gasped, "and muscle tightenings."

His face was distorted by effort and, mostly, by pain. Sweat stood out in glistening streaks on his forehead and neck. The thigh muscles at the top of his cast clenched and unclenched as he tightened and relaxed without let-up.

"What are you doing?" I asked in astonishment.

He kept on flexing the muscle, eyes fixed on his knee.

"If I can do one thousand leg raises...and two thousand muscle clenches...a day...I figure I can avoid...atrophy of the leg muscles...Isometrics, Digs...tightening of the muscle...without moving...the joint..."

His breath came in pants as he spoke, the pain obvious in his voice. No wonder. With a leg newly operated on, he should be doped-up on painkillers, resting quietly—not killing himself with this drill instructor's regimen. My limited medical knowledge told me it was too soon, and instinctively I reached out to him, like a father with his rambunctious son, placing both hands on his chest.

"Swoop, it's too soon, you'll hurt yourself," I said. Even I was surprised by the gentleness of my voice.

Swoop kept flexing, his glance never wavering from his leg. He shook his head as he spoke.

"No, I've got to strengthen the leg muscles."

"But Lefkowitz will tell—"

"No! Lefkowitz said I couldn't hurt it." His breath rasped out of him. "It's just a matter of standing the pain."

"You checked?" I was almost shocked. I imagined him telling the doctors to go to hell, then tearing off the cast himself.

"Yes. I speak to him every day."

I nodded and he continued his exercises.

The heavy book by his side was one of his kinesiology texts, and I picked it up. Swoop's notes were on every page, personal exhortations like, "Keep feet hip-width apart when working the gastrocnemius," and "Don't arch the back when doing pelvic lifts for the glutes." The tissue thin pages bore thumb prints all over them.

I watched him for hours, unwilling to let my eyes roam, staring as a slave would at the actions of a free man. I felt like a selfish bastard, who wouldn't have cared if international crises wracked the globe. Swoop looked up.

"I spoke to the physical therapist," he said.

"About your leg?"

"About *yours*."

"Mine?"

"That's right. You have an appointment to see him the day after the team gets back. Two PM. Be there."

I sat silent for a moment, then I felt something clutch at my stomach.

"Swoop, I…"

"What?"

He could sense the reluctance. There was something in his eyes, hard and unyielding, like an ice-cutter.

"Talk," he said.

How could I tell him? He had no experience of this, no point of reference by which to navigate in such a world. He couldn't hear the unsummoned voices, the taunts, the laughter. He had never seen the sneers directed at him, had eaten neither the dirt nor the shame.

"Talk," he demanded, interrupting my musings.

I had been staring at the floor, but now I looked at him. I knew that, this time, hard eyes were no danger. So I told him.

"Autumn Blossom! Autumn Blossom!" Mitch Schotheim had called when I showed up in Kelleher's backyard to play football. Schotheim was fourteen, already in high school, and he'd lounge over the neighboring fence, watching the younger kids play ball. Kelleher was big for eleven, going on later to star in football at Central East.

"Come on, Autumn Blossom," Schotheim yelled, "let's see you tackle Kelleher! Hey Kelleher, I bet Autumn Blossom rips off your balls!"

The other kids smirked as they looked at my skinny frame and the way I dragged my right foot. Kelleher looked at me in disgust.

"You think you're going to tackle me?"

"I can p-p-play," I stammered.

"Did you hear that?" Schotheim boomed. "Autumn Blossom can p-p-play!"

Mike Uhing threw Kelleher the ball.

"Let's see."

And Kelleher came at me across the backyard like a semi; he blasted his shoulder into my chest and knocked me flat; he stepped on my solar plexus and kicked me in the mouth; then he continued past me.

"Autumn Blossom down! Autumn Blossom down!" Schotheim laughed. The other kids clapped their hands. Kelleher towered over me then.

"Get out of here, Autumn Blossom. And don't come back."

I was raging. I got up and spat blood in his face.

"You're a scumbag, Kelleher, you're a rotten son of a—"

And he hit me. His right fist smashed my nose, breaking it, blood spurting all over my face and shirt. I was on the ground again, and I couldn't breathe, crying in pain and shame and helpless rage, tasting the dirt and blood in my mouth.

I crept away, Schotheim's voice booming behind me. My father's office was on the other side of town, and I staggered toward it,

using my handkerchief, then my shirt to stop the blood. A passing
driver stopped then and drove me there.

My mother, an R.N., was at the desk when I came in.

"Oh my God!"

She rushed me into an examining room and gently washed the
dried blood off my face.

"Jarrett! Jarrett!"

My father came in and calmly examined me.

"Is it broken? Is it broken?"

"Yes, it's broken."

She seized my father's arm. "He must go to the hospital. Do
you hear me?"

I pulled away.

"No! No hospital!"

"I'll set it right here, Duggan," my father said. "You'll be fine."
He smiled. He was a powerful man, not tall, but thick across the
shoulders and chest. He had endurance, he worked long hours at
the hospital, the clinic, his office. These were his domains—I almost never saw him at home—and he ruled them with calm
strength, oblivious here to the birdlike chirping nervousness of
my mother.

"Jarrett, it's broken," she said, her hand pressed to my forehead. "Are you sure?"

"Yes," he answered, and that was the end.

But after my father set it, she clutched my hand.

"I'm taking you home, you're going to bed."

"No! I don't want to go to bed, I'm O.K.!"

"It's all right," my father said to her. "He doesn't need to go
to bed, he can watch TV, he just needs to take it easy."

"He's going to bed, his nose is broken, he must rest." As always my father was beleaguered by patients. He had no time for
this.

"Go with your mother, Duggan, and listen to her. I'll see you
later." He returned to his work.

So I left him, though wanting to stay in his office, near to his
instruments, his surroundings and his work. I left and went home
with my mother, who put me to bed.

But I only pretended to sleep. Even later, when I was tired, I
fought to stay awake. And when my parents finally went to bed, I
got up, quietly turned on the light and read for hours.

The next day she made me stay home from school. When she

left for the office in midmorning, she kissed my head and made me promise to stay in bed. Looking in her eyes, I answered with conviction.

"O.K., Mom, I promise."

But as soon as she left, I got dressed and trudged across town. Across town to the Kelleher house, where I stood across the street, looking in anger, in outrage, in yearning.

Still yearning, years later, by the bedside of another cripple— but one who stared pitilessly, and who didn't take his eyes off of my face.

"Where's Kelleher today?" he asked.

I shrugged. "Pumping gas probably."

He nodded. He hadn't stopped working his leg. He kept lifting.

"And where are you?"

"Ready to kick some —"

"Ready for a resurrection," he interrupted, not letting me finish.

I said nothing. I merely nodded in reply, and when I left, hours later, it was with a sense of confidence that nothing could stop me. At the door, I stopped. "In six months, I'll dunk it in your face, boy!" I shouted and swaggered down the hall, Swoop's ringing laughter following in tribute.

I didn't feel quite so confident when I returned—but for other reasons. Our western swing had been disastrous. We had played nine games in nineteen days, and lost six of them, six more than we had lost in the entire season prior to Swoop's injury. The team was struggling without him, still hustling but barely competitive. Huntington had moved into first place, we clung to second and were fading. Although there were still die-hards around campus and town—a hundred fans greeted our return at the gym, and the sports columnists of *The Independent* exhorted us to build on the positive foundations we had lain—Hoppo Valley fever had been fueled by Swoop's leadership. It could not survive his downfall.

Talk at the downtown bars was that we were through. Season ticket holders tried to sell, rallies of team support ended and sales of Swoop posters at souvenir shops dropped to a trickle. Members of The Swoop Troop hung their heads and Drew Doherty, starting at point guard again, smiled more often, though we repeatedly lost.

At the same time, things reverted to the way they had been

before. A story in *The Daily Iowan*, the campus paper, claimed that Dean Pearsall's contract renewal was in doubt. The author averred that, according to informed sources, President MacPherson was quietly interviewing other candidates, nominees more amenable to the ethical precepts traditionally ascendant in Hoppo Valley. Pearsall's probable demise didn't bother me. But it was disturbing when one of my professors, a parishioner of the First Presbyterian Church, said in class that he'd been surprised to hear muted expressions of relief at Sunday services regarding Swoop's injury. Nobody, however, was surprised that Judas Bittner's proclamations on the topic were not muted. For weeks, his message had trickled out of the smaller denominations scattered throughout the Valley's poorest sections. But one day just before my return, he brought the word to campus.

He spoke before two dozen students at a meeting of the Campus March for Redemption. His words echoing throughout the cavernous reaches of Marian Auditorium, he spoke simply, starkly, eloquently. "God's justice has been served," he stated. "We must make sure it is not served similarly on us."

When I arrived at the hospital, Swoop looked hard as a fist. He hadn't shaved since I left, and his beard bristled like a pirate's. He'd worked out continuously, sitting up in bed to lift weights, and relentlessly flexing and clenching his leg muscles. His body was a razor's edge, and he looked mean.

"What the hell happened out there?" he snapped as soon as I walked in.

I opened my arms. "What, no 'hello,' no 'hi, how're you doing?' Just 'what the hell happened?'"

"Cut the bulls—t, Digs. How'd you lose six games?"

I had never seen him like this. No bravado or laughter, no aura of gaiety and a self-confidence that sparkled—just grizzled determination and a relentless drive that bordered on hostility. I was surprised at the change, although its aptness under the circumstances was clear.

"What the hell did you expect—that we'd still beat everyone without you?"

He rubbed his fist across his stubble.

"No, I guess not."

"Relax," I said.

"I'll try," and he returned to his leg raises, the white cast of his leg rising and falling in a steady beat.

I sat by his bedside, beginning the absorption process again. Swoop lifted the cast ceaselessly, straining like a slave until beads of sweat stood out on his body like jewels. Sitting in his presence, time seemed a mythical conception. I was a prisoner of my own budding ambitions and my consciousness admitted no external concerns. I had no idea how much time passed, and Swoop was still at it, when there was a soft tapping at the door. I looked up, startled by the realization that other people still existed in my private universe. Swoop had no such realization—he kept grinding. At the door stood Freddie Zender.

He stood there for a long time, staring at Swoop. As if by gravitational attraction, his sad eyes were drawn to Swoop's cast, to the heavy, white, hospital pallor of it. His face showed no recognition of the soaring, springing Swoop, who had performed unparalleled feats—nor of the glinting hardness of Swoop's eyes—nor even of the remorseless creature sitting by his side. He paused in the doorway staring at the cast as it rose and fell. Then he advanced into the room.

Swoop looked up.

"Coach tells me you're planning to come back."

"I'm not planning to come back. I am coming back."

Freddie nodded and though he looked at Swoop's face, the ceaseless motion of the cast was a constant on the edge of his vision. His athlete's eye noticed the sweat streaking Swoop's neck and shoulders, and the muscles in his chest flexed involuntarily, as if in sympathetic communion with Swoop's.

"I believe you," he said.

Beside me, he was the first person who did.

"But not without help," he added.

A pair of nurses walked past the door. The hushed, serious tones of their voices reached us faintly. An orderly bustled by with a tray of medicines on a cart. It rattled in the still hospital air.

"I'm in my third year, pre-med," Freddie said. His voice was soft, solemn, not unkind. "The top student in my class. Ask him." He jerked a thumb at me. "When he was in the program, he was the only one better."

Swoop stared without expression. The white bulk of the cast rose and fell.

"I'm going to Columbia's med school," Freddie continued. "Their College of Surgeons and Physicians. I'm sure to get in."

A wheelchair bumped past in the hall outside, pushed by a mem-

ber of the hospital staff. They were taking an orthopedic patient
for x-rays. Through the open door I saw his leg held stiff in front
of him. He didn't look happy.

Freddie's eyes were on the kinesiology text lying open on
Swoop's bed.

"The repaired ligament connects the articular extremities of
bones," he said, repeating Lefkowitz's words but in a hard clinical
tone. "It will never withstand sustained stress."

No response from Swoop. The cast rose and fell.

"You can't do it alone," Freddie said. "You need help."

His voice was softer now.

The seconds passed. Swoop didn't speak.

"Will you answer me?" Freddie asked finally.

"He's answered you already," I said, keeping my voice calm.
"His whole life's an answer to you."

Freddie stood motionless by the foot of the bed, listening to
the soft sound of nurses' voices coming from the next room. They
were helping a bed-ridden patient turn onto his side, relieving the
pressure on his bed sores. From the sounds, it was a struggle.

"God forgives," he said.

I saw an image of his face as Swoop writhed on the floor, but
he wasn't talking to me, so I bit off a reply.

Swoop stopped hefting the cast.

"I've nothing to forgive," he said.

Freddie sighed and looked around the room, as if seeing cen-
turies of boasters laid low for their vanity. Swoop resumed lifting.

"Pride blinds you to the Redemption," Freddie said softly.

"Pride is the Redemption."

"But look at you," Freddie pointed at the room, the hospital
bed, the cast. "How will you do it alone?"

"I'm not alone."

"I'm talking about God."

"So am I."

"How you going to do it?"

"You see how. Rehabilitative workouts. Full time."

"Every day?"

"Every minute. Every hour. Every second I'm not in class."

"For the next year?"

"For the rest of my life if necessary. Watch me!" He leaned forward at the waist even as he continued to heft the cast. "I'll swim
before dawn, lift weights in the morning, run in the afternoon,

ride the exercise bike in the evening, do calisthenics at midnight. You know why?"

Freddie nodded, transfixed. His eyes were riveted on Swoop's leg as it rose and fell, and they were starting to gleam like Swoop's own.

"The muscles."

"That's right," Swoop panted, sweat streaking his face. "Do extensions, presses and squats for the quads—curls for the semi-membranosus, semitendinosus and biceps femoris—heel raises for the gastrocnemius and soleus—and dozens of different exercises for the glutes. Build every muscle group in my right leg. Until they're twice as strong as an ordinary athlete's. Then more. *The muscles must take the stress.* Super-strong!"

Freddie stared at him now like I did.

I looked at his hard frame standing by Swoop's bed. He had brown hair wrapped around his head in tight curls and a long face like a horse, eyes often filled with sadness. Nobody could doubt either the sincerity of his compassion or the relentless intensity of his work habits. Though I had never liked him, I couldn't withhold my grudging respect. He stared at Swoop, and for the first time there was a question in his eyes.

But for me there was no question, not with the memory of a gloating face growing stronger before my eyes. Not with the triumphant "I-told-you-so" look that flashed from the recent past and pressed itself on me. I got up. They could talk all they wanted and Freddie could look at him as a Greek sailor at Odysseus. I wanted no part of it. I started for the door.

"Where are you going?" Swoop's voice had a note of urgency.

"To the dorm. I'll be back."

It bothered me for a long time. I didn't like bottling it up like gas in a cylinder. Too much of Swoop had rubbed off now, and I was a walking gas leak, set to go off, caused by big things or small, directed at anyone who got in my way, Swoop included.

But it wasn't all bad. For, if you're angry, you can't be afraid. And I was angry enough now to do something about it; angry at myself for being such a goddamned wimp all my life, running from the problem. Well, I was running no longer. I attacked the problem. I kept my appointment with the physical therapist.

He kept me in his office for hours, putting me through a series of tests appropriate for a linebacker. He took stress tests, strength tests, flexibility tests. He made me bend, stretch, run, jump and lift with it. He worked me with such a gung-ho, Parris Island approach that it made me wonder what Swoop had said to him. And made me want to strangle Swoop for saying it. But Swoop had been right. The regimen he prescribed, though paying careful attention to the legs, focused on building the gluteal muscles. He assigned bent-kick crosses, raised-leg curls, standing kickbacks and a dozen other butt-breakers. At the end, he punched my arm, grinning in his toothy, drill instructor way, saying:

"Go get 'em, kid."

Yeah, go to Hell, I thought to myself, faced with the brutal realization that physical development for a soft intellectual was going to be torture.

"Thanks," I said and left in tight-lipped determination.

Swoop didn't laugh when I told him the story. He had interrupted his exercises to listen to me, paying attention to the details, staring at me like we sat at an evangelical revival. When I finished, he said:

"Go get 'em, kid!"

"What's this bulls—t?" I shouted, bristling at the stupid jock-mentality familiarity.

Swoop looked at me for a long time. He didn't laugh. He looked, but he never laughed.

"Digs," he said like a mother. "You're scared."

"So what if I am?"

"So nothing. Do it, that's all. Feel the fear, and do it anyway. Don't let the fear stop you."

Suddenly, I realized how deeply I needed him.

"You been scared, Swoop?"

"Of course."

"And what'd you do?"

"I did it anyway."

I stared at him. Some quiet rectitude with which he said the words, not just the words themselves, jolted me to an internal stop. Underscore this, said an authoritative voice within. Write it in bold lettering on the transcript of your soul and don't forget. After all, what did it mean to be a hero—to feel no fear when bullets were aimed at your chest? Or to summon the courage to defend your home and freedom in the face of an overwhelming fear of those bullets?

I nodded. "All right."

He spent the entire vacation in the hospital, lifting weights, reading Virgil, flexing his leg muscles. And I got started on a light training program—at least Swoop called it light—beginning slowly with the intention of gradually building up. I used the whirlpool and started to lift weights with my leg. I had to learn to swim, because swimming gave the legs exercise without strain. But I was afraid of the water, always had been; and when I went to the YMCA for my first lesson, I had to grit my teeth and do it anyway. But the real punishment came when I began to jog.

It was an icy morning in late January, the wind blowing like a silent knife, all the deadlier for its stealth. I pulled on my sweatsuit and laced up my high-top sneakers, flexing my knees all the way to the track. I looked up at the gray winter sky, pregnant with snow. It was a big moment for me. The beginning of the end—or more accurately, as Churchill had once suggested, the end of the beginning. For I was on my way, starting with a half-mile run. Or so I thought. I had never run in my life, limping everywhere I'd gone. And when I started now, the impact on the frozen ground pulsed shocks through my body. I gritted my teeth and kept going. Despite the frigid weather, I sweated like a horse. I kept going, not running, not jogging even, but more like half-hobbling, half staggering. But I kept going. Four times around the track equaled a half-mile. I staggered on, blind with pain, eyes more than half-closed, wind knifing my breath like a frozen scalpel—and when I made it, I collapsed on the track like a junk-yard heap, sobbing with pain and terror at the realization that I'd never have the courage to withstand this every day.

But agonizing or not, I had made a start. And maybe I didn't have the courage to face it every day—but I forced myself out there on a regular basis. Swoop didn't laugh at my struggle or my fear. He looked at me with admiration and said:

"Way to go, kid."

I got enough energy from one of those looks to last for days.

Swoop got out of the hospital in time for the start of spring semester in February. He had decided to stay on campus near to the gym and classrooms, and Coach had understood. I was with him when he left and moved back to the dorm. He was almost white, pale as the winter sun; but he was lean and hard from exercise, biceps rippling like wave crests as he walked down the hall on crutches. For weeks after, you could see him hobbling around campus, crutches supporting his weight, right leg held stiff in its rigid cast. He couldn't put any weight on the leg at any time throughout that long winter—but he had undying optimism. The cast was scheduled to come off in early April, and he had a weight program worked out two months in advance.

But he didn't wait for the cast to come off to begin exercising. The night before classes started, he took me down to the gym, navigating gingerly over the ice. The team had collapsed and could barely win a game, but Swoop didn't mention its dependency on him. There was a change in him, a growing maturity. I saw now that his earlier bragging had been playful, part of a youthfulness, a child-like energy that bubbled and couldn't be suppressed. But now he was playing no more—his kitten quality was gone, and his life lived in deadly earnest. I still respected his determination and drive, but I yearned for the child-like Swoop that I had come to love. I suspected that I'd never see him again.

The school had recently installed a complete Nautilus set in our battered weight room, its metallic skeleton gleaming amid old barbells and a heavy bag covered with dust. Swoop led me to one of the machines and put me to work on my leg. Then he stretched his length on a rickety bench and alone began to bench press several hundred pounds. Without breaking rhythm, he called across the room to me:

"When you finish on the quads and glutes, you're going to start on your upper body."

"What?" Unlike him, I couldn't concentrate on exercise while I spoke, so I stopped.

"We're going to build up your chest, shoulders and arms, not just your legs. You're going to ripple like a bodybuilder."

"What are you, nuts? I don't want to look like some muscle-bound jerk. What are you trying to do?"

He never stopped pumping iron as he spoke.

"You're going to be a muscle man, bulging in every part of your body. Wait till you see yourself as a physical specimen—you need to see it and feel that way about yourself."

Here his voice quivered, whether with emotion or strain I couldn't tell. "We're rebuilding you, Digs, from top to bottom, remaking you, not in God's image, but in Swoop's."

"Oh, yeah? What if God doesn't like the new image?"

Swoop laughed impatiently. "Don't be ridiculous. God likes everything I do." He floored the weights and got up in one fluid motion. "Fifty," he said. "Come on, let's get started."

I didn't move.

"Everything? He likes everything about you?"

He fiddled with the Nautilus equipment, adjusting the setting, and didn't look up when he spoke.

"What's not to like?"

"Right," I said, nodding emphatically. "You have all the humility and charity necessary. It's clear why He loves you."

Swoop looked up from the machine.

"God loves audacity," he said quietly. He completed the adjustment with a brusque jerk of his wrist. "You have the goods. Let's go."

"But I'm an atheist," I whispered.

"The most religious men are."

It was the way he turned from me then, the glance of impatience, of challenge, of impending triumph that he fixed on the weight machine, that hit me harder than the words. How had Heracles stared at the Nemean lion despite the beast's impenetrable hide? Here was a creed known previously only in legend and fable, a code embodied now before me. It did more than thrill me with feelings of Achilles and Odysseus—more than make me taste the wild vigor of sword thrusts or smell the salt air surging through the rigging of my ship. It made me look down at him with a new understanding.

"You've got the heart of a pagan," I said.

But he wasn't listening. He had the workout regimen formed in his mind and could attend to nothing else. He knew what to do and all that remained was to act. I gripped the sides of the machine.

"Show me the exercises."

And so, I began a program of systematic body building, working not merely to strengthen my butt and legs, but to develop every muscle in my body, to transform my skinny frame into one bursting with power. I was going to be a physical specimen from head to toe—lean, fit, strong. The more I thought about Swoop's suggestion, the more I fell in love with it. I wanted to see myself that way, needed to—and this need drove me to rise at five A.M. every morning for two hours of grueling torture before class. I had gotten a key to the gym from Coach, and I'd get there by five-fifteen every morning. But I never had to unlock the place, because no matter how early I arrived, there was always someone there before me—Swoop, who didn't need sleep, was already grinding, relentlessly strengthening his body.

On Thursday mornings I had Advanced Logic, Nineteenth Century Comparative Literature, and Philosophy of Science one after another, starting at eight-thirty. But I was determined to get to the gym first. I got up at four, threw on sweat pants and sneakers, and jogged between patches of ice to the gym. To my surprise, the place was dark. I had done it, I had beaten him. Strangely, what I felt was disappointment. In my mind I had this picture of him as a tireless physical specimen, a mighty hero from Mount Olympus who needn't bother with such mundane concerns as sleep or relaxation. My picture permitted him only to work out ceaselessly, break for class, then head back to the gym. Reality smashed this picture now, and caused a stab of betrayal.

Until I got to the weight room. There, hitting the light, I flooded the room with brightness, revealing a sleeping figure curled on the wrestling mats in a corner. It was Swoop, of course, dressed in tank top and gym shorts, his white cast stretched straight on the mat. He had the Pope translation of *The Iliad* tucked under his head as a pillow. Evidently, he spent the night here sometimes, straining for hours, then sleeping briefly before rising at dawn to begin again. Even I was stunned by this level of devotion.

In sleep, he was peaceful as a child, face serene, muscles relaxed like a cat in the sun. He breathed easily, his back rising and falling slowly, in a smooth rhythmic flow that reminded me of waves rolling to a far shore; one could imagine them coming forever. The hard lines of his body were sculpted even in repose, and a soft strand of hair fell over one eye. Without thinking, I reached down and smoothed back the hair. My hand brushed his cheek.

Letting Swoop rest, I hit the Nautilus equipment, beginning the torture again; I lifted for hours, first with my legs, then my upper body, pumping metal until my muscles burned and bones creaked. Some people like to work out, enjoying the sense of exhilaration, the experience of a healthy body in action. But not me. I hated it with a loathing so intense it was almost painful. I hated the groaning grind of it, the long hours of wracking pain as I pushed muscles beyond their limit. Libraries, classrooms, bookstores— these were places for a civilized man—not this tight-lipped pit of Hell. No, it wasn't pleasure that drove me—but results. So I lay flat, pumped iron, grit teeth, and withstood pain.

I groaned through half an hour of it, my body sheened in sweat, before Swoop woke up. He stretched luxuriously on the mat, yawning like a lazy yellow cat. He rubbed his eyes like a little kid and looked up at me, blinking, hair tousled like a boy's.

"Digs," he yawned again, "go get 'em," and sank back on the mat.

"Come on, you lazy slob," I demanded. "You're never going to amount to anything with your attitude."

Swoop giggled like a pre-adolescent girl, openly, with no defensive reaction. He stretched again on the mat.

"I know it," he responded dreamily.

For all his aggressive energy, Swoop loved to do this, lolling in bed after one of his brief naps. He was a devoted hedonist, reveling in every pleasure his healthy body provided, and it was as if the lolling rather than the sleeping provided his energy renewal.

He rose quickly now, and we worked out together for two hours until it was time for breakfast. We parted after that, I going to my Advanced Logic class, and Swoop to his in the Literary Epic. As he walked the length of the hall, his hands gripped his crutches and he had a paperback copy of his text jammed in the back of his jeans. I faced him outside the cafeteria.

"How long before we get there?" I asked quietly.

"Less time than it took Odysseus."

"It took him ten years."

"I know it."

"And he had Penelope waiting."

He paused, letting both my words and my yearning hang in the space between us.

"So do you," he enunciated carefully.

I looked at him, reading his meaning in his glance, surprised at my own lack of surprise. I had never mentioned this to anyone, not even to him. How much had he guessed?

"This is torture," I whispered.

He nodded.

"But it's great torture."

He started toward his class. I looked after him, motionless, not even shaking my head.

"That's a goddamn oxymoron!" I shouted at his back.

He didn't stop or turn around, but merely projected his voice over his shoulder.

"Like studying Greek and Latin," he said, and laughed when I groaned. Then he was gone.

It went on this way for the entire winter, he and I driving ourselves like warriors, involved in nothing but schoolwork and physical
torment. And yet, though I didn't realize it at the time, I was happy.
I was happy to push forward against a deeply entrenched foe. I
was simply too busy to notice it. Even our loss in the conference
play-offs to Huntington made little impression on me. For next
year was going to be different. Swoop—who had been at all home
games, exhorting his teammates and who had continued supervis-
ing The Troop's grueling workouts—promised an undefeated
season climaxing at the national finals. I had no difficulty believ-
ing him—for I already knew that next year was going to be different
for me.

Swoop's cast came off in the first week of April. Jonathan
Lefkowitz flew in personally to do it. Lefkowitz removed the cast,
examined Swoop's reconstructed knee and growled: "Take better
care of your new leg than you did the old one." Then he flew to
Chicago to operate on one of their big-league pitchers. Swoop
still couldn't walk on it, but he was using the whirlpool now, swimming for long hours in the pool, and bending and flexing it. By
the first of May, he was walking again. I taped his leg then until
the right side of his body looked like a mummy, and we walked
slowly to the track.

"How you feeling?" I asked, knowing that both Lefkowitz and
the physical therapist disapproved of running, walking even, so
soon.

He was grimacing in pain already, and we hadn't even started
to run.

"I'm all right," he insisted.

Nevertheless, I was worried. "Swoop, you sure you want to do
this? Lefkowitz said to wait. He says you're making great progress—
he's amazed, in fact—but don't overdo it. He says you're not ready
yet. Come on, let's go back..."

He cut me off with a brusque wave, sweating already. His answer came in gasps.

"I'm ready...Know my body...better...than him...This will
hurt...that's all...No damage."

I was amazed. "How can you tell?"

He looked right at me. "I can *feel* my body. Can he?"

We started a slow jog, taking it easy, allowing Swoop to get
loose with a good sweat. His face was contorted and his breath
came in pants. He limped noticeably. He looked like I felt, yet he

pressed on, and me too, until we had staggered to my half-mile limit.

"That's enough," I gasped, unable to go on.

"Keep going," Swoop panted, staggering on. "A mile or bust."

"A mile?" I could hardly breathe, much less talk. "Are you insane? You can't run a mile so soon." I was aching all over, every muscle clenched in agony, but here I was truly thinking of him. It was too soon for him to be running at all, much less a mile.

He kept going, sweat pouring off him. "Yes, I can. Could run two if I had to." He looked back to where I was limping in exhaustion. "Come on, Digs, let's do it!" I was sobbing at the pain shooting up my leg. I had neglected my running because of this, and now it showed.

"Swoop, I can't!" I cried.

"Come on, you goddamn pussy!" he roared. "Come on, or I'll bleeping kill you!"

My head was swimming with pain, and I didn't think the anger could penetrate it, but I was wrong.

"Kiss off, you crippled bastard!" I roared back, taking off after his limping figure. "You ain't killing no one!" With a savage burst, I pushed on, catching up to him despite the pain-wracked world spinning before me. "You're no better than me," I repeated over and over.

Swoop looked at me hobbling abreast of him, hair pasted to his face, sweat dripping into his eyes; looked at me through his own nightmare of torment, and smiled a grimace of a smile.

"Go get 'em, kid," he gasped. It was only then that I noticed the blood spurting down his jaw from where his teeth had bitten through his lip.

We made it, staggering the final laps like crippled birds unable to fly. As we crossed the finish line, I collapsed on the track, oblivious to the harsh gravel tearing my knees. My lungs burned like Nagasaki and my leg was ground to bone meal. I lay whimpering, and Swoop hobbled over and collapsed on me in a heap, and we lay together, lungs heaving, legs and arms intertwined, sweat and grime and tears and Swoop's blood all mixing until I couldn't tell where one battered body left off and the other began. And suddenly it didn't matter any more, for Swoop had his arms around me and his head on my chest and I was stroking the softness of his hair and he was gasping, "no pain, no pain, no pain," over and over until there wasn't any any more—there was only me and him and we lay there together for a long time—and the world didn't scare me any more, didn't even exist, nothing scared me any more, and there was only me and Swoop together.

We ran every day after that—and soon it became a common sight on campus to see us limping together toward the track. Sometimes various Troop members ran with us, continuing their off-season training; occasionally other students would pat Swoop's back, offering warm smiles and encouraging words, as he hobbled to the starting line; and once a group of them spontaneously rose, cheering long and loud as he staggered to the end of a two-mile run. *The Daily Iowan* did a feature story on his comeback, complete with pictures of him in the weight room and on the track—and *The Independent* ran weekly progress reports in its sports section, proclaiming Swoop's boast that next year Hoppo Valley would win it all.

Kathryn Gately painted a canvas depicting Swoop soaring and slamming over an enemy's front line, and was amazed at the demand for it. She sold the original to Dexter Bullock—one of the Valley's most prominent attorneys, who was both a team supporter and a man who had attended last year's "Celebrate Self" party. But first she made up prints, which did a brisk business.

But it wasn't all support and encouragement, for the enemies Swoop had made were ready neither to change their minds nor go away. On an afternoon in May, with the sun's warmth flooding the earth, Swoop and I entered the weight room, our chests heaving from a two-mile run. E.J. was alone, straining on one of the Nautilus machines, his wiry muscles taut with exertion. He saw us and continued for several moments until done with his current set of reps. Then, with neither a word nor a glance, he got up and left the room.

Nor was it merely E.J.. Drew Doherty and his beer-drinking buddies grinned openly whenever they saw Swoop limp by, and one night as we ran laps I heard taunting cries of "Crip-ple! Crip-ple!" waft down from the dark upper reaches of the stands. Though some of Swoop's foes visited his bedside now, others made it clear that they had very different intentions.

But no one dared voice open opposition to his return—in broad daylight and to the face of his friends—until one day when Swoop himself wasn't even present.

It was an evening in mid-May, the semester was ending, and my Philosophy of Religion class was completing a long section on the major religions' comparative theories of human nature. To my disgust, Judas Bittner had enrolled in the course, and all semester had subjected us to his interpretation of the Bible. He had kept up a running commentary with Kathryn Gately on the ambiguities of his favorite Scriptural passage. Hilda Simonson, the seventy-year old professor, was called out of class in the middle of their discussion.

"Samson's depravities," Bittner intoned. "Are typical of the creature known as man."

"What depravities?" I asked.

He snorted. "Mr. Claveen makes a joke. I didn't realize that comedy was included among his other intellectual proclivities."

"He's not joking!" Kathy said. She was seated to my right, but now she turned fully to face Bittner. "Samson's flaws are a side issue. Essentially his life was one of stature."

"Stature!" Judas sneered. "Sure—with drinking, whoring and violence to match Jack the Ripper—there's your stature."

"No," Kathy's hard eyes were calm. "Chasing bar-flies, prostitutes and brawlers is your style. The substance of Samson's was to save his people from the Philistines. He lived—and died—heroically. Don't you forget it."

"How can I forget it," Judas drawled. "With you and your comic side-kick here to remind me?"

"Remember it then."

"But there are other things we must not forget."

"Such as?"

"Oh, lots of things." He leaned back easily, his torn monk's robe oddly contoured to the thin lines of his body like the uniform of an honor guard. He smiled, his supercilious, sneering manner gone, not warmly, but in the manner of one certain he held the high card. He looked at Kathy and me, but I doubted he saw us; he rarely saw persons at the best of times, and never when preaching; he saw only abstractions, the essence of sinfulness and Godliness. It was clear which one he saw now. "Like shaven-skulled, blinded weakness," he said. "Like being an imprisoned laughing-stock before one's enemies. Like being torn down by a crippling injury for the sin of overbearing pride. Things like that."

"Who are you talking about?" Kathy asked, her voice low.

"Samson, of course. Isn't that who we were speaking about? You're not going senile on me, are you? Look at the similar stories in the Bible—or at those of Mr. Claveen's precious Greek culture.

Not only Samson—but also Arachne and Tantalus, think of Pha-
eton—all those of haughty distinction, who, thinking their talents
exalted, turned from God or challenged Him. All laid low in the
end. A familiar theme, my friends?"

"If you mean to imply that—"

"I? I imply nothing. I state only that those who, so full of their
own bodily prowess, feel themselves able to ignore God's teachings—like Samson—find themselves torn down in the end by
crippling afflictions, possessing strength no longer, dominant no
further, unable to run or leap, forced to limp and hobble, staggering now where once they soared and sprang."

I started to rise from my seat, but grabbed the sides of my desk
at the last second. I noticed the other students looking on, their
eyes tense. "Damn it!" I shouted. "You're not talking about Samson. You're talking about—"

"Faust, Claveen. Ever read it? The man who sold his soul to
the devil for the wisdom of the ages. But there are other objects
for which a man might sell his soul—aren't there? Things like
wealth, love, fame, athletic prowess, perhaps. Or maybe an impossible comeback. What do you think?"

I was too astounded to think anything, and in another context
I might have laughed in contempt. But when I remembered the
response of certain people on this campus, in this town, all desire
to laugh was removed, replaced by something else.

"You're insane, Bittner."

"Am I? Let's see, what were your own words that day in the
hospital? 'Don't you know when to quit? Lefkowitz's assistant,
Lefkowitz himself, the top man in sports medicine—they both say
you've had it. Isn't that enough for you? Whose authority would
be enough?' Am I quoting you correctly? You—with your medical
background."

"Hey!" one of the students in back interrupted. "What are you
talking about? You've strayed from the text."

"Have I?" Bittner's voice grated across his words, all but oblit-
erating them. "I don't agree. We're discussing the Old Testament
view of man, aren't we? What better context in which to discuss a
man who has bartered his soul to Satan?"

"Oh, are we discussing you?" Kathy asked. "Funny, I thought
we were discussing your betters." She was relaxed in her chair, her
long red hair falling casually across the shoulders of her green

blouse, the slender, shapely lines of her legs curving under the taut planes of her skirt. She leaned back, her head resting on the chair back, poised slightly to my side, lightly brushing my arm, which was resting on the back of her chair as I leaned sideways, glaring at Bittner. For a second she turned and smiled at me, and I felt the soft, hot touch of her breath; it was one moment, and then Judas's voice cut through it.

"You know damn well whom we're discussing. We're talking about the orthopedic marvel—the Adonis of Hoppo Valley—about that hero of yours, who has defied every medical precept, every known principle of biology, to return from a crushing blow that would have shattered a regiment, and once again run, leap, and lead his troops. What do you think has made that possible?"

"Integrity," Kathy said. "Dedication to the true God."

"Evil," Judas replied. "Dedication to Satan."

The classroom was hushed and the students looked at Judas with faces white, knowing clearly now what he was talking about. But before I could interject, Kathy dropped a grenade.

"Your God is a stunted dwarf," she said. Her smile was never sweeter.

Bittner didn't move. For one second his eyes narrowed to slits, as if trying to modulate the heat they released. Then his shoulders relaxed. He nodded in acceptance.

"God has places for those who blaspheme."

"I trust you'll be happy there."

"I?" He laughed, its nasal sound somehow rich and resonant in the crowded room. "It's not my soul in jeopardy."

Now Kathy laughed, a hard, glittering sound of contempt.

"If God looked," she said carefully, "could He even find a soul?"

When his lips curled to sneer at her needle, Kathy leaned in.

"You don't get it, do you?" she said in a voice not of scorn but of scholarship.

"God's *all-wise*," she emphasized. "*All-powerful*. Do you think He's insecure?"

He looked at her in incomprehension, unused to being on the receiving end of a religious lecture. His expression reflected not rancor but puzzlement. She shook her head in impatience, her red hair flowing at his inability to grasp her truth.

"Only a creature who feels inferior demands blind faith and unquestioning obedience. Don't you see? But God is fulfilled, He's perfect. Nothing threatens Him. Such a God expects development, excellence, courage. We have health and strength because He gave us these. From us He expects prowess!"

She had risen as she spoke, addressing not just Judas Bittner but the entire class.

The students appeared trapped, caught between unyielding theological forces. The specific content of the course discussion was forgotten, and the two forces stared at each other, for one moment without hatred, with nothing but devotion to their respective deities.

"I am an angry God, a jealous God," Judas whispered. "I punish the sinful."

"I am a joyous God, a fulfilled God," Kathy breathed, her eyes closed. "I glorify the excellent."

"Amen," came a voice from the back.

Kathy didn't react to it, Judas did.

"Heaven is not attained by questioning the one God," he snapped.

"On the contrary!" she shouted. "It is attained only by questioning Him." She looked at me. "Sometimes I think only atheists go to heaven."

"He lets in a few theists," I allowed.

She turned back to Judas. "I'll write a book on this one day. I'll dedicate it to Jews and Christians." She thought it over. "Maybe I'll dedicate it to you. *Your God Is A Stunted Dwarf* makes a great title, don't you think? Catchy." Her angelic smile was back.

"Write any drivel your delusions require," Bittner said. "It is of the Apostate that I speak."

"Is he an Apostate? Or a Prophet?"

"A Prophet who bartered his soul to the Fiend." Bittner smiled. "Put it on his tombstone."

"No," Kathy said. "On yours."

"Amen," the voice in the back said.

Judas refused to turn his head in acknowledgment.

"They flock back even now," he said. "To a cat's-paw of Lucifer. To a Force from the Pit." He shook his head sadly. "Fools never learn."

I got up to leave. I'd heard enough, the period was almost over and Professor Simonson had yet to return.

"Come on," I said to Kathy. "Let's go to the library. Pelagius's teachings on free will are relevant here. We should read up on them."

"In Duchesne's book? You're right. But what a shame to miss the Reverend's scintillating conversation."

"Sure," I said, only half paying attention, my mind focused on Pelagius's denial of original sin. "We can read it in the comic strips."

But as I turned to leave, the grating voice of Judas Bittner brought me back.

"Comic strips, Mr. Claveen? Do you read them? Then read this: When Judas Bittner takes this truth to the God-fearing men of this town, what do you think will occur? What will they do—E.J. Speed and those like him? Will they passively submit to this Beelzebub of the basketball court...or what? What will happen when certain members of the un-Godly—such as Drew Doherty and his cohorts—have as an excuse that there exists a Satanic presence among them? Do you suppose that there will exist any constraints on their behavior? And who among the men of this town will care to lift a finger in opposition to the forces then unleashed? The outcome of it raises fascinating questions—wouldn't you agree?"

"The police, civilized people," Kathy protested. "They won't stand for this. This is the twenty-first century—not Calvin's Geneva."

Judas spread his arms in a gesture of helplessness. "Life is filled with unfortunate events—as you know. One may cross the street and get hit by a fuel truck—or get bumped on the stairs—accidentally, of course—and topple to the bottom. Who can know what's coming?" He paused. For one second his eyes glittered at Kathy. His voice washed us gently then, with soft currents of menace. "Your hero's made enemies throughout the valley." He let the words linger in the air, then leaned back and closed his eyes. "For one so smitten, Jesus is the sole refuge."

Kathy's mouth opened silently, forming a perfect red oval. But I saw Bittner's eyes glinting as they had in that one signature moment—saw his eyes, nothing else. My sensory capacity was limited to sight, leaving me cold, deaf—and mute. It wasn't because logic had deserted me that I had nothing to say, but because its function had been performed, its conclusion impelling me now to deeds, not words, pushing me across the room toward his face, intent, in the middle of this Philosophy class, to smash his mouth into a splintered mass of bloody chicle—uncaring that they'd expel and arrest me, concerned only to punish this creature before me who would have Swoop hurt again.

Professor Simonson entered the classroom and saw the bomb about to fall.

"Duggan!" she screamed.

But it was Kathy who flung herself around the bulging hardness of my chest, attempting to pin my arms.

"He's not worth it," she said, her eyes piercing Judas's as her arms wrapped around me. "Let it go."

It wasn't her words that held me back or the hard, unyielding way in which Judas stood his ground or the frantic plea that issued from the lips of the professor—but only the fact that, for the first time in my life, Kathryn Gately had her arms around my waist. Ignoring Bittner and Professor Simonson and a class full of gaping students, I wrapped my arms around her and pinned her to my chest. When she looked up in surprise, I pressed my lips to hers. For one second she responded, a woman in the arms of a man—then she ripped herself away.

"Are you crazy?" she screamed, oblivious to the crowd of on-lookers. "Freddie will kill you!"

I laughed. "No, he won't," I said. "Freddie loves his rivals."

"Not about me!"

"Bring him on," I said. "Bring the son of a bitch on. It'll be fun."

I flexed my shoulders and grinned through my teeth. Then I headed for the library.

They suspended me from the last week of school, but allowed me to take finals. Unfortunately, I didn't hear from Freddie Zender, but I did from my mom who called to scream about my suspension. I hung up the phone at the first sound of her voice. "I know," I muttered to the broken connection, and returned to my studies.

Swoop's eyes gleamed when I told him about Kathy, but he was silent for a long time after I told him about Bittner. He'd been lying in bed in his dorm room, a copy of Ovid's *Metamorphoses* in his hands, lifting ankle weights for his leg, looking at me as we spoke. But now he gazed somberly at his knee, his entire torso unmoving.

"What's the matter?"

He didn't answer at first, then held out the copy of Ovid. "Good stories," he said. "But not as respectful of the gods as they should be."

"Not all men respect the gods," I conceded.

He laid the book down with no further comment.

"But forewarned is forearmed," I said hopefully.

"Yeah."

"Swoop, I—"

He waved his arm brusquely. "Forget it."

"How can I forget something like that?"

He shook his head, as if clearing from it the cobwebs of a foreign universe.

"Kathy's right. They can't stop me. This will never happen again. Don't be afraid."

He resumed hefting the ankle weights.

But I couldn't forget it; it stayed with me; and one night, several weeks later, I dreamed about a crusade of small-town Bible-beaters, who burned books, attacked university science departments, and threw suspected atheists in prison. Nailed to a cross, high above a public intersection, the body of Swoop swayed slightly in the wind.

CHAPTER EIGHT
THE GENESIS

I hit the gym at seven. Somewhere inside Swoop was winding down from a full day of exercise.

"Swoop!" I called.

"Over here," he answered from the weight room.

The place was deserted in the summer, but Coach trusted us with keys. We had the gym to ourselves and we made the most of it. I went straight to the Nautilus equipment, married to the hated thing, and began the grind again. Swoop, having completed the heaviest part of his daily workout, jumped rope with enthusiasm, leaping with the tireless energy of a child. I pumped iron for two unrelenting hours, straining every muscle of my body, but concentrating on the legs. At nine o'clock, Swoop and I locked up the gym and jogged to the track. We laced our running shoes tight and, with no taping now, proceeded to run five miles in twenty-five minutes.

Swoop, his lungs tireless, chattered relentlessly the whole time.

"I can feel it, Digs, I can feel it, the leg is going to be there by the fall, just like I said, and guess what—when I talked to Lefkowitz the other day, he said nothing the whole time I reported—and you know what that means for him, he'd snap your head off for grins—but when I finished he took this long breath and said, 'Swoop, can anything stop you?' and I was about to say 'Hell, no!' when it hit me that coming from Lefkowitz this was a big deal, that the go-to guy had never seen it, so I said, 'When Polyphemos devours Odysseus's men, the captain doesn't quit, he puts out the monster's eye, then fights on,' and Lefkowitz just grunted—and hey! Digs, that reminds me..."

Running by his side, my lungs heaving, a knife wound in my side, I just wanted to ram my elbow into his mouth and shut him up. It had been like this for over two months. It was late July and once the term had ended after graduation, we'd sublet an apartment in town from a student going home for the summer. I got a job driving a delivery truck for the Valley's largest bakery while Swoop had scrounged enough of his scholarship money to last the summer. We were both taking a class in summer school—Swoop in Ancient Greek and I in the History of Modern and Contemporary Philosophy. We'd rise at dawn, work out for two hours, then go to class after breakfast; Swoop would then return to the gym for a grueling all-day session while I went to work; in the evening I'd join him for the second of my daily workouts, then we'd return to our apartment where we would shower and study. Turning in late, rising early, and working like a Spartan slave—I was a chronically cranky SOB. But I was pushing ahead.

As we completed our run, Swoop showed no sign of relenting.

"...these workouts are going great—the running, swimming, weight lifting are rebuilding us, absolutely, but it's not enough. We have to do more."

I had ignored him as best I could, but this registered.

"What?" I asked, panting. "What else do we have to do?"

"We have to climb."

"Why?"

"Because climbing builds the quadriceps in ways that no other exercise can. Besides working the rectus femoris, the vastus lateralis and the—"

"Spare me," I interrupted. "What are we going to climb? This isn't the Rockies, you know."

"Don't worry, I got just the thing."

"I bet. What?"

"What's the tallest thing around? What towers over the other buildings in town?"

I turned to face him. "No! Not the..." I couldn't finish.

Swoop leaned closer, so that our chests almost bumped as we ran abreast.

"That's it. We're going closer to Athena, we'll rise like Daedalus. We'll bring a message from the true gods to the top of the Catholic church steeple."

"What message?" I tried to keep up the same pace, but suddenly my legs didn't work as well.

"That Hoppo Valley is meant to win, that the gods command victory, not mercy, that Jesus got this point scrambled and we need to straighten it out—that message."

I stopped running.

"Swoop, are you crazy? They'll crucify us if we…"

I stopped only because as his back receded my words could no longer be distinguished above the sound of his laughter.

The following night, we climbed to the top of the steeple. The Holy Rosary Catholic Church was situated on a wide sweep of green lawn near the northern end of the Salvation Mile. Jogging towards it, we passed the major Protestant churches on Broadway, their dark bulks looming over us in the night. But the Catholic Church, though not possessing the largest congregation, was the Valley's most formidable edifice, its fieldstone structure providing a solid base for its tapering steeple aspiring for loftier heights. As we jogged up the street, we could make out its towering form while we were still two blocks away.

It was a dark night with clouds obscuring the moon. Swoop had done his research, picking a steeple with a jagged surface, providing jutting footholds and handholds for any fool intrepid enough to climb it. He had made up a banner, white, with the brilliant yellow rays of a rising sun, proclaiming: Helios and Hoppo Valley Ascend. In the lower right corner stood our signatures.

He had me go first. "Why?" I asked suspiciously. "So I can grab you if you fall," he replied. His eyes glinted hard and metallic in the night, determined to pull this crazy stunt, and his body was electrified, as if countless watts of current flowed through it. "How you going to grab me, hold me, and hang on yourself? It's not possible." "Digs, I swear I'll do it," was all he said—so I started up the wall.

The climb was arduous but Swoop whistled Marine marches all the way, and once, near the top, he let go with his right hand and allowed his body to swing way out from the wall, holding on with only his left hand.

"Come back, you crazy bastard," I hissed. "How the hell you going to grab me out there?"

"Sorry," he said and swung immediately back.

The view from the top was striking. There was no light from the moon and the twinkling stars were faint, but even at four in the morning enough lights were on in town to let me sweep the area. Swoop laced the banner so tightly to the bell that I doubted it would toll.

He grinned when I said so. "Ask not for whom the banner flows," he replied. "It flows for thee."

We started down.

Swoop went first and though he continued whistling jauntily, I felt his eyes on me the whole time. When I hit the earth, I bent and kissed it. Straightening up, I felt the strain in my thighs and calves.

"You're right about climbing," I groaned. "I think I used muscles I never used before."

"Wait until tomorrow," Swoop replied cheerfully.

But tomorrow had other troubles to bring.

When the monsignor discovered why his bell wouldn't ring, he could not be described as delighted. The police found our names emblazoned on the banner and arrested us for trespassing and defacement of private property. Coach bailed us out, and thanks to the esteem in which he was held, all charges were dropped. Still, it stirred a minor fuss during this sleepy Iowa summer.

One irate parishioner wrote a letter to the editor arguing that irreligious people received preferential treatment because they were jocks. An editorial on local radio chided that religion had become a joke today, a butt of obnoxious pranks and warned of "the self-indulgent spree to come." Judas Bittner, in a sermon delivered before two dozen people at the First Commandment Missionary Church, blasted the arrant Satan-worshipper running amok in the community.

Coach chewed our butts plenty in his office.

"Of all the stupid, bonehead, suicidal stunts to pull! Are you crazy?" He turned to me. "You especially," he said. "I might expect it from this madman"—he pointed at Swoop—"but from you, the budding genius, I would expect more sense. What the bleep's gotten into you lately anyway—getting suspended for threatening to cave in another student's chest cavity, kissing Freddie Zender's girl in front of a whole class, and now risking your life to pull a wild stunt dreamed up by someone who's probably certifiable. What in blazes is wrong with you?"

During the tirade, Swoop had gradually edged around behind Coach, where he stood, pointing at me, laughing in deep, silent guffaws as I got bawled out.

"Does your family know what you've been up to?" Coach continued. "Do they know what you've been doing?"

Ignoring Swoop, I turned on Coach.

"Would it make any difference?"

"What do you mean?" he answered. "Your Mom calls all the time and—"

"Sure, and tries to keep me the teacher's pet she always wanted—while my dad just leaves me to my fate."

"Your dad is—" Coach began, but I didn't let him finish.

"The hardest working man I've ever met. I know. There's no more conscientious general practitioner—anywhere." I stopped and looked away. "I only wish he'd taken the slightest notice of what went on at home."

Coach looked at me intently, perhaps seeing something for the first time.

"No," I pointed to Swoop. "This is my family. If he wants me to risk my life with him, I will—and we'll do it together."

Coach was silent and Swoop had stopped laughing. Finally, Coach nodded.

"O.K.," he said. "Just keep your bleeping butt out of jail."

But later, in our apartment, I turned on Swoop.

"The next time you want to climb, get a ladder."

I expected him to laugh, but he didn't.

"It was always like this," he said sadly.

"What do you mean?"

"I mean growing up, with my parents, at Catholic school—before I got expelled, that is. It was always this way."

Suddenly all thoughts of climbing, Coach and town furor were gone, and one thought filled my head: What was it like to have grown up Swoop?

He laughed when I asked him.

"What was it like to have grown up Swoop?" he repeated.

"Yes, what was it like? Why'd you get expelled from Catholic school? What did you do? What were you even doing there? Were your parents religious? Tell me what it was like. I got to know."

"Why? What's so important about it?"

"Are you kidding?"

After all these months it had finally occurred to me that I knew nothing about Swoop's development—about the decisions he had made, in the face of opposing alternatives, that caused him to be the man he was. After all, despite what I had come to think, he wasn't Pallas Athena, he had grown, not sprung full-blown from the head of Zeus.

"Swoop, you got to tell me," I pleaded.

"The whole story?"

"The whole story."

"It'll take a long time."

I reached over and yanked the plug on the kitchen clock.

"I got plenty of time."

"All right," he said.

* * *

Sister Mary Keenan heard the commotion while still inside the convent. She ran to the door, fearing the worst, and when she saw the white face of Sister Kathleen staring at her from the top of the stairs, she clutched her rosary.

"Did you hear what he's done..." the gasp in Kathleen's voice was only partly from the strain of racing up the stairs.

Sister Mary didn't wait to hear more. She bolted down the steps, dimly wondering whether she ran toward a resolution or fled from it. It had been this way for ten years—one incident after another—ever since he was a seven-year-old cub in her second grade class at St. Patrick's Grammar School.

The first time he'd been caught, during Catechism, poring over the tale of the Argonauts' victory over the Harpies, he'd merely gazed in rapt forgetfulness at the nun's face. When he'd received an "F" for writing his term paper on the boast of Perseus to Polydectes rather than on the words of Jesus to the adulterous woman's accusers, he'd replied to the priest's questions with the perplexed innocence of an eight-year-old, "But heroes *are* without sin." But when as a fifteen-year-old sophomore he'd stood in front of Father Malone's Religion class and described in picaresque detail his preference for Aphrodite over the Virgin, no amount of solemn earnestness was sufficient to avert judgment from on high: he was suspended.

By then he was universally-recognized as the outstanding high school basketball player in the country, leading St. Patrick's to both the city and state titles in his sophomore and junior years. He was hailed as a conquering hero in both his native Bay Ridge and surrounding Brooklyn neighborhoods.

But now it was different. This time, she knew, reconciliation might be impossible. For on a November evening of his senior year, intoxicated by the warmth of a prolonged Indian summer, he had gathered his teammates and fellow students for a midnight raid on the church. With his friends, who were as loyal to him as were the Trojans to Hector, he jimmied the door's ancient lock and slipped inside. Slowly, at painstaking care to do no damage, they removed all stained glass windows, opening the house of God to wind, air and light. They stayed the night, discussing their quest for a third consecutive city title, as well as their plans for the future, and when apprehended in the morning issued no denials. Reaction from school and church officials was swift. No matter his fervent expostulations that "The sun god commands we ban murk," the priests had the windows replaced and the vandals punished.

He and his friends were ordered to stay after school, and to receive training from Father Malone in proper Catholic principles. As a condition of continuing enrollment, they were required to do volunteer work in local nursing homes and hospitals. His friends and fans complied. He declined.

He worshipped, he said, in Fort Hamilton Park, overlooking the passage to the sea, and on the shoulder of the highway high atop the Verrazano Bridge, amidst the clouds, the mist and the brilliant sun.

The basketball coach protested that the players would miss practice and games. Father Flynn, the ex-boxer and senior English instructor, pointed out that it detracted from his best student's study time. But the clergy recognized a doctrinal issue when they saw one and were determined to quash the mini-revolt.

He ignored the priests' pleas that a young man of his gifts should not discard them wantonly; he laughed at their warnings that God punishes sinners who fail to relent from a wayward course; he left unheeded their calls for obedience to Holy Mother Church.

He attended practice and games. He urged his teammates to reject the priests' commands and do the same. When several of them wavered, it left the administration with no choice. They suspended, once again, their star athlete and top English student.

Still, he attended his senior literature class, where Father Flynn bade him welcome. He arrived punctually for basketball practice, and the coach threw his arms around him. He walked the halls of the school amidst students who cheered spontaneously, but then turned suddenly away.

Finally, administrators had security remove him from the premises, generating ripples of protest from students and faculty. But it was the next day, when the sports pages of the New York tabloids criticized the school for banning such an individual from class and practice, that the clergy started to panic. Seeing clearly that Swoop's unrepentant presence could only continue to foment spiritual unrest, they felt compelled to take a final stand. They expelled him and, like Pilate, washed their hands irrevocably of the problem.

The final meeting and decision, Sister Mary remembered, had come on Friday afternoon. The priests, in their dark garb, had voted somberly, one by one, and listening to the death verdict she had been unable to choke back either the flood of memories or the tears, the second flowing from one ineradicable component of the first—his shining eight year old's face when he stood to recount the tale of Jeanne d'Arc.

She had tried, in the intervening day and a half, to push the memory of that face aside, but her sense of foreboding could not be shaken, as if his expulsion were not the end but only an over-ture, as if the death blow of such a spirit could never be thrown externally but only from within—and that it would be thrown im-minently.

Following the small crowd gathered outside the convent, she made her way across the courtyard to the church. The wind blew snow across her face and the dark shadows of early morning loomed on the ground. Outside the entrance a crowd had gathered, and from the stunned, numbed expressions of their faces it appeared that all that kept them from stamping their feet against the cold was their stare fixated on a huge white placard nailed to the door. Though she hadn't taken time to throw on a coat, the chill run-ning through her as she read was not from the weather.

It occurred to her, later, as she trudged blankly back to the convent, too soul-weary even to attend services, that someone who urged the church to replace Jesus with Odysseus as the earthly representative of God—who pleaded to scrap the cross and cruci-fix and replace them with a replica of Nike, goddess of victory, sword upraised in triumph—who desired to hold services for He-lios—who clamored to scrap the Bible and the Catechism, replacing them with *The Iliad* and *The Odyssey*—who demanded the utter repudiation of the doctrine of Original Sin—who urged an end to the celebration of virgins and celibacy and a birth to the worship of Aphrodite—who punctuated the point by insisting all clergy be required to have sex and that those who didn't, wouldn't or couldn't be immediately fired—it occurred to her that someone who wrote all this and more, who nailed it to the church door under the heading of "Ninety-Five Exhortations," might be head-ing for more than expulsion from high school in his official dealings with the Catholic Church.

Days later, after Cardinal Mulrooney himself had been notified and made an appearance, causing quite a stir in this backwater

Brooklyn parish, she met with the terrified mother—an unfortunate, harried woman, who had seemingly lived for twelve years in
the principal's office—and the two women spoke aloud the six syl-
lables they most dreaded: excommunication.

But while they sat and prayed, the object of their anguish was
recruited by the local public school, and by every other high school
in the city, all promising to move him into their districts—and by
scores of colleges who cared not a damn if His Holiness himself
renounced him.

Swoop did not have the heart to tell either Sister Mary or his
family that he was already an excommunicate from the Church.
The only other soul who had access to this precious truth was Patricia Boyle, and she was even more proud of it than he.

Basketball had been a demanding mistress. Other elements of
his life were arrayed around it in secondary order, ranked in accor-
dance with their ability to promote the quest. Practice,
conditioning, inspiration from literature—these occupied the uppermost tiers of his personal pantheon. Early on, it led him to
pursue the reigning god of sports medicine.

Swoop had just turned fourteen on the day he burst, for the
first time, into Jonathan Lefkowitz's office.

Lefkowitz, even then the greatest living authority on sports
medicine, worked out of the Hospital for Special Surgery on the
Upper East Side of Manhattan.

Entering Lefkowitz's office, Swoop strode to the receptionist's
desk and announced:

"I'm here to see Dr. Lefkowitz."

"Do you have an appointment?"

"No."

"I'm sorry. Dr. Lefkowitz never sees a patient without an appointment."

"I'm not a patient. And he'll see me."

"Oh, really? Who are you?

"I'm Swoop."

"Who?" she asked.

"Swoop. I'm the greatest basketball player, if not the greatest
athlete, on the planet. Surely, you've heard of me?"

"Oh, surely," she replied, rolling her eyes. "Are you sure you
want the Hospital for Special Surgery and not Bellevue? I think
you'd better leave."

"Not until I see Dr. Lefkowitz."

She called for security, but when the guards started dragging him away, he called at the top of his lungs:

"Dr. Lefkowitz! Dr. Lefkowitz!"

Lefkowitz banged through the door to one of his examining rooms.

"Let him go," he snapped to the guards.

He strode to the young bum and grabbed him by the arms and waist, ready to throw him out himself. Swoop, knowing who it was, offered no resistance; he relaxed in Lefkowitz's grasp—and the orthopedist, feeling the musculature under his hand, stopped. He stared at Swoop carefully. Then, oblivious to the patients in the waiting room, he unbuttoned Swoop's shirt. Silently, he examined the lean lines of muscle structure; he looked, pushed and probed; he took a long time. Finally, he looked in Swoop's eyes.

"Go wait in the examining room," he said. Swoop turned to go. "And button your shirt. It's not polite."

Jonathan Lefkowitz had been born in the mid-1930s in Vienna, where his father was a prominent surgeon. His entire family died at Auschwitz, but Jonathan Lefkowitz survived. He was medium height but six-four across the chest and shoulders—and in college, at Princeton, had played four years of football. He worked out every day, by himself, for two hours—not at Jack Lalanne's or the New York Athletic Club, not by riding an exercise bike or swimming laps or doing Nautilus—but at a fighter's gym on 137th Street in Harlem, where he lifted free weights and pummeled a heavy bag.

He bought his clothes at the most expensive shops in the city—custom tailored slacks, fitted dress shirts, silk ties—but never wore a jacket; he rolled his sleeves up at work and ignored the pitying glances of those who stared at the numbers scorched into his skin.

Members of his staff referred to their office as "Parris Island" because of its boot-camp atmosphere—appointments were kept to the minute and staff members were allowed no latenesses. Other than medical business, Lefkowitz didn't speak to his staff or colleagues, never inquiring about their homes, their families or their feelings. But his patients put their careers, even their lives, unquestioningly into his hands—and though several of his nurses, who were religious, wondered why in their own minds they thought of their hard-bitten, atheist boss as "the miracle worker," one Catholic patient, who'd been told by several orthopedics that her tennis career was over, supplied the answer, saying that "she didn't pray to St. Jude but to Jonathan Lefkowitz."

He received top dollar for his services and growled "get a job" at beggars in the street; he rejected all New Deal welfare programs and was a free market capitalist—but when a talented young dancer was hurt, who, unable to meet his fee, offered to "pay it off over time," Jonathan Lefkowitz snapped, "Don't worry about it. You'll pay me when you're a star." Years later the kid did become a star— but by then Lefkowitz had forgotten the debt.

In the examining room, Lefkowitz examined Swoop from head to foot, leaving his regularly-scheduled patients waiting.

"But Dr. Lefkowitz," one scandalized nurse said. "This patient doesn't even have an appointment."

Lefkowitz pulled out a pen and appointment slip, and scribbled the date and time on it. "Now he does," he said, handing it to her. "Get out."

For an hour, wordlessly, he studied Swoop's body, physically gesturing the movements he wanted performed. He checked Swoop's reflexes, his breathing, his heart. He took X-rays and blood work. Finished, he said his first words.

"You've got the greatest body I've ever seen."

"Of course."

Lefkowitz stared.

"You don't understand," he said. "The best athletes, the top dancers, they're all my patients. But I've never seen anything like this."

"I understand," Swoop said quietly. "Now you do, too."

In the hush a chair scraped next door and at the reception desk a voice demanded to see the doctor. Lefkowitz seemed not to hear. His hand rested on Swoop's shoulder, but he looked at a photograph on the wall. It was an aerial shot, showing a ring of mountains, their sides hacked as with a machete. A storm swept across them, a wall of white, spitting snow. The summits rose to meet the wind as it hurled itself against them, as though each knew that in eons the peaks would be reduced but would still stand. The wind would howl on.

"Took it myself," Lefkowitz said. "And more like it—rivers, canyons, oceans. Even the glaciers of Antarctica. I fly." He turned to face Swoop. "I pray."

Swoop looked directly into his eyes.

"Then you understand."

"Yes," Lefkowitz whispered.

Swoop got up and dressed. They didn't look at each other and they didn't shake hands. Swoop left the office without another word between them. But he had only one image before his eyes on the subway ride home. Even crossing the Manhattan Bridge, he saw it: squall clouds caressing the eternal peaks.

Two days later, Lefkowitz called. Over the next few years he gave Swoop a library of textbooks, met with him in his office, had him to his home in Connecticut, talked to him on the telephone. He lectured, answered questions and prescribed workouts. He became more than Swoop's mentor—he was his personal physician and trainer. Watching Swoop in action, Jonathan Lefkowitz knew he would never take a penny from this young star—and knew that no one else would ever pay him as much.

From the time they met, Swoop never let another doctor touch his body.

Nobody could touch; they could merely watch. The only other individual on the face of the earth accorded this privilege was Patricia Boyle—and she could touch where, when and howsoever it pleased her.

If basketball had been a possessive mistress, Patricia cut into its ownership and made it share space in his soul. She was sixteen when he met her at the start of his junior year, but nobody could think of Patti Boyle as a child.

She attended St. Agnes Academy for Girls on Fourth Avenue in Brooklyn—the school's best student, top athlete and most hated individual.

"Get your head in the game!" she snapped at a teammate who dared flub one of her passes against rival St. Theresa. Then, moments later, she pounced on a loose ball and, darting upcourt, hurtled her petite frame into the thicket of larger girls camped under the basket.

Swoop, sitting in the stands, watching his sister's team, was on his feet in applause.

"Good action! Good action!"

For the next game he arrived early and positioned himself behind the St. Agnes bench. Watching her slash to the basket time after time, he found himself spontaneously on his feet, roaring his approval.

Patti noticed the lean jaguar staring at her from the stands. She didn't know who he was or care. But for one second she stared back with the smoldering look usually reserved for the opposition.

Patti's teachers knew that look and described it in similar terms. She was a slow-burning fire, they said—TNT, but in the hands of an explosives expert. The best student at any school she'd attended, she had her life planned by the age of thirteen: she would attend Columbia University where she'd study History and Political Science, then the best law school in the country. Impatient with the vacillating weak-mindedness of people, she scorned social contact and threw herself into excelling at all things—in school first, but also in sports and at work. Her acquaintances—she had no friends—claimed that if a potential obstacle had consciousness to know better, it would get the hell out of her way.

One day, Swoop waited for her by the locker room exit. Showered and changed, she was fresh as a May morning in Ireland. With chestnut hair falling to her shoulders, a complexion fair and clear as mountain water, and brown eyes trembling behind the fierce will, she stopped in front of the door and gazed at him. Other girls were shocked that Patti noticed anything outside of herself. They gaped but Patti neither noticed nor cared. Classmates were strangers and she was alone with him. She'd lived her years like a projectile and motionlessness was her sole tribute. She felt—with the shock of clarity that transforms one in an instant—that if life were a train ride, this was her stop. She had to get off; it was the reason she had boarded. He crossed the distance to her slowly, eyes merciless as at all great moments—and if words came only later, communication did not. He stood in front of her, equally motionless, holding himself back, and when he spoke it was with no preamble.

"I never had a girlfriend before. You'll be the first. You'll like it."

Patti, who hadn't been seen to smile in the ten years since her father's death, started to laugh, then held herself back.

"You've certainly never had one like me. Maybe you won't like it."

Swoop thought it over.

"Try me," he said.

The next day, they ran ten miles together at the crack of dawn, Patti wrapping herself in his oversized sweatsuit against the frigid January cold. They danced on Saturday nights in violent exertion that exceeded the energy they spent in the morning. They lived at the library, Swoop reading the love songs of Sappho, Patti poring over Gibbon, Milton and mountains of calculus notes. Mostly, they spent wordless private moments, exploring something too precious to be shared with others, moments that neither would talk about, moments that neither would forget. Mrs. Boyle watched Patti come in at dawn with tangled hair and radiant eyes, and bit off all comment, knowing it would be easier to move Mount McKinley than to change her daughter's mind.

Patti had two younger sisters, whom she began to care for at age seven when her mother started working two jobs to support the family. Patti unplugged the television, gave Mary and Kathleen picture books, then watched them with one eye and did her schoolwork with the other. She cooked, cleaned, washed, sewed for them, and never cried; the responsibilities had to be shouldered, and with tight-lipped determination she shouldered them.

She even withstood the religious fervor that Mrs. Boyle embraced after her husband's death. Patti was never suspended, expelled or even assigned detention at school; she wore the skirt, mouthed the Catechism, attended mass and addressed the clergy with the most rigidly-formal respect. But though the nuns praised her work daily, she ignored them. Crowded into a basement apartment, lacking her own room, rising before dawn for extra research and shivering in the kitchen before the heat rose, Patti's eyes were fixed from earliest schooldays on one shining goal: Columbia. She lived for her studies, read constantly and had to be ordered from the building when sick. When her teachers asked her to help others less talented than she, she complied immediately without question or complaint. But something in the ruthless efficiency with which she performed all tasks, something that neither sought nor granted the least personal of bonds, raised their eyebrows in question marks, and though none would admit it, there was not one undaunted by this slim child with the gangster's eyes.

It seemed that nothing could intimidate her. On one summer evening, after working eight hours at her job in the local supermarket, she accompanied Swoop to the ultra-competitive playgrounds of Foster Park, where the city's top black players, many of them future NBA stars, gathered to kick ass and talk smack. Swoop was known and accepted, but when the slender female with a book in her hands crouched under a lamppost to read Voltaire, she didn't know—or care—that she was breaking the rules.

Two players approached her. "Yo, girl," the shorter one said.

"Don't be bringing no books in here. The brothers not about writing essays now."

Patti just shot him a contemptuous glance and went back to her reading. But James Watkins was not one to be silenced so easily. Known in the uptown playgrounds merely as "Street," he had been orphaned at age eight, and survived knocking from one relative or acquaintance to the next, living mostly on the avenues and alleys of his native Harlem. He was a six-two point guard, with the wing span of a condor and the left-handed range of a Cruise missile. He and his homeboy, Miller the Killer Hayward—a seven-foot, two-hundred and fifty pound engine of destruction—had led De-Witt Clinton of the Bronx to the public school city championship, and had kicked tail in dozens of high-stakes pick-up games. Behind his brash, trash-talking ghetto rap, Street hid a calculating, cerebral character; he scored 680 on his verbal SATs, and shunned all drink, smoke and drugs. "I be going NBA *and* MBA," he said—but only to those few he trusted.

"We get it on now," Street said as he brought the ball upcourt, guarded by Swoop. "You Catholic boys wimp out on us, not play us for an undisputed city title. We find out here." "Don't hurt yourself now," was his later comment when Swoop, with a lunging dive on asphalt, slapped away his dribble. "My bad boy be airborne," he said, wagging his head, when Swoop skyed over Killer for a rim-rock. "Be suffering from oxygen deprivation and s—t."

But he met his match with the hard-eyed girl on the sidelines. "What you think, babe?" he turned to her after threading a deft pass through traffic for a Killer cram. "Street such a sweet mother, he be having sugar diabetes." "Street be having irreversible brain damage," she replied, mimicking his style.

Later, when Swoop and Patti departed after two hours of intense competition, Street left them with a final benediction. "Yo, library girl," he called. "Make sure the man carry your books now." As the bystanders snickered, Patti turned. "That's a job for illiterates like you. Here, want to touch?" she offered, holding out the copy of *Candide*. Street laughed. "That a sister with an edge," he said admiringly.

It was an edge felt by all who came in contact with her. Even the one crisis of her adolescent years—her abortion at age eighteen—cut her up for reasons quite different than those held by her teachers, the parish priest or Cardinal Mulrooney.

"I could have your child," she whispered, clinging to him outside the doctor's office.

"I know."

He looked at her in his arms, her brown hair tousled, eyes wide, never so feminine as at this moment.

"We can't do it, Patti. We've got things to do."

She closed her eyes and her hands left red marks on his arms. She buried her face in his chest and from the way her back shook he knew that the sounds coming from her throat were not words. He held her, and after a while she stopped.

"The priests say that if we do it, we're immediately excommunicated whether the Church knows about it or not."

Her response came without hesitation and from deep within the fold of his arms.

"Well, that's something, at least."

He didn't laugh, nor did she, and with money saved from working three part-time jobs between them, they did what they knew they must.

But such unanimity of spirit did not extend to all matters of faith, and when the final break came, less than a year later, it resulted from long-standing wrangles over Swoop's college choice, and was a direct result of the religious controversies that swirled at the center of his life.

The year Swoop took off after high school pleased her. He worked at the Classic Book Shop on lower Broadway, unloading crates, stocking shelves, surrounded by the Greek and Roman texts he loved. He enrolled as a non-matriculated student in the Classics program at Fordham University, and began to study Ancient Greek. He spent long hours at Jonathan Lefkowitz's home, learning the principles of kinesiology, fine-tuning his training regimen. And he scrimmaged often and hard, mainly against pros, both in New York and out of town—in Philadelphia, Boston and New Jersey. But the year off, far from changing his mind, as she hoped, was, in actuality, an integral part of his plan, readying him for his mission.

"Don't save the souls of those Dark Age Bible-beaters!" she railed when he revealed his plans for transfiguring Hoppo Valley. "Let them rot in their own ignorance."

Swoop said nothing but his eyes shone, and Patti knew she must stay calm.

"Just go to class, get your education and lead the school to the national title. Isn't that enough?"

"But Patti," he said, as though not hearing her. "Imagine the tragedy of never knowing the true gods."

She buried her face in her hands.

"There are no gods," she said into her fists, then raised her head. "There's only you and I—and those like us—and our will."

He was silent briefly, letting her words wash over the space between them.

"What better gods for whom to crusade," he murmured.

"Swoop," she made one last effort. "Crusades are struggles between zealots. Lots of them die."

"Everybody dies," he said. "Only a chosen few crusade."

Where Patti was infuriated by Swoop's decision to descend upon rural Iowa, major college recruiters were simply flabbergasted. Sports writers on the college beat scratched their heads, trying to remember the last time a can't-miss blue-chipper had spurned the basketball factories and opted for some jerkwater burg barely on the map. Nobody had an answer.

Swoop kept his own counsel, and it was only after his arrival in tiny Hoppo Valley that his grand plan for the future of the community became apparent. At least, to those who were willing to see.

* * *

It was late. The unplugged clock said eleven-twenty but I knew it was closer to five. The sun would rise soon, and I had to go to work. I was just getting tired, but my attention was riveted by the drama unfolding before me.

"The cards with pictures of skyscrapers and mountain peaks," I said. "The girl in New York."

Swoop nodded.

"Have you spoken to her?"

"No," he whispered.

"It's been over a year."

"It's been a year, two months and seventeen days," he said.

I stopped, unwilling to push it.

For a long time we sat at the kitchen table in silence, and the next thing I knew Swoop was prodding me, waking me up.

"Come on," he said. "Go to bed."

"We got to work out," I protested.

"Not today. The body needs rest. Come on, I'll wake you for class."

I skipped the exercise grind that day, going only to class, work and the library. By nine that night I was asleep.

But Swoop was ready for me the next day.

He pushed me past my limit on the Nautilus, upped our run to six miles, then accosted me as we panted along the track, cooling down after the run.

"You're not limping," he said.

"Good."

"You're walking like a normal person now."

"That's right."

"But it's not right," he insisted.

"Why?"

"Because you're not a normal person."

"Then what am I supposed to do?"

"You have to learn how to swagger."

"Swagger? What do you mean?"

"I mean 'swagger'—you know, to 'walk with an air of arrogant and overbearing self-confidence.'" He said it with a precise matter-of-factness as if quoting from Webster's.

I stopped and turned on him.

"Forget it," I said. "Philosophers don't swagger. It isn't fitting."

"No? What do they do?"

"They just sort of stroll. Maybe, on good days, they amble. But they never swagger."

"That's pitiful. At least they could saunter, couldn't they?"

"I don't know. Amble, saunter—what's the difference? But swaggering is out. Definitely."

Swoop turned away, muttering to himself.

But moments later he turned back.

"At least you could strut."

"Swoop, what did—"

"I know! Philosophers don't strut. But that just means they haven't in the past. You could change all that, start a trend, be an innovator in the philosophical community, show them the meaning of—"

"All right! I'll learn how to strut—O.K.? Anything to shut you up."

"Fine. But if you strut, you can definitely swagger. They're very closely-related."

I whirled on him. "You don't give up, do you? Is it that important to you?"

He'd been laughing. Now he stopped.

"If philosophers don't swagger, who will? They're the ones to teach us wisdom—right?"

I stared.

"If they've grasped a deep point or written a great chapter," he said. "Don't you think they should? What kind of philosophy tells us: 'Do good, but don't be proud'?"

I didn't need to say anything. We both knew.

"Well?"

My answer was unhesitating.

"Let's swagger like pirates."

And so Swoop taught me how to bounce on the balls of my feet as I moved, how to strut the hallways with a jaunty spring. I worked on it at the right moments—after writing a forty-page paper analyzing Descartes' influence on Kant, after a grueling two-hour workout of pumping iron, after mastering the gears on the truck I drove at work, and after setting a new personal best for our six-mile run. I found plenty of opportunities to work at it over the last weeks of that Spartan summer—and when one morning it hit me that it was almost Labor Day, I didn't wonder where July and August had gone. I knew.

Every time I moved I felt those months in rippling cords of body tissue—and every time I looked at Swoop, I saw them in the growing, bulging re-birth of his right leg. September was coming, bringing the advent of a new school year, and though the campus still lazed under the last summer sun, its unsuspecting ambiance was about to be gate-crashed by the return of two lean and panting tiger cubs.

And one of them was so cockily flexing his young muscles that it was only a casual question in his mind whether Hoppo Valley was ready.

CHAPTER NINE
THE SECOND COMING

I moved back into the dorm the day after Labor Day.

The summer sun blazed on the concrete of the rear courtyard as, dressed only in tank top and gym shorts, I lugged crate after crate of philosophy texts up the three flights to my room. People looked at me on the stairs, not recognizing me—for I had put on twenty-five pounds of muscle since January, bulking up from 145 pounds to 170, a weight at which my 5' 9" frame quivered. Donna Axford and several other girls shot me double-takes as I swaggered down the hall, and I grinned, thinking of Aristotle's proud man with his "slow step and deep voice."

Classes started two days later. When I walked into the first class of my senior year—Philosophy 400, Advanced Seminar in Aristotle's *Metaphysics*—I noticed the three other students blink. The professor looked at me dressed in tight black shirt and dark slacks, and shook his head.

"Duggan," he said. "I wasn't sure it was you or a wrestling villain."

I flashed my battered McKeon *Aristotle* at him.

"It's me."

Then I settled in my seat, ready for a year of straight Philosophy courses and the graduate entrance exams.

There were changes at school as well as in me. The Board of Trustees had gone along with President MacPherson's decision, and had not renewed the contract of Dean Pearsall. It was done quietly, over the summer, with no fuss and for reasons that seemed obvious to some. He was replaced by David Keyes, a former assistant of MacPherson's, from his days as chancellor of Knox Freedom College in Dayton, Missouri. In his announcement, MacPherson stressed the Dean's responsibility to assist the President in leading the University back onto the path of its sacred mission. Kathryn Gately wrote an article in *The Daily Iowan,* pointing out that in an essay entitled "The Ethical Foundations of Liberal Education," published some years previously in the academic journal, *The Theist*, MacPherson had argued that the purpose of education is to "instill in the mind of the student the high-minded moral and social principles that form the core of traditional Western theological teaching." The new dean, like MacPherson, did not smoke, curse or gamble—and was on public record as agreeing with the president's educational goals. Together, they promised new leadership down an old path for the university.

Swoop was running well now, putting full pressure on the leg and beginning to leap. Although nine months had passed since the injury and neither of us had dunked, there were no complaints, for our lungs were in great shape and our legs coming around. When basketball practice started in mid-October, he was almost ready to play. He still put in long hours of work after classes on the exercise bicycle in the weight room, pedaling hundreds of miles each day, not stopping till he was bathed in glistening sweat. He jumped rope like an antelope, springing and soaring in long moments of graceful motion, legs pumping like organic dynamos—and he lifted weights with his right leg until the tendons and muscles bulged with power and the veins stood out in red streaks on his neck.

One evening after practice Swoop made his nightly pilgrimage to the weight room. He hadn't played in the intra-squad games, but had dominated all exercises, running lines with tireless ease, finishing Coach's five-mile run four minutes ahead of everyone else, and doubling all others' total of push-ups, sit-ups and jumping-jacks. Members of the Swoop Troop encouraged him, pounding his back and flashing wide grins. "Great going, Swoop!" they hollered. "Better than ever!" E.J. and Doherty stared in stunned silence.

After completing my chores in the training room, I joined Swoop with the weights and grunted through hundreds of reps for my upper body while Swoop did the same for his leg. Twenty minutes later, when I dripped sweat as profusely as he, I noticed someone standing in the door and looked up. It was Freddie Zender.

"Damn," he said, shaking his head. "Don't you guys even break for dinner?"

I couldn't talk while lifting, so I ignored him. But Swoop gasped a reply even while his leg pumped hundreds of pounds.

"Food Service packs us a ...box lunch...We eat...later."

Freddie said nothing, but his eyes kept switching from the grow-ing definition of my chest and shoulders to the bulging authority of Swoop's leg. Though my eyes were focused on the machine, and Swoop grunted nothing else, it was a long time before I heard footsteps walking from the door.

Several weeks later, in early November, Swoop led me to the gym. He grabbed a basketball, walked onto the court and stood quietly at the foul line, looking at the rim as if to say: "Here I am again, you bastard!" Then he took two steps, catapulted into the sky and rammed the ball through the basket.

He walked up to me, eyes burning like wires, and handed me the ball.

"Now you do it."

I tried. I tried until I felt my lungs poised to burst and my calf muscles turn to jelly—but I couldn't do it, couldn't even come close. And, of course, we both knew that I'd never do it, had al-ways known it. But I was jumping. I was jumping, walking, running now. Hard as a tire iron, I had earned my strength—and earned, too, the hard look of respect in Swoop's eyes. I walked up to him then and threw my arm around his shoulder. He didn't back off or move away, but let his head rest against my arm, like a girl. And when we walked out of the gym, we walked out together, my arm still locked around him. People stared at us like we were two lov-ers flaunting our illicit bond. But we didn't even bother to laugh. In a sense it was true.

The season started near the end of November. Swoop wasn't quite a hundred percent, but getting there fast. He scrimmaged for the first time several days before opening night.

The day after Thanksgiving was cold, and the damp wind whis-tling off the Nebraska prairies to the west promised an early snowfall. But when I came up from the training room to the gym that afternoon, the sun might as well have crested to its zenith—for Swoop stood on the court ready to play basketball. It was the first time in eleven months.

His teammates pretended not to notice, but when he walked onto the floor they dropped the basketballs, turned from the rim and faced him. They burst into spontaneous applause.

"Swoop! Swoop! Swoop!" they chanted. Bobby and Davy laughed like exultant children and Dandy threw his huge arm around Swoop's shoulder; several of the guys whistled, a few whacked Swoop's back, and Freddie smacked his hands together, eyes riveted on the chiseled mass of muscle surrounding Swoop's knee. Although most of the guys didn't approach Swoop, and their smiles were tight with a reserve that was not resentment, they clapped and stomped in vigorous approval. Only E.J. and Doherty remained apart, standing together under the far basket, scowling, heads down. None of the others cared or noticed as they cheered for Swoop.

When the pick-up game started, we could see that Swoop's specific basketball skills were rusty with disuse. He fired errant passes, threw up an air ball from the perimeter, and once, comically, watched in open-mouthed disbelief as the ball rolled out of bounds after he bounced it off his foot. But nobody even noticed, for those skills would return with practice. What everyone did notice—in gaping, head-shaking silence—was the complete resurrection of Swoop's athletic talent.

I wasn't surprised when he sprang two feet over the rim to slam home an offensive rebound, and I wasn't shocked as he cut, changed speeds and veered direction with the grace of a deer—but others were. They hadn't been there when he'd hefted iron eight hours every other day—they hadn't seen him sprinting mile after mile until his teeth bit through his lower lip and blood spurted down his jaw. They didn't know, maybe couldn't understand, what drove him—all anyone knew was that his career was supposed to be over, but wasn't—and so they stared, eyes bulging, and said nothing.

By opening night, Swoop's readiness inched toward the verge of game competition. Coach took him aside in the locker room just before tip-off.

"You're on the bench tonight, Swoop, no matter the score. Understand?"

"I can play," Swoop insisted.

"I know you can play. I've watched you in practice. It's unbelievable that you've come back at all, never mind so quickly."

"That's why I should play tonight."

Coach smiled. When around Swoop, he seemed more alive—not younger, but healthier. His mannerisms were crisper, more energized, and his slumping carriage seemed somehow more erect. He liked to touch Swoop, his hands moving with their own consciousness to rest on Swoop's arm or back. Now he clinched both hooks in Swoop's shoulders.

"No, son," he replied. "That's exactly why you sit. Do you think I would jeopardize your career for a few games?"

Swoop opened his mouth to protest, but Coach waved him off. "That's it! You sit—got it?"

Coach pulled to his full bulk and jabbed a finger the size of a night stick. All dispute ended.

But Swoop's play in practice over the next two weeks made further dispute irrelevant. He dominated scrimmages as both skills and timing returned, and by early December he was ready for game competition. On the road, against Pierce College of Minnesota, Coach brought Swoop off the bench for his first action of the season. It was our fifth game and we were one and three.

Eight minutes before half-time, Coach looked down the bench. "Swoop!" he called.

Swoop tore off his sweatsuit and bounded toward the scorer's table before the air molecules had ceased trembling with his name. Coach blocked his path as he streaked toward the court. His gut sagged and his skin was white like a limp sweat sock. The fragile final embers had left a last glow in his eyes—never, perhaps, to be rekindled, but not yet extinguished; they sparked briefly as Swoop drew near. His voice was a croak— but I was able to hear, and his words caught me off-guard.

"Most lie down when it's all against them," he said. "A few like it that way."

Swoop's eyes held his, then he stepped onto the court.

As he walked onto the floor, the Pierce students and fans rose, bursting into spontaneous applause—stomping, banging, hollering, spitting a barrage of sound. Swoop lowered his head and stood motionless, hair blowing as if in the breeze from the crowd's lungs. His teammates, swept to him by the torrent of noise, engulfed him.

"Welcome back! Congratulations."

They shook his hand and pounded his back while the enemy crowd stood and roared. Freddie approached him last.

"Swoop," he said. "It's about time."

There was no pity in his eyes and his voice, though hushed, carried clearly in the din.

Swoop stood straight, saying nothing, and Freddie lowered his eyes, not from shame but from an irresistible attraction to Swoop's re-built leg. They stood together, saying nothing more, until the crowd tired of cheering and play resumed.

Coach had Swoop playing shooting guard, with Bobby Stenaker on the point until Swoop got his timing back. On our first trip upcourt, Bobby handled the defensive pressure and whipped the ball to Swoop on the wing. Swoop, single-covered, put his man in the air with a silky head-and-ball fake, then blew past him and drilled the pull-up jumper. Our guys leaped from the bench, sensing victory, but Swoop ignored the hub-bub and raced downcourt to play defense. He skyed for the defensive rebound and, later, slammed one home at the offensive end, rising cleanly over the backs of Pierce's big men to put it down with his left hand. But, in his short stint, he also got whistled for two fouls and bounced a pass into the crowd on a delicate timing play inside. Coach pulled him after the second foul, not wanting to overwork his star in his first game back. Eventually, with Swoop sitting and fuming, we lost by twelve.

Swoop's play improved gradually as his timing returned, rustiness dropping from him like a shabby cloak. With each game his jungle instincts asserted themselves, his confidence swelled, and other players, both friend and foe, shook their heads at the increasing number of mega-plays. Coach still brought him off the bench, but his playing time increased with his re-born skills, and by the time conference play began in late December, Swoop was, again, on the verge of dominance.

Ironically, he started his first game just before Christmas at home against Jabez, a team whose only disappointment was that Swoop wasn't crippled by them. He was announced last, and when the loudspeaker blared his name the packed house bellowed in a standing ovation. The fans stood now, even those who had previously rejected him, and roared his name.

"Swoop! Swoop! Swoop!"

Swoop stood at center court with his teammates as thousands stood and cheered. Some perhaps felt pity for this recent cripple and some no doubt felt guilt, but there was at least one in attendance whose hard eyes showed nothing of the kind. Freddie Zender wrapped both arms around his neck and even from the bench I could see the words formed by his mouth.

"Kick some tail, Swoop. God knows you've earned it."

Swoop didn't nod or utter a reply. But his hand gripped Freddie's wrist like a cuff.

From the opening play, Swoop took it at Jabez's throat. Their hulking center easily won the tip, but Swoop stole it in their offensive end and cruised the length of the floor, cramming the game's first points on a winging, two-handed slam. Getting all over their point guard, he applied remorseless pressure, playing defense offensively. He stole the ball at mid-court and, blazing to the hoop, eyes seeing only rim, he fired a blind, last-second pass to a hustling Bobby Stenaker for a lay-up. On Jabez's next possession, he blanketed their shooting guard when Bobby got picked off, forcing him to throw up a wild shot; then knifed to the glass and grabbed the rebound a foot above the rim. He dribbled through traffic, weaving like a running back, emerging on the left sideline, where he out-raced all defenders to the baseline, then paused, and when the defense caught him drilled a pass to Freddie wide-open in the lane. Our guys pumped their fists as Freddie scored the lay-up, but Jabez's players looked stunned: in forty seconds Swoop had a slam, a rebound, two steals and two assists. We led six-nothing and they called time.

The home fans stood, stomping their feet, banging the chairs. "S-w-o-o-o-o-p!"

His teammates milled around him as we huddled on the sideline, grinning as if we'd just won the conference championship.

"Looking great, Swoop!" Bobby said. "Congratulations!" several others called. "Glad you're on our side!" the front row fans gushed, swinging towels.

Freddie's face loomed like a peak behind his teammates. He shook his head, but his eyes looked like they witnessed the unfolding of events that had been ordained.

"Better then ever," he said, his voice hoarse. "How'd you do it?"

Swoop's eyes glittered as he turned to face the captain.

"It's not enough to be born," he said. "You must be born again."

Several laughed, somebody whistled, even E.J. merely gaped. But Freddie didn't move. He stared at Swoop in silence, then he turned back to the game.

We crushed Jabez by thirty, raising our record to three and six, but more importantly, making us one and oh in conference play. Coach let Swoop play thirty-two minutes, pulling him only eight minutes from the end when our lead stood at thirty-four. His stat line read: thirty-six points, twelve assists, ten rebounds, ten steals, zero turn-overs. Troop members spent the night celebrating, not just this win but the ones they anticipated. By the time they got home it was past three, and they paid the price when Swoop woke them to run at six.

But members of The Troop were not the only townspeople to celebrate. Two weeks and three victories later the Main Street Merchants' Association threw a dinner for the team at the best steak house in town. We had won in routs, Swoop was better than before, and the town buzzed with his promise of a national title. The two-hundred-dollars-a-plate dinner didn't just sell out the restaurant's private room, but filled it with professors, several university administrators, the county's most prominent realtors, bankers and insurance brokers, the deputy mayor, town comptroller, two members of the city council, and even the Unitarian minister. The Association's president, Bob Geronda, was an entrepreneur from St. Louis who owned a small chain of drug stores throughout the Valley. He stressed the impact the team's success would have on local commerce, several of his colleagues added points corroborating his claim, and Coach gave a snappy talk in which he punched home his theme of pride as the ultimate reward of a man's attainment. But it was Swoop, as guest of honor, who spoke to thunderous applause regarding his guarantee of national dominance. The atmosphere was giddy with success, we stayed until two A.M., and local businesses did not open until ten the following morning. A week later, following two more blow-out wins, the Chamber of Commerce declared "Hoppo Valley Basketball Day," a twenty-four-hour period in which all season ticket-holders would receive fifty-percent discounts at every shop and restaurant in town. Season tickets were sold out the day after Swoop's first start and the sports page of the local newspaper was the section to which most readers turned first.

Just as they had done when Swoop first arrived, crowds gathered again at the gym on Saturdays, Sundays and late weeknights to watch him put The Troop through its drill. Coach excluded fans from formal practices, but Swoop welcomed their psyche-up potential and allowed them to teem along the sidelines and clamber in the bleachers for all informal scrimmages. From the first day of school, since the moment of The Troop's return, Swoop had made sure that the gym's confines were home to them more than their dorm rooms. The Troop members were learning, like their leader, to live on less sleep—and now they had company.

The injury had shown people Swoop's vulnerability; but the better-than-ever return had convinced them of his invincibility.

Frederic Westegaard asked Swoop to write a feature on his come-back, stressing the theme of the human spirit's indomitability, and many of our fans read and loved it. They also knew that the news-paperman himself could have written it.

Frederic Westegaard was in his early sixties, a tall, lithe, silver-haired figure who looked like a patrician but who came from a family of Missouri dirt-farmers. He'd worked his way through the University of Iowa, and when he'd first started on the paper he eventually re-christened *The Independent*—as a reporter forty years ago—there had been three small papers in a one-hundred-square-mile radius. Now there was one—his. He was an outspoken defender of the First Amendment. He interviewed everybody—including Communists, Klansmen and religious zealots; and didn't care what anybody—clergy, state legislators or judges—thought of it. He excoriated both rural bigots who harassed a black family new to the area, and University of Iowa administrators who ex-pelled a redneck student for racist remarks. "Monopolies are the last bastion of freedom," he'd once written. "But only when they're owned by renegades, mavericks and outcasts."

Westegaard had fought relentlessly against the extreme elements in town who upheld religious censorship. Just several years previously, he had driven two hours through a heavy snowstorm to deliver an address on "Our Sacred Right to Free Thought" to thirty students in a rural backwater high school. He saw in Swoop the spiritual tonic he believed the community needed.

Swoop's feature, accompanied by a drawing of Pallas Athena, goddess of civilization, was entitled "Man Also Aspires." In it, he argued that the Greek commitment to bodily, mental and moral excellence formed the basis of "the only proper religion," and that any creed attacking man's nature was "damned by that alone and from its own mouth."

Swoop-mania was growing. Both local and campus radio inter-viewed him repeatedly. Prints of Kathryn Gately's painting—a vision of him soaring above Huntington's big men, poised to slam, his lean musculature rippling—sold like newspapers; soon it appeared in store fronts and homes all over town. Swarms of kids surrounded the gym clamoring for his autograph.

But it wasn't until Swoop held sunrise services at Krandell Lake that the fever approached epidemic proportions.

"The sun god must receive homage for his triumph over dark-ness," he proclaimed in a January morning interview on local radio.

When the host asked him his purpose, he replied that the return of the light must be used as inspiration for our own feats of valor. When several admirers stopped him the following day before The Troop's early workout, and told him that *he* was the inspiration for their feats—of enrolling in college, becoming engaged, seeking a black belt—he smiled and said that we too, like Hermes, could fly.

There were scores who remembered the Celebrate Self party, hundreds who yearned for victory, and some who, feeling the need for positive change, saw Swoop as the means to effectuate it. They called the radio station, listeners from around the Valley, wanting to know where and when services would be held. Bob Geronda financed an ad in *The Independent*, stating location and time, proclaiming the Valley's need to be "up-lifted in a holy quest."

Geronda had battled unsuccessfully for two years against local ordinances to keep his stores open all day on Sunday. The Catholic church he'd been attending supported the blue laws, and when relentless negotiation had failed to move the priests he'd walked away, fuming at the old-fashioned restrictions they still imposed on the most entrepreneurial people. He'd played baseball at the University of Missouri, had supported both the Hoppo Valley football and basketball teams from the day he entered the Valley and had publicly stated numerous times that the great virtue of athletics was its dedication to winning championships. He'd embraced Swoop's crusade from the start.

We had a game at home on Saturday night against tiny Warwick College of Nebraska, then left Monday morning for a road game against Concordia. Services for the sun god were scheduled for dawn on Sunday.

The hills overlooking Krandell Lake six miles outside town were the highest point in a fifty-square mile area. They stood on the west shore of the lake and faced east across the water. The sun's rising rays struck here first, before any other spot in the Valley.

Saturday night was cold and crisp as an apple. Hundreds of fans quietly celebrated our 87–52 thrashing of the Nebraskans, a mismatch in which Swoop had twelve steals and sixteen assists. Sunday morning broke clear, with slivers of ice hanging from the trees like a statewide chandelier. The first rays of the rising sun glistened on the frosty breaths of nearly eighty worshipers who half-ringed Swoop at the top of the hill, facing him and the east behind.

With the wan rays sparking flecks off his hair, standing bare-headed, wrapped in his Hoppo Valley sweats, he raised an invocation to Helios.

"Sun god," he said simply. "The sky is your domain and you flood it with light. We will do the same in our spirits and in our lives."

Their faces were turned upwards, hundreds of them, their cheeks receiving warmth from the dawn's rays and their souls from the speaker's radiance. Over and again, they asked about his guarantee of a national title; over and again, he assured them. "We will use the championship as fuel to push forward in individual quests, for the Olympians more highly prize the homage of an exalted man, like Odysseus, than that of one who relents." In the waxing light, he read aloud the tale of Daedalus, describing his ascension, his flight, his achievements as the first aviator and his escape from Minos. But as he spoke, it was unclear whether the audience observed the discrepancy, whether they noticed that, in Swoop's version, Icarus rose higher and higher, far outstripping his father, and the heat of the sun's rays had no effect on his wings, because Daedalus, the far-seeing inventor, had had the wisdom to fasten them not with wax but with bronze—so Icarus soared ceaselessly higher, and never plummeted.

When he was done, they gathered around him; nobody left; they stood at his side, in front of him and in neat rows behind others, reaching out to shake his hand, to touch his arm, his shoulder—and, especially, his leg. The sun struck off their glittering eyes; and when they asked about basketball, he answered politely, then segued smoothly to education, career and love.

The following day, the snapshots taken by the photographer sent from *The Independent*—showing scores of locals surrounding Swoop, reaching upward in yearning aspiration—appeared on the newspaper's front page, under the caption "Communion in the Sun." The accompanying story made it clear where, how and with whom many Hoppo Valley residents now spent their day of worship. The article also made clear that such services were not about to end.

We got back late that night after clubbing Concordia by twenty-five at their place. Swoop had twenty points and twelve assists in the first half and Coach sat him for most of the second, though he squirmed like a child on the bench. On the long bus trip home, I sat in the back with a copy of the *Metaphysics* on my knees, a pen in my right hand and a pencil flash in my left. Swoop lay stretched on his back, his head on my lap, reading Ovid's *Heroides* by the same light. When we reached campus it was two A.M. and I was whipped.

Two hundred people waited for us in the parking lot. They clapped and waved towels; they stomped their feet and hefted posters of Swoop. When he got off the bus, they asked two questions about the game, one about the national title and ten about future services in the sun.

On Tuesday morning, Swoop—who never sought publicity— made call after call to The Buzz, finally getting through, and announcing on air that Sunday services this week would feature exclusive devotion to champions and the requirements of becoming one. He exhorted all listeners to "relinquish the creeds of sin and humility and embrace the code of pride." Zatechka told him he would end on a crucifix but wished him luck. Most subsequent calls, whether pro or con, discussed Swoop's invitation—and rural Hoppo Valley, previously undiscussed, was now a hot item on Des Moines radio.

Bob Geronda advertised it daily in *The Independent* and, on Sunday, though flurries fell lightly, greater than one hundred residents drove their pick-ups to worship with Swoop at Krandell Lake. One young entrepreneur with a van made money by shuttling people back and forth between various points in town and the appointed place.

The morning was dark with heavy snow clouds hanging over us and a damp, cutting wind blowing off of the lake. Swoop, dressed simply in letter jacket and jeans, snow flakes glistening on his face and hair, walked among us as he spoke.

"Astylos," he said. "Unfortunately, few remember that he won dual wreaths in consecutive Olympic Games, competing for different cities." He stopped in front of me, and I felt one hundred pairs of eyes staring at me. "You're a Classical scholar. What do you know of Milo of Croton?" My answer came unhesitatingly: "Not a goddamn thing." Swoop didn't smile as he laid his hand on my chest over my heart, pressing so hard through my thick sweatshirt that he almost forced me back. "He was a boxer who carried a calf every day of its life until it was a full-grown bull. That's how he developed his strength." I stared at his back as he continued through the crowd, stopping periodically to address some worshipper individually. It took him only several minutes to work his way back to the front.

He looked at the sky, as if hoping for the sun to break through. He smiled for the first time when he looked back at us, communicating the need to create our own light despite the weather.

"One writer made the point succinctly," he continued. "It was under the rubric of athletics that we find the real religion of the Greeks—the worship of health, beauty and strength. That quote—and the great athletic feats of the Olympians then and now—can continue to be a source of inspiration, showing that excellence is still possible." We were silent as he quietly concluded: "Citius, Altius, Fortius." The only sound was the steady wind through the trees. The fresh evergreen taste of a snowflake was in my mouth, but only the words, "swifter, higher, stronger," were in my mind.

The crowd remained hushed, motionless, the soft flakes landing lightly on their upturned faces, and when, after more than an hour, they finally pivoted to depart and return to their lives, their eyes had not lost the glow of this momentary intercourse with divinity.

The road leading from the lake was jammed for twenty minutes and word the next day was that attendance had been down at more than one Hoppo Valley church.

But Swoop was only beginning. He had already fired the first shots of his campaign, it is true, but these were mere bullets from an arsenal that included nuclear weapons. It was not until ten days later—at a celebratory team dinner held by the Chamber of Commerce, a shindig thrown after three more crush-jobs, toasting our undefeated conference record and co-ownership of first place—that Swoop unleashed heavier artillery; stating publicly from the dais that "the championship is symbolic of the new religious fervor sweeping the area, a faith that will blast aside the debilitating codes of the sin peddlers." When these words were greeted by rousing applause from dozens, it became apparent to everyone in the community—friend, foe and non-combatant alike—that a strike force not to be despised had gained a beach-head in Hoppo Valley.

As if to corroborate his words, the number of supporters seeking to train with The Swoop Troop—seeking to run, lift, spring, soar—started growing in exponential proportions. Buoyed by the drive to a national title, inspired by the new worship of excellence, they flocked to Swoop now, not to kneel, follow or obey, but to take private lessons in how it was done. On the late January morning after we trashed Bellemore College—blowing them out of their own gym, running our conference record to nine and oh—Swoop had fifty fans milling outside his dormitory in the pre-dawn cold. They ran mile after mile in pursuit of stamina, lung power, fitness, pride and something beyond even these that, perhaps, they could not find anywhere else. After the next Sunday service—dedicated to the undying spirit of Thermopylae, with candles flickering but not gutting in driving snow—the number exceeded eighty; after a rousing home victory over Templeton, with fans thronging the parking lot of the over-stuffed gym, it approached one hundred.

They ran through the streets at seven o'clock in the morning, and bystanders noticed that Swoop hung back, always encouraging one of the others to lead. Pedestrians also noticed that many wore a basketball medallion around their necks, hanging outside their shirts. Some were of bronze, some of stainless steel and a few of gold. Their route took them around campus, through the business district and past every major church in town. They chanted as they ran: "If you don't know, best listen in, only priests are born with sin." Some spectators beeped, some waved and stomped, some turned deliberately away. But none could ignore them.

There were those who said that his presence in the community could no more be ignored than an outbreak of the Black Death. They pointed not merely to the battalion of runners snarling Main Street traffic during the morning rush, not only to the raucous crowds teeming outside the over-brimming gym during games and Swoop Troop practice sessions, and not just to the hard-jawed townies swarming in the school's weight room, clamoring to work out with Swoop—but to the new spirituality taking root and sprouting plants in every outpost of the Valley.

For weeks, clergymen throughout the area had spoken out, in private discussions and in public sermons, against the idolatrous blasphemy festering in the Valley like gangrene. But now they were ready to do more than talk. At the same time that Swoop spoke of Thermopylae, they pow-wowed at the Unitarian Church on Front Street—clergymen from every major denomination, two professors from the Religion Department, several town councilmen and a few prominent businessmen. A student I knew from school also attended, and *The Independent* printed a detailed account in Monday's edition.

Though the Unitarian Church was constructed largely of glass, with windows belting the structure, the curtains were drawn, preventing the entry of sunlight, befitting the occasion's somber mood. The audience of sixty did not sit in pews, as in a traditional church, but rather in collapsible metal chairs set up in the church's meeting room. The assembled clergy sat in the front row, waiting their chance to speak. The Reverend Davidson Autry of the First Presbyterian Church went first, and the audience hushed.

A rotund, red-faced man in his fifties with little hair but a hearty laugh, Pastor Autry was widely liked by both his congregation ånd the broader community. But his tone today was pained and worried, not convivial.

"It's no good mincing words," he said. "A primitivistic, pre-Christian sun-worship has been born and is catching on in our community."

Father Schaefer of the Holy Rosary Catholic Church reiterated his colleague's message. "The new observances cannot be called 'religious' in any proper sense. Rather, they are cultish in manner and method." In the dim light, the tall, powerfully-built young priest reached out to his interdenominational audience, seeking not to frighten them but to inspire them to redoubled commitment to their Christian faith.

But it was Whitfield Buttle, pastor of the Episcopalian Church and minister to the town's elite, who, despite his calm, dignified way, generated the day's greatest excitement.

"While upholding our sacred right of freedom of speech," he said, "we must nonetheless protect the community from disruptive activities springing from licentious principles. We must meet with University President MacPherson and with Mayor Pedersson."

While the interdenominational summit planned meetings with the university and town leadership, Judas Bittner called for a different form of action. Bittner, who was not invited to the meeting at the Unitarian Church, delivered a Sunday morning sermon at the First Commandment Missionary Church on Burleigh Street on the edge of town. E.J. was in attendance, and spouted Bittner's message all over our locker room, though most players ignored him.

The church was a small clapboard affair near the train tracks in the town's poorest section. An abandoned home stood directly across the street, bricks crumbling from its outdoor, roof-to-ground chimney. Across an empty lot could be seen the smokestack of the valley's sole foundry. Inside, Bittner stood on the pulpit before

twenty-odd worshippers, many of whom were young men from
the farms circling the area outside of town. He did not speak in
the refined terms of those at the Unitarian Church.

"The Maccabees pointed the way. They did not merely worship—they warred for Yahweh—and resisted the pagans in every
stratagem of conflict. Can we, as their spiritual heirs, do less?"

His slight figure seemed to grow, to become taller, more robust as he hammered home the word of God.

"We must take action, not merely spout words. Moses wasted
no time on verbal recriminations of those who abandoned God
for a golden calf. He slew them. Though the legal system currently
restrains us from delivering the infidel to such a fitting end, it is
not necessary that all we do is talk. A Christian action group is
imperative, a community watchdog to hound the enemy, to moni-
tor and plague him at every turn."

He said nothing further regarding the specifics of such a group.
But within seven days and for weeks following, intense, close-
cropped young men toting Bibles and "Jesus saves" leaflets showed
up in the college dorms, banging on the doors of Troop members
and pasting flyers to the walls. Based on descriptions from students, it sounded like there was only a handful of them, but what
they lacked in numbers they made up for in zeal. They broadcast
in severe voices the threat of impending Hell fire and they refused
to go away. In some cases, campus security was compelled to escort them from the buildings—but they never failed to return the
following day. They gained admittance to the offices and work-
places of those who attended sunrise services; they followed them
home and stood beneath their windows; they said nothing but
merely held lonely vigil for lost souls. In no cases did they offer
violence or threats, only plain wooden crosses thrust high in their
hands. One followed me around campus for most of one morning, though none ventured near Swoop.

But when the controversy spilled onto the team itself, when it
rumbled and shook and threatened to tear at the fabric of what we
had accomplished, then it hit Swoop right where he lived—and
then it was that Coach interceded.

It started in the hallways with E.J. and his cohorts confronting
Troop members for stern harangues; continued during practice with
the infliction of flying elbows after those harangues were ignored;
accelerated when Swoop's foes refused to pass him the ball, though
Coach demanded it be in his hands at all times; and climaxed when

Swoop told them to their faces that "their Dark Age bigotry undercut the team's drive to greatness."

When E.J. whirled and went for his throat, Coach stepped in between. He placed one hand on E.J.'s chest and shoved, sending him tripping back, almost sprawling flat. He hooked an arm around Swoop's neck and, with his other hand, jabbed the air. "We're winners finally," he said and looked around. "Anyone doesn't like it, clear the bleep out." Nobody moved as Coach glared from face to face. But later, there was grumbling in the locker room and more than one sullen look, especially after Freddie moved his locker next to Swoop's.

By early February, it seemed that nobody in town spoke of much besides basketball and the swirling ideological conflict that engulfed the Valley. *The Independent* featured continuous basketball coverage in an expanded sports section and front page pictures of Swoop's private army streaking through town. Though seventy miles away, Ron Zatechka had on the air every clergyman in town to proclaim their views, then concluded by calling them ninth century superstition mongers. Merchants along Main Street hung in their windows basketball medallions, pictures of Swoop or unvarnished wooden crosses to announce their allegiances—and several street corners were sites of serious disputes, replete with red faces, upraised voices and gesticulating mannerisms.

For me, it was the start of my final college semester, and nothing short of world war could have deflected my attention from philosophy courses and applications to Princeton's, Harvard's and Yale's graduate programs. But then that's what the struggle was about, and so, as part of my studies, I immersed myself in it.

We played three nights out of four on a road trip through southern Minnesota, a sequence in which we routed our first two foes and in which Swoop rallied his exhausted troops for a heart-stopping, overtime triumph against the third. On the crawling bus trip home through heavy snows, we celebrated—for the final victory gave us an unshared conference lead for the first time in the school's history. Holding a one-game lead with six to go, we could almost taste the conference crown and the ticket to the district championship that accompanied it; it was no wonder then if even Freddie Zender and a few others who rarely touched alcohol made an exception and sipped champagne with a free conscience.

But our return home met with mixed reception. The effusive multitude we'd come this year to expect didn't wait for our arrival

on campus but met us at the town line, their waving banners as
white as the snow whipping in the wind. It was after midnight
and the drifts piled high on the shoulders and sidewalks. With a
snow-plow scraping clean the streets before us, with a raucous
crowd milling the bus on either side, we inched our way toward
school.

We pulled up in the backlot behind the gym. It was empty save
for a lone female figure that approached the bus. Though wrapped
in an ankle-length coat and boots, she was bare-headed, and the
glistening white specks melting on her hair gave a sharper clarity
to its red hue. She kissed her fiancé right in front of me, then
turned to Swoop.

"I trust you like being the center of attention?"

Swoop smiled as the snowflakes and the adoring fans swirled
equally around him, but he said nothing.

"I like it," I said.

She looked at me, her arm tightening around her boyfriend's
while at the same time her eyes glittered with a hard look of heightened respect.

"Great minds should have students," she said. After a moment
she added, "They also make enemies."

Knowing what was coming, I kicked at the snow with my sneakers, ignoring the wet stuff drifting over the sides and seeping
through my socks.

"Go on."

"President MacPherson will announce tomorrow that non-stu-
dents will no longer be permitted access to campus facilities. Any
student found guilty of encouraging such use will be hauled before the Dean of Student Life for disciplinary action. That's a fact.
There's more, but it's only rumor."

Swoop listened and though he still said nothing, I could have
sworn that a slight smile tilted upwards the corners of his mouth

"All right," I said with disgust. "I'll play straight man for you.
What is it?"

So she told us.

At the end of the week, Mayor Pedersson proposed a new ordinance before the city council. Gunthar Pedersson held a Masters
degree in Education and was former headmaster of Calvary Prepa-
ratory School in Des Moines. He was a critic of the local culture's
undue dependence on the dual addictions of alcohol and basketball, and an outspoken champion of a bi-sectarian moral front

united against the encroachment of hedonistic, urban depravities into the heartland. A stalwart of the local Lutheran Church, his ordinance would prohibit teeming throngs of runners from congesting traffic on the community's downtown streets. It was passed the following Wednesday after a fair amount of heated debate.

On Sunday morning, when one hundred people showed up for services at Krandell Lake, they were met by deputies of the County Sheriff's office who informed them that a permit was required to hold mass rallies or demonstrations on county grounds. They told Swoop that there was a waiting list of applicants, that he would have to submit one, then wait his turn.

"What do you mean?" shouted several angry voices.

"Nobody's ever stopped people from getting together at the lake," said others.

When some members of the crowd responded with anger, Swoop shooed them away.

"This isn't the place," he said.

When Swoop promised that there would be future services, and that attendees would be informed, the crowd gradually dispersed. But on our way back to the car, we were accosted by a powerful figure in a black leather jacket.

"Swoop, this is a hell of an opportunity," said a firm voice, and we turned to find Bob Geronda by our side.

Geronda was a tall, muscular former athlete, who, though now in his mid-forties, worked out consistently and was still lean and hard. He had a full head of dark hair now graying at the temples. He didn't dye it and, though he spoke softly with just a trace of a Southern accent, he didn't mince words.

"Think about starting an organization," he said. "An official group with a name and a charter. Even if you meet at the home of one of its members. You can get your message out, and nobody can harass you. The Merchant's Association has issues with the town's current leadership. It will support you."

I looked at him with interest.

"Business people are notoriously reluctant to rock the boat," I said. "They don't get involved with social change. What makes you think this lot is any different?"

He smiled, a wry, patient look that spoke of years of frustration trying to mobilize his colleagues. I knew that he'd worked his way up from a poor family, and had heard that he'd studied history at Mizzou.

"They're a conservative lot," he conceded mildly. "Almost as bad as the clergy. I wonder sometimes," his voice and his eyes grew mischievous as he answered me, "how they managed to forge an Industrial, and later, a Computer Revolution. I wonder, too, if those events might have impacted social change."

"All right, you win," I acknowledged. "So the merchants will support Swoop?"

"Some," he said. "The few who came up from nothing. They don't like political interference. Or religious."

"They're opposed to the blue laws, I assume?"

He nodded.

But Swoop's focus was not on the legal dispute.

"And the rest?" he asked.

Geronda's look was sad, and he pointed at me.

"Like the philosopher said. They follow."

I didn't speak as we walked away, and Swoop's look was thoughtful all the way back to campus. But he and I both knew that there were successful, hard-working people who attended his Sunday morning services. A few well-chosen phone calls to Fredric Westegaard, to campus radio and the student newspaper, even to Ron Zatechka could set forces in motion. Back in my room that morning, I took half an hour to make certain that at least several of those phone calls were made. I was not the only one.

When the conflict erupted across *The Independent's* front page and permeated local radio—when some commentators cried that Swoop's Constitutional rights were violated and others that he was a "Satanic presence running amok"—when Dexter Bullock contacted him pleading to represent his case against the school, the town council and the county administrators—when shouting matches broke out in Ethics classes and melees in local bars—when fifty protesters surrounded the mayor's office and dozens hefting crosses surrounded them—while this stew of controversy simmered to a boil, Swoop laid low, and could be found only in the library, in classrooms, in the gym.

"Is that all you're going to do, let your supporters speak to the press?" I demanded one morning on the way to class. "They control the school and the government. They're putting you out of business."

When he didn't respond, I continued.

"There's Bob Geronda, Dexter Bullock and others. Don't forget Janet McMenamin. They're on your side. Why don't you let them help you?"

He smiled benignly.

"I will," he said. "Their day will come. But you're a philosopher. Remember what you know about cause and effect."

He knew that he had set forces in motion—and that the drive of onrushing momentum could not now be quelled. The ensuing collision would demonstrate that the law of inertia applies as fully to men as to inanimate matter, and that high velocity impacts are capable of consequences more benign than the sheerly destructive.

But mostly it would establish that human beings experience religious needs that run deeper than anyone has suspected.

Swoop couldn't hold services at the lake, he could neither work out at school nor jog the streets with his supporters. His admirers were dogged by stern-faced crusaders against sin, and ominous rumblings emanated from certain of the town's poorer denominations. The sentinels of conventional theism starting to array against him were formidable. But despite the tradition of religious martyrs, I was beginning to suspect that perhaps—just perhaps—this time the Messiah would not be scorned.

CHAPTER TEN
THE DEFENDERS OF THE FAITH

For the foes of a messiah, danger lurks everywhere, and characteristically they resort to desperate means in the struggle to stop him.

Sensing that, like Samson's hair, the source of Swoop's power lay in basketball, they knew it was insufficient merely to restrict services and physical training; they had to diminish the Swoop-glorifying success of the team. Sound strategy required the nullification of Swoop's base.

The escalation began innocuously enough with church sermons and letters to the editor, muted growls that basketball had been elevated to such a level of prominence in local culture. But it was at a Town Hall meeting on a cold Sunday afternoon in late January that the protests began to turn into action.

"Sunday must be reserved for the Lord," said a slender, dark-haired woman of thirty. "No other activities. I want my children to grow up in a community that respects God."

"Emigration to Iran is still open, isn't it?" whispered Kathryn Gately, leaning over to speak to the stranger sitting by her side. The man looked at her briefly, then shifted away.

Kathy told me later that there were one hundred people crowded into the small auditorium, although neither Judas Bittner nor members of the basketball team attended.

Gerald Hopkins Tolliver, president and CEO of the Iowa Union Bank, the Valley's largest financial institution, moderated the session. Tall, spare and in his seventies, Tolliver was a member of Pastor Buttle's congregation, and a man whose personal integrity was as impeccable as his financial judgment.

"Serious-minded members of the community are concerned," Tolliver, a World War Two vet, agreed calmly. "But preserving a proper reverence for God does not require suppressing freedom of choice and action within our community."

But one by one, people from both the school and the town

rose to protest the increasingly rowdy behavior within the community. An earnest young man whom Kathy didn't know, wearing glasses and a brown dress jacket, agreed with the previous speaker, arguing that all gyms and parks should be closed on Sunday. Richard Peterson, an administrative assistant to President MacPherson, mentioned that for the first time the school was concerned that unrestricted access to gym use would overburden both the school's electric bill and students' time. He said he urged MacPherson to treat the gym like the library, closing it at ten, and to curtail all forms of workout regimens. Arlene Thole, a tall girl with shoulder-length blonde hair and a choir girl's expression, spoke last. She was a Religion major at school, and such a fervently-compliant follower of the Lutheran faith that she prompted Kathy to paraphrase Confucius. "If the goody-goodies are the thieves of virtue," she said to me once, "then Arlene is Al Capone." Arlene quoted from an interview with Dean Keyes in the Sunday supplement of that day's *Independent*. "Student-athletes should be devoted primarily to their studies and to traditional precepts of self-abnegating behavior," she read.

I was too busy with classes, reading and two-a-day workouts to pay attention, but the emerging threat to gym availability had Troop members walking around campus for days with eyes narrowed to slits. Others had more extreme reactions.

Team supporters resented the outside interference and the new breed of worshipers, incensed already at the restrictions placed on them, mobilized to take legal action. Hundreds of fans, both within and without the gym, made home games seem more like a political convention than a sporting event, waving banners displaying a replica of a gold basketball and chanting: "Don't *stop* our drive to the *top!*" Kathryn Gately, in an interview on campus radio, exhorted all free-thinkers to uphold as their champions, the Hoppo Valley basketball team—and as their banner, a man's right to pursue greatness. Twelve students formed a vigilante group to guard the gym and ensure that its doors remained open. They held a poster reading "Home of the Champs" and rotated their hours of duty. But the greatest encouragement came not from students, but from one in a greater position to provide it. Dexter Bullock called Swoop one day to inform him of the tortuous progress of his lawsuit. ·

"But don't worry," the lawyer growled near the end of their conversation. "I'm used to the perverse contortions of the legal system. You might have heard that I represented, and continue to

represent, Dr. Wechsler, who was convicted of helping a terminally-ill patient end his life painlessly in Cedar Rapids. I'm not the
only civilized person in this area—just one of the few. There are
others ready to take on the high and mighty. Some will get into
this brawl with you."

Swoop didn't know of the Wechsler case, but I did. My father
was an outspoken champion of a terminally-ill patient's right to
die, and of a physician's right to assist him. He wasn't popular
with the clergy back home in Hutchinson.

But Swoop didn't get involved in the tumult and he didn't wait.

"We have to find a gym outside of town," he said to me. "A
place that's ours, that nobody can take away from us."

"Right," I said. "But where?"

He didn't answer. He sat staring, eyes unblinking.

The following day, Saturday, we hosted Pierce College of Minnesota, who had beaten us in Swoop's first game back. They had a
rock-hard six-seven forward and a tandem of laser-guided shooters in the backcourt. They came into our place so pumped-up on
"Swoop-itis" that their adrenaline rush threatened to sweep us out
of our own gym. They had us down thirteen in the first, before
Coach switched Swoop onto their Cro-Magnon forward and
Swoop kept the ball from touching his hands for nine consecutive
minutes. With their leading scorer throttled, we came from behind and inched ahead in the waning minutes on a steal and
breakaway slam by Swoop. We ended up winning by five, our closest game at home since Swoop's return, and the late-night bars
saw heavy traffic until dawn.

But Swoop was in bed before midnight, and we were up Sunday morning at five for two wrenching hours on the weights and a
six mile run. After a shower and light breakfast, we were in my
room, studying—Swoop savoring the bawdy verse of Catullus, I
poring over "The Sophist" of Plato. After lunch, we met The Troop
at the gym.

It was locked.

Both Swoop and I had keys but the doors were padlocked.
Swoop immediately called Coach, who informed him that the decision to lock the school's gym on Sunday had come from the top,
from University President MacPherson. He had sent in campus
security in midmorning, swept away the gym's guardians, and
locked up shop. "Let's take it to the courts!" I raged, but Swoop
silenced me with a glance. Without a word, a scowl or a wasted

second, Swoop whirled, strode to Campus Maintenance, and borrowed a pair of ice choppers from the two guys—both basketball fans—on duty; then we piled into Raif's pick-up, drove to Healy Park, scraped the courts clean and, though the temperature was barely in double digits, practiced outdoors.

Tuesday night we blew out Wakefield on the road at their gym, a non-contest in which Swoop convinced Coach to play him most of the game, a massacre in which he totaled fifty points, sixteen assists and ten steals. When we arrived back at school, Kathryn Gately informed us that Mayor Pedersson had introduced a bill to the city council that would close all parks on Sunday and at dusk on other days. The newspaper said it had solid support among his grass-roots constituency in the poorer areas on the outskirts of town. It was well-known to be adamantly supported by at least one member of the city council.

That weekend Swoop disappeared immediately after basketball practice on Friday afternoon and didn't return until his first class on Monday morning.

"Where the hell you been?" I asked, when we sat alone at lunch.

"Dykstra's," he said.

"Jumbo's?"

He nodded grimly.

"Doing what?"

He nodded at the battered, bulging gym bag on the floor next to him.

"Winning," he said.

When I got on the floor and opened it, I wasn't surprised to find it crammed with large bills, filled to the seams with fifties and hundreds.

"How much?" I asked.

"Lots."

I sat, dazed, and though I knew the answer, I asked the question anyway, for the record.

"What for?"

He turned and faced me, triumphant, and for the first time he smiled.

"We're going to buy a gym," he said.

Jumbo Dykstra was the greatest player to ever come out of the state of Iowa, a recently-retired NBA superstar, a six-ten banger with an arching stroke. Throughout his career there'd been whispers that he bet on his team's games—always to win—and that he'd made a bundle, but nothing was ever proved. He owned his private gym on a piece of wooded property outside of Dickerson, Iowa and, retired now, openly consorted with gamblers as well as with professional athletes and former NBA stars. His place was a high-stakes hotbed where wealthy athletes and hot-shot wannabes competed at every sport from pool to arm wrestling.

But Swoop was concerned to compete at only one sport.

The following weekend I drove there with him, though I complained bitterly about the two-hour drive.

"The further from Hoppo Valley, the better," Swoop said, and I shut up.

The road cut through Iowa's rolling hills, a straight-line ribbon unspooling toward the horizon, and as we whipped past corn fields and grain silos I had time to wonder if the designers of highways were themselves the ones to traverse the interlocking network in its sweep toward the horizon or whether they left it to unknown, hard-eyed voyagers. Swoop drove Raif's pick-up like he played—the vibrant horsepower under control—and we passed local traffic without strain.

"What gym we going to buy?" I asked when we stood at the entrance.

"This one."

"It's for sale?"

He held the door open, but turned to me before entering.

"Not that I know of."

The gamesters were wary of Swoop, their eyes filled by "Proceed With Caution" signs as they shook his hand. Starting with a few hundred of his scholarship money, Swoop had won more than cash at Jumbo's; he'd kicked the cockiness out of them and engendered fear. He had to raise the stakes.

When he strutted to center court and bellowed, "I can whip any man with my left hand!" the bets flooded in. I held the money as Jumbo tied Swoop's hand behind his back. Swoop turned to the big man and said, "You're last, Hoss." The old pro tried to keep his voice hard, but the twinkle back of his eyes gave something away. "Beat these guys, Killer."

Even Swoop's range was limited with his off hand. Knowing this, his opponents backed off, giving him the jumper, trying to deny him the basket. It forced Swoop to play the greatest defense of his life—to swipe dribbles and swat shots—and to devise moves to the basket—springing, hurtling, soaring—that made him re-

semble a bird more than even such land-bound creatures as chee-
tahs or pumas. After two hours of intense struggle, Swoop had
dispatched three foes, sweated like a horse, and held winnings in
big numbers.

"Double or nothing, Hoss," he said. "You're next."

Jumbo couldn't hold it back. He shook his head and burst out
laughing.

"You got it, Kid."

At six-ten, two-forty, Jumbo could box out a freight train and
was unstoppable around the basket. But Swoop, taking a deep
breath, buried lefty jumpers—then jerked and shook and rock-and-
rolled along the baseline—then flashed by his man with a slashing
lefty dribble to the *right*.

Hardened gamblers screamed like fans and Jumbo—sweating
more profusely than Swoop—played with a smile made equally of
determination and appreciation. When he drilled a twenty-five
footer from the left wing, it sent the game into overtime.

The gamblers still roared, a minute later, as Jumbo pounced on
a loose ball in the corner. With Swoop needing one basket to win,
the big man rose straight up for the tying shot. He let it fly, an
arching sky-bolt arrowing true, and it seemed the game would never
end. But Swoop rose from under the basket like he belonged to
neither ground nor sea but to the sky, elevating like some mythical being exempt from such mundane concerns as gravity—and
his knees were level with Jumbo's eyes when he caught the shot.

He didn't block it but tore it from the sky. Bystanders gaped,
and later one said he was afraid Swoop would split his damn skull
on the rafters. Though he hovered interminably in the air, neither
fans nor opponent could react—neither to cheer nor defend—because first they had to collect their jaws from the floor. When Swoop
whirled and slammed home the winner, it seemed anti-climactic
and irrelevant, jarring briefly in the consciousness of all onlookers
the memory, "Oh right, they were playing a game."

Swoop panted, alone under the basket, and nobody spoke, not
even in whispers. Jumbo recovered first. "That was worth the
price," he said, speaking to all and to none. It was several minutes
later that he approached Swoop.

"How do you want the money, Kid? I'll pay you now."

"I don't want the money."

"What? What do you want?"

Swoop neither paused nor blinked.

"I want the gym."

"The gym's worth a lot, Kid. But not this much."

"Keep the change," Swoop said.

"We're talking big money."

"Carrying charge. But I want the gym."

Jumbo looked around, gazing at the baskets and the hardwood floor, breathing in the deep sweat-stained fragrance of the place. He'd made millions from basketball and endorsements. This wasn't about money.

"Rent it to me," Swoop said. "Lease me twenty-four hour, carte blanche access for two years. I come in, anyone here clears out. Give me two keys."

"Deal," Jumbo said.

"Put it in writing. We'll both sign. I got witnesses. Then we'll go to a notary."

"Done." Jumbo had been grinning as Swoop spoke but now it faded. His eyes were not far away, but riveted on the court on which they'd played; they were not gazing at events of a distant past, merely of some moments ago—but it was clear he'd see them for whatever days of his future remained.

"Keep the money, Swoop. You earned it."

Swoop could not miss the tone—it was his native language— and his eyes answered in this, his mother tongue, even as he shook his head.

"Got no use for it. Just let me have the gym."

"O.K. But I'll put the money in trust. You might change your mind."

"S—t." Swoop grinned. "Blow it on pool or arm wrestling or something."

"Can't." Jumbo grinned wider than Swoop. "I don't ever lose."

"Hardly ever," Swoop said.

Two days later we were on the road at Weber College. Despite his determined stare, Coach barely had the strength to walk, and his jacket was an oversized tent. Whispers around campus were that there was far more wrong with him than just a failure to eat— and looking at his pasty jowls, you didn't need medical expertise to guess that he was close to joining wife and daughter.

But not in the Gospel according to Swoop.

Swoop sat next to him the entire bus ride, haranguing him with guarantees of a national title. At first Coach beamed, knowing Swoop's ability to deliver. Then he started to squirm as the deeper import of Swoop's meaning carried through. Finally, he turned as Swoop refused to relent, shouting with a red face: "All right, we'll win in Kansas City! Shut up now, will you?"

But Swoop refused to shut up—ever. By the time we reached Weber, he had Coach begging for the nearest medical clinic.

But right before half, one of the Weber guards tripped Swoop in the back court. When Coach got off the bench, raging for a foul call, he collapsed on his face. He whacked his forehead on the gym floor and blood spurted in a red stream.

As they loaded him on a stretcher, he was barely conscious. He grabbed Freddie Zender's arm.

"You're team captain. You're in charge. Run the team."

They were wheeling him away from the other players. Only Freddie and Swoop were with him as they passed me on the sideline.

"Coach," Freddie said. "I'm a player."

"Listen to Swoop," Coach gasped. "He knows the game like a pro coach."

Flecks of foam drooled at the corners of his mouth as he struggled to speak. His hands hung like wash rags on a rack and his breath was stertorous. We walked at his side in anguish and in mixed reaction: helpless before the inexorable outcome of his own policy—angry because the policy had been chosen. The taut lines of Freddie's frame held the tension of a gladiator torn from battle— but his eyes held a medical man's grim knowledge regarding a fallen comrade. His hands were outstretched, pleading for Coach's life, but he was too proud to beg and no sound came from his mouth.

Swoop spun him by the arm as they pushed Coach out the door.

"His life is in the hands of the doctors," Swoop said. "Ours is in our own."

He was angry. I could see it in his eyes. He felt cheated. He hadn't had enough time. Not enough time to save Coach, to resurrect him—by inspiration, by example—to uplift him as he had so many others. He'd run out of time, he'd lost one, and his hard eyes would neither grieve nor lose another.

"Fine," Freddie snapped, jerking loose his arm. "But an honest man knows his limits. I'm not a coach." His eyes also glared, but at Swoop, not at the world.

Swoop didn't wait. He slammed Freddie so hard with a stiff arm to the shoulder that the big man fell back.

"You know enough!" he punched the words harder than the blow. "Run the team!" He turned, prohibiting a reply, and strode onto the court. The mercilessness of his gaze was commensurate with the facts that condemned Coach.

"I run the team now," Freddie rasped at the head ref. He kept himself in the game and brushed past defenders to his offensive position. Sweat flowed from the hard lines of this merciful man turned warrior. He ignored Swoop but scowled at Weber's center. The game resumed.

Swoop made Freddie's job easier. By half he had twenty points and twelve assists and we led by sixteen.

At half-time, Freddie turned to him in the locker room.

"Swoop, we've had trouble playing zone all year. Some of the guys get confused on their assignments, and—"

"Junk it," Swoop cut in. "It's too passive. Let's go man, play a high-pressure defense. Turn me loose to press their ball-handlers all over the floor."

"But, Swoop," Raif said, puzzled. "We're not familiar with a man-to-man system."

"I know. We can't do it today. We'll start practicing it tomorrow and be ready to play it in a few weeks."

"That zone is Coach's baby," Freddie said. "It protects the slower and smaller guys. Allows everyone to play without getting burned individually on defense."

Swoop looked straight at him. He said nothing.

"Of course, it also forces the better defensive players to cover for the weaker guys," Freddie continued. "Keeps us packed in. Opens holes around the perimeter."

"We're giving up a lot of open jumpers," Bobby added. "Swoop's right. Junk it and go with the pressure man-to man."

"If we do that, then only the best defensive players can play," Freddie said.

"Who do you think is supposed to play?" Bobby asked.

"Coach wants everyone to play. Every game."

There was silence after Freddie's comment. Gradually all eyes shifted to Swoop. It was Freddie who finally spoke.

"Swoop, what do you think?"

"I think you're right. Coach wants everyone to play. What do you want?"

Freddie hesitated only a moment.

"I want to win," he breathed.

"Then you've answered your own question."

"What about when Coach comes back?"

"Let's hope Coach comes back."

"What if he does?"

Swoop laughed softly. "Winning," he said, "will be the best cure."

The conflict was etched in Freddie's face.

"Isn't there a way to make the zone work?"

"The zone's ineffective," Swoop said. "We need more defensive pressure. But there's still a chance for everyone to play."

"How?"

"If they join The Troop, work out regularly, they can upgrade their defensive skills. But not everyone's willing to do it."

Freddie looked around, seeing the vitality of his teammates' faces, hearing the energy of their excited murmurs, and he turned back to Swoop.

"Are you sure?"

"I'm sure," a sharp voice cut in, and all heads turned to the speaker.

It was E.J., who had risen to his full height and looked down on his teammates. He ignored Swoop.

"Like the Biblical Judas," he said, and stared at Freddie.

In the silence that followed, it was the almost total absence of positive response that was startling. Doherty nodded. Everyone else looked at E.J. with no sympathy and no remorse. E.J. looked at his teammates, his hard eyes softening momentarily, filled with the sincerity of his cause. He reached to each of his comrades in turn, although he refused to look at Swoop, as if the very sight of him was painful. "He's a Satanist," he pleaded. "Can't you see? He's intent only on seducing control from Coach." But they backed away from him, standing behind an invisible line, leaving only Doherty at his side. When it was clear where Freddie stood, E.J.'s head bowed briefly, in apparent grief for a fallen comrade. Then he whirled and strode from the locker room without another word. Doherty muttered several choice obscenities, then joined him. Freddie stared after them. Then he turned and spoke to the team.

"I agree with Swoop. As long as I'm in charge, we'll play the pressure man-to-man. We're not going to play all twelve guys anymore, but only the best players. When Coach returns, he'll change back if he doesn't like it, and discipline me."

"Me, too," Swoop said.

"Stay out of it," Freddie snapped. "It's my decision."

Swoop lowered his head, but not before I caught the gleam in his eye.

"And incidentally," Freddie finished. "We're going to kick butt. Any questions?"

There weren't any.

But Coach had one a few days later when we visited him at the hospital.

"Speed called Swoop *what?*" he asked.

"A Satanist," Freddie repeated.

Coach was silent for several moments as Swoop, Freddie, Kathy and myself sat around the bed looking at him. Finally, he looked at Freddie.

"Tell Speed I want to see him. Now. Today. Understand?"

"Yes," Freddie replied. After a while, he asked: "You going to can him, Coach?"

"If he backs off on this swill, no. Otherwise, yes."

"Good," Freddie said.

"Speed's a good ballplayer," Swoop put in. "He hits the boards, he plays tough 'D,' he hustles all the time. We'll miss him."

"That'll give you a chance to do more," Freddie said.

"Yeah, thanks."

"Isn't that the point? After all, you came here to carry a bunch of stiffs to the national title—right? If we cut down to five players, think how much more you'll get to do."

Kathy smiled, coughing into her hand, and Swoop looked away, unable to disagree.

"Freddie's right," Coach said, looking at Swoop. "As long as you're healthy, we'll beat anyone. I think you've proven that to everyone, son."

Swoop said nothing, but lowered his head in acceptance.

"No, with or without Speed, we'll win now," Coach said and he lay back on the pillows.

The four of us stared at him in silence. The medics said he'd suffered no complications as the ambulance transferred him to the hospital in Hoppo Valley. But the doctors believed that it could be stomach cancer, and that if he didn't submit to treatment he would die. They wanted to run tests, but Coach just shook his head. "We're almost there," he said. His skin was white, his forehead was bandaged and he had intravenous tubes jutting out of his arms.

Lying helpless on his back, his protruding belly resembling a beached whale, he was still a formidable mass—but gasping.

"Coach," Kathy said, interrupting his rest. "I know it's none of my business, so if you tell me to shut up I won't mind. But the real problem is Judas Bittner. He preaches all over town that Swoop's sold his soul to Satan. There are people who believe him, Speed is only one. God knows what they'll do. Isn't there some way to shut him up—strangulation maybe?"

"What's he after?" Coach asked, looking at Kathy.

"Swoop's soul," she said.

"Or his hide," I interjected.

"No, his soul. He doesn't want Swoop killed or silenced—but torn down, spent, his pride broken, so that he'll beg for redemption. He wants to use Swoop's charisma to spread the Word."

"He missed his chance," I snarled.

"He never had a chance." It was Freddie who said it and I stared at him, wondering how he knew that.

"No, he never did," she agreed. "But the dumb-ass doesn't know it."

"He's not dumb," I pointed out. "Would that he were."

"He is about this," Freddie said.

"You're both right," Kathy concluded. "He's dangerous—but not to Swoop."

"To whom then?" I asked.

"To the weak-minded," she replied.

"Or the guilty," I burst out, and involuntarily my gaze fixed on her fiancé.

But Kathy missed the point. She was eased back in her chair, next to Freddie, her right hand clasping his left, her legs brushing his thighs. Despite the gravity of Coach's illness, regardless of the tense, brusque sound of her voice denouncing Bittner, her eyes did not fail to notice that Freddie's gaze returned ceaselessly to Swoop, and a half smile threatened to become permanent at the corners of her mouth, an impish grin of triumph and of the reckless, go-to-hell daring she worshipped. It wasn't clear whether the triumph was Swoop's, Freddie's, hers—or all of the above—but though Bittner and the Reaper hovered together in the room's darker corners, Kathy could sustain only limited interest in them. As her god rewarded only free-thinkers and heretics, so she prized only champions and heroes—and the rest of creation was merely a minor irritant. Dressed in jeans, heels and a clinging sweater, she rejected the looks she received from the nurses—as she rejected the presence of death in the room—and she guessed neither the righteous lethality of my thoughts nor its cause as she turned her implacable eyes on me.

"If only the weak-minded and the guilty are at risk, then you're as safe as can be, aren't you?"

"Me? Damn right."

Kathy knew that I had spent two hours on this Saturday morning pumping iron and running with Swoop, and four more in the library researching Aristotle's conception of "ousia" or primary being, before coming to the hospital in the evening. She knew that I planned on attending either Harvard, Princeton or Yale the following year for my doctorate—and when she looked at me now, with her hand, legs and life intertwined with Freddie's, her smile hinted at things that might have been had circumstances been otherwise.

I scowled and jerked my attention to Coach.

"What about Bittner? I was ready to dismember him once. I'm still available."

Kathy laughed and even Freddie grinned but Coach cut them off.

"What did I tell you after your steeple-climbing stunt? You want to go to the state pen? You keep your hands to yourself and go to graduate school. You hear me, Duggan? Flex your muscles in the gym."

"O.K.," I said.

"There's only one thing to do about Bittner," he continued. "I'm not going to forbid my players to associate with him or attend his sermons. I would never do that. But if they swallow any of his 'Swoop-as-Satanist' trash, they better keep it to themselves. If they put it into practice on my team, they're out. Clear? Now send Speed to me tonight."

"Got it, Coach," Freddie said, and we left.

Coach was in the hospital for weeks. He never said a word in objection to our new defense, but he said tons of them to E.J. When Speed refused to back off on his accusations, Coach gave him a simple choice: keep his mouth shut or quit the team. Speed answered angrily that he'd sooner quit the game than play for a seduced and fallen figure who postured as a man of God. Coach calmly replied, "Suit yourself," to E.J.'s back as he strode out the door. Doherty muttered something about "the way that loudmouth runs this team" when he heard the news, but the rest of the guys ignored him.

Swoop never said a word. With no singing, bragging or laughing, he grimly played the greatest basketball of his life. When Coach returned two weeks later, against medical advice, we had won five straight games by an average of thirty-five points. He let our new defense be, and Swoop responded by attaining a level of defensive excellence that might have throttled pro stars. With a week to go in late February, we had won twenty-one straight games, gone undefeated in conference play, and held a one-game lead over our old rival, Huntington State. Our closing game of the year was against them at home. If they won, they could still tie us for the conference crown, setting up a one-game playoff to be played at their gym. Excitement ran high in both towns, but in Hoppo Valley, where Swoop's admirers did not forget the violent events of the previous year, there was talk of payback and fear of mayhem.

"Things are stirring," Swoop whispered to me one evening as I sat at a small desk amidst the library's underground stacks.

It was a week before the Huntington game and Swoop paced restlessly back and forth in the aisle in front of me, whispering even though the huge room was deserted.

"But it's not enough. We got to do more."

I waited. Though immersed in the technicalities of Aristotle's *Physics*, I had been silently thinking for weeks about the religious turmoil in Hoppo Valley. Swoop failed to notice the paperback copies of *The Iliad*, *The Odyssey* and *The Aeneid* that lay scattered around my hardcover McKeon.

"One more push in the right direction and this town will go to the next level."

His hands were in the pockets of his jeans as he walked and talked, his head on his chest, forehead furrowed. I sat back in my chair, watching a field marshal at work, interested in the campaign; amused, but only mildly, too caught up in the excitement of personal change to remain coolly detached.

"Heroes, Swoop," I said, letting my thumb riff the pages telling the stories of Achilles, Odysseus and Aeneas. "That's who will galvanize people in a positive direction."

"Heroes, yeah..." he looked out the small basement window as he walked, trying to gaze past the shrubbery surrounding the library building to the town beyond. He was thinking about something else, and only half-heard my words.

"Isn't that what you said at the Celebrate Self Party last year?" I insisted. "That you modeled your life after the lives of every hero you could read about, real or fictitious?"

He turned to me now, interest showing in his eyes.

"That's right. What are you driving at?"

"That you should put two and two together. What does it do for people? What did it do for you—to read incessantly about George Washington or Louis Pasteur or Marie Curie? What lesson is there for anyone intelligent and daring enough to see it? Just that some rare individuals are capable of extraordinary accomplishments in the face of opposition that would daunt a lesser man? I don't think so. Isn't there something more than that?"

"What?" His voice was not even a whisper now, it was so low, I could barely hear it. But he knew the answer, had always known it. He had lived it, and thereby taught me. I said nothing, but let him answer his own question, because his words would mirror his life and consequently say it better.

"It's inspiration," he said, not looking at me, but not needing to, because our souls were in deeper touch than eye contact. "The awareness that, whatever my ability, I can and must be the hero of my own life."

"You've been doing and showing us that for years," I said, and now I was whispering, not from respect for a library's quiet but because it was difficult to speak through the rockslide that had clogged my throat. "You just need to do it now in a new form."

"Bob Geronda," was all he said, and I nodded, remembering the entrepreneur's words. Then I remembered something else. "And Janet McMenamin," I added. "Don't forget her."

Swoop said nothing else, but he looked at me now and his eyes told what was coming.

The next evening after basketball practice, Swoop and I ate a light, quick dinner and then paid a social visit.

Dexter Bullock was expecting us after the call he had received from Swoop. He was one of the Valley's wealthiest men, but lived alone with his wife in their large home on Douglas Avenue, several blocks from the Episcopal Church. The four bedroom house was set back from the street, and Bullock waited for us by the front door as we drove up the tree-lined driveway. He didn't smile when he greeted us, but gripped each of our hands firmly.

"A couple of kids," he said, his harsh voice grating but not contemptuous. "But, then, how old was Mozart when he wrote symphonies?"

Bullock was known as a fierce courtroom fighter, chronically embroiled in conflict with authority. He swore during trials, was cited for contempt and was hated by all except his clients. Moreover, he was a hard-nosed skeptic regarding the traditional religion, and a crusader against the legal consequences of all forms of dogmatism. He had defended, in court, in addition to Dr. Wechsler, parents who opposed the introduction of prayer into the public school. In politics, he'd been active in the local Republican Party until the state leadership had booted him out for his outspoken disagreement with its religious platform. His involvement on behalf of an individual's legal right to die was so vociferous that it prompted one of his party opponents in Des Moines to remark that he would change his mind and support such a right only on condition that Bullock would exercise it.

The lawyer stood at least three inches below six foot but was a barn door across the chest and shoulders. His hair was black, short and sharp as bristles. The stubble of his chin was so thick that he'd given up the fight against it; his beard was coarse and rough, though clipped close to his face. He was a graduate of Annapolis and the University of Illinois law school, had flown combat missions in Vietnam and—after being disowned by his Presbyterian family for marrying a Jewish girl he'd met in law school—had repudiated the Presbyterian Church, which had not been sorry to see him go. He had attended the first, and every subsequent service at Krandell Lake, though, rare for him, he'd stayed in the background. In his study, he listened as Swoop explained his idea.

"A society to spread the virtue of personal courage?" he bellowed. "Meeting at eight o'clock on Sunday mornings? What do you want to do—roust people out of their cowardice and lethargy?"

"If that's what holds them back," Swoop said. "But they think that courage applies only to life-threatening situations. We want to show that—with all the obstacles there are in life—valor is fundamentally required to pursue the things you love."

Swoop spoke quietly, earnestly as Bullock listened and I gazed at the stacks of books lining the lawyer's walls. There were far more than merely law books. He had texts on the history of Western Civilization, economics books by well-known free market writers and Nobel Prize winners, biographies of Jefferson, Madison and Franklin and a thick two volume set on the complete history of the United States Navy. Copies of Swift, Voltaire and Montaigne occupied a shelf above the lawyer's chair.

"There's only a few open to it, kid," Bullock said, shaking his head. "The rest won't go for it, because the hardest quality to renounce is a self-imposed stupor. Democracy was never a good idea. Elitism was always a more accurate gauge of the human spirit."

Swoop didn't argue. He merely listened, might even have agreed, but his eyes acquired the impatient look I was so familiar with, as if he yearned to brush away human weaknesses and fears with his hand, opening men up to a vision of life's far-flung boundaries.

"If that's true," he said, "then those are the ones we'll reach. The rest will cling to their self-chosen limitations." He paused, and his eyes were no longer sorrowful, but hard with an edge that was not hostility. "But you might be surprised."

"Doubt it," Bullock answered immediately. "Nature has immutable laws. You can't expect a bovine herd to acquire the instincts of individuality."

"True. But we're not talking about bovine creatures. You in or out?"

"I'm in. What'd you think? That I'd miss a shot to shake up the herding instinct of the flocks? This'll be the greatest upheaval since they brought in evolution. We can knock this community cockeyed."

"We might even change some lives," Swoop murmured.

But Bullock didn't hear. He pointed at Swoop and me jointly, his finger gesticulating emphatically.

"But just remember—I'm commander of this squadron. I join no organization where I don't lead. That was the problem with the Navy. No offense to you whelps, but I don't follow bureaucratic assholes."

"No assholes," Swoop was agreeable. "And you set the agenda. But let's reach everyone who's open to our message."

"Sure, both of them. By the way, what's the name of this outfit?"

Swoop turned to me, wanting me to state the name I had chosen.

"The Society for the Propagation of Heroism," I said quietly.

"The Heroes Society," Bullock said, and stopped respectfully. "It can only do good."

Frederic Westegaard evidently agreed when Bullock broached it to him, because he ran an ad in Wednesday's *Independent*, announcing the formation of the Society and its first meeting at Bullock's home on Sunday morning. When the local radio station called to interview Bullock, he was smart enough to refer them to Swoop, who went on the air on Friday morning.

"Members might disagree on other points," Swoop said. "But we agree on this: that whatever the depredations that surround us in society, each one of us has the power—and must develop the will—to be the hero of his own life. We believe in goals, in purposes, in achievement and in the joy of living. We repudiate any and all codes that uphold sin, guilt, shame, suffering. We proclaim the power of one and the stature possible to each."

Bullock's shortened version stuck, and the organization gradually became known throughout the Valley simply as "The Heroes Society." Swoop's words on the air also stuck when he described Sunday mornings as "a proper time to celebrate the potential glory of man." Bullock's first act as president of the Society was to appoint Swoop director of Sunday morning services. Each week Swoop opened by reading tales of the great heroes—of Theseus and the Minotaur, Alcestis and her willingness to face death, the devotion of Odysseus and the undying integrity of Penelope, and the great feats performed by heroes and heroines of more recent time. But the bulk of each service was devoted to contemplating the courageous deeds of individual members who had fought, often against daunting forces and remorseless foes, to reach their own goals.

Over time, the Society marveled at the relentless drive of Lindsay Walken, the twelve-year-old classical soprano, who practiced six hours daily while still maintaining straight As in school—applauded the courage of Megan Rentzler, who left her violent husband in Wisconsin, moved hundreds of miles to Hoppo Valley and worked two jobs to support her children—and stared in silent reverence at Josh McGibbon, the nine-year-old child who battled leukemia with the nerveless calm of a combat veteran. These, and others, were drawn to the Heroes Society because of its purpose: to celebrate the daring feats performed by individuals in their own lives—and to be inspired to do the same.

The new breed of Hoppo Valley worshipers found what they were looking for in the Society and they joined by the dozens. Swoop's phone rang so persistently that eventually he left it off the receiver and fled for refuge to my room. He permanently changed the announcement on his answering machine informing callers to contact Dexter Bullock.

They came from across the area and from beyond it, from towns as far away as Lockfield and Dumars, a distance of nearly one hundred miles. Williams, the banker, came, who had served three years in the Marine Corps; and Byron, who had come from a poor family in Davenport and, working three jobs, paid his way through Drake University without a penny of financial aid. Jane Kurtzhals, a feature writer for *The Independent*, who doubled on the weekends as a sky-diving instructor at Lefferts Airfield was there; as was Kelsey Jensen, the area's leading fitness expert, who rose before five to do thousands of sit-ups and crunches, and who treated her body like a temple. John Kraeger, a local farmer, who, after his wife's death, had raised three girls alone and put all of them through college, came with two of his daughters. Brady Cavanaugh—who ran her farm independently, had a son out of wedlock and told the rest of the Valley's residents where to go—came alone. A number of the town's leading professionals also attended: Thom Kolotourous, who owned the local movie theater, who came from Chicago, and who had battled town officials for years for the right to show movies other than those rated "G" was an eager participant. Butch Bratton, the crusty English teacher in his mid-sixties, who taught whatever books he deemed educational, regardless of state guidelines or church pressures, also came, as did Virginia McBride, who held a Master's degree and had lived for six years in the Mission District of San Francisco. Donald Ryan, the former priest, who had rejected celibacy for love, and who now had two children, joined immediately. Janet McMenamin, of course, signed up on the first day. Nicholas Bradlee, the fresh-faced, recent Ph.D. doing his supervision under her likewise joined—for, despite his baby face, Bradlee had grown up under the most squalid of rural conditions; he'd worked exhausting hours to earn both his scholarship to Iowa State and—through eight years of psychotherapy—his own mental health. Pastor Peter Kracjek, the renegade minister, who had fled Communist Czechoslovakia in a hail of bullets, also became a member; Kracjek had converted from

Catholicism to Unitarianism, and routinely told members of his flock that they weren't sinners but dolts.

All of these came to the Sunday morning services of the Heroes Society and made clear, by word or deed, that whatever their differences, they experienced a deep hunger for spiritual sustenance, a hunger left unfulfilled by the conventional religions. All of these, and many others, came to the meetings of the Heroes Society. Most came back.

In the midst of this, the desperadoes from Huntington State came crashing into Hoppo Valley, though with different purposes in mind. With the conference title, a berth in the district championships and hegemony in the rivalry they had so long dominated all at stake, they had more than sufficient motivation to want to whip our butts, to do so on our home court and to humble our charismatic leader in front of his most enthusiastic admirers. And basketball fans throughout the Valley responded to the challenge. They rallied the night before, giving speeches regarding the championship's meaning to the town, dredging forth images of Swoop's injury and burning, in effigy, Tetzel and other Huntington heavies.

But there was more, there was an edge to it that was difficult to diagnose but impossible to deny. The sounds emanating from Huntington contained a sullen quality, a whiff of resentment, just a hint that there was more involved than a long-standing sports rivalry. Swoop's enemies in Hoppo Valley also made noise—though their concerns were different—when Judas Bittner's loyalists claimed that God's justice sometimes takes the form of conquest by the Philistines. The gauntlet thereby thrown to the turf was immediately snatched up by Swoop's more zealous admirers, who vowed to form a posse of bodyguards, to surround him if necessary and to wreak vengeance on anyone, local or out-of-towner, whether motivated by intentions secular or religious, who did him bodily harm.

The game was played in a gym packed to the rafters, with virtually the entire population of the Valley surrounding the building listening on loudspeaker, and with a cordon of local police stationed within the gym and without.

In the locker room before the game, nobody but one spoke a word to Swoop. Freddie Zender looked him in the eye and spoke a single sentence.

"Beat hell out of these guys, Swoop."

And the way Swoop started the game gave strong evidence that his thinking and Freddie's were fully congruent on this point.

When he snatched the game's first defensive rebound, with Huntington's guards already in full retreat, with the crowd instantaneously on its feet, he blazed down the court with such unconstrained quickness that friend, foe and onlooker alike must have believed a roadrunner, not a man, had been turned loose in the gym. When he bore in on the rim like a homing missile, defenders collapsed around him and he left it for a trailing Dandy, who crammed it. When he pumped his fist, the crowd roared, teammates smiled and just a puff of air seeped out of Huntington's balloon.

Swoop went at their throats from baseline to baseline, on offense and defense, from the opening tip to the end of the half. Coach turned him loose and let him play, and Swoop ripped into them like they were the Persians descending on Marathon. By halftime, he had eight steals, countless deflections and tips, and had turned Huntington's offense into a mad scramble resembling the Keystone Kops. He had also been knocked to the deck four times, flung into the first row, trampled once as in a stampede, and elbowed so often that he had welts under both eyes and blood trickling from his nose. But we led by fourteen and he smiled.

In the locker room, nobody spoke but Coach, who concentrated on the technical details of the game. The possibility of the team's first-ever appearance in post-season play hung in the room like air scented by the perfume of a beautiful woman, but nobody mentioned it. Coach leaned against the wall as he spoke and Troop members sat, listening, but with looks of men who recognized that their dream stood right outside in the gym waiting for their touch. In Swoop's eyes, there to read for any who understood him, was the realization that, for him, the stakes were larger even than this. But he, too, said nothing and took the floor for the second half like a man who knows he has a task to finish.

From the opening seconds, Swoop harassed their guards with such all-consuming ferocity that Huntington struggled to bring the ball across half-court. At the other end, with Swoop penetrating and dishing, our guys got one open look after another. Inexorably, we pulled away, and before the ten-minute mark our lead exceeded twenty. Huntington's rough stuff didn't diminish, but they were a beaten team and it was visible in their faces. When Coach pulled Swoop with eight minutes to go, the crowd rose in standing ovation, but when the applause ended, the standing didn't; they remained on their feet and stared at him, their silence rendering tribute more profound than their cheers.

But interspersed amidst the sea of solemn faces, like uninvited representatives of Pluto at a Bacchanalian feast, sitting not standing, a small cadre of hard-faced, close-cropped young men looked conspicuously disenchanted with the outcome of events.

But the rest of the area did not agree. With Hoppo Valley now champion of the Iowa Valley Conference for the first time in its 47 year history, and with the school's inaugural appearance in post-season play, the town launched into a celebration that, old-timers said, the locale hadn't equaled since V-E Day. Fireworks were set off in Healey Park, and motorists honked in the streets and stopped their cars. The bars disregarded all blue laws, refusing to close, and a large segment of the population did not sleep that night. The next day many Main Street merchants held celebratory sales and the Chamber of Commerce issued a national press release describing the attractions of the town and surrounding areas. Most local farmers came to town, teachers were more lenient with students who cut class, and not much work got done in Hoppo Valley that day.

Mayor Pedersson looked the other way as revelers violated several ordinances, but his office issued no words of congratulations. President MacPherson proclaimed several days later, in an announcement to the university, that "the basketball team has done a splendid job and certainly deserves the unqualified support of administrators, faculty members and students alike." But he had misgivings, he said, and warned that "athletic achievements do not, and must not be taken to, justify a licentious disregard for all established norms of ethical conduct." There was only silence from the churches of the poorer denominations sprinkled throughout the back-roads of the Valley.

But we had seven days before the district championships got underway in Des Moines, and the activities of the Heroes Society had barely begun. Swoop had not just led the conference in scoring, shooting percentage, free throw percentage, assists and steals—he had not merely accomplished this despite sitting out the extended garbage time at the end of our many blow-outs—but he

had also succeeded in leading the town to a new vision of itself.
He had performed spiritual alchemy, taking men's visceral belief
in prowess and transfiguring it, elevating it to a higher plane, dem-
onstrating the profound need shared by all to incorporate such a
faith into their own lives. Perhaps not all could be saved but most
would be touched. Some, no doubt, would throw off the gift such
a touch brought to their lives, snarling from the vantage point of
an opposing faith—or from the emptiness of no faith at all. But
some would smile beneficently and let it in. The Troop members
barely slept any more, burning as they did with feverish intensity
to win the national title. I felt that Philosophy doctorates and body-
building prizes were light stuff, that I needed to find a real
challenge. People from out of state started to inquire about the
Heroes Society, about starting their own chapters, about the inspiration it would bring to their areas. Even Coach—when he
looked at Swoop, you almost missed the pasty face and sagging
gut, you saw only the "V" for victory signs in his eyes. Freddie
also beamed around Swoop; he pounded Swoop's back and threw
his arm around his shoulders during practice or games.

Freddie was with Swoop now on a pulsing crusade to win the
national title: he worked out regularly with The Troop; he studied
game films alone with Swoop; he trumpeted to anyone who listened that a healthy Swoop would sweep us to the summit. He
still attended church, not Heroes Society services on Sunday mornings, but nevertheless, I overheard him one day in the cafeteria tell
several members of the Campus March for Redemption that
"Swoop was a favored prodigy of God," and when they walked
away he shouted at their backs that "Swoop alone was unblem-
ished with Original Sin!"

It was Freddie who stepped out of the car that early Sunday
morning in late winter when Judas Bittner strode from the courtyard into The Troop's path. We had just pulled away in two vehicles
for the long drive to Jumbo's; he stood there, motionless, not letting us by. The Troop members stared and Swoop looked on calmly.
Only Freddie moved. He neither argued nor hesitated, but hoisted
Bittner over his left shoulder, held him like a sack of meal, and
waved the cars through. He put Bittner down on his feet and got
into Bobby's car. He said, "Let's go."

We pulled away. Through the rear window I saw Bittner standing—motionless, watching.

Freddie was losing his old friends, certainly among Bittner's followers, and the zealots around town referred to him as an apostate. He didn't care. In his born-again fervor, he had somehow reconciled Swoop's proud heathen demeanor with the Bible's injunction to serve the meek. All traces of his earlier animus were gone, and nobody seemed to question it.

But one did.

We were heading into the crucible of post-season play, we faced the district tournament upcoming, then the national championships in Kansas City. Swoop's dream loomed on the horizon, the town was gripped with religious fervor, and for me the nation's top universities beckoned.

But Freddie had once gloated as Swoop writhed in crippled agony on the floor.

Only one knew or cared. But that one was an ascetic priest of moral philosophy, who, rejecting mercy for justice, knew that one's transgressions are paid for.

But, as it turned out, with the escalating activities undertaken in the week leading to the district tournament by Swoop and the Heroes Society, I wasn't the only one intent on getting payback. Nor was Freddie Zender to be the only target.

CHAPTER ELEVEN
THE UNGODLY

The district championships began with a bang. Every top team from five states was there and not one was uninfected by the Swoop-mania that had ravaged the Midwest like the flu. Writers from national sports magazines covered the games, commentators unanimously predicted Swoop to dominate, and all foes came to the arena with one unrelenting thought: to club the brash upstarts from rural Iowa.

Back home the furor approached a declaration of war. Bands played in Healey Park, crushes of people milled on Main Street, and hundreds walked our bus out of town the day we left for Des Moines. But Swoop kept our guys from being swept up in the fever. "It's only beginning," he said.

And when towering Westlake College of Illinois hit us in the first round with a front line that averaged six-foot-ten, anchored by a bruising six-nine center and flanked by a bookends pair of six-ten forwards, his words were proved prophetic.

Swoop stole the ball in the backcourt on their first possession and whipped it inside to Freddie, but the captain's lay-up was snuffed in a tangle of hands and arms that resembled a redwood forest more than a basketball team. Their guards knew better than to try dribbling the ball upcourt; they passed it up instead, lobbing it high into the rafters, making their big men stretch like rubber figures to reach it, keeping it far from Swoop's thieving hands.

The ball floated in to the high post where the bruiser went up and snared it. Towering over our front line, he had unhampered visibility and he socked it in to one of the book ends on the right wing whose soft shot kissed in off glass.

Swoop raced it into the frontcourt like he burned jet fuel, but Westlake had both guards shadowing him over every inch of the floor—so he pulled up at the line and whipped it to Bobby, who, though open on the wing, rifled the shot a trifle long. As the ball caromed high towards the far corner, both guards thrust their butts and backs into Swoop's solar plexus, boxing him off the offensive board, permitting the bruiser a free hand in sweeping it clean.

Westlake brought it up deliberately, each pass describing a gentle parabola, hitting their big men with geometrical exactness across pre-appointed spots on the floor. The result was that though the second bookend's shot bounced hard off the back-iron, his partner and the bruiser battled each other to gobble it off glass, as Swoop waded through bodies to reach the rim. The first bookend wrestled it from his hulking buddy with surprising strength, then went back up and crammed it with his left hand.

Swoop's face was red and his jaws worked.

"Five men to the glass!"

He waved his teammates into the frontcourt as Coach roared at them from the sidelines, "Block off the defensive boards!" Swoop's shadows ringed him under the basket and he didn't hesitate. Jabbing left then right, he threw them off balance, then sliced like a poniard between them. Shedding them like jetsam, he hurtled into the frontcourt. Tearing into the paint, he feinted neither to left nor to right but skyrocketed toward the rafters, clearly intent to take on the trio of giants mobilizing beneath the rim. As the three meat-eaters rose to swat it back, Swoop soared higher, as if he had helium, not carbon, as a constituent element and, wearing his best game face, descended in a rush, hitting them simultaneously with a slam and a message: he was here to kick ass and take names.

After that, the war was on. Our guys charged the defensive backboard and with Westlake expending two men to block off Swoop, we had numbers, but they had overpowering size. Time after time, the bruiser shouldered back our frontline and gave the bookends free play on the offensive glass. Swoop had six buckets, but with ten minutes to go before half, they led 22–14. Coach called time.

"Their whole game plan is inside," he told Swoop. "Drop off the guards and let them shoot. Get position."

Swoop proceeded to take his advice and go him one better. He not only ignored their guards at the defensive end, he ran them ragged at the offensive. There were times when he had a clear shot or open lane and passed it up, waiting for their beaten guards to catch him, seeking to make them ceaselessly chase. It worked. By half, their guards were dragging and often left Swoop an alley to the defensive glass.

We went off tied, but the momentum had started to switch.

Coach exhorted them at half and the guys drank up his words, but Swoop remained silent, like a man who holds the final ace.

"Just keep hitting the boards," he said.

Not eight minutes into the second half, his strategy became clear. With their starting guards wilting, with their reserves too slow to keep up, Swoop crashed to the defensive glass time and again, forcing their big men to fight three against five for an offensive carom. Then the brutal conditioning of The Swoop Troop began to kick in in our favor, and when their giants started to droop, we won the battle of the boards.

After that, our first post-season game was history, and we had earned a hard-fought ten-point win. But nobody looked to party yet, though word was that the streets ran with wine back in Hoppo Valley.

"We play tomorrow," was all Coach said. "Get some rest," Swoop said to The Troop. "Stay out of the bars." Then he went back to our hotel room. Swoop, who thrived on naps rather than on long hours of sleep, stayed up most of the night with a Greek original of *The Iliad*, several dictionaries and a loose-leaf reamed with paper. He was still going strong at three-thirty when I reached up to turn off the reading lamp by my bed.

"You plan on getting some sleep?"

He shook his head impatiently.

"Later."

"You must know the text by heart. What the hell are you doing?"

"Studying."

"Studying? Studying for what?"

I craned my neck, glancing at the pages of notes he'd scrawled, observing the list of vocabulary words, the highlighted sentences, the dictionaries spread open before him.

When he looked up, he did not smile, but looked at me with an air so full of expectation that I could imagine Shackleton or Magellan looking at their peers with the same expression. It was a gaze not primarily serene with the sense of accomplishments already reached—or even one of pride, recognizing personal worth—but one of undiluted excitement at the prospect of great adventures to come. Then it hit me.

"Aspiring heroes need appropriate texts to inspire them. Is that it?"

He nodded, without speaking.

"What about the existing translations—Rouse or Pope, for instance? They're not good?"

He rubbed his hand across his jaw as he thought about it.

"I don't know," he answered honestly. "I'm not qualified to say. But I think that we need a version that captures the story's heroic action and language in the colloquial English of our day. Think how many people it might reach."

Briefly I stared, not quite shocked by any goal he might choose, but struck with the ambitiousness of the undertaking.

"How long will it take?"

"Years." He smiled ruefully. "Maybe decades. Fortunately, I know someone who's a Greek scholar. I'll recruit him to edit it."

I nodded.

"You're willing to put in the years?" I asked, but knew the answer before he spoke from the soft smile which lit his eyes.

"Just like practicing jump shots or studying with Lefkowitz. Hour after hour. Day after day." He paused. "There's no other way." His voice, husky with conviction, held the same quality of restrained energy responsible for the accomplishments he mentioned.

"And the years that you'll be playing professional basketball?"

He laughed.

"Digs, do you realize how much time professional athletes have on their hands? Do you think I'll spend it in the clubs, carousing and chasing skirt?"

"Sure, Broadway Swoop," I said, but he was so earnest I couldn't laugh. And though I shook my head and went to bed, twisting my glance away from his lamp, I knew damn well that skepticism had no place in the world I now occupied; that Swoop's truth was told in his deeds, not in his words. They were deeds that went far beyond his exploits in basketball—beyond the way he buried Holbrooke of Wisconsin with thirty-one first-half points in the tourney's second game, significantly past the quadruple double he laid on Burlingame State to take a breathless, to-the-wire struggle in the third; deeds performed off the court, though not unrelated to it, that had ripple effects beginning only now to be felt back in Hoppo Valley.

For the Heroes Society had not been inactive in the seven days between our conference-clinching victory and our arrival in Des

Moines. Like strategists plotting a carefully-wrought campaign, Bullock and several other members had used Swoop's ever-growing notoriety to thrust at the enemy again.

It was four weeks since the Society's formation and, fueled by the hoopla surrounding the team's championship run, its form of worship was taking hold in the Valley. Even before we left for Des Moines, its Sunday morning service had the highest attendance of any religious observance in the area. They came from outside the Valley, they arrived early, stayed late, and flooded the interior of Bullock's mansion. It was clear after a matter of weeks—as dozens trampled across the lawyer's lawn—that the Society had outgrown its original home, and needed to move to more spacious headquarters. The problem was resolved by Thom Kolotourous, owner of The Acropolis, the movie theater on Main Street. For years, Kolotourous, a long-haired son of immigrants, with a dark, sweeping mustache, had campaigned for the right to show all films against the local ban on obscenity. Though single-mindedly devoted to film and holding no interest in sports, he was galvanized by the ideals of the Heroes Society. He offered use of The Acropolis, and the Society moved its activities there on the morning before the start of the district tournament.

Swoop inflamed them with a reading of Apollodorus's poem of the great hero, Perseus. He stood on the stage of the theater, his long hair combed and still, but seemingly ready to flow with the anticipated motion of its possessor. Though it was comfortable in the theater, he refused to take off his Hoppo Valley letter jacket, wearing its navy and white colors as a symbol over his dark turtleneck and jeans.

"Garbed in the winged sandals of the nymphs of the North," Swoop began, "armed with the sword of Hermes and the shield of Athena, Perseus flew to the island of the hideous Gorgons. For he had to slay the monster, Medusa, upon whom a single glance would turn a man to a pillar of stone, in order to save his mother from the evil tyrant, Polydectes."

As he told the story, of how, with the aid of Hermes and Athena, Perseus slew Medusa, rescued Andromeda, and brought justice to his homeland, the audience stared raptly, captivated more perhaps by the speaker's earnest involvement with the content than by the stately elegance of the language. They stared too at the print of Tiepolo's *Perseus and Andromeda*—depicting the hero's triumphant escape—that hung on the wall behind the speaker.

"So over the sea rich-haired Danae's son,
Perseus, on his winged-sandals sped,
Flying swift as thought.
In a wallet of silver,
A wonder to behold,
He bore the head of the monster..."

That Athena agreed to proudly bear Medusa's head upon the aegis, Swoop concluded, was symbolic of the heights man could achieve if he first brought his soul into proper relationship with the gods.

But the real star of the day, as Swoop had planned, was Theresa Ringsmayer, our colleague at school, who had overcome both asthma and a severe bout of rheumatic fever to speak fluently three languages, spend a year as an exchange student in Germany and excel on the girl's volleyball team. When she stood calmly at the podium, the crowd hushed. She was tall, sturdily built, with blonde hair cropped close to her ears. She wore neither makeup nor jewelry, but her clean-scrubbed face exuded the fresh air of the Minnesota lake country she came from.

"The men's basketball team has pointed the way," she said. "But they are not the only ones dedicated to excellence. The women's volleyball team, too, will rise out of rural obscurity to reach the national tournament."

She was interrupted by people rising to their feet, applauding vigorously, and by several cries of "hallelujah!" that rent the air.

She waited until the excitement died down.

"Win or lose," she concluded, "our lives are committed to reaching the best possible to us."

When she sat down, Swoop mounted the stage again, his face holding the determined look—distinctive to him—that Kathy had once described as grizzled joyousness. He wasted no words.

"Heroes do not permit their quests to be thwarted," he said. "They push forward with dauntless determination until their goals are fulfilled. When the Hoppo Valley Crusaders win the national basketball championship, we will have proved—"

Bullock, seated in the front row, was inspired to rise and interrupt him.

"We will have proved that heroes do not languish under the stifling yoke of Dark Age superstitions," he said, his voice hoarse but carrying clearly. "When impacted by the oppressive consequences of medieval swill, they rise up and take a stand."

The lawyer's chest was outthrust as he drew a breath to continue. His right hand came up in an overture to his signature gesture of jabbing the air, but Swoop cut in before he got warmed up.

"Thank you, Mr. Bullock," he said softly, "for reminding us of that." He was trying not to grin. "But the championship will prove mostly how much is possible to all of us in our own lives."

Swoop returned immediately to his theme of personal inspiration to be drawn from the team's success. But others, though empathizing with him, agreed with Bullock and were more immediately concerned with the social struggle taking form in Hoppo Valley. Bob Geronda, for one, had called a meeting with Bullock and Fredric Westegaard. The publisher was not a member of the Society because he refused, as a matter of principle, to join anything. But he was in firm support of the Society's goals. Geronda also invited Swoop, but busy with school and preparation for the upcoming tournament in Des Moines, he declined. Bullock, however, kept him informed of the businessman's goals regarding social change in Hoppo Valley.

After six days and three victories in Des Moines, we were left with two games to win and a stream of news trickling in from Hoppo Valley. We took our next step toward Kansas City, when we took the floor on Saturday afternoon against undefeated Williams College of Omaha. Williams was a track team of greyhounds, who raced from end to end like Olympic sprinters juiced on amphetamines. Though even smaller than we were, their explosive quickness had proven irresistible all year, and earlier in the season, before Swoop's return, they had knocked us cockeyed at our own gym. They tore into us from the opening gun to the final horn, flashing past our heavy-footed plow-boys like all the devils of hell streaked in gleeful pursuit.

Swoop laughed. This was basketball as he loved to play it, the baseline-to-baseline action full-bore and unremitting. There were no elbows flying, no midair collisions, no players knocked to the deck or pole-vaulted into the third row; only five men sprinting the floor, four chugging uphill and one hurtling at mach three.

On one possession late in the first half, a haggard Raif Lockett missed a baseline jumper, which was rebounded by their jackrabbit forward on the far side. Instantaneously, he revved upcourt, four cohorts flanking and trailing like a biker gang, outstripping our staggering defenders, thrusting at the hole, surging head-on at Swoop, back alone. Swarming into the frontcourt, they fanned out and bore in, eyes seeing only rim. The jackrabbit faked right, faked left, then exploded for the hoop. Swoop refused to bite at the feints; he crouched directly in his path, low to the ground, waited for the last moment, and when the shooter was committed to the slam, he sprang. The blow was falling, the shooter's arm swinging down, and Swoop went up as from a launch pad, hands clawing for the ball as he rose, finding it, scratching it from the shooter's grasp, clutching it in midair, laughing aloud as he fell to earth.

The bikers thronged at him, swiping for the ball, and Swoop weaved through traffic like a startled deer, darted into the clear and fired the ball upcourt to Dandy Halliday for an unmolested cram. Then he dropped back into the paint to play defense.

No matter the degree of speed to which the greyhounds accelerated, they couldn't outrun the big cat poised against them, and although they outnumbered him—five clawless dogs against a cheetah—the realization could be seen dawning in their eyes as he bloodied them repeatedly that, when the battle was fought on his terms, Swoop could not be defeated.

And as we advanced into the finals against twelve-man-deep Rivington State, the news streaming in from Hoppo Valley indicated that a number of people at home had come to the same conclusion.

Swoop's championship quest may have concerned only basketball, but it symbolized something to people. The Sunday morning meetings of the Heroes Society, and the earlier services leading to its formation, had struck a chord. There was a fever, a new spirit taking root in parts of the Valley, and it emboldened those who had chafed for years under the prohibitions of the dominant creed.

Several members of the Hoppo Valley High School PTA, led by Butch Bratton, presented to the administration a revised reading list for the English program that included previously banned literary classics. Bob Geronda's Main Street Merchants Association announced its plan henceforth to keep stores and shops open all day on Sunday, and to take its battle against the blue laws into the courts if necessary. With Janet McMenamin mustering support among the town's medical practitioners for an abortion clinic—and Thom Kolotourous passing a petition among filmgo-

ers calling for an end to the Valley's cinematic censorship—the spec-
ter of social change no longer loomed on the horizon but was
taking center stage in Town Square.

"You plan on fomenting political revolution?" I asked Swoop
the morning of the district finals against Rivington.

He turned away, but not before I saw a smile turn up the corners of his mouth.

"Nah, I'll leave that stuff to Bullock. That's not why I'm here."

As we walked onto the court on Sunday to play for both the
district title and a ticket to the national tourney in Kansas City, it
was difficult to determine whether the excitement ran higher in
Des Moines or in Hoppo Valley. Two hundred of our supporters
had journeyed to the capital at the start; more had poured in with
each victory; now a thousand made the cross-state trek, and since
most couldn't get tickets they thronged the entrances and door-
ways, stomping, stamping, waving banners, shouting: "None can
stop our drive to the *top!*" When we arrived two hours before game
time, they mobbed Swoop at the players' entrance—and though
he stood patiently, talking with each, he refused to sign autographs,
explaining that their own accomplishments, not his, should be the
center of their concern, and asking each individually what he had
done that day to improve his life.

In Hoppo Valley, responsible citizens weren't sure which clamorous event to attend to first. In defiance of all blue laws, the bars
had remained open throughout Saturday night and Sunday morning. Dozens of people were there continuously in a state of
mounting excitement and by afternoon their number swelled into
the hundreds. They gathered around televisions in the Main Street
taverns, roaring at the pre-game introductions, as they had roared
all night, and though several of the community's traditionalists registered complaints with the authorities, no legal consequences
followed, because most off-duty police officers were bellowing in
the bars, and several of their working colleagues desired to be.

Fans thronged the streets through the night and morning, and
by afternoon, despite the March temperatures, several people
around town set up their televisions outside, grilled hot dogs and
burgers, and with their friends and neighbors howled at the events
of the game.

Amidst the pre-game fervor, the Heroes Society conducted Sunday morning services as usual. Thom Kolotourous opened the
doors of The Acropolis at seven, and the worshippers were joined

by dozens of drunken revelers who staggered in from bars up and down the street. When Dexter Bullock decided himself to conduct services in Swoop's absence, several Society members cringed, but their objections were overruled. The lawyer mounted the stage that morning, wearing a black jacket and a white open-neck dress shirt, his chest thrusting forward as if in generalized challenge to the world. When he attempted his most genial smile, audience members reported that he succeeded only in displaying a mouthful of incisors. "They say all life originated in the sea," Janet McMenamin once remarked. "Seeing Dexter when he's happy confirms that claim—and that the missing link is not a monkey but a shark."

Bullock gazed out over the audience, and rubbed his hand across his bristles. "The sanctimonious lords of this community never anticipated a brawl with men of greater principle than themselves." He paused for effect. "But now that it's here, they'll wish they had never heard the name 'Dexter Bullock.'" Attending the service, sitting in the front row, Fredric Westegaard interjected in a resigned whisper, "I'm sure they already do, Dexter."

But Bullock ignored all gibes.

"Swoop will make good on his promise—and soon. I don't think anyone in this room doubts it. The soon-to-be-won championship makes this a prelude to a holy day."

The lawyer spoke in earnest, all bombast dropped from his manner and voice, and members of the audience who had chuckled, now stopped. For a moment, there was no sound in the theater, and those who had spent the night partying seemed to sober quickly.

"Our next speaker, though still wet behind the ears, is a perfect example of The Society's ideals. He didn't want to speak, but I gave him a swift kick in the rear to get him up here. That and Swoop asking him. Anthony!"

A boy of around sixteen, stiff in jacket and tie, came up the stairs and approached the podium. He was slender, with short dark hair, neatly combed, and he smiled nervously at the lawyer.

"Now don't be nervous or we'll chop off your head!" Bullock boomed.

The boy didn't wait for Bullock to seat himself. He plunged in, as though seeking to get his address over with as quickly as possible.

"I'm Anthony Prudente," he said, looking down, almost mumbling the words. But then he lifted his head and his words grew stronger, as if an unseen presence whispered to him, buttressing his courage.

"I received nothing but 'A's' all through Catholic school," he said proudly. "But I was always in trouble. I raised doubts, asked questions, refused to recite the Catechism. Eventually, they expelled me." He continued for several minutes, expressing confusion and pain that he'd be punished for what he regarded as a virtue—free-thinking.

"But now I'm on track to graduate as valedictorian of Hoppo Valley Academy," he said, referring to the Valley's one secular private school. "My teachers welcome every question. They point out problems in my theories—and we argue. They never grade me down for failing to parrot them." He concluded in words that were quiet, but which carried with some inner conviction to the theater's rear. "I know what I think, and I'm not afraid to say it. Now I've found teachers who welcome it."

The members of the audience rose in unison and stood erect, gazing quietly at his figure looming under the picture of Odysseus. When services ended at noon, the worshipers departing The Acropolis shared the exits with dozens of recent drunks, all of them heading to places around the Valley to watch undisturbed a man pursue his vision.

But the vision was not similarly inspiring to all. A few might have remained indifferent; many, certainly, were troubled. With traditional academic curricula now challenged, with all blue laws coming under heavy fire, with one movement pushing for the legalization of abortion and another for the de-regulation of film, with the Sunday services of the Heroes Society consistently outdrawing every church in the area and with thousands following a brash, self-proclaimed Messiah, it took no genius to discern that the community was in upheaval. Similarly, it took no great insight to predict the reaction that would follow.

I tried to push it from my mind, but it troubled me—this holy war that was brewing. And Swoop didn't help. By deliberately stressing the belief in man's sinfulness held by the other side—by lambasting their self-effacing approach to life—he fanned the flames rising higher against his crusade. Finally, I put my concerns to him.

"You know what men of integrity most of your opponents are," I said. "Why do you intentionally antagonize them?"

We were leaving the hotel after breakfast, walking toward the bus to carry the team to the arena. It was a brilliantly-sunny winter day, though cold, and I had my parka unzipped to let the yellow rays closer to my skin.

"Men of integrity belong on our side," he responded immediately. "They have to see the conflict more clearly."

I continued walking steadily by his side, but his answer stopped me.

Our game against Rivington was scheduled for one-thirty five. When we emerged for warm-ups at one-ten, the fans screamed by the thousands. "Swoop! Swoop! Swoop!" they chanted, and roared: "None can stop our drive to the top!" But in Hoppo Valley they roared something else. The Reverend Buttle had called for a one-thirty meeting of all citizens concerned about the direction in which the community was heading. They came to the First Episcopal Church by the hundreds, of all denominations, from all over the area, some of the Valley's most prominent citizens and some of the college's best Religion students—and as Swoop took an outlet pass from Freddie and tore into the forecourt against three defenders on our first possession, the true defenders rose to speak in Hoppo Valley.

"I have long been a champion of freedom and the traditional American conception of rights," Pastor Buttle declared. "My father fought for freedom against the Nazis and I have persistently reached out to my fellow worshipers—Protestant, Catholic or Jew—in the spirit of religious toleration. But when liberty becomes license, when every moral principle of the community is assaulted and anarchy threatens to reign, then it is by no means un-American to conclude that the liberty of some endangers the safety of all."

The members of the congregation arrived early, listened carefully, spoke earnestly, and though their mood was solemn, even somber, they sensed an opportunity to take decisive action, and clamored for the mayor and university president to speak.

When Mayor Pedersson, his face lined with sleeplessness, tight with duress, rose to the pulpit and addressed the assembly, even his bitterest of political rivals could not doubt the genuineness of his distress.

"Never in my years in this community, as resident or public servant, have I witnessed such an orgy of licentiousness, such flagrant disregard for both the letter and the spirit of the ethical precepts underlying our local ordinances. The secular authority," he vowed, "while also retaining a reverence for the Founding Fathers' commitment to religious freedom, will not, indeed cannot, stand idly by while our home town degenerates into the Midwest's equivalent of Sodom and Gomorrah—or worse, of the Bronx."

But it was President MacPherson who made the biggest splash. In addition to stating that the town and university faced the gravest moral crisis of his tenure, he revealed that the school was in the midst of two ongoing investigations that could turn the ethical tide of battle. The administration, he concluded, would take every appropriate action to ensure the triumph of the time-tested, tried-and-true values that formed the core of the community's spiritual lives.

There were three minutes until half in Des Moines when MacPherson concluded—three minutes left when Coach Bakken sent in five Rivington reserves who had yet to play, a fresh wave of reinforcements to deliver a challenge, a gut check and an assault on our 37–32 lead. As thousands of our fans rose—then and throughout the day—urging our warriors to stand firm against the foe's superior numbers, just so, when President MacPherson concluded his address in Hoppo Valley, did the congregation rise to applaud its champions, lending energy and commitment to their quest to take on the infidel's burgeoning power in the Valley.

But today the infidel's power source resided in Des Moines, untouched by events in Hoppo Valley, by the rumbling pronouncements of a contrary faith; confronted only by a full contingent of athletes as equally determined as he that the season would not conclude on a March afternoon in Iowa, but would live on to reach the final celebratory rites of Kansas City.

Swoop had allies in his crusade, he had inspired foes, and he had never asked for more. The two sides—one outmanned and drooping from its relay races against Williams, the other pouring forth interchangeable parts like Xerxes's millions against Sparta—clawed, scratched and flailed for every point, rebound and loose ball.

Leading by two midway through the second half, Swoop crashed to the deck with a defensive board, wheeled like a cornered mountain lion and darted upcourt. The enemy troops raced back, poised to repel his one-man thrust, but our guys lagged behind, mired in the backcourt as if their sneakers were filled with sand. Coach waved his arms and roared, "Slow it down!" Swoop stopped at the key and brought it back out, observing that after the streetfight with Westlake, the track meet with Williams and the war of attrition with Rivington, even the savage conditioning of The Swoop Troop was not sufficient; his teammates staggered up the floor.

We were down to one time-out, which Coach would preserve for the final minutes. "Go four corners!" he bellowed above the crowd.

Swoop set it up like a traffic cop, and our guys took their appointed spots at the far extremities of the frontcourt, leaving him alone in the center to weave his way through pursuing defenders. But inexhaustible Rivington was not content to let Swoop's exquisite ballhandling skills eat precious minutes off the clock. They overplayed the ball and chased aggressively, hoping to trap him with sheer numbers. But heading full-bore toward halfcourt, he whipped a no-look strike to Freddie at the far midcourt, then spun a one-eighty on one leg, reached to the floor with both hands for balance, pushed off hard and burst into the clear streaking for the hoop. Freddie arced the lob high over the front rim and Swoop, never willing to slacken his in-your-face style, catapulted for the rafters, caught and smashed downward in one flash of motion. He and the ball descended to the floor simultaneously, but on opposite sides of the iron, and our lead had grown to four.

Rivington substituted again and stormed at our gates like a homeland army desperate to oust a conquering invader. They came in waves, punching the ball from the key to the wing to the low post, looking to draw reaching fouls from opponents too spent to move their feet. Swoop forsook their guards and dropped into the paint, swarming at the swarmers, hands flashing like a pickpocket's for the leather.

"Go strong!' he urged our beleaguered defenders, and Freddie and Dandy were with him, reaching deep into their afterburners for the remaining fumes, bodying hard against their center, forcing him either to kick it out to an open guard or barge rimward against an armful of heaving beef. He chose the latter, and when he put it on the floor and spun, Swoop left his feet in a dive that carried his frame horizontal to the deck, reaching, clawing, striking with his fingertips, deflecting the ball away in a dribbling roll that carried it toward the baseline.

As Swoop struck the ground chest first, his face pressed to the wood, his mouth sucking dust, the precious leather was gathered by Raif Lockett, who clutched it to his chest, crouched and encircled it with his six-seven bulk, swinging his elbows to ward off the foe.

Though Swoop lay motionless for an instant, none rushed to his aid, not because he didn't rate it but because it was inconceivable to all that he could need it. After a quick blow, he sprang upwards and screamed "Ball!"; then received Raif's pass fired through a crush of defenders. The Rivington players scattered toward the backcourt like a pack of dismayed wolves.

Swoop tore upcourt, dribbled to the left baseline, came under the basket, out the other side and—zig-zagging between ravenous defenders—brought it up past the key, where he again set up our four corners.

The look of panic on the faces of Rivington's defenders as they ceaselessly chased was manifest. Swoop laughed with a child's brilliant fervor as he wove a tapestry with the ball, dribbling in, out, through and around his foes as if they were boyhood pals, not ignoring their desperate lunges or swiping paws but using them, needing them to complete his artistry, and so, befriending them.

But camaraderie was not in the eyes of the foes as they ignored our other players and hounded Swoop with three and sometimes four men. They hunted him across every square inch of the forecourt as Swoop rhapsodized on his theme and the minutes ticked away. No matter the frequency of their substitutions, the toll of the chase wore on the predators, not on the bounding prey—and at the final horn, with the rat-a-tat staccato of Swoop's dribbling still pounding in their skulls, the bitter realization creased their faces that, if a man pursues the wind across a continent, in the end it is all over him—his face, his back, his hair—but it sings through his clutching fingers and is not to be grasped by his hands.

We had won the district and were going to Kansas City.

There was no celebration in Des Moines—only a squad of exhausted men embracing Coach and the hard eyes of Swoop gazing south. Our fans, so raucous and jubilant throughout the day, stood now, neither applauding, cheering nor speaking, only staring at us with taut bodies prepped for action and with hungry eyes yearning for more.

In Hoppo Valley, too, the celebration was restrained. Thousands of residents, in smaller groups, gathered in the homes of their closest friends and quietly savored the triumph, waiting for the team bus that would bear us home. When we arrived at eleven that night, they waited for us, not in screaming throngs at the edge of town, but in a hushed group on campus, waving, smiling, holding signs reading "Kansas City," their eyes, like our hearts, filled with the radiant awareness that the tiny school from nowhere would play the country's best for the national championship.

We stood outside in the crisp March night for over an hour, talking quietly with our supporters, not as conquering heroes to an adoring crowd, but as achievers to those who craved the same. Swoop mingled freely, shamelessly reveling in the attention, but discussed neither the national championship nor the Society's campaign. Rather, he asked each individual for details regarding his own dreams and quests.

Swoop and I slept for five hours that night. We rose Monday morning before six for ninety minutes on the weights, followed by a six mile run. The workout left time for a quick breakfast but not for a shower, and we walked in our still-damp sweats to the Humanities Building for our first classes at eight-thirty.

On the steps we parted, I going downstairs for my Senior Seminar in the Pre-Socratics, Swoop upstairs for his class in Roman Love Poetry. But before I had taken three steps, the figure of Freddie Zender strode through the front door and loomed in front of me. Kathryn Gately was by his side. As Swoop's footsteps receded up the stairs, the captain wasted neither time nor words.

"They burned a cross on Bullock's lawn last night."

Though I was hit by surprise, and even as a flood of foreboding possibilities flooded my mind, the reaction that surged irresistibly from within was so tinged with the impact of one who recognized no limitations that it stamped me as either a groveling follower or a dauntless hero. I laughed exultantly.

"That's not all," he snapped. "They pasted signs all over The Acropolis, with one line, a single theme: 'Death to the Un-Godly.' They're signed: C.R.U.S.H."

"C.R.U.S.H.?"

"Christians Resisting Un-Godly Satanic Hedonism."

Kathy had said nothing to this point, but though I'd been looking at her lover I'd felt her eyes on me the whole time.

"It's so wonderful to find people who are clever at acronyms, don't you think?" Her laughter was a rich, deep throated sound, expressing joy at the fitness of it all, at the symmetrical perfection of events in God's world. She observed me nodding in approval. "I wonder who C.R.U.S.H. is?" she murmured.

"Yeah, I wonder."

"I'm glad the two of you find this funny," Freddie said. "But you're wrong. They're dangerous."

Though Kathy's words answered him, her glittering eyes looked at me.

"It's true. They might exhaust the letters of the English language. Then where will they be?"

"In the same place they are now," he answered grimly. "In their cellars, planning to censor books and movies, heave their bodies at Dr. McMenamin's patients and cripple Swoop. That's where."

The chill that stifled our laughter was not primarily the result of his words but of writhing images burned into our memory banks. I turned from the group.

"May God smite the bastards. I've got class."

"God?" Kathy's grin, never gone long, was back, teasing me.

"Well, whatever's out there protecting Swoop."

"Let's hope there's something protecting him," Freddie said.

His words stayed with me through the day, so much so that I didn't tell Swoop, never even asked him if they did. Over the "V for Victory" sunlight that flooded Hoppo Valley in those days, Freddie's words cast a single appalling cloud. Though I pushed away those thoughts and thrust into classes, preparation for graduate entrance exams and hours of brutal workouts, I found that I couldn't shake free of them. The events of the next few days bore them out too forcefully.

CHAPTER TWELVE
THE HOLY WAR

Practice was brutal all week.

The national tournament began on Saturday, for us the pilgrimage to Kansas City took place on Friday and, briefly, nothing else mattered. It was the end of the line—put-up-or-shut up time—and Coach knew this was his one chance. He worked the guys like slaves.

On Monday he ran defensive pressure drills for three hours without a break. Then he drove both units up and down the floor in a breakneck fast break scrimmage, each squad ordered to drive the ball relentlessly at the other.

It was after eight by the time he finished and we had missed dinner. Coach took the whole team to the Black Steer at his expense, though most everyone just sat in numbed exhaustion and stared at their steaks. Swoop—who ate little meat—had a chef's salad, a loaf of French bread and skim milk; he topped it off with a bowl of fruit salad. Freddie sat at his right hand, and between mouthfuls of sirloin, baked potato and buttered bread, spoke of the blood they would shed in Kansas City. I sat across from them and devoured filet mignon as I did everything else—with an appetite insatiable and merciless. Coach ate light and stared hard, and everyone else sopped up water but picked at their food.

After dinner I hit the weights for two hours, then showered and was in my room by midnight, stretched on the bed with the Greek original of Aristotle's *Metaphysics* side-by-side with Ross's English translation. Swoop was at my desk, writing a paper on "The Renaissance Vision of Eros," comparing Petrarch's idealized Laura to the Greek myths of Aphrodite. Editions of Petrarchan sonnets lay sprawled open before him. The window was cracked and the cold, hard, scented promise of the March night seeped in. Neither of us said a word.

At two-thirty there was a banging at my door. It was Bobby.

"Trouble," he said to the room at large.

Swoop was on his feet and down the hall in a blur. Bobby and I struggled to keep up.

We got my car out of the lot and Bobby explained as I drove.

"It's Raif and Davy. They're drinking at The Cockatoo, that dump out on Route 46. Some guys come up to them, say they're team supporters, start buying them drinks. Get them plastered. As soon as Raif and Davy pull away, state troopers nail Davy for DWI. Get Raif for buying for a minor, too."

"The Cockatoo," I said. "That's outside Wahlsberg. No cop in Hoppo Valley would arrest them."

"Coach don't like drinking. That's where we go."

"What did they look like?" Swoop asked.

"The guys? I don't know."

I turned to him.

"Think they're close-cropped and fresh-scrubbed?"

"Want to lay odds?"

I shook my head. "No bet."

"But, Swoop," Bobby protested. "Those zealots don't drink."

Swoop turned on him, and for one second the hardness of his eyes was directed at his teammate.

"But you guys do. Why wouldn't they use your own vices against you?"

Bobby stared.

"But that's entrapment. Isn't it?"

Swoop said nothing and, after a moment, I responded, musing in general as much as answering Bobby.

"The Puritans physically tortured women to extort phony confessions," I said. "Then burned them at the stake as witches. Calvin had people drowned for fornication, and once beheaded a child for striking his parents. The heads of Catholic France lured thousands of Huguenots to Paris under pretense of a marriage ceremony, then slaughtered them while they slept. The Pope celebrated the massacre of the heretics. Should we believe such zealots would hesitate at entrapment?"

When I received no answer, I looked at Swoop.

"What's the plan?"

"Let's get Coach."

"Swoop," I said. "He's got no juice in that burg."

"He's connected all over the area. He's got enough."

We found Coach at home. Although it was three A.M., he was

awake. He was in the den, where clothes hung over the backs of chairs, basketball books cluttered the shelves, and a movie projector stood in the room's center, running game film of upcoming foes. The house was immaculate, the dining room chairs preserved in plastic as if they were museum pieces. In the living room a shaded lamp burned all day, shining on a picture of his family. An unvarnished wooden cross hung across from the portraits, giving the room a pristine ambiance, unlived-in, like a shrine.

He showed no reaction when we told him; he merely lifted his bulk and drove with us to the Wahlsberg lock-up, where he bailed out his players.

But the next day at practice, he took a stand. After three hours of grueling workouts, he sat his exhausted players around him in the middle of the gym floor.

"This is an ultimatum," he said. "You stay out of the bars and off booze altogether—for the duration. Or you're off my team. Understand?" He spoke in the same gentle tone he always used, but the look in his eye was something different.

"Yes, sir," said several players quietly.

Swoop and I had worked out in the morning, so after practice we ate dinner and were back at our studies in my room by eight.

We'd been silently absorbed in our work, and the clock on my desk said 10:35 when I was startled by the shrill clamor of the telephone. It was Jumbo. Swoop spoke for several minutes—mostly he listened—and when he hung up, he did not smile.

"Jumbo's spotted strangers skulking around the gym for the past week. He wasn't sure, at first, what they were up to, Now he is."

I said nothing, waiting for him to finish, and after drawing a breath, he did.

"They've been snooping around, talking to some of Jumbo's crowd, and taking pictures. The pictures are of us—you, me, The Troop."

"So what?" I asked, but the answer hit me a split second before Swoop's reply.

"The strangers are clean-shaven and short-haired."

The next morning, after a workout even more charged than usual, I was stopped at the front door of the Humanities Building by the associate dean of student life.

"The president wants to see you. Now."

"I got class now," I said, and started to shoulder past him.

"If you want to go to grad school," he said softly, "I suggest you don't keep him waiting."

Robert MacPherson, though a stern and disciplined administrator, was known for keeping his door open to students. But when we arrived at his office, it was shut. The dean knocked once, opened the door, let me in, then shut the door behind me. The president was alone. He waved me to a chair.

"Duggan," he said, in the deep voice that, coming from such a spare frame, always surprised people. "I know you have class, so I'll make this brief."

"Go ahead," I said.

He sat behind a huge mahogany desk, flanked by bookcases stuffed with scholarly theology texts, several of which he'd written. He was tall, painfully thin and gray-haired, with an austere smile but a wry, mocking humor that often left visitors wondering whether they'd been had. His intimates testified that he'd never smoked, cursed, cheated or philandered but did have a refined taste for single-malt Scotch. His wife, his children, his faith were his life. None of the storms or tribulations of sixty-two years, including a two-year bout with stomach cancer, had prompted one inch of shift on these.

"Duggan," he said. "You are, without any doubt, the most brilliant student we've had in my fourteen-year tenure as head of the university. So it deeply pains me to bring up these criticisms. But consider: you are going to an Ivy League university as, no doubt, our valedictorian, with glowing recommendations from us. Several members of my staff and myself, I must add, are troubled by your involvement, even founding member status in, that new society which threatens every Christian value dear to this community. Do you understand what I'm getting at?"

, The look on his face was so earnestly sincere that I almost hated to disappoint him. But I shook my head.

He sighed, then got quickly to the point.

"All right. I am deeply reluctant to place in jeopardy such a brilliant academic future. But I also have a moral responsibility to the best universities to inform them that they are admitting one who is becoming as much of a troublemaker as he is a scholar."

"Troublemaker?"

"It is difficult to think of one with your gifts in such terms, I acknowledge. But when a student is arrested for trespassing on private property and suspended for threatening another student's physical well-being in class, I don't know what else to call it." Then the president did what he did so rarely—he raised his voice in anger. "And above all, when the student is a key member of that hooligan society which literally runs wild in our streets, he contradicts every principle this institution stands for."

Then I understood. I got up.

"So any future involvement with the Heroes Society places in danger my recommendations and, consequently, my admission into the top philosophy programs?" I asked. "Is that it?"

The president was not an angry man, and immediately he caught himself and took several breaths. There was no doubting the genuineness of his pain. He shifted uncomfortably in his chair, and his eyes looked appropriate to a funeral.

"I'm sorry, Duggan, but it might. I have to be just, and surely you see—" he continued, but I was already on my way out the door, and didn't hear it.

After classes, I pleaded with Coach to join Swoop and me for lunch. His normally sad, benign look grew dark as I told the story.

By the time I was done, Coach looked grim.

"You entered a peaceful community and started a bleeping holy war," he said to Swoop. Looking at me, he added, "And I doubt he could have done it without you—so you pay a price for your rashness." He stared from me back to Swoop, and when my glance moved upward to his eyes from the chain and cross around his neck, I noticed where his gaze was focused—on the gold chain Swoop wore ending in the medallion under his shirt. Coach shook his head. "But what you've said and done...I can't altogether condemn it, can I?"

"Kansas City," Swoop whispered involuntarily, and Coach nodded.

Though Coach was calm as we left the cafeteria, he had a look that spelled trouble for anyone in his way, including those who had been long-time friends. He didn't say a word before practice, he merely lashed the team through four hours of boot camp hell, snarling orders at his men as he had under fire at Inchon. The guys were in great shape, but after three gut-breaking hours began to droop. Swoop and Freddie kicked ass then, urging, pushing, exhorting—and doing it themselves. When it was done, Coach spoke only two lines.

"Stay in the dorm at night for the rest of the season," he commanded. "Keep your sorry butts out of trouble."

The guys were too exhausted to object.

It was Freddie who spoke to Swoop as the others crawled off to shower.

"Coach thinks we're at war."

Swoop nodded, his eyes like slits.

"We are."

"After what they did to Raif and Davy, I guess so."

"Among other things."

"Shouldn't we hit back? I mean *hard*."

Swoop turned to him.

"Against your friends at the First Commandment Missionary Church?"

"That's not Christianity," Freddie snapped. "They're no friends of mine."

"Not Christianity?" I interjected. "They stand for the sinfulness of man, the need for abject obedience to God and the evils of secular living—don't they? What do you call it?"

He didn't answer at first, and then Swoop jumped in, addressing the second of Freddie's claims.

"Not even Bittner?"

They'd been walking to the lockers. Now Freddie stopped.

"Judas is a man of God," he said softly. "He would never get involved with that."

"Is he?" Swoop asked, ignoring the second statement.

"Yes," Freddie insisted. "He recognizes the sinfulness of..." He felt Swoop's eyes on him "...of other men. He just doesn't realize that it's a transgression to oppose...one on a sacred quest."

"Do you?" I almost blurted, but the way he hung his head made me pause.

"Stay away from him if you value your soul," Swoop said, then he walked away.

That night I shoved aside my worries and threw myself even more relentlessly into my studies. I chafed only slightly when Swoop invited Freddie to join us. "He's starting to see the light," Swoop said. "Let's keep showing the way." We got a chair from the lounge and placed it next to my desk. He sat in it, placed his feet on the radiator, and without a word pored over a medical text.

"Where's Kathy?"

He looked up.

"At the library. I don't have to be with her every evening."

"No?"

It was pushing eleven, hours later, as Freddie was at the door to leave, that we got the word.

He jerked open the door, saying good-night, and Dandy stood there with cotton in his nose and a bandage over one eye. His hands were behind his back. He held his head high looking at Swoop. But he said:

"I a dumb-ass."

Swoop looked calmly and I gaped. The question that hit like a snarl came from Freddie.

"Who were they?"

Dandy shook his head.

"Strangers. Redneck motherf—kers."

"They provoked you?" Swoop asked.

"Word. Be downtown after dinner, do some shopping, get my ass back to the dorm, like Coach say. They lay for me outside the drug store, three big motherf—kers in overalls blocking the door. When I say, 'excuse me, cous,' they just lean up close, all over me, like we lovers and s—t, and now I getting scared, so I try to slide my ass between them, but one grab me, so I push him off, and when he topple over, all hell more or less break loose. They ace me, swinging all wild and s—t, and when I shove their asses down, must be twenty people out of nowhere all at once, screaming, 'He's trying to kill them!' and I beat it, running the wrong way, they chase my ass all the way back to school."

Swoop nodded.

"So they have twenty witnesses to nail you on assault."

Nobody said a word, and Dandy stood there, his broad face long now, distorted by despair. Freddie spoke first.

"Who are they? What did they look like?"

Swoop turned on him.

"We know what they look like. Do you have any doubt of it? The question is: What do we do?"

"Let's find those—"

But Swoop had other priorities.

"We're going to Bullock. Then to the cops. This is self-defense, and you're turning yourself in."

"Word of twenty white people against me, Swoop. They going to lock my ass up."

"I know it. And Bullock's going to get your ass off."

He turned to Freddie.

"Make sure everybody's in."

Freddie nodded.

"You don't still preach with Bittner, do you?"

"Not since you came back. My preaching," he almost grinned, "takes a different form now."

"Good. You may get a chance to do some this week."

"How's that?" Freddie asked the question, but we all looked at Swoop, puzzled.

"Because you were right. We will hit back. Now."

"It's a short week," I said. "We leave on Friday."

"Then that leaves tomorrow, doesn't it?" He turned to Freddie. "You still upstairs in Whitby?"

"That's right."

"O.K. Get over there, lock yourself in and stay put."

"Right."

"Digs, you too. I'll see you in the morning."

"Where you going?"

"Bullock's first. Then to pay some visits. Dandy, I need you to come with me."

"Word."

"It's late, Swoop," I said.

His grin, as he stood outside my room in the dim light of the hall, was like a wolf's.

"With these people, it doesn't matter."

"Got it."

"Get on the phone and make sure everyone on the team has each other's numbers. We'll stay in touch by phone."

"O.K. But you think there's danger even in the dorm?"

"No." He looked around the hall. "But I won't be happy until we hit Kansas City."

I let his words hang in the air for one beat, then I finished:

"Or Hoppo Valley, after we torch Kansas City."

Nobody spoke after that, then Swoop and Dandy were gone.

On Thursday morning I met Swoop at the gym at six. He looked fresh, his workout more super-charged than ever, so I didn't ask if he'd been to bed. I asked only about Dandy.

"He's in custody for questioning. Bullock says he'll be released by noon."

"We got Raif, Davy and Dandy all facing charges, Swoop. They going to be able to come with us tomorrow?"

"I don't know," he said, his face grimmer than I ever saw it. "Bullock is working on it."

We had classes from eight-thirty to eleven-fifty, and when we broke for lunch, Swoop said:

"Tighten your belt. No pasta today."

"What do you mean? We're this active, we got to eat."

He grinned.

"Today we eat life—rare. Pass the pepper."

I stared at him, at the tint of reckless vitality surging in his eyes, and I nodded. Somebody was about to get side-swiped.

We met Freddie in the parking lot. Kathy was with him and when The Troop members joined us a minute later, we gave Dandy a warm reception. Then we piled into Freddie's car and pulled away. Swoop gave directions.

As we drove through the back streets and alleys on the edge of town, it didn't take a genius to figure out where we were going. The noise started to hit me when we were still two blocks away. Cars jammed half the length of the street, parked and double-parked on both sides—of all kinds, several Cadillacs and a Mercedes convertible mixed with the Fords, jeeps and mini-vans. People hung from the windows of clapboard houses, gaping at the commotion, and mothers held back their ragged, dirty-blond children. There were at least fifty people on the sidewalk, many I knew, including Dexter Bullock, Thom Kolotourous, even Janet McMenamin. They held placards and signs at their sides, not yet aloft, but clamored at the top of their lungs, and Bullock jabbed vociferously in the face of an elderly man dressed in black with a white collar.

The First Commandment Missionary Church was under siege.

"It's a church!" Bullock snarled as I opened the car door and got out. "It's supposed to be open for worship!"

"I told you," Pastor Loomis explained calmly. "We hold regular morning services. After that the church is closed." He was white under the verbal assault but held his ground.

"Why? What are you hiding?"

I turned to Swoop as we stepped onto the sidewalk in front of the minister.

"What the hell are we doing here?"

He gazed at the throngs roaring and gesticulating at the church's closed doors.

"Listen."

I strained to make out the words they shouted.

"Open for worship—now! Open for worship—now!"

I turned to him, to the glitter of his eyes, to the joyous smile at the outrageousness of it, and I could think of nothing to say. I merely grinned in silent communion and left Swoop to put it into words:

"The Heroes Society is conducting services at the First Commandment Missionary Church."

"And when they refuse to let us in—what then? We bust down the gates?"

He laughed in simple delight.

"Let's see."

I looked around at the street we were on. Though I'd been to churches of similar denominations, I'd never before been to this one. The house next door had the rotting hulk of an automobile in the front yard, and the one next to it had tarpaper siding on the first floor. A tire lay strewn in the gutter, and across the street an old house had been abandoned. The neighbors had turned the front lawn into a dumping ground: a box spring with twisted wire and a rain-soiled mattress littered the driveway, and a kitchen table missing a leg lay cockeyed in the yard. I turned back to the argument.

"Open the doors now!" dozens of Society members yammered, but Pastor Loomis was steadfast. The church was closed.

"A house of worship must be open to all who seek spiritual sustenance," Bullock's foghorn could be heard demanding above the crowd.

"The church is closed," Pastor Loomis stated again.

Swoop stood back as Kathryn Gately, with Dandy on her arm, thrust into the circle surrounding the minister.

"Is the church also closed to bigotry and violence, Reverend?" she asked, pointing at Dandy's nose and bandaged eye.

"The church knows nothing about that," Pastor Loomis replied instantly.

"Does it know anything about burning crosses? About warnings posted all over the Acropolis? About persecution of the Hoppo Valley basketball team?"

"The First Commandment Missionary Church is an institution of God. It neither engages in nor condones acts of wanton..."

"Nice speech," Bullock cut in. "How will you like it when Swoop goes back on The Buzz and tells the whole area that you're harboring a nest of Bible-beating, Dark Age, cross-burning fanatics?"

The minister was shaking as he stared at the vociferous horde, but he hung in under Bullock's bullying. He was a slight man with white hair, and it was easy to feel sorry for him as Bullock thrust a thick finger again and again in his face. His kindly expression held a naïve, almost otherworldly, quality and I wondered if he knew what some members of his flock were involved in—and what he would do if he did.

"I think you better get off church property immediately," he said. His voice quavered slightly with a hint of fear at the potential physical confrontation, but with no sign of guilt or malice. "You're trespassing. Leave or I'll call the police."

"Do it," Bullock snapped. "I'll pay the fine for trespassing and you'll explain to the cops why you're accessory to acts of criminal desecration."

"And perhaps," Kathy added sweetly, "you'll allow *them* inside your premises. Especially when the Big Man in Town," she pointed at Swoop, "files a complaint and they come with a warrant."

"Perhaps also," Bullock turned to her. "Since I called every member of the press not fifteen minutes ago, he'd like to explain to reporters, and on local radio, some of the more stimulating extra-curriculars that the church now engages in."

Several members of the press had already arrived, including a newswoman from the Hoppo Valley radio station. But when a reporter and photographer from *The Independent* arrived a few minutes later, it was the moment Bullock had been waiting for. He corralled them into a group and converged on the clergyman.

"Now here's a true man of God," he boomed. "An enlightened man, the very embodiment of religious toleration."

He pointed at Pastor Loomis, and when the elderly minister saw half a dozen media sharks—jaws open—descending on him, he didn't require further warning. He spun and darted through the crowd toward the safety of the church.

Bullock turned to Swoop and laughed.

"What do you think?"

"Good job."

"Thought you'd like it. Something else you might like. The court won't be able to try your teammates for several weeks. Until then, they're free on their own recognizance."

"Able to cross state lines?" Swoop asked immediately.

The lawyer nodded. "As long as they inform the authorities of their specific whereabouts."

Swoop turned away, satisfied.

At a signal from the lawyer, dozens of Society members raised their signs and posters and began slowly to circle the building. They sang as they walked, and I could hear the beautiful soprano of Lindsay Walken hitting perfect notes high above the crowd. Their signs read "Let my people go." Their song was "We Shall Overcome."

Two police cars drove by in the next fifteen minutes. The first stopped across the street, and when Bullock stepped to the curb and glanced over, the cops waved. But the second pulled into the church driveway, and when its two occupants piled out they looked annoyed.

"Break it up!" one shouted.

But before they could wield their authority, the other cops crossed the street and stood in their path.

"Leave it be," they said.

As they argued for several minutes regarding the Society's right to demonstrate, I sidled to the edge of the crowd nearest them. One of them wore a stainless steel cross around his neck. One wore a gold chain, displaying something different.

But while dissension plagued the Hoppo Valley Police Department, there was only interest among the members of the press.

"The First Commandment Missionary Church is a sanctuary for a small number of Bible-beating fanatics who wish to dictate moral law as if this were Calvin's Geneva," Bullock snapped at a reporter from *The Independent* as Westegaard's photographer got shots of the protesters and their signs. "Print that."

"The persecution of a free man's creed will stop—today," Thom Kolotourous told Hoppo Valley radio, his sweeping mustache looking fiercer than ever. "This extends to works of art, as well as to members of the university's basketball team."

"C.R.U.S.H.E.D. will add several letters to its name," Kathy remarked to the writer from the campus newspaper. "Perhaps Mr. Bittner will do it personally," she added lightly, looking at me.

Swoop politely declined to be interviewed. He stood in the background, letting others speak, observing the successful professionals and talented students who had taken up—as a conscious code—the cause of self-actualization. He didn't smile, but there was a softening of the facial muscles, especially around his eyes that gave to his countenance the light, untroubled expression of a child.

The peacefulness of the demonstration and the presence of the press convinced the second group of cops; they departed by one o'clock; the first pair spoke to Bullock, then left several minutes later. By one-thirty people needed to get back to work or school. There had been no sign of Bittner, E.J. Speed or close-cropped young men. Bullock pulled a brand new Wilson basketball from Townsend Sporting Goods out of the trunk of his Lincoln. Someone else had a gallon of gasoline and Dr. McMenamin brandished a gold lighter. "When I gave up smoking eight years ago," she said to me with a wink, "I knew I'd still have use for this thing." They laid the goods on the front lawn of the church.

"Swoop, they're not going to..." Freddie began, but Swoop turned to him.

"You wanted to hit hard, didn't you? Well, Bullock agrees with you."

He didn't wait for an answer but turned back to the lawyer. His eyes were slits.

"Torch it," Bullock said.

As the ball went up in a blaze, all watched in silent reverence, except Kathy who whispered in my ear: "Silly, you forgot the marshmallows."

As we sped away, I could see in the rear view mirror the spurting flame and billowing smoke on the church lawn, and could hear Bullock's booming voice—his head arched way out his car window as he drove—"Burn, baby, burn!"

I had no classes on Thursday afternoon and spent two hours in the library, writing the first pages of a paper entitled "Pre-Socratic Themes in the Metaphysics of Aristotle." At four, I packed my bags and headed to the gym for practice.

Freddie collared me on the steps outside the building. Despite the March breeze, he was sweating. He wasted no words.

"Do you know why Bittner wasn't at the church?"

"No idea. Why?"

He leaned toward me and lowered his voice.

"I just got the word. He was on campus meeting with President MacPherson."

"*What?*"

"That's right. He spent two hours in MacPherson's office."

"Doing what?" My mind raced with possibilities—all of them bad—but could find no answers.

"I don't know," he answered grimly. "But MacPherson's scheduled a press conference for six o'clock tonight."

"Great." I shook my head. "Come on, let's go."

It was our last practice before Kansas City and Coach looked like an executioner. After thirty-two years in the profession, he finally had a team capable of competing at the highest level. He walked into the gym dressed in black and barked commands like a dictator.

Our first game in the tournament was against Ballston College of North Carolina, whose attack featured Walter "Rock of Gibraltar" Tompkins, a six-nine, two-fifty-five, post-up strong man. "Rock Man," as he was called, was unstoppable on the low blocks, and had the mean streak of a back-alley D.C. gangbanger, which he had been.

Coach made us practice low-post defense for hours, double and triple teaming, swarming into the paint, charging the big man like starving predators at red meat—assaulting, attacking without letup until our guys puked on the sideline, then staggered back to the fray.

Swoop laughed exultantly. He stole the ball from Rock Man's impersonators so often that they flashed their elbows by reflex, seeking to ward off their tormentor, whether he was there or not. When Doherty, only six-two but built like a linebacker, was sent by Coach to simulate Rock Man, Swoop swiped with especial gusto.

Late in the day, with Doherty hounded mercilessly by defenders, Swoop slapped it away, then ducked as Drew's slashing elbow glanced off the side of his head. Coach blew his whistle and pointed at Doherty. Swoop scooped up the loose ball.

"Offensive foul, Sweet Pea," he said, blowing his antagonist a kiss.

When Doherty came for him, Swoop laughed in his red face. "Like the slavering Cerberus," he said. Though Coach sent the cursing Doherty immediately to the showers, practice was not done. Coach put Swoop himself into the post and ran guys at him till it looked like Custer's last stand with the Indians running out of gas. It was almost eight, players reeled, even Swoop wheezed. Then Coach called it a day.

"The bus leaves tomorrow at two," he said as they crawled away to whimper. "The championship express."

He strutted from the gym as if confident he held a fistful of aces in a last round of five card.

But when he reached the Athletic Department, he pulled up short. The red bulb flashing on his phone, he said later, appeared to pulse with a sense of special urgency. He stood in the doorway and stared—hesitant—and when he finally started across the room it seemed like it took the full duration of his career to reach the desk. The message on his machine was short and unambiguously clear: President MacPherson had announced at an evening press conference that, based on evidence incontrovertible and conclusive, Swoop was suspended indefinitely from the Hoppo Valley State College basketball team for gambling and conduct unbecoming. There would be no appeal.

CHAPTER THIRTEEN
THE CRUSADER

Hoppo Valley was in an uproar.

With the team leaving for Kansas City the next day, and with our first game in the national tournament the day after that, championship fever had reached an apogee never before approximated in the Valley. Swoop's suspension was a death blow to the town's hopes. The storm that burst now over MacPherson was a typhoon.

He faced it like a man convinced of his rectitude.

He stayed in his office, with the doors of the building and of his rooms unlocked; he didn't go home to subject his family to the deluge. He said what he had to say, then openly faced all comers. They came.

Team supporters let up a howl that could be heard in Minnesota.

"He bet on himself to win access to a gym? That's wrong?" they asked. "He wouldn't have even been at Jumbo's were it not for official interference in Hoppo Valley," blared Westegaard's editorial in Friday's paper.

The Executive Committee of the Heroes Society, without Swoop in attendance, met hurriedly on Thursday night in its original quarters at Bullock's home. By the time the members got to campus, it was pushing ten-thirty. MacPherson was still in.

The line stretched out the president's door and along the hallway to the stairs. Dozens of responsible citizens from across the area, feeling the inspiration torn from their lives, rushed immediately to meet with the administrator, to plead, cajole, reason, thunder and threaten. MacPherson met patiently with all.

He sat at his desk, calm in the eye of the storm, sad but certain of his action. Several visitors remarked that his spare frame never seemed quite so bent before.

"I understand the basis of your alarm," he told Deborah Raftery, an aggrieved thirty-eight-year-old mother whose fifteen-year-old twins had, within the year, begun to excel in school. "But the university charter is, and always has been, unequivocally clear regarding the status of gambling. The success of our basketball team has been a source of proud distinction for everybody associated with this institution, but I think you'll agree that the wording, 'Neither administrators, faculty members, other employees nor full- or part-time students will have occasion to bet money or material possessions on any game of chance whatever,' leaves me with very little room to maneuver on this matter."

A commotion in the hall outside his office interrupted him.

"You can place any interpretation on this you like, Robert," a familiar voice boomed through the door. "But this is a witch-hunt, plain and simple, and you damn well know it!"

"Ah," the president said to his guest. "I believe counsel for the accused has arrived."

Bullock burst in, and, ignoring the seated woman, reached across the desk and jabbed his index finger in the president's face.

"Eight o'clock tomorrow morning, you know where I'll be?" He didn't wait for a reply. "At the county courthouse, seeking an injunction to lift the suspension pending an investigation into the evidence. That's where."

When he finished, the sound of his breathing was the only thing audible in the room, and the hard bulk of his frame loomed in rigid pose over the desk.

MacPherson let the lawyer's words hang in the room, then he leaned back in his chair and calmly folded his hands over his stomach.

"That is, of course, your right, Dexter," he said. "In a free country the legal system must be open to the expression of every grievance—"

"Stow it," Bullock snarled. "You guys are great at talking about freedom of worship while suppressing it in action. I'll see you in court."

Without another word he stomped out and banged the door shut.

MacPherson sighed as the books rattled on their shelves, and he turned to his shaken guest.

"Don't be alarmed. Mr. Bullock's charm has always been his greatest courtroom asset."

Disappointed and a little shaken by the events of her meeting,

Mrs. Raftery spoke for an hour with visitors lined up outside the president's door, and gave an interview to a reporter from *The Daily Iowan.*

But it wasn't only on campus that protests were lodged. Several dozen team supporters who would leave for Kansas City in the morning gathered outside MacPherson's house on Oak Street that night. Several students were there, and they kept silent vigil for hours, lighting candles and hoisting action shots of Swoop. They picketed without a fuss in front of the administrator's home, and the only noise they made was when Butch Bratton, accompanied by several other Society members, arrived to announce that, from this time on, the Senior Thesis for all Hoppo Valley High School English students would be a paper on "The Traditional Religion's Suppression of Man's Striving for Greatness." The crowd softly cheered.

Talk radio shows, both in the area and throughout the state, lit up with calls on Friday morning, most voicing consternation at the college's action, a number expressing vehement support. One of Zatechka's competitors in Des Moines nominated MacPherson for the "Dark Age Pin-Up Boy of the Month" award, and Zatechka himself introduced a new call-in contest—a vote on the question, "Betting on One's Self to Win: Virtue or Sin?"

Though no one heard from Judas Bittner in these hours, E.J. Speed led a small contingent of clean-shaven young men in rapt communion outside MacPherson's office—on their knees, waving signs reading, "The Lord Has Spoken," some beseeching the president's dissenting visitors to see the error of their ways, others rising, threatening with the furies of Hell. Pastor Buttle stated in a front-page interview in Friday's *Independent* that, "The entire spiritual community breathes a heartfelt sigh now that this tameless apostate has been brought to God's justice." Pastor Loomis, questioned by reporters for the first time, held up a handful of ashes and said merely: "The boy is Satan's seed."

Swoop slept on the floor in my room to avoid the crush of people wanting to question him. He sneaked out of the dorm at dawn to get to the Humanities Building unobserved, and Campus Security unlocked the door for him. But a reporter from *The Independent* collared him on the stairs as he headed to the cafeteria for lunch.

"Swoop," the writer asked, "the administration regards your gambling as a sin. What's your assessment of your action?"

Swoop stopped on the step above the reporter and looked down at him. Though it was early Spring, the day was dark with gray clouds, and a raw prairie wind blew that made it feel like February. Swoop's glittering stare provided a brief flicker of light.

"Like Commodus, the Emperor, living with the gladiators, fighting in the pit against men and beasts, betting on himself to win." When asked if the suspension would stop him, he replied only, "Wait and see."

Coach said nothing in public. He went home immediately after practice on Thursday evening and stayed there. Members of the press besieged his door, but the house remained dark, except for a shaded lamp in the living room. They said they saw a huge shadow in that room until dawn. It was kneeling.

When Coach emerged at six A.M. on Friday, his face was drawn, lined around the mouth, and it was obvious that he had not slept. But his eyes were calm, even serene, and he smiled graciously as he told the reporters, "No comment."

He went straight to campus and when he left a long meeting with President MacPherson at eight-thirty, it was the administrator, who, for the first time, showed brusque indications of displeasure in his manner.

"Not now, not now," he snapped as reporters descended on him.

But Swoop's suspension wasn't the only source of turmoil. Pastor Buttle and other leading clergymen had been pushing for weeks for some form of restriction on the Heroes Society's activities, but even with Mayor Pedersson in support it took the basketball-burning incident to ignite action. With members of prosperous denominations now lobbying for results, the City fathers felt the time had come. In the early afternoon on Friday, over heated objections from several members, the City Council drafted a resolution requiring newly formed groups who claimed religious affiliations to apply to the local government for certification. Failing that, there could be no legal right to hold services or engage in religious demonstrations.

I heard about it only the next day from Freddie, who had spoken to Kathy by phone. The captain shook his head.

"They're crazy," he said. "Such a law must be unconstitutional as hell. How will it hold up?"

I nodded.

"It is. But don't forget that teaching evolution in the public

schools was illegal in Tennessee for forty years. Who knows how
long it might take to get a law like that repealed?"

A scant half hour before the law's passage, when morning classes
had ended, Coach rounded up the team—including Swoop—and
we boarded the bus two hours before the announced two o'clock
departure time.

We slipped hurriedly out of town, dodging the main roads,
avoiding the royal send-off planned for us. Coach said nothing as
we sped south on the interstate, and was still silent hours later as
we crossed the Missouri state line. It was only when the skyline of
Kansas City appeared in the distance that he turned to us, his cheeks
sunken, his jacket three sizes too big, but his eyes shining like a
knight's before the gates of Jerusalem.

"Swoop plays," he said. "We kick butt. Understand?"

He addressed us as if some unseen enemy hovered in the recesses of the bus, but when all he received were silent nods his
stare turned inwards and he added, as an afterthought, "Perhaps
some fall in battle."

It was eight-thirty by the time we checked into the hotel. Coach
went right to his room but not before he ordered everyone in by
eleven.

"You're not in, you don't play. Team breakfast at seven."

He went upstairs. After seven hours on a bus, some of the guys
joined him. I turned to Swoop.

"The dinner for us, I assume?"

"Absolutely."

The athletic association was holding a reception at eight, with
defending champion Maryville Baptist of Louisiana as guest of
honor. The champs, featuring Swoop's former schoolyard rivals,
Street and Miller the Killer Hayward, were thirty-two-and-oh,
routed foes by an average of twenty points and were heavy favor-
ites to repeat. Despite the school's official dicta upholding humility
and grace in victory, Street used the affair as a personal press conference.

"We be talking ay-troc-ities, yo," he answered a reporter's question as we entered. "Maryville be decimating, devastating and
decapitating these hapless chumps."

Though his coach and teammates sat on the dais wearing blaz-
ers and ties, he wore a silk sweat suit, a white turban and blue
wraparound shades shielding his eyes. Some of the players stared

at the floor in embarrassment and a few wore plain crosses outside their shirts, but Street, on a roll, paid no heed.

"Who we got?" he demanded of the room at large. "Who get it first up the poopy?"

"Danesville," a reporter from a Denver paper answered. "Of Utah."

"Utah?" Street looked around the hall, perplexed. "There be universities in Utah?" As some of his teammates laughed involuntarily, his mouth wrinkled upwards in a delicate sign of distaste. "Street be in Utah once. Do an all-star gig in Vegas, get sidetracked out there," he waved his hand vaguely west. "Pig farmers, yo! There be no schools in Utah. That be rumor, 'g,' mere hearsay. Next?"

When a writer from a national sports magazine asked his estimate of the gambling scandal at Hoppo Valley, his eyebrows arched with interest behind the shades.

"They best let that boy play," he said. "Or this tournament be nothing but trav-es-tie."

When members of the audience snickered, Street carefully removed his shades and leaned over the dais. His dark eyes scowled at the crowd.

"You think this be a joke? Street serious—he serious as hemorrhoids—and you best be listening, money, because Street give you the cold dope, and he don't say this more than once: This tournament about being the best. I know this homeboy and I tell you, he got a terrible game. Nobody else give us a run, I not even bother to suit up, play them in my streets. He bet on hisself to win? That a bulls—t rap, yo, how you think we make money. All the homeboys do that, me and my man *clean up* all the loose change on 155th Street, buy us a Mer-ced-es-Benz, 'g,' drive us around like we dukes and earls and s—t, how you think we do that—drug money? S—t. I don't do no drugs, I be *winning*, yo, Street tell you that, you take it to the bank. Square business. That the way it is, money. Let the boy play. We the best."

Killer Hayward coughed loudly into his hand, and looked as if he wanted to shrink his seven-foot frame under the dais. Just two years prior, Killer—after a teenage period of chronic troubles with the law—had found Jesus, and shed bitter tears for his fallen state. Street, a picture of consternation on being offered the word, replied, "Jesus saves only if you dominate the boards, yo," then walked away. Eager to keep the championship partnership together, he agreed to accompany Killer to Maryville Baptist—but he did not agree to quit talking smack. Now, nobody in the audience paid any attention as Killer and his teammates bowed their heads during Street's monologue. I leaned toward Swoop.

"Maybe you can get a little side-action on the championship game. Put me through grad school."

He grinned.

"If you get in," he said.

"Yeah, thanks."

I turned away.

But the following day, nobody turned away from our opening game against Ballston or from the events surrounding it. We got to the arena early and strode in through the players' entrance, seeking to avoid the crush of reporters and their questions regarding Swoop's suspension. People clamored outside for hours before the gates opened, including hundreds of our supporters from Hoppo Valley and across rural Iowa, and they crammed every seat in the house within moments of the doors swinging wide. Dozens of Society members were there, using the event as an occasion to press home their attack. They brandished signs reading, "Betting on One's Self to Win is Pride," and "Confidence is Not a Sin." No counter-pickets were there yet but nobody doubted that, in time, they would be. I shook my head thinking of the scenes that must be playing out then in Hoppo Valley.

From the locker room, I could hear the crowd noise building, and ducked quickly out to walk through the gym. Nobody in the stands knew yet what Coach would do. I could feel electricity in the air, but there was a sense of foreboding, too. When it became clear that Coach would play Swoop in defiance of administrative ruling, the stuff back home would hit the fan. Although my intellect understood how Swoop's foes construed the conflict, somewhere in my viscera I ached. I could never reconcile myself to a world in which people opposed the principles Swoop stood for. Back in the locker room, I mentioned it to him, and he stopped stretching, sensing my sadness.

"We got to give ammo to the Society," he said. "Let's bring home the gold."

As the players stripped for action, nobody spoke but the uneasiness was in their eyes. An expectation of impending doom hovered in the locker room and only Doherty smiled. Nobody would ever know Coach's exact words to MacPherson the previous morning, but their import was clear, and we weren't shocked when, forty minutes before tip-off, a telegram arrived from Hoppo Valley. It was for Coach, who shared it with us. "Board of Trustees in firm support. If university policy not obeyed, Coach Betorsky to be terminated immediately. Deepest regrets. Robert." Coach crumpled it and pitched it in the trash.

"No speeches, guys. Let's kick ass."

We looked at each other in silence. It was the first time he hadn't said "butt."

Only Freddie pulled Swoop aside as we prepared to take the floor for warm-ups.

"You swear you'll blow Rock Man away?"

Swoop nodded, then asked suspiciously: "Why?"

Freddie's look, as he responded, was neither sheepish nor cocky but filled with a seriousness that bordered on the grim.

"I bet my life savings on us to win."

Swoop's answer came with no hesitation.

"Then you'll be able to pay your way through medical school."

It was then I noticed that beneath his warm-ups, Freddie wore something in addition to a stainless steel cross; it was a gold charm in the shape of a basketball. Swoop's eyes followed my gaze, then flicked back to me, gleaming with excitement. I shook my head.

But it was the fans who shook their heads just minutes into the first half. They roared upon seeing him emerge for warm-ups, his wavy hair flowing as he soared toward the rim. They howled during introductions when his name was announced, making the old arena rock to its foundations. They called his name from the opening gun, their chant of "Swoop! Swoop! Swoop!" sending a message to whoever threatened his quest for excellence.

Swoop's play sent a message back. He stole the ball from Ballston's guards—he fired a no-look, one-hop, length-of-the-court dart for an easy lay-up—he went three rows back of the right side-line, a full-layout dive into the ample bosom of a middle-aged matron to a save a loose ball—and, with six minutes gone, he came on the double-team with such gleeful abandon that he bowled through Raif Lockett, then catapulted high to pin Rock Man's shot to the top of the box, his sneakers five feet off the deck if they were an inch. The ref and Rock Man gaped, the Ballston bench screamed for a goaltending call that never came, and the fans just screamed, an arena-ful reacting with one mind and one throat. They were on their feet after that—thousands of them, seemingly the

whole world—roaring and stomping till half, refusing to sit or relent, expressing support for such a man, doing it the only way they
knew how—with their voice and their hands—delivering their vote
on matters far weightier than their preference for national champion.

Though the game was over by half—we led by twenty-six despite Rock Man's nineteen—the fans didn't slacken or abate, we
heard their din through the thick walls of the locker room.

In the second half, Coach let Swoop play even when our lead
exceeded thirty. Normally, he sat him down to avoid running up
the score, but not now. He turned him loose to race both ends of
the floor like an overactive child, then watched in satisfaction from
the sideline, arms folded across his chest, eyes like slits.

The first game was in the books and the scores were on the
board. We had another one tomorrow—Sunday—but that evening,
around five o'clock, word started to trickle in from Hoppo Valley.
At an afternoon press conference, President MacPherson, flanked
by members of his staff, had announced officially the discontinua-
tion of Coach Betorsky's contract.

"It is with the deepest regret, but as a matter of unshakable
principle, that I am forced to carry out the termination, for insub-
ordination, of a valued friend."

The president's words were greeted, in Hoppo Valley, by sad
approval from some, by stony, silent hostility from most.

In Kansas City, reporters besieged Coach with questions.
Though he called no press conference, at least a dozen showed up
and interrupted Saturday evening's team dinner. They surrounded
our table, yammering questions, and Coach rose shakily but reso-
lutely to his feet.

"That's enough!" He leaned on the table with both fists, his
shirt sleeves rolled up to his elbows. He looked around, his cheeks
gaunt, but his eyes skewering each individual they stopped on. "I
have only one thing to say, so take it down and clear out. If the
administrators of Hoppo Valley State College wish to terminate
my twenty-year tenure as coach of this team in the midst of our
first-ever appearance in the national tournament, they are free to
do so. But they will have to send police officers to arrest me, to
drag me physically from the arena, and to prevent me from coaching my team. No further comment."

He swung his right arm in a gesture of finality, and sat down.

A long-time team supporter and contributor from Hoppo Valley, eating at a nearby table, overheard Coach's comments. He accosted me on the way out.

"He's as convinced as is MacPherson that he's right. They're crusaders."

His word choice struck me and I nodded, speaking almost to myself.

"It's catching."

Swoop was on the phone to Hoppo Valley far into the night. By midnight I grew tired of studying with sound suppressers jammed in my eardrums, so I threw him out and made him use the lobby phones downstairs, then returned with satisfaction to the passage on pride in *The Nichomachean Ethics.*

When our phone refused to stop ringing, I disconnected it. I found out only on Sunday morning that the president had ordered the athletic director to fly to Kansas City and assume immediate control of the team. The athletic director—a fierce supporter of the team—replied: "Fine. But when I'm coach, Swoop plays." MacPherson was forced to ask for his resignation, the athletic director refused and MacPherson canned him.

With Coach and the athletic director fired, members of the Hoppo Valley State College administrative staff—some of whom were in Kansas City—started to protest. The academic dean, the bursar and two assistants to the registrar threatened to quit. Many administrators supported Swoop's right to play, and were troubled that two of their colleagues had lost their jobs over the controversy. The Heroes Society moved immediately to take up their cause. One of Swoop's phone calls on Saturday evening was to Bullock at home.

"Focus tomorrow morning's services on the great individuals who opposed the beliefs of their societies," he insisted.

"And were persecuted for it?" the lawyer asked. "Way ahead of you, kid. Already made notes regarding Socrates, Bruno and Galileo. And I'm really going to hammer on the Scopes trial. Don't try giving me advice."

"Sorry," Swoop said in a contrite tone, but hung up smiling.

That Sunday morning's service drew over one hundred worshipers, more than any previous meeting had, including a number of the university's administrators, teachers and students. In Swoop's absence, Bullock was going to conduct services himself, but Thom

Kolotourous and Bob Geronda, concerned that people would then be driven away en masse, convinced the lawyer to let Janet McMenamin do it.

The psychologist took the podium at precisely eight A.M., dressed simply in black sweater and slacks, her hair down, as she always wore it, sweeping along the line of her shoulders. As was her style in class and in general, she wasted no time.

"Aspiration in this community is now a crime," she said quietly, and attendees reported that though her eyes were untroubled and her voice unraised, the room became electric as she stood calmly on the stage. "The great, unfulfilled yearning in the lives of most individuals is to reach some lofty goal, the highest possible to each. The youth who has become a healthy symbol of such a quest for excellence is now under attack in this town, as are his supporters. Consequently, so are our dreams." She paused, and when she continued her voice was so low that listeners strained to catch her words. "I came here to tell you that we will not allow this to continue."

They were with her as she recounted the struggles of Columbus, of Darwin, of Fulton, of Pasteur—not merely to identify important new truths but to convince their unseeing countrymen, as well. Moving to her own field, she made no denials regarding the errors of Freud, but told also the saga of his pioneering efforts to found the practice of clinical psychology. Her voice rose for only one moment—when she described the struggle of St. Joan to overcome all prejudices regarding her youth and her gender, to take command of the French forces and to sweep before her victorious army the English invader. "The triumphs of the seventeen-year-old Maid of Orleans are symbolic of the potential that lies dormant in mankind, and in the female spirit in particular." She spoke quietly of the dedication of these heroes, their social conflicts and, above all, their triumphs.

"There must be a Law of the Conservation of Moral Principles," she concluded. "The issues change their specific form, but the underlying fundamentals can be neither created nor destroyed. Freethinkers with important new truths are ever opposed by the majority. It is so today in our community. The inspirational figure—and, as a result, the inspiration—in our lives is now under fire. It is from fear and guilt that most individuals hold themselves back from pursuing their dreams. We require the vision of heroes to inspire us to rise up against our own trepidations. We cannot permit political and religious authorities to augment the internal forces of suppression. Our souls cannot afford the price we will pay if we permit this to occur. Therefore, we will not."

When she finished, attendees reported a peculiar phenomenon. Though she neither shouted nor gesticulated, the energy level of The Acropolis rose to where many felt an impetus to immediate positive action. But the applause she received—projecting the same quality of restrained intensity as her presentation—indicated the crowd's recognition that the deepest conflicts would not be resolved over the ensuing weeks or months, but only over the full course of their lives.

The Society's Executive Committee met after services with a small number of founding members. They decided, for the present, to channel their limited resources into one overriding goal: to undermine the president's influence with all figures central to the university's successful operation.

Though Swoop smiled benignly when he heard that Janet McMenamin campaigned among both the school's faculty and contributors to exert pressure on the Board of Trustees—and when word trickled in that Butch Bratton met with former students currently enrolled at Hoppo Valley and their parents—he was too focused on the national title and Sunday services to pay much attention. But a few of the Valley's educated elite heard what the psychologist and the English teacher said. They sided with Swoop's mission and favored a different aspect of the battle.

The result was that on Monday morning the Registrar, the Admissions office and the President's staff were hit with a small but steady stream of calls from top students and their families, all promising to transfer to other institutions if the college did not cease its persecution of the town's hero. One parent—a physician at the local hospital who was a team supporter and a friend of Janet McMenamin's—stated emphatically to the president's secretary that if the school was sufficiently ignorant not to recognize that it had someone who represented the eternal striving of man to reach higher, then it would pay a price in terms of an inability to retain its most discerning students.

Dexter Bullock, in the meantime, scarcely paid heed to the new law requiring religious certification. "Its manifest unconstitutionality dooms it," he told members of the press. "It will die an early death in court." But there were those who did not agree. "The Founding Fathers did not favor anarchy in the streets," Mayor Pedersson stated in an address to the Hoppo Valley Christian Women's Association. "Religious toleration does not include hooliganism." The two hundred attendees rose in a spontaneous standing ovation. When informed, by a reporter, that Saturday afternoon, of the mayor's words, Bullock responded: "We will not apply for certification and we will not cease our activities." "Services as usual, tomorrow morning?" the writer asked. "Damn right," Bullock said.

On Sunday we had our second-round game in the tournament, a two o'clock start against Martinsville College of Oregon. Though they had gone twenty-five and two and were led by a pair of whippet guards from Oakland, a backcourt tandem proclaimed by the press as the only guards in the country quick enough to match up with Swoop, Swoop's preparation was for other battles. He paid scant attention to the social upheaval in Hoppo Valley, but spoke incessantly to Bullock regarding his plans for Sunday morning services. Finally, at one-thirty in the morning, I chided him for being on the phone with prospective members of the Heroes Society. He was discussing the personal significance the Society's values could have in the lives of each, and whirled at my question.

"The national championship?" he asked, flabbergasted. "Digs, we're going to win the national championship. This is about changing lives in Hoppo Valley."

But then he heard something from Bullock that rocked him. "Got a message on Friday afternoon from a college kid in New York, said Constitutional law would be her specialty. Said she was coming on the next bus, would fight for freedom of religion as a volunteer. She said to tell you there *are* some crusades worth fighting for. Dopey kid. I'll send her packing as soon as she hits town." Swoop caught his breath. "Send her packing and I'll rip out your voice box," he said. "Hire her, pay her and get the hell out of her way."

The battle raged on several fronts simultaneously. Even as we took the floor on Sunday afternoon against Martinsville, President MacPherson sent a private message to Collier Denton, president of the intercollegiate athletic association, at his home in Chicago. Denton was a former national wrestling champion, who spent Sunday afternoons neither playing golf nor watching sports on television, but pumping iron in the private gym in his basement. He was not one to be distracted when he had a goal before him. For decades he had conducted a withering campaign against both national and international Olympic committees, excoriating them

for their ban on professionals, demanding that they drop their hypo-
critical cant and let the world's best compete. When he returned
MacPherson's call that evening, and received a plea to ban Swoop
from the national tournament, he dismissed it on the spot. Going
public, he announced to the press that the athletic association had
no policy on bets that did not involve its own games, that it was
up to a school's coach who played and that, personally, he thought
that "out-of-shape administrators should keep their hands off and
allow the true spiritual value of athletics—the contemplation of
epic struggle between superior competitors—to shine forth unre-
strictedly."

With or without MacPherson's approval, the unrestricted competition shined forth on Sunday in Kansas City. Martinsville sent
both guards at Swoop in a relentless double-team from the opening tip to the final horn, a blanket coverage that shadowed him
across every inch of the floor, from baseline to baseline. They threw
caution to the breeze, left men open and dared other players to
beat them. There were times when they harassed Swoop with three
and even four defenders, swarming at him in waves, seeking to
strip, steal or deflect the ball, at the very least to force it from his
hands.

Swoop cut across every millimeter of the gym floor, describing
long circuitous routes, 180 degree pirouettes and breath-stopping,
against-the-grain cutbacks, never giving up his dribble, always maintaining an angle, keeping open slivers of an alley through which to
shoot one-hop bee-bees to open teammates spread along every
square foot of the frontcourt.

Time and again our players possessed clear looks for a fraction
of a second, but Martinsville's hurtling defenders reversed direction and threw themselves across space in orgiastic abandon,
distracting, deflecting, intimidating until the scene more resembled
a pier-six melee than an organized game. The recovery time of
their defenders was hair-trigger slight, our guys could match their
intensity but not their velocity, and in the ensuing scrambles we
were consistently beaten to loose balls, deflections and rebounds.
Their troops roared upcourt then and flung themselves at our basket like the dervishes of The Mahdi against the walls of Khartoum.
Swoop was back alone, standing like Gordon before the maniacal
hordes, except instead of spears through his chest he took charges,
swiped passes and crammed shots off the craniums of opposing
gunners, sending ricochets bouncing at every angle into the stands

in the far recesses of our backcourt. For all the quickness and maxi-
mum-impact energy expended, neither side could score—the
defenses dominated like swirling hordes—and the score looked like
a football game until Swoop took matters into his own hands late
in the first half.

With three minutes to go and their lead at 17–14, Swoop
hurtled from the weak side, blocked their small forward's shot on
the baseline, then won the battle for the loose ball. With the ball
in his hands, Martinsville's guards leaped at him, seeking to pin
him to the baseline. Swoop waited until the exact moment before
their onrushing momentum stopped in front of him, then, with
their propulsion still thrusting forward, he sliced between them
and broke out in the opposite direction. Leaving their guards in
his wake, he sprinted upcourt as if he raced the hundred meter
final. His shadows trailed him like state troopers in hot pursuit,
but for a second only their center was back, standing between him
and the basket. Springing high over the seven-footer's outstretched
reach, he threw it down with a savage intensity reflecting neither
frustration nor hostility but hope. With the backboard rocking,
with the whack! of the ball off hardwood ringing through the arena,
Swoop roared at his comrades, "Step it up!"

They came on the press with renewed vigor, and though Martinsville broke it, lobbing it down the sideline, firing up a mortar
shot from the deep corner, it bounded high off iron, arcing toward the stands on the far side, torn from the sky like a bloody
prize by Swoop, high over the fracas like an eagle.

The crowd gasped as Swoop floated down, searching, like a
skydiver, for a place to land. He hit the deck with feet pumping,
caught his balance as he scrabbled forward, rocketed upcourt with
defenders thrashing and surged into the lane like a wave. It was
evident, as he hurtled rimward, that neither guards nor forwards,
nor coordinated teamwork, but only an act of God could stop
him—and with the Olympians no more willing to desert him than
Odysseus, the defenders' plight was hopeless. Their searching hands
and threshing limbs flailed like the suitors of Penelope, and with
the same effectuality. Swoop thundered down with a slam that this
time, shook not just the rim and the board, but the floor, the stands,
the glass in the windows. It was a blow that rattled the bones and
the confidence of the defenders. They stared, like fans, with a look
not of dismay, but of hushed, solemn stillness. Swoop stood panting under the rim, momentarily motionless; nine players and two

benches stared; and thousands of souls in the arena realized that, though Martinsville would not relent, the game's outcome had now been decided.

Though the score remained close until well beyond half, Martinsville's resistance seemed performed by rote, a lesson learned but no longer believed, and late in the day—with Swoop slashing ceaselessly at their vitals—we gradually pulled away.

But it was the silence of that signature moment, the hush of thousands as they stared at a man with chest heaving, that stayed with me. Hours later, even months after, all I could remember of that Sunday was the stillness in Kansas City, the calm peace of contemplation, not the roaring hub-bub of the fans' earlier reaction, not even the louder and far weightier hub-bub of events back home in Hoppo Valley. For though all of us who witnessed his exploits could focus on little else, there nevertheless remained a battle raging in Hoppo Valley, one kicking up a ruckus that the town had not seen in one hundred and sixty years of its existence.

That morning, Bullock and Thom Kolotourous had been arrested at The Acropolis shortly after the conclusion of services. Although Bullock had gone quietly, he threatened legal action all the way to the Iowa Supreme Court. Later, when released on his own recognizance, he stopped briefly at his office and found a disheveled, brown-haired girl waiting for him on the steps. "What kind of trouble are you in?" he barked. She smiled like a wolf, showing a lot of teeth. "I'm not the one in trouble," she said.

Sunday night, after the Martinsville win, hundreds of team supporters rallied spontaneously on Main Street. Fired by our success at the big dance, unwavering in their support of Swoop, they beat drums, tied up traffic, roared at the top of their lungs. They poured into town from across the Valley and beyond, from towns and farming communities over a hundred miles away, all caught up in championship fever. Merchants kept their stores open late, and business boomed; scores of people swarmed in and around The Acropolis where they mingled with members and signed the petition. Though many were strangers to him, Thom Kolotourous approached one after another, his stocky frame bristling with joyous energy as he hosted his domain. He grasped hands and clapped backs not like a business proprietor but like the last of an endangered species—a sincere politician. "How will you use a hero's deeds as inspiration in your life?" he asked each, his mustache curving fiercely as he smiled.

Hoppo Valley was in a state of bedlam. Stores and taverns were now open all day on Sunday. Thom Kolotourous vowed henceforth to play all films in Hoppo Valley and to fight any injunction in court. Butch Bratton and his supporters worked for high school reading lists to include previously-banned books, and his students now wrote against the conventional code. With Swoop's admiring hordes clamoring by the hundreds in public thoroughfares, and with God knew what depredations to come, it was clear to the town's traditionalists that Hoppo Valley was undergoing cataclysmic change. The old time faith was being swept away, and drastic measures were needed. On Monday morning, Pastor Buttle led a delegation of concerned citizens to meet at City Hall with Mayor Pedersson, a group that included, for the first time, Judas Bittner.

The mayor met with the press in the small media room of Municipal Hall in the early afternoon. Commentators reported in *The Independent* and on campus radio that his normally benign demeanor was absent and his face lined with the stress of sleepless nights. His message was brief and heartfelt.

"Maybe I'm dead wrong," he said simply. "But I always thought that honest faith in Jesus was the meaning of a good life. It seemed clear that we needed blue laws and administrative channels to determine the appropriateness of specific books and movies. Or else—what happens to our character?" His tone was gentle, reproving but not reviling. As he spoke, his shoulders seemed to straighten, and his voice grew forceful, not in the manner of a politician gaining confidence from the audience but of a devout man gaining aid from the divinity.

"The Hoppo Valley State College basketball team has reached great success," he continued, "far more than any in the past—and deserves our warmest congratulations. But all celebrations must be kept orderly and—preferably—indoors. It is regrettable but necessary that any overexuberant public displays will be broken up and punished by arrest and charges of disorderly conduct."

But nothing broke up the demonstrators that evening in Kansas City. With traditionalists disgruntled by the university's lack of decisive action in the face of Coach's stand—with Swoop's enemies disgusted by cheering throngs and banner-waving demonstrators—they organized a counter-demonstration of their own. When we arrived at the arena, two hours before game-time, they were already there, picketers and counter-picketers, their numbers swelling by the second. Some waved signs of gold basketballs and chanted,

"Heroes win championships!" Others waved signs of wooden crosses and chanted, "Sinners fall!" The first group ringed the arena, walking slowly; the second group ringed the first, walking at the same pace. They glared at each other, they shouted but, as of yet, made no threatening movements. When they saw Swoop alight from the bus, both sides let up a howl, their cheers and jeers reverberating off the arena's hard outer walls. Swoop blew kisses to each, then ducked into the player's entrance.

When Swoop came out for warm-ups, it was clear in his eyes he wanted to finish Drummond quickly. He had that ability—no matter the conflicts swirling elsewhere in his life, he could push them aside and focus on the task at hand. He came at Drummond's players now as if they were the sole obstacle between him and his dreams. With thousands of his fans roaring, he turned the Texans' first six possessions into nightmarish experiences, stealing the ball three times, and forcing their guards—great shooters but mediocre ball-handlers—into one errant pass after another. As the game wore on, Swoop's flashing hands stripped the ball incessantly, driving their frustrated starters to commit foolish reaching fouls. Barely midway through the first half, with Drummond's starting guards sitting with three each, Swoop ran roughshod over their reserves, building a huge lead, though their coach called time-out repeatedly. By half-time, the dazed look of their backcourt told the story even more than did the score: Hoppo Valley was one win away from the national finals.

Friday night was our semi-final game against Colton State of Pennsylvania. Though Coach kept the pressure on, preparing us as for war, Swoop's look made it clear that his mind was elsewhere, thinking about someone else. Though he didn't call her, he got daily updates from Bullock.

Bullock and Thom Kolotourous had been arraigned, and though disagreement wracked the D.A.'s office, as well as the Police Department, it looked like they would come to trial in late spring. With other matters pressing, Bullock and his new assistant worked feverishly to prepare their brief against the moral propriety of the law.

Bullock spoke to Swoop about the case by phone on Thursday afternoon.

"I fell asleep, kid. This morning, a little before dawn. Working long hours."

Sitting at the desk in our hotel room, I saw Swoop nod. Bul-

lock couldn't see it, but the smile that softened the corners of
Swoop's mouth, and the look of appreciation in his eyes, were a
testament to the lawyer's dedication.

"This girl's unbelievable," Bullock continued, referring to his
assistant. "I start to nod off, and she turns on me from her desk.
She's been working longer hours than me, her eyes are red and
her hair's a mop. She says to me, all haughty, 'I thought you were
a man.' I almost choked, but I got back to work. I was afraid not
to."

I kept looking up from my books. I couldn't hear Bullock's
end of the conversation, but Swoop was laughing silently to himself, not disturbing the lawyer's story, and I was interested.

"But fear or not, I fell asleep," Bullock went on. "The strange
thing is, when I woke up, I found myself covered with her trench-
coat. I'm not sure if it was a dream, but I think she kissed me on
the right cheek."

Swoop stopped laughing.

"Easy," he said.

"Shaddup," Bullock snorted. "You think I carry on with children? I'm not that much of a degenerate."

Leaving the brief against the "Anti-Hero Resolution"—as the
law had come to be known in Hoppo Valley—to his assistant, Bullock spent hours on Thursday haranguing various members of the
Board of Trustees. His action forced the president to divert attention away from Swoop and Coach, impelling him to spend precious
time bolstering his foundations at home. With controversy raging
among administrators and faculty, the Board of Trustees was not
as unanimous in its support of MacPherson as they had been merely
a week earlier. With every victory we won, our foes' resolve wavered just a little. As we approached the final turn, our momentum
was building.

We were the first game on Friday night, Maryville Baptist the
second. But though they were the defending champs with the killer
record, it was obvious, long before game-time, who the fans were
here to see. Swoop's battle in Hoppo Valley, his resulting suspension, the deeper issues that swirled around it, brought to the sports
world—and to small-college basketball, in particular—a heightened
attention it had never before received. This was a story. It wasn't
merely sports writers from major newspapers or reporters from
national sports magazines who were here for the first time. Feature writers for the influential news magazines and papers were

also here. "Culture Shock in the Heartland" ran the headline of a prominent article in a major news weekly. As the skirmishes over fundamental issues accelerated in Hoppo Valley, and boiled over to Kansas City, the battles became news, not merely in rural America, but in Chicago, Los Angeles and San Francisco, making it a story increasingly difficult to ignore, even in New York City and Washington. Die-hard basketball fans with no prior religious loyalties found themselves swept up in the controversy, taking sides, bellowing in support of Swoop's innocence or sinfulness, arguing—in a distinctively-basketball setting—more vehemently over theology than over shooting percentages.

With the press row jammed with successful journalists from the country's most influential publications, our guys took the court with some degree of trepidation. Raif, who prior to this month, had never been in a town larger than Fort Dodge, Iowa, said with a glance half disbelief, half fear, "We're going to be in the *New York Times?*" Swoop swatted his back. "You claw to the top, you're an inspiration. Let's kick ass!" Perhaps Colton, a tiny school from the backwaters of the Alleghenies, was less accustomed to controversy than our guys had become, for at the opening tip they looked jittery. They had been a superb defensive team, second only to Maryville Baptist, but their whole squad and coaching staff had witnessed the Martinsville game—the destruction Swoop had rained on a smothering defense—and the look in their eyes betrayed a fear they couldn't hold him. They were right. Colton's guards were sure of hand but slow of foot, and Swoop flared by them at will, his eyes seeing rim as he drew interior defenders, then dished no-look feeds to open teammates on the baseline and wings. With Drew and Raif raining jumpers, with Freddie and Dandy punching home short-range bank shots, we shredded their defense in the opening minutes without Swoop taking a shot. We were up fourteen before they knew what hit them and Swoop had yet to throw a blow. When they called time-out three times in the first eight minutes, it served to boost our confidence rather than slow our momentum, and with our guys feeling it, Colton was caught in an impossible bind: double Swoop and let confident shooters fire at will or single Swoop and get killed. They chose the former, and though our guys cooled eventually, the lead seemed insurmountable. At half, we were up eighteen, and early in the second, when they started to creep closer, Swoop threw it into the sixth gear no other player had, taking two and sometimes three defend-

ers off the dribble. In a five-minute stretch, he launched six as-
saults against their rim, slamming over their big men, pulling up
for hanging baseline jumpers, getting fouled, nailing his free throws
and Colton's coffin lid simultaneously. They were down twenty,
there were twelve minutes left, and the outcome had been decided.
Colton's players hung their heads, the fans screamed when Swoop
touched the ball, and the reserves on our bench sang "National
champs!" But Coach knew Maryville would have something to say
about that, so he pulled Swoop with eight minutes to go, resting
him at the end of the bench, where he chafed like an incarcerated
speed freak.

Fans poured out of the stands when the game was over, swirling around us as we fought our way to the locker room. Basketball
enthusiasts from across the country, seeing Swoop play for the first
time, pumped his hand and whacked his back. Supporters from
Hoppo Valley, seeing again what they'd observed all year, were
content to surround him and, without touching, just stare greed-
ily as he walked past. But our date in the national finals was not
taken as inspiration by all. Several voices from the overhanging
stands cried "Ban the gambler!" and a group on the crowd's pe-
riphery thrust forward signs reading, "Romans Wagered for the
Robe of Christ."

Swoop was out of the shower and on the phone to Hoppo Valley within fifteen minutes of the game's end. He did not speak to
Butch Bratton regarding the teacher's upcoming presentation to
the Spring meeting of the school board. Nor did he call Frederic
Westegaard about the publisher's editorial campaign to demand
the ouster of President MacPherson, and his replacement by one
of several accomplished educators belonging to the Heroes Society. He did not speak to Janet McMenamin about her upcoming
appearance on Ron Zatechka's show, in which she planned to call
for private funding and public support for her proposed abortion
clinic. He welcomed all of these events as positive developments—
but they were not his primary concern. The sole call he made was
to Nick Bradlee, Janet McMenamin's young protégé. "We ready?"
Swoop asked. Whatever was the psychologist's response, Swoop
smiled "That's right. A week from Sunday is Easter. That's exactly
why we're going." He nodded while listening. "Don't forget, the
Campus March for Redemption has scheduled a prayer meeting
for nine A.M. They especially want to reach the crippled and orphaned children. We have to be scheduled not just at the State

Hospital, but *at the same time in the same wing.* Let's see who the kids respond to." The sounds of Bradlee's excited voice could just be made out in the room and Swoop laughed at his reply. "The Heroes Society will clean up. You got it. Right. Bye."

When Swoop got off the phone, Maryville's game was about to begin. Coach was still in the visiting staff's office, but some of the players had already gone up to take their seats, though most waited for Swoop. I was on my knees, storing supplies in the cabinets under the trainer's table. Freddie sat across from the phone, staring anxiously at Swoop. Throughout the brief conversation with Nick Bradlee, Freddie had become increasingly agitated, nervously extending then retracting his legs.

"What the hell," he said when Swoop finally hung up. "Are you going to conquer the town?"

He was dressed in a dark blazer, gray slacks and loafers. With his short hair and clean-shaven face, he still looked like one of Bittner's followers. The steel cross and gold basketball were on individual chains showing outside of his tie.

"Could be," Swoop said absently, his thoughts not yet back in Kansas City. "Town could use it."

When Freddie objected that Swoop was only a student at Hoppo, that he was too young to exert such influence, he caught Swoop's attention. "How old was Alexander when he conquered the Persians at Issus?" Swoop asked, turning to him. When Freddie hesitated, Swoop's voice answered clearly. "Six hundred thousand foes massed against his thirty thousand infantry and five thousand cavalry—and the King but twenty-two."

In the quiet that followed, all that could be heard was the roar of the crowd drifting faintly into the bowels of the great arena as Maryville's game began. Coach was preoccupied with his own troubles and only silence emanated from his office. Freddie stared at Swoop.

"Swoop and Alexander," he said. "Swoop and Caesar—why don't we add a chapter on Swoop to the next edition of Plutarch's *Lives?*"

"You know," Swoop began thoughtfully. "That's not a bad—" but Freddie cut him off.

"Swoop and the Heroes Society subjugate Hoppo Valley. Why not all of Iowa while you're at it? Why not the whole country? Swoop for President, Swoop for God." He shook his head. "It all fits." When Swoop didn't respond, but merely stood waiting,

Freddie's voice lowered. "The State Hospital is not the right place for the Heroes Society."

Swoop's eyes narrowed as the captain named his real objection. Unlike Freddie, he wore merely jeans, sneakers and his letter jacket. The gold basketball was tucked inside his football jersey, next to his skin.

"I don't agree with you," Swoop said. "The State Hospital is the ideal place for heroes."

"But these children are crippled," Freddie protested. "Some are retarded. They can't run five miles, lift weights or study Homer. They can't even walk."

Upstairs the crowd roared as the early minutes of Maryville's game unfolded and, even at this distance, the excitement of the national semi-finals could not be missed. Swoop's eyes turned upward immediately, glittering like a tiger's, and when he lowered them to Freddie the look was still there, only its object had changed.

"Can't they?"

Now Freddie looked puzzled, his honest workingman's face etched with questions.

"What do you mean?"

"I mean," Swoop said, his reply tinged with the effort to control his impatience, "that these are the ones who need heroism the most. I mean that there are men who play international basketball though they've lost a leg, who write books though they've lost their sight, who compose symphonies though they've lost their hearing. I mean, who the hell is somebody else to tell one of these kids what he can or cannot do? How do you know who can lift weights, run five miles or read *The Odyssey*?"

"I know because I've been there. These kids need pity, not Nautilus equipment. I've seen them. Have you? They can't reach the exalted goals you're demanding of them. You'll only set them up for frustration."

He got up to face Swoop, his voice earnest with conviction, his back to the trainer's table. He couldn't see me as I rose behind him, couldn't feel the seething quality, lying buried for sixteen months, starting to rise, too.

"Pity?" Swoop was too incredulous to express contempt. "Anybody give me pity when I was crippled, I'd rip their lungs out."

"That's you! You think everybody else is like—"

"No! That's everybody. What they need is respect—not pity—respect. You understand me, Zender?"

"I understand you," I said, and all eyes turned to me in that locker room like a graveyard. "I understand respect," I repeated and though my words were to Swoop, my eyes were not on him.

The captain said nothing, merely stared at me through the increasing volume of the Maryville game, and though our opponent in the crowning contest of Swoop's quest would be decided, it barely registered, other issues overwhelmed it, and all I knew was that Freddie Zender finally—after sixteen months—stood revealed before me.

"Pity, that's your specialty, isn't it?" Though I had received years of it from him and his friends, and more from a source much older and closer, none of this mattered now. Only one image was there, had ever been there, through all the months since his conversion, bursting now into consciousness, free finally of compunction or restraint; thrusting aside even awareness of the crowd's roar, the trembling of the ceiling and walls, as Swoop's merciless foe trampled over its next-to-last victim.

He looked at me and some flicker of his eyelids made clear that he knew what was coming, had known all along a reckoning was due, had dreaded it, avoided, it, yet in some sense welcomed it. He stood straight, his body tensed as if to receive a blow, and just when I thought I couldn't do it, pictures of Swoop's first days on campus—of soaring energy through sunlit weeks, of laughter that couldn't be suppressed until the animus solidified into a crippling blow—flooded into consciousness, and then I couldn't be still.

"You loved him from the start, didn't you?" The irony of the words dissolved in the sudden roar of the crowd, and Swoop's eyes, lifted upwards, reflected images of Maryville's champions racing the floor, joyous images of challenge and anticipation, and it was the very contrast between them, the unbreachable chasm, that fueled my resolve. When I hit him, then, with the reminder that he, like others, had spurned the original bounding Swoop, that he, too, needed Swoop crippled before embracing him, that he, a prince of kindness, had gloated as Swoop writhed in crumpled agony on the gym floor, he lowered his head and offered not a sound of protest.

"You knew Bittner's agenda," I spat at him. "You were at the First Commandment Missionary Church the night he compared Swoop to the Philistines, and claimed that jawbones and slingshots become sanctified simply by virtue of being used against him. Sure, you love Swoop so much—what did you do to discourage those zealots? You could have protected him from those bigots then and there. E.J. was your boy, wasn't he? You could have held him back, could have warned him against harming Swoop. But what did you do?" When he gave no response—when it was clear to everyone that he had no response—I answered the question for him. "You left him to his fate, that's what."

Swoop stared momentarily at my words and at the captain's lack of denial, stared at me not Freddie, but only for an instant. Then he turned on his heel and walked to the door, leaving Freddie slumped in a chair, his head in his hands. He strode from the room without a further glance, the disgust evident in his expression, not directed at Freddie's deeds of the past, but at the way we wasted his time, at the minutes we had taken from contemplation of the sublime. My work done, I joined him, as did the other players. Freddie didn't budge. We trailed him by several yards as we strode down the hall, the sights and sounds of the national semifinals brought closer with every step. Here, the noise was deafening, as Maryville's legion of supporters roared, stomped, clapped and whistled. The bright lights glared, ushers swarmed in the halls and vendors hawked hot dogs, screaming to make themselves heard. But as we turned into the aisle leading to the competitors' section of the stands, the action immediately ahead, a large figure loomed in front of us, blocking our path. It was one of the team supporters from Hoppo Valley, a successful businessman, an alumnus, a solid financial contributor. He carried a mobile phone and a worried look.

"I just got word," he said to us. "He left Hoppo Valley this afternoon. He's on his way. President MacPherson will be in Kansas City tonight."

CHAPTER FOURTEEN
THE END DAYS

I have never seen a basketball game like our final against Maryville. But whether it was the game itself that shocked us—or the death struggle surrounding it—was unclear.

President MacPherson arrived in Kansas City, with several members of his staff, just before midnight on Friday. Nobody met him at the airport. At six-thirty on Saturday morning, he called first Coach, then Swoop. Coach hung up, but Swoop agreed to meet with him.

When we walked into the president's hotel room that morning, he was waiting. He sat at the desk in his suite, flanked on one side by his executive assistant and on the other by the Dean of Student Life. His carriage was erect, his body tense and his eyes bored into us as we crossed toward him.

"You broke university rules," he said without preamble to Swoop, ignoring both me and the rules of etiquette. "You knew that. You've got to accept the punishment."

Swoop didn't answer at first. He looked around the room, taking in the spacious dimensions, the king-sized bed and the thick carpeting. He took his time. Strangely, though he made us wait for his response, his appreciation of the president's taste made his silence a respectful, not an insolent one.

"President MacPherson," he said earnestly, as to a favorite though misguided son. "You don't understand. The rules need to be changed. The ones you enforce just put obstacles in my path. That's not right."

MacPherson gripped the arms of his chair, as if to keep from rising, but it was no use. As if with no choice, his legs propelled him up.

"Those rules, young man, are based on two thousand years of religious teaching." Despite the tremor in his voice, the president stayed true to his policy of never shouting. The discipline with which he modulated his tone gave to his words a hard-earned dignity. "Gambling, I remind you, is a sin."

Swoop could not doubt the sincerity of the president's tone. Briefly, they stared at each other, two souls sharing a devotion but separated by a faith.

"And yet, Idomeneus bet Ajax a tripod over the chariot race in honor of Patroclos," Swoop replied.

As we left the president's room, we passed a group in the hall waiting to enter. There were eight of them, all men, generally middle-aged or older. I observed that at least half of them wore collars; then I realized that they were clergymen. I heard later that they represented every denomination the city had to offer—a cross-section of ministers, a Catholic priest, even a rabbi. I saw a jolt of recognition in several pairs of eyes as they noticed Swoop, and though they parted respectfully to let us pass, I could have sworn I heard repeated in a low murmur, "The flocks will rise. The flocks will indeed rise."

At the pow-wow, the clergymen swore to use every ounce of their influence to bring judges, city councilmen, state legislators, the police commissioner and even the mayor to heel. The flocks would rise, they vowed. The flocks would rise.

That same day, when we arrived at the arena for our last practice session, we were met with vehement picketers, a host of fifty or sixty who rushed at the team bus, gesticulating and brandishing placards. These were not the well-fed, suit-and-tie attired members of Kansas City's mainstream denominations; these were lean, fierce, wind-burned countryfolk in overalls and work boots, with sandy hair, scraggly beards and hard stares. They pointed at Coach as he tottered down the stairs.

"Self-serving old hypocrite!" sneered one balding, red-faced man, holding a child high to see the object of contempt.

Another, a tall powerfully-built young man, waving an open Bible above the crowd, gesticulated at Coach with his left hand. "Judas!" he cried. "Who sold the true faith for profit."

The crowd alternated between jeers and exhortations that "Christ saves" as our players emerged one by one and walked slowly through their midst to the locker room. But when Swoop stepped down, eyes shining in the afternoon sun, they hushed and made not a sound as he walked through their ranks, merely stripping the crosses from around their necks and holding them straight out, at arm's length, as if to ward off a ghoul. He stepped through the curtain of crosses at a slow, ambling gait, and the only sound was when he turned once to each side and murmured, "Thank you." I ignored them, looking at the arena over their heads as I hurried to the door—and ducking quickly behind one of the ticket booths about fifty yards down the street, I could have sworn was a slight figure in white. But it was merely a fleeting glimpse of a face in the crowd and then I was inside the building.

"I think every evangelical denomination in town is represented out there," one of the stadium ushers said. "Who do you think organized them?"

"No idea," I answered, my mind on other matters.

Freddie had missed the team bus. In fact, no one had seen him all morning. He had been silent since my locker room revelation, had not attended Maryville's game and had kept to himself. Coach waited several minutes before starting practice, but the captain didn't show. This had never happened before and the looks on several faces were worried.

They were even more worried when practice was over. With Freddie now missing, it meant increased playing time for Drew Doherty. Though Drew was a fierce competitor and a good shooter, he was too cumbersome to play the racehorse style Swoop favored, and more importantly, his brutal, elbow-to-the-head temperament kept us in chronic foul trouble. Coach was loath to give him extended minutes, but had no more experience on the bench. It was Swoop who piped up and, right in the open, spoke what was on everyone's mind.

"Play K'nada or Ding," he said, referring to two little-used freshmen. "They're quick enough to run the floor."

Doherty opened his mouth but then shut it, and not only Coach but every player in the room knew it was the right move.

"You'll still play, Drew," Coach said softly. "You're the only experienced reserve I got."

Doherty played the one guard for the scrubs that day and came so hard at the basket that he left welts all over Raif's face and Dandy's chest.

"Maryville's the enemy," Coach said. "Save it."

But as Swoop stripped, stuffed and slammed over him, Doherty was not one to save it. He stuck out a foot and tripped Swoop as he flashed into the lane, sending him hurtling through the air. He landed on his knees and skidded four feet, losing skin but not the ball. Maintaining his dribble, he grimaced in pain but not in surprise. When he glanced up, it was without rancor.

"Many are called but few are chosen," he said. "Your time's running out."

"What's that supposed to mean?" Doherty snarled, but before Swoop could answer Raif stepped between them.

In the locker room after, Coach's face was white. "Get with the program, Doherty, or get out." He was in the football player's face, then turned without another word and walked away. When Doherty stripped his sweaty things and flung them into his locker, everyone ignored him. But when, without showering, he put on jeans and heavy work boots, then slammed shut the locker door, several guys had seen enough.

"Be at peace, fool," Dandy said, grabbing his arm. "Game be tomorrow."

"What the hell's it to me? I don't play."

"Coach give you some run. Give you more, you lighten up."

"Lighten up?" Doherty spun from Dandy and pointed to where Swoop sat on a stool in front of his locker, placidly observing. "So I can be one of his trained seals, like you?"

"So you can win the national championship, chump."

"So he can win the national championship, you mean, and get the whole town to kiss his ass."

"So we can win it," Raif said. "Now calm down."

Doherty looked at Dandy and Raif advancing on either side of him and balled his hands into fists.

"Go ahead, defend him," he sneered. "But since God's gift got here, things ain't been the same."

"Damn right. We been winning."

"Bulls—t," Doherty's face got red. "He's taken over our lives. He runs the show around here and everyone knows it."

I looked around the locker room, involuntarily searching for Freddie, and when I remembered why he wasn't here a stab went through me. I came up off the trainer's table and started toward Doherty.

"I tell you again, sucker," Dandy continued. "We be right at the top because of him. Now ease off and enjoy the view."

"You can kiss my ass. You follow him like a damn dog. You run with him, lift with him, work out with him—all of you! And what's he do? First he gets E.J. kicked off the team, then Freddie. Who's next?"

Observing the buildup in his eyes as I advanced into his space, I picked my words and thrust them at his head.

"It's clear, isn't it, who'll be the next one off the team?"

He stopped. Then he started for me. Dandy grabbed him.

"Don't be a bigger chump than you got to be, man. Just do what Coach says and play the game. We got a championship ring coming!"

He pushed Dandy off. Some of the guys stepped in front of me. Raif grabbed his right shoulder as Dandy closed from the other side. He was surrounded and overwhelmed, but for one second he had a clear shot at Swoop. He swiveled on the ball of his left foot, brought back his right and, with tremendous force, smashed his steel-toed boot into Swoop's reconstructed right knee. Swoop sprawled to the floor and the stool clanged against the metal lockers.

"There goes your national championship!" Doherty screamed.

Swoop writhed on the floor, his teammates looked on in stunned silence and for one second Doherty's face contorted openly with glee.

Only one force animated me. Ignoring Dandy's arms wrapped around him, spitting at any sense of fair play, I crossed the space between us and smashed my right fist into his nose, breaking it and splattering blood onto Dandy's jersey.

Some of the guys grabbed me from behind, jerking me away. Doherty sagged in Dandy's arms. Swoop struggled onto his left knee as Coach emerged from his office and started across the room. He grabbed Doherty from Dandy, placed one hand under each armpit and, with strength amazing in one so gaunt, lifted him like a hydraulic jack and crashed him against the far-wall lockers.

"Get yourself to a hospital, Doherty, and remember this: If I ever lay eyes on your carcass again, I'll snap your neck like a twig. Now get your gear and get out!"

No one moved to help. Coach let him go and he slid down the lockers to the floor. Stumbling to his locker, he held a towel to his nose, stanching the blood. Then he threw on a shirt and a jacket and headed out. At the door he turned. Tears were in his eyes but he said nothing. Then he turned and staggered out.

Coach coughed into a handkerchief. Everyone turned to Swoop

and no one noticed that the red stain flecking Coach's jaw and handkerchief was not from Doherty. Swoop hobbled onto one leg. The blood was drained from his face but had somehow flowed to his eyes, which were on fire, not with anger but with something else.

"Swoop, stay off your leg, we'll get a doctor," one of the guys said.

"No, I don't need a doctor. I'm OK."

"Swoop, you want Lefkowitz?" I asked.

"No! I'm OK! I'm going to walk it off. It's only a deep bruise."

"Are you sure?" a chorus went up from the guys.

But Coach waved them to silence. Painfully traversing the distance between them, he wrapped one polar bear paw around Swoop's shoulder.

"Lean on me," he said. "Put weight on it only gradually."

They circled the locker room, Swoop hobbling, pain etched in his white face each time he stepped down on his injured leg.

The rest of us watched in silence.

When we left the locker room, reporters stared with mouths hanging as Swoop hobbled slowly past them. When we left the arena, the hooting roar died in the throats of the picketers as they witnessed what, to them, could only have been an act of God. They too gazed with wide-eyed looks, and neglected to strip free their crosses and thrust them at Swoop as he passed.

Though he kept it iced constantly, the knee swelled painfully that evening. The phone in our room rang ceaselessly as word of the injury got around, so, again, I disconnected it. But one message lifted Swoop's spirits: word that the odds on Maryville had gotten progressively heavier. Maryville had been favored from the start, the smart money betting on Swoop to run wild but on their defense to crush the rest of us. Now, with word out that Freddie was missing, Doherty canned and Swoop re-injured, the odds went through the roof. Swoop waited until late that night, when he heard they had reached ten-to-one, then he called Jumbo at his home in Iowa.

"Bet everything in trust on Hoppo Valley to win."

"But it's in trust. I can't get at it that quickly."

"Then bet your own money for me and I'll pay you back from my winnings."

"You got it. And, kid…"

"Yeah?"

"I already bet twenty K on you to win."

Swoop smiled. "Double it."

When he hung up, he sat pondering for several moments. Then he turned to me.

"You kicked Freddie in the groin."

Though it was said without anger, as a statement of fact not an accusation, I couldn't help but react.

"Swoop, I—"

"Don't defend yourself. He had it coming." He smiled ruefully. "Your sense of timing wasn't too great, though."

I didn't answer and we sat in silence briefly. Then his face got serious.

"Where do you think he is?"

"I don't know." Despite myself, it came out sounding like "I don't care." Which wasn't true.

"Yes, you do."

"Where?"

"Maybe not where exactly, but why."

I stared at him and we both knew the answer, but Swoop put his own spin on it.

"He's overcome with sin, what happens to him and Kathy?"

"Beats me."

"You got no interest in it?"

I stopped. I had never discussed this with anyone, not even him.

"Swoop, what makes you think I have—"

"Am I blind? I can't see the way you look at her, the way your tongue hangs out when she walks into a room? You think I don't know what it means to look at a girl that way? That I don't know what it feels like?"

I didn't respond. There was nothing to say and Swoop's words hung in the air between us.

"Call her," he said finally. "She's a player in this game. She needs to be here."

"You don't think she's heard?"

"In case she hasn't. But mostly, because she should hear the full truth from you, not from somebody else."

I nodded.

Meanwhile, as Swoop rested in our hotel room, icing his knee and reading Plutarch, events were popping across two towns.

The struggle between Swoop and Hoppo Valley authorities had long since passed from sports sections to the front pages. The papers in Kansas City were no different, nor were the results. Swoop's face was plastered across TV newscasts, as well as the papers, and stories appeared regularly on the Heroes Society.

People clamored by the thousands for seats long since sold, and many lined up outside the arena for one glimpse of Swoop. Though he paid scant attention to the hoopla, he perked up when several individuals approached him about organizing a chapter of the Heroes Society in Kansas City. Though besieged by reporters, team backers and fans, Swoop ducked away from them to meet with the aspiring heroes. He put them in touch with Bullock and members of the executive committee in Hoppo Valley. Daniel Blaine, the leader, took out an ad in the Kansas City papers on the Wednesday of our quarterfinal game, announcing the formation of a society dedicated to the worship of human greatness against those who insist on man's depravity. On the day after, following another electrifying performance by Swoop, they had more than fifty responses. The day after that, they had a site and announced their first service, to be held on the Sunday morning of our game against Maryville.

But evidently, there were those not entirely in favor of the founding of a new creed in their town. On Friday afternoon, ministers of several prominent denominations announced a press conference to be held on Saturday evening, a non-sectarian summit to reaffirm the community's enduring commitment to traditional religious teachings. It was well-attended. The city's most respected pastors, the bishop of the Catholic archdiocese, the rabbi from the town's synagogue, even several successful Islamic citizens, representatives of Middle-Eastern import-export firms, spoke for two hours to members of the press. The essence of their message was succinct— an impassioned, from-the-heart warning against a re-birth of the spirit of paganism, with its emphasis on prowess, on pride, on the unaided capacities of man. They got spots on the nightly news and coverage in all the Sunday papers.

At the same time, the authorities at Maryville Baptist had something to say, though in private. They held a prayer meeting at one of the smaller Baptist churches on Saturday evening, led by their coach, Dance Wilkins, a deacon of the church, and by the school's athletic director, the Reverend Bryce T. Lomax, an ordained minister. It was open to the public, but there was no hype or press release, just a devout expression of their faith. All players were re-

quired to be there, and all but one wore suits. They offered thanks
to God for the honors He'd bestowed on them, and prayers for
the strength to overcome their remaining foe. In the finale of their
service, they beseeched Jesus to redeem the soul of the gambler
who opposed them, to extend to him the bounty of His deliverance, and to preserve themselves from those very temptations to
whose allure he had fallen. "I don't be falling to no allure, yo!"
affirmed Killer Hayward, amidst rich baritone salvoes of "Amen."
Several athletes and team backers fell to their knees and wept in
joyous remembrance of their deliverance. But not all participants
displayed such unanimity of sentiment. "Jesus help us more, we at
the gym," a worried Street told supporters as he left the church,
shaking his head.

Meanwhile, the area's Pentecostal churches were not idle. On
Saturday night, in a huge tent pitched in a field of one of the members, located twelve miles outside the city limits but attended by
several hundred of the faithful, a quartet of evangelical preachers
from Missouri and Kansas joined forces to hold a revival meeting.
This was more than a fervent, gut-bucket appeal to sinners to re-
habilitate their ways. This was a sweaty-palmed, panic-driven defense
of hearth and home against the invading alien horde. "We cannot
stand by and watch as the infectious disease ravaging Iowa spreads
to our towns and communities!" warned the Reverend T.B.
Arbuckle of Dry Branch, Kansas. Amidst the crashing organ tones
and the caterwauling, groaning cries of "Hallelujah" from the assembly of the saved, the local preachers thundered home one
focused, unrelenting message: the beloved homeland was under
siege. Flitting in the shadows behind the stage, bobbing periodically to the surface amid the shifting lights and noticed by the
trained eye of a Kansas City reporter, there appeared a slender,
silent figure in white. The newspaperman, wondering who it was,
observed him in earnest discussion with each of the speakers who
mounted the pulpit.

Swoop was up before five on Sunday morning. He had slept
with his leg elevated, the knee encased in ice packs, and though
the swelling was down, it was still painful to walk. He limped around
the hotel room for ten minutes, flexing and bending, putting weight
on it only gradually, loosening it up. Then he coaxed me from my
lolling.

"Workout for you, then we got a day," he said.

We took the elevator to the hotel's exercise room, where Swoop supervised me through sixty non-stop minutes on the weights. Then, with no time even for a shower, still dripping in my sweats, I joined him in a cab ride across town.

The Heroes Society of Kansas City held its inaugural service in a cluttered warehouse in an industrialized section near the river. The chapter's founder, Daniel T. Blaine, was a lifelong union guy who had clawed his way to the top of the meatpackers' local by scourging every gangster, thug and gravy train rider that a massive witch hunt could uncover. "You work a hard day for an honest buck or you answer to me," he snarled at recalcitrant elements. Apparently, some did answer to him—personally—as his toothless grin could attest.

He was short, stocky, dressed in denim and work boots, and kept a hardcover copy of Kipling in his office. He boasted that his income now exceeded one hundred thousand dollars, added quietly that he earned every nickel, but drove a panel truck and lived with his wife in a one-bedroom apartment. His assistant told us, when Blaine was out of earshot, that he donated large sums of his own money to unions struggling under dictators around the globe—and that he made no complaints against wealthy capitalists, but fought Communists to the death. He had moved the local's meeting hall to the warehouse district where its membership worked, away from its former downtown location where the tentacles of city government exerted their greatest influence. He had erected a stage and a podium in one corner of the warehouse and, today, alongside the union banner and American flag he flew a streaming white sheet embossed with the symbol of a gold basketball. "You started a great thing, kid," he told Swoop when we entered. "Now we got to convert the rest of the bastards."

Blaine wanted us to sit with him on the stage, but Swoop politely declined and we sat in the last row of chairs instead. By eight o'clock, there were barely fifty people in the hall, but Blaine started exactly on time and personally rebuked every latecomer who arrived in the midst of the service. He briefly explained the Society's purpose, stating that, "when the battle's done, the guys in the white hats are the only ones left standing." When he concluded his introductory remarks with, "Just like we cleaned the deadbeats and dirtbags from the union, so we got to run them out of the country!" he received loud applause from the majority of the crowd. But they quieted when the next speaker, a twenty year veteran of the Kansas City Fire Department, recounted in exact detail the actions by which he had single-handedly pulled a family of four from a building engulfed in flames. And they hushed utterly when the main speaker, a twenty-nine-year-old immigrant from India, mounted the stage and spoke her piece.

Asani Nakrishnan might have been diminutive in stature and calm in demeanor but her words were brief and blunt.

"I'm not a public speaker," she said, "and only one point matters. It wasn't the struggle to complete medical school—not the battles with my family or with old country prejudice or with immigration officials, and not with local rednecks or fellow students envious of my grades. These were real, but just minor nuisances in comparison to the goal. They couldn't prevent me from graduating next week with high honors." She shook her head. "The point does not involve conflicts with other people. It's something else."

She paused, looking around the room, but her eyes contained a dissatisfaction that had nothing to do with her audience. Though she did not speak for several moments, the silence felt not awkward but one of genuine wrestling with some unspoken yearning of her own.

"I've always lacked faith," she said, her head high. "I'm a scientist. The Hindu and Christian religions are not for me. They lack..." she groped briefly, straining for some understanding not contained within the conventional..."a certain reverence...something hard to define." She looked at her audience now, and it was her face even more than her words that spoke of years of longing for some unidentified element missing from her life. "The best I can do," she said, her voice falling to a whisper. "Isn't that what's holy? Worshiping virgins and succoring the poor were not what I needed. I wanted something higher—something I never had—that caused people to look at me as if I were from the moon, so I could never explain. I gave up trying." The expression on her face now was neither pain nor joy, but some untroubled gaze that spoke only of release from suffering. "But when I read about the Heroes Society, I knew I had found it. I don't give a damn about sports, but I knew I had found it."

We left at ten, after the conclusion of services, with Swoop in an uplifted frame, and I didn't need to ask why. "Soon-to-be-Doctor Nakrishnan set the tone for the day," he said. "Let's win us a national title." We got to the hotel minutes before the start of the team breakfast at ten-thirty.

Coach was pallid and boisterous at once as he addressed the team, as if a man whose last day on earth would be his best. "I don't know who's going to play for us," he said. "And we're going against the greatest team in college basketball history. But I do know that—win or lose—this day is a celebration of how much is possible." Though Swoop's friends and teammates devoured large helpings of steak and eggs, he himself ate oatmeal and drank fresh orange juice, eating moderately as was his wont. "'A night's march gives me an appetite for breakfast, and a light breakfast gives me an appetite for dinner,'" he said, eyes gleaming, knowing I would recognize the quote.

At noon, our pre-game strategy session ended, and it was time to leave for the arena. But as we waited for the team bus, Swoop excused himself to make a few phone calls. He returned as the bus pulled up in front of the hotel.

"Who'd you call?" I asked several minutes later as we approached the arena.

"Just a few media guys in Hoppo Valley and Des Moines."

I eyed him suspiciously.

"For what?"

"Had a few things to tell them." He smiled coyly, like a teenage girl discussing her first date.

"Swoop, cut the bulls—t. What did you tell them?"

"Not much. Just that I bet all money held in trust on us to win, that the winnings will be dedicated to building a temple in Hoppo Valley—a new home for the Heroes Society—and that all residents who support us should bet and contribute to the temple. Other than that, nothing."

I looked at him, speechless for a moment. "This will be announced on the air?" My voice sounded unusually low.

"Immediately."

"Swoop..." I was groping, looking for the words. "You don't think that a public call for gambling will stir trouble in Hoppo Valley? Especially for this cause?"

He did not grin. The look of his eyes matched the solemn tone of my voice, and that was his sole reply.

We had pulled to the curb by the players' entrance. Hundreds of people swarmed the sidewalk, some hefting crosses and anti-Swoop posters, some cheering and stomping as the bus stopped in front of them. They rushed the bus as the front doors swung wide. "Stop the anti-Christ!" screamed an overweight woman, waving a Bible opened to Revelation. "Swoop! Swoop! Swoop!" chanted dozens of fans.

He reached for the purple gym bag under the seat and pulled from it an English translation of *The Iliad*.

"Sometimes, to be the good guy, you got to stir trouble."

And as he swaggered off the bus into the sunlight, his aviator shades shielding the crowd from the brilliant stare of his eyes, he succeeded in stirring plenty. "The Beast is among us!" shouted a lanky man wearing overalls and a hefty steel cross. "He's against the Bible!" roared a protester by his side. They converged on him, dozens of gesticulating country folk, and though it was Bibles they brandished in their mitts, their eyes made clear they would have preferred pitchforks. For a moment we were lost in their midst, engulfed, and in the one moment before arena security rushed to our aid, as Swoop's supporters formed a human wall, warding off the protesters, I noticed that in their hands the evangelists clutched something in addition to their Bibles: tickets for this afternoon's game. "How'd these jokers get seats?" Raif yelled in my ear, as we fought our way through the door. "Christian radio's got a lot of juice in this burg," I said, remembering a feature in the Kansas City papers. "They bought a ton for the faithful."

If Swoop wanted his announcement to stir trouble, he got his money's worth, in Hoppo Valley as well as in Kansas City. Coming less than two hours before tip-off, it did not spur a large amount of betting—though it did generate some—but it got people's attention across the Valley. "He's irredeemable," some said sadly, shaking their heads. "He is the Redeemer," others said joyously, plunking down their cash.

Though Swoop was not fully abreast of the Society's social struggle in Hoppo Valley, he supported its goals, and acted on the conviction that boldness was the key to victory. In keeping with the spirit of its founder, the Heroes Society had not been quiescent during Sunday morning hours.

Incensed rather than intimidated by the Anti-Hero Resolution, such educated professionals as Janet McMenamin and Butch Bratton were ready to fight for their rights. "Let's hold services at my place," Dr. McMenamin had said, referring to the cottage she owned on Twelfth Street, at the other end of town from The Acropolis. "It's small," Bullock had objected. "So was The Lyceum," she said.

The focus of morning services was Bill Falkenberg, a man who'd two years previously moved to the area from Virgil, Missouri, where he had been pastor of the Lutheran church. He had been a true believer, he said, until the day his daughter was born. When she had been brought home from the hospital and with wide, clear, untroubled eyes reached for her daddy for the first time, he knew in his heart that Luther had been wrong; that he would kill with his own hands any being with the effrontery to claim that this child was with sin. She would be named Penelope and she would not be baptized. That night, he took down the cross from the living room in his home, drove to the church and left it lying, face down, on the altar. The next day, he informed his superiors he had given his last sermon. He resigned from the ministry. He had received a degree in math from Concordia College before entering the seminary. He returned to school then, to the University of Missouri, for a Master's degree; then got a job, teaching elementary school, in Hoppo Valley, Iowa. He knew many of the teachers in the public school system, and was friends with Butch Bratton. His story had been widely-known to Bullock and other Society members before the meeting at Janet McMenamin's. Six-year-old Penelope was not at the meeting, he explained, because her team had soccer practice at Healy Park. She was, however, conducting services on the field.

At 2:05, when the two teams emerged for warm-ups in Kansas City, members of the Hoppo Valley Heroes Society were scurrying to reach Bullock's home in time to hear the game. It was a beautiful day in early April, sun shining, temperature in the fifties, and Bullock—free on his own recognizance—had set up speakers on the lawn. He had dozens of chairs lined up in the sun, and arriving guests parked in his driveway until it overflowed, then parked in the street.

"In a few years we'll be doing this at a champion's temple," Bullock said. "Contribute if you like."

They listened to the game in hushed, clustered knots, at least forty or fifty of them, with a golden emblem waving over their heads and the sun blazing on their faces. Some wore sweats, having just run, lifted or completed calisthenics; some were in jeans but carrying briefcase or book bag, having arrived from library, office or—in the case of two professors—from the research labs at school. There were couples, young, old, middle-aged, sitting together, bent forward, listening intently, their legs pressed to each others', hip to ankle. In the back, alone with his wife, sat the elementary school's new math teacher, Bill Falkenberg. The

six-year-old soccer champ, having completed a careful solo inspec-
tion of the mansion's grounds, sat on her father's knee—haughtily,
some thought—befitting one with exclusive property rights. Her
eyes blazed at the sounds coming from the speakers.

Tip-off was scheduled for 2:20. At 2:15, as the two teams approached the sideline for a final pre-game huddle, one of the
wealthy team backers in the front row leaned across the intervening space and whispered to me, "MacPherson's been busy." I turned
to him. "I'll bet. Doing what?" So he told me.

With neither Coach nor Swoop guilty of a crime, the Police
Department could take no action. When MacPherson's allies in
the clergy put him in contact with the state's lieutenant governor,
the official told him that as a devout Episcopalian he empathized,
but that as an officer of the state he could do nothing.

It left the president no choice. He would have to go through
the courts. Ambitious citizens intrigued by the values of the Heroes Society were not the only ones united in support of Swoop's
right to play. They were joined by sports fans, free speech advo-
cates and several popular talk radio hosts and their listeners. The
total formed a sizable chunk of the local electorate. Politicians were
reluctant to intercede. MacPherson knew that the judges they con-
trolled would be equally reluctant. But the establishment clergy,
and the members of their flocks, also represented a significant por-
tion of the voting public. The ministers knew it, the politicians
knew it, the judges knew it. With the town's leading clergymen
applying remorseless pressure on the secular authority, with ministers and priests calling in Sunday morning sermons for decisive
action to restore God's supremacy in Kansas City, MacPherson finally caught the break he needed.

He received a call from Pastor Jonathan Stevenson of the West
Shore Presbyterian Church, who bubbled excitedly in his ear. The
minister had just gotten off the phone with the Honorable John
R. Templeton of the First District Court for the state of Missouri.
The judge, Reverend Stevenson said, had been scandalized by
Swoop's open call for a pagan temple to be financed by gambling.
He was prepared to entertain a plea for a restraining order against
both such an athlete and a coach who would back him. There was
time.

But not at the arena. As the two teams walked onto the floor
for the opening tip, eighteen thousand spectators rose to their feet
and roared for what they had anticipated. Seventeen thousand-plus

cheered for one side or the other, and focused on the game. But several hundred swung Bibles and crosses and, silently, with hard stares, focused on one player. As barely two miles away, President MacPherson hurried into the state court to meet with the Honorable John Templeton in chambers, Killer loomed over the gym, seven feet of bone and sinew, the cross around his neck concealed now under his jersey, his face an open snarl of feelings more primeval. As our guys stared at the lithe frames of the foes towering above them, Street made the circle, shaking hands. "We make this quick," he told our players. "You be back in Hippo Valley by nightfall." Swoop, limping to his position, barely acknowledged him. He stared at our basket and looked like he would kneel. Coach, coughing on the sideline, did.

The ref held the ball balancing in his fingertips, ten players bent at the knees and, for one anticipatory moment, the arena hushed. Then, as the ball arced slowly towards the light, as Killer tensed to spring out of his crouch over poor, out-classed Raif Lockett, eighteen thousand pairs of eyes riveted on the action and one, unable to bear the sight, looked away. As Killer soared a foot-and-a-half over his straining foe, as he batted the rock toward Street and as Swoop sprang for the steal, I was the only one to notice a slouching figure work his way from the entrance toward the edge of the gym floor. Eighteen thousand throats roared as Swoop's thieving hands flicked the ball from Street's grasp and the final battle began. I saw only the haunted figure of Freddie Zender, standing at the baseline, gazing on the game from which he was barred.

CHAPTER FIFTEEN
THE ARMAGEDDON

The ball bounced off Street's fingertips and immediately Swoop dived. He skidded across the gym floor, eating dust, scraping elbows and knees, stretching for the ball. As he grasped it, Maryville's lithe horde assaulted. Tyrone Gates, their six-foot whippet of a point guard, dived from Swoop's blind side and Street closed from behind. Swoop rolled and, in one motion, flicked the ball to Dandy at half-court, then swept to his feet. Dandy, moving nothing but his hands, caught and pitched, a sidewards flip, corralled by Swoop on the run. Swoop dribbled twice past mid-court, then exploded for the rim, intending to soar twenty-five feet and cram. But Killer was back, along with Floyd Jackson, Maryville's six-nine, shaven-skulled hit man of a forward, and, looking like a trio in unison, the three bodies flew above the basket. Jackson and Killer stretched to the limit of their wingspan, two feet above the rim, but Swoop plummeted from the sky, an eagle above springing cats, and crashed it through, smashing both elbows on the rim as he descended.

The crowd was on their feet, so electric with energy, it looked like they would never again sit. Raif and Bobby swatted Swoop's butt and the Maryville bench looked stunned. Swoop ignored them all. He saw only Gates about to inbound the ball, and he sprang toward the baseline.

"D-up!" he roared.

But Gates fired the ball high into the rafters, forcing Killer into the air, stretching every sinew to haul it in. Our guys swarmed at him at half-court, wind-milling in his face, but Killer went up-top, airmailing it to Jerome Handley, Maryville's sensational sophomore, on the far right wing. Swoop, sensing the opponent's strategy, forsook their guards and hurtled straight up the center of the court. He tore across the key, flung himself down the lane and arrived at the rim at the exact moment as did Handley's arcing lob to a springing Jackson. Flailing in mid-flight like some winged creature, he flicked the tips of his fingers off leather, spinning the rock just beyond Jackson's reach, to carom high off the back iron. The ball was snagged by Raif Lockett, who clutched it to his chest in the lane as Swoop landed just inside the far baseline, a scant five feet from where Freddie Zender stood in the crowd milling under Maryville's basket.

The captain stood tall, erect to see over people in front, and the hard lines of his chin bore the same sculpted features I had known for years. As he watched Swoop land under the basket surrounded by Maryville's troops, his eyes gleamed and for a moment I thought he might suit up and play. Then he turned away. Swoop waded through defenders toward the beleaguered Raif, not seeing him.

"Ball!" he cried.

In the game's early minutes, Swoop was fresh, his body swimming with adrenaline, and he threw off the painful sensations of his swollen knee to patrol the court like some omnipotent cop of the hardwood. He deflected passes, swiped dribbles, raced the floor and slammed so often that the game's start looked like a track meet, with one superb athlete dominating the sprints and the high jump. He not only had Maryville down twelve–nothing two minutes in, but drew two fouls on Killer Hayward, forcing Dance Wilkins to go the better part of the first half without his best player. The Maryville supporters in the stands looked shocked; nobody played this kind of searing number on their team—ever. But Street rallied his troops, swatting backs and kicking butt. "We the champs, yo!" he said over and again. Then he brought the ball upcourt.

But as Maryville struggled to get untracked against the ferocity of Swoop's onslaught, a different kind of struggle broke out in Hoppo Valley. That morning, several Society members on their way to services at Janet McMenamin's had noticed that they were followed from their homes to their destination. Looking back quickly, they noticed the bright, freshly-washed faces of those trailing them.

Dexter Bullock merely scoffed when he heard the word, but Mayor Pedersson did not when the chief informed him what the clean-shaven young men had reported: that against city ordinance, the Heroes Society still conducted Sunday morning services.

"How many officers can we count on?" the mayor asked.

When Chief Sanders himself, flanked by two of his subordinates, arrived at Bullock's home just minutes into the game, he was met at first with disbelief, then with anger.

"We're under arrest for what?" the lawyer spluttered.

"You know what the law says," the chief snapped. "There are no religious services in this town without prior certification by the City Council. Let's get moving."

There were dozens of solid citizens, including two of Chief Sanders's own men, flanking Bullock. When one of the cops, a six-three bruiser who had stopped drinking and undertaken massive renovations of his home since Swoop's arrival, stepped forward, he did not speak merely for himself.

"I took part in this morning's service, Chief. You going to arrest me, too?"

Heavily outnumbered, confronted by an irate group of some of the community's leading members, facing dissension in his own ranks, Chief Sanders appealed directly to Bullock.

"I expect you to come peacefully, Dexter."

"You expect it because you know what we stand for," the lawyer replied. "Tell the mayor we're on our way. Get Pastor Buttle, too. We'll have this out right now."

But even as the conflict seethed within the Hoppo Valley Police Department and among the town's most prominent figures, opposition to Swoop's quest stiffened on the floor in Kansas City.

With eight minutes gone in the half, Swoop's kick-to-the groin play had built our lead to sixteen. He panted, sweat poured off his face and he grimaced against the pain in his knee. But he looked invincible. At this point, Dance Wilkins took a gamble and put Killer back in the game. But perhaps it was not a gamble—for with Killer on the bench, the game was out of hand.

The move paid immediate dividends. Coach Wilkins had Tyrone Gates bring the ball upcourt, starting his offense as far from Swoop's thieving hands as possible. Gates was a slashing penetrator, a great passer and defender but a weak shooter. Too quick for Bobby Stenaker, he shook loose and cut into the lane. But anticipating like a hungry predator, Swoop dropped into the lane, stopping Gates cold. With tremendous body control, Gates braked, avoiding the charge, and kicked the ball back to Street perched beyond the circle. Swoop tracked the ball like he had sonar, leaping in Street's face, swiping at the ball. But panic was an alien emotion in Street's impassive universe. Gripping the ball overhead in two hands, he peered inside for Killer, and finally, the positioning right, he arrowed a taut shot a foot-and-a-half above the rim. Killer went into the stratosphere to grab it, and watched by our interior defenders, came down like a load, slamming it through with two hands.

Maryville was on to something. They had made all of their baskets on slams, and there was no reason to think this would change. Swoop raced the ball upcourt, but Maryville's defense had set up after the basket, and Swoop found himself confronted at the foul line by Street, Gates, Handley and Jackson, circling him like a noose. He rifled a pass to Davy open on the baseline, then broke through the circle, heading for the rim. He was open in the lane, unspotted by Killer, who was going hard for the ballhandler with mayhem in his eyes. But Davy didn't see Swoop either, intent on taking it at Killer. He went up for the lay-up, but Killer soared two feet over him, not blocking the shot, but ripping it out of his hands. In the air, Killer twisted, firing a pass to Gates, who, releasing on Swoop's pass, was already past mid-court. Gates flipped the ball ahead to Jerome Handley, who, outracing even his own guards, roared in for a solo that carried his entire head above the rim.

Swoop flew down-court, in-bounded the ball to Dandy, took the return pass, and rocketed back at Maryville's defense. Again he was confronted by the same quartet of defenders, but this time he took the ball straight up for the first jumper of the game. With Handley and Jackson skying with him, waving their huge fists in his face, Swoop's shot was off, rebounding high over Killer's head. Swoop knifed into the lane, and rising four and a half feet into the sky, ripped down the offensive rebound and spun in on Killer. Everybody pump-faked Killer, nobody took him straight up, so when Swoop went up on him it caught him by surprise. Swoop was over him before he could react, and all he could do was catch him hard with the body. Killer's hip unintentionally swung broadside, catching Swoop's knees in midair. Knocked off balance, Swoop's slam attempt smashed off the rim, bounding past half-court. Swoop hit the deck flat, unhurt, while the ref whistled number three on Killer. Dance Wilkins shook his head as Swoop calmly buried both free throws. Killer stayed in the game.

This is the way the first half went, until the final minutes. Maryville was in offensive gear, getting the ball inside to Handley, Jackson and Killer, who slammed over our earthbound big men, drawing fouls. Protecting his center, Dance Wilkins shifted Jackson into the low post defensively, swinging Killer to the baseline, away from Swoop's lethal thrusts to the rim. It prevented Killer from picking up his fourth while allowing him to terrorize our interior defenders at the other end.

Though Swoop shut down their guards, stealing the ball repeatedly and racing the floor for breakaway slams, our front line wasn't the faintest match for theirs. Their big men played volleyball all night off the offensive glass, especially Handley, who scored on one put-back after another. Swoop scored in every way possible, but the rest of our players were out-gunned and worn down, exhausted well before the half.

Maryville substituted freely, playing nine men, coming at our five in waves. Relentlessly pounding the ball inside, they drew one foul after another on our undersized front court; Davy and Raif each had four; one more and they were gone. But when Coach looked down the bench, all he found were empty spots where his reserves used to sit; shaking his head, he turned back to the game and kept them in.

Two-and-a-half minutes until the half, we clung to a two-point lead, 48–46. Swoop had 32 and assists on all other baskets. Gates, fouled on the drive, was at the line. His free throws could tie. The crowd screamed.

I looked at our guys. Bobby dripped sweat, trying to stay with Gates. Our big men, Dandy and Raif, were bent over, hands on their knees, gasping, as they were at every dead ball. Swoop limped, his face white with strain, but he was among them. He swatted Bobby's butt and threw his arm around Dandy's shoulder. He urged, threatened, exhorted.

"Just two-and-a-half minutes to half," he gasped. "Pour it on!"

Dandy and Raif grimaced, trying to nod, but they were running on fumes. Maryville's fresh troops sensed it, smiling like hunters with their prey in sight. This prey was fighting back—but its claws were dulled in the struggle; it needed reinforcements.

Looking involuntarily toward the Maryville basket, I could see that the captain was still here. But a second later, it became clear that reinforcements were not coming—not for our side anyway. For through the milling sea of excited faces along the baseline— faces with mouths gaping, roaring, chanting—I caught sight of a shadowy figure in white, a fractional glimpse at most, not a clear shot, but more than enough, because I knew he was here, had known all along. Freddie bent briefly, listening to a few words whispered in his ear. Then he backed away.

But as Gates stepped to the line, bedlam erupted behind the Maryville bench. Spectators, bench warmers, even the players on the floor turned and stared as hundreds of fans rose in unison, as if on cue, waving open copies of the Bible in their hands. Their faces were seared from sun and wind. The men wore overalls and workboots, the women floral dresses, and they gazed in unison at a lone figure, their eyes burning, and chanted: "Devil's seed!"

On the court, Gates looked at them, then finally turned away and took a deep breath. But the rest of us had temporarily forgotten the game. Only Swoop seemed oblivious to the ruckus, staring intently at Gates, noting the shooter's body language as he squared up to face the rim. Five hundred strong, the evangelical brigade blared their cry, swinging their Bibles overhead in their left hands, gesticulating at Swoop with their right.

"Devil's seed!"

The arena, now otherwise silent, rocked with their cry, and seventeen thousand fans, previously riveted by the most hotly-contested national championship game in memory, stared transfixed at events occurring in the stands.

From the corner of my eye, I saw Freddie Zender's back as he followed the scrawny figure in white toward the exit, but then my attention shifted to the game.

Despite the resounding racket, Gates drilled the first free throw. We led by one. But Swoop ignored both the game's tension and his enemies' vehemence. Simultaneously relaxed and focused, he held inside position on Handley, and crouched, staring at the placement of Handley's feet, at the angle of Gates's release, judging arc, velocity, spin in one instantaneous calculation. Gates's second shot missed, wide right, and Swoop took one stride to the spot and sprang, snatching the carom a nanosecond before Maryville's predators. But as he floated to the ground, the hundreds-strong revivalist segment let loose a chorus of boos so lusty that it sounded like an echoing clap of thunder. Swoop looked up, momentarily startled, glancing at the stands, trying to recall who they were. Then Gates swiped at the ball and Swoop came back to reality. He darted around the defender and swept up the left sideline.

The jeers of Swoop's foes came with an intensity so great it bordered on loathing. It rocked the arena for several seconds, startling everyone, not just the players. Then from around the stands circling the court, rising like the notes of a hymn from men fighting for freedom, came the cheering, chanting cry of thousands:

"Swoop! Swoop! Swoop!" The sounds ascended as if pouring from the floor, aspiring to go higher, until they reached the ceiling and reverberated back on themselves. Thousands of fans rose, gazing at Swoop's streaking, sweat-soaked figure, their eyes unable to leave the sight of his struggle, but their lungs and throats answering his detractors.

In Hoppo Valley, the cheers washed from the speakers of Bullock's boom box, cradled in the huge paw of Doug Smith, as the members of the Heroes Society, accompanied by Chief Sanders, started up the steps to City Hall. Smith, a construction crew foreman, majoring now in Liberal Arts in the college's Continuing Education program, strode at Bullock's side as they mounted the stairs. He lowered the volume to a whisper as they entered the building. Mayor Pedersson and Reverend Buttle were waiting for them inside. One of the mayor's aides arrived several minutes later.

"I've got to make a phone call," Bullock announced before any of the authorities could speak, and Chief Sanders nodded.

As Bullock left the room, Pastor Buttle—despite the presence of the secular power—assumed immediate control of the meeting.

"Nobody denies the stature of any number of your members," he said. "But running amok in the community is not an accomplishment."

For decades, Whitfield Buttle had stood like a granite pillar of the township, against licentious, undisciplined behavior of all forms. He was tall, with broad shoulders and big-knuckled hands that looked capable of strangling fire hydrants. Though sixty-two years old, he was lean, hard, and, as his wife of forty years liked to say, still at the same weight as he was at sixteen. He rarely carried or read from the Bible, but his demeanor reminded parishioners of an austere Old Testament prophet. Yet, when he smiled, it was with a soft, paternal glow that recalled to them their fathers, and impelled them to reach out their hands for physical contact. He towered in this town—over his flock in physical stature, over the community in spiritual clout.

"I love sports, too," he said. "The quest to win a championship at any level involves hard work, dedication to a goal, teamwork. All good values." He smiled. "And your young basketball star is undoubtedly a precocious, commanding presence." He shook his head. "But there are limits to the degree that anyone may properly challenge the legitimate moral and legal authorities."

When he completed his mini-sermon, the mayor, his aide, then the chief of police took their cues. The message they delivered to the Society's membership was succinct and unequivocal: worship in private, but cease all clamorous demonstrations and involvement in public issues or be prepared to serve jail time. By the time Bullock returned, governmental blows had been landed like body shots.

"What's the score?" Bullock asked.

"You and your group refrain from social activism," Mayor Pedersson said. "Or face the consequences. That's the score."

Several seconds passed. Bullock's voice was barely louder than the radio.

"What does that mean?"

"It means," one of the Society members answered, fists clenched. "That we desist from working for new high school reading lists, for the right of stores and bars to be open on Sunday, for the freedom to show all films, and for the rest of our program—or else they bring us up on charges, under the new law."

Bullock nodded thoughtfully.

"I see."

From the radio, the broadcaster's vibrating voice spat forth the action, his excited words carrying through the air despite the muted volume, describing the drama as, with the score tied and less than a minute till half, Swoop surged up the sideline, whipped a blind shovel pass to Dandy at the line, then cut to the rim. He took the return pass—a BB to the numbers—on the run, and launched immediately into the rafters. But before he could slam it home, the hurtling frame of Jerome Handley inadvertently crashed into his side, sending him pinballing—out of control—through the air. He cartwheeled to the deck at an awkward angle, and landed off-balance on his right leg, twisting his injured knee. With a grimace and a cry, he sprawled forward and lay, momentarily, still. He appeared too exhausted to move, even to react in pain—and for one heartbeat the hush in the arena was complete.

The stillness among members of the Heroes Society at City Hall was identical. Only the Reverend Buttle moved.

"This young man has a brilliant future," he said with genuine concern. "But God shows us all, sooner or later, how much we depend on Him. You're older. Don't let him be led astray."

In Kansas City, Swoop pushed himself to his knees, but seemed incapable of rising further. A number of us on the Hoppo Valley bench stood, but nobody rushed to his aid. After several deep breaths, he reached both hands to the floor and pushed himself upright. A foul on Handley—his second—had been called, and Swoop hobbled painfully to the line, where he drilled both free throws, putting us up two.

Maryville then came down on the last possession of the half and tried to ram the ball inside to Killer on the low blocks. But in the final seconds, Swoop got his fingertips on Gates's bounce pass, and during the wild melee under the basket the buzzer sounded, ending the half. Swoop lay flat where he had dived, half-across the baseline, and though there had been no contact he didn't move.

I walked slowly from the bench, with Coach wheezing behind me. We got our hands under his armpits, hoisted him upright and carted him to the locker room. The fans were hushed.

Swoop collapsed into a chair in the locker room. His right knee was a balloon and his face a contorted mask. I immersed both in ice, and he winced.

"You need to stay off it."

"One more half...you can carry me on your back...for a week."

I nodded.

Coach flopped next to him, his face as white as Swoop's. He said nothing, but his hand rested on Swoop's shoulder. I looked at my watch.

"Kathy's bus is due in the station in six minutes."

"Meet it," Swoop gasped. "Grab a cab."

"But I don't want to miss anything."

"You got to be there. Hurry."

I looked at Coach and he nodded. Though in a hurry, I hesitated. I had information he needed to know, but I couldn't bring myself to tell him.

"Freddie's here," I finally blurted out. "I saw him in the crowd."

Coach's eyes flickered with interest. For years, Freddie had been more than a player.

"Can you bring him here?"

"He left with his mentor," I said, and immediately regretted the tone of harsh sarcasm in my voice.

I saw the look of immense sadness in his eyes, one that included issues and people beyond Freddie. He nodded slowly, almost as if making a point to himself.

"He's crushed by guilt," he said. "Maybe those people who say there's a better faith are right." He closed his eyes. Then he remembered something. "Meet the bus, Duggan."

I bolted for the door. I gave the driver every cent I had and he rocketed through the Sunday traffic. I told him to wait and sprinted into the depot. Kathy's bus was on time.

Her skin was pale, and even the bright luster of her hair seemed somehow dimmed. But her eyes were dry.

"Where is he?" she asked, without greeting.

"The 'where' is not the problem. It's the 'who' you need to worry about."

Her eyes narrowed.

"I haven't seen Bittner around school for several days."

I nodded, and we said nothing else.

We got back to the arena with ten minutes to spare. I left Kathy directly behind our bench, and hustled back to the locker room. It looked like a scene from a combat hospital. Raif Lockett lay sprawled on the floor, unmoving except for his chest gulping huge draughts of air, a small puddle of sweat pooling on the tiles beneath him. Dandy sat hunched on the other side of Swoop, his head between his knees, one hand tight around the side of his chair, the other gripping Swoop's thigh. Swoop lay, rather than sat, in his chair, his red face packed in ice, as was his knee. Swoop's voice, trying to croon his words, was a halting moan, not a song.

"Twenty minutes...we the king. One more half...got the ring."

I sat down next to Coach, and lay my head on his shoulder. In the almost complete silence, all we heard was Raif's breathing and Swoop's broken song. I was still leaning on Coach, when Dandy spoke.

"We bleeding, Swoop. You need rest. What we going to do?"

Raif, still sprawled on the floor, pushed himself onto his elbow and nodded.

"Got no reserves. They're murdering us with fresh troops. What's the scoop?"

Swoop didn't rise from the chair. He pointed to his open locker, to the copy of *The Iliad* lying on top of his clothes.

"Hide yourself and pull your bow," he said, eyes closed, envisioning the scene. "Stand up and fight like a man, and much good will your bow and arrows be."

We stared at him, not one of us moving, and his figure filled our eyes even as the proud words of a wounded Diomedes filled our ears. The scene from Homer's world gripped him, it showed in the lines of his taut frame as he laid it in front of us—the Greek champions, Odysseus and Diomedes, holding back the Trojans,

Diomedes wounded cowardly by an arrow fired from hiding, responding contemptuously. "As Diomedes spoke, Odysseus came and stood in front to protect him, while Diomedes sat down and pulled the arrow through his foot with dreadful pain."

Swoop stopped. In the silence that followed, the only sound in the room beside the players' quiet breathing was the voice of Dandy, repeating, "dreadful motherf—king pain—you got that right." Swoop looked at Coach, and as if by some unspoken message, the rest of us turned to him, as well. The ex-Marine nodded. "That's how wars are won."

No one spoke. We were still silent thirty seconds later when there came a loud knock on the door. Davy staggered off the wall and opened it.

"Two minutes," said a male voice.

Davy shut the door and leaned against it.

Someone banged at the door again.

When Davy opened it this time, two uniformed Kansas City police officers stepped in.

"Peter Betorsky?"

He turned to me gently, and I could see the look of foreboding in his eyes. I pulled back to let him rise, and he got up slowly. The cops turned to him.

"You have a player named Drew Doherty?"

"Had. What about him?"

"Had a car wreck. Drunk. He's in bad shape."

"When?"

"Night before last."

"How is he?"

"The docs say his spinal cord's snapped. He's paralyzed. Chest down. He'll never walk again."

Coach stopped. He said nothing. Everyone in the locker room was still.

"We need to know if he has any family," the cop said.

The hush in the air went beyond silence to breathlessness. I looked around at a row of faces that neither gloated nor grieved. Nor looked shocked. The concern in their eyes was not for Doherty but for Coach. At one time he had possessed a roomful of sons. Now there were few left.

"Any family at all?"

Coach shook his head.

"Not here," he said. But his eyes were closed.

When they left Coach stayed by the door. He stared at the floor and he didn't move.

"Game time!" the male voice shouted.

Coach looked stunned. When he raised his head his glazed eyes told the story. A fighter trying to go the full fifteen, he had taken one shot too many. Doherty may have been like a distant relative, but Freddie was a favored child. Swoop and I started for him but it was too late. By the time we reached the door, Coach's body was on the deck. Swoop hurled open the door.

"Get a doctor!"

He was on his knees by Coach's side as I cradled the big man's head. He was still conscious.

"What a kid," he whispered, looking at me. His hand reached out to grab Swoop's.

"Coach," Swoop began, but Coach cut him off. "He was right...all along..." he gasped the words, looking only at me, as I nodded, holding him, rocking his huge body in my arms. "A national title...and I won't be allowed to...taste it...like Moses..." He shook his head, and even this simple action contorted his face. "He was right..." For the first time he looked at Swoop. "None of this win it for the Gipper crap. Just win it." He passed out.

"Stretcher!" someone called as the doctor in attendance arrived.

"Get an ambulance!" I shouted over the crowd noise. "He needs a hospital."

"Game time, gentlemen!" the usher shouted.

Swoop looked in my eyes.

"Go to the hospital with him."

"No way."

"Digs, he'll die."

"I won't."

He stopped and looked at me. I saw the swallow in his throat. When he spoke his voice was low.

"Being here means that much to you?"

Tears were starting in my eyes.

"You can ask that question after all—"

He grabbed my arm.

"I'm sorry," he said. "You're right. Sure as hell. You're right. Let's go."

I nodded.

The guys were on their feet, heading out, as Coach was carried through the door. Raif was bent over as if he had a knife wound in his side. Swoop threw an arm around him and I threw another.

"You going to make it?" Swoop asked.

Raif's face was as white as Coach's. He looked at Coach being carted off, then at me, then back at Swoop.

"Now more than ever."

Swoop nodded. Together the three of us started for the gym floor.

Maryville had completed its warm-ups and was growing restless as we arrived. They looked at us without curiosity. We didn't look back.

Swoop notified the refs he was running the team in Coach's absence and then inserted K'nada in the starting line-up, resting Raif Lockett and his four fouls.

The crowd, having revived during the half-time breather, quieted as it saw the six-foot Ding Royster shift to forward and the five-seven K'nada Lewis enter the game. When Swoop hobbled painfully onto the floor, they stared. I ignored them and sat on the bench, directly in front of Kathy.

The second half began.

We had first possession and Swoop brought the ball across half-court as Maryville dropped back into a sagging zone, trying to protect its foul-plagued big men.

Swoop cut into the key with a decision to make: he could slash to the rim, initiating an aggression that would endanger our own foul-troubled players or he could back off, selecting a laid-back pace that would protect players on both sides. He didn't hesitate. He drove the ball at back-pedaling Street and Tyrone Gates, as if he would ram it down their throats, and when they collapsed on him in the lane, he hurtled airborne, sliced them sideways and threw up a dazzling underhand scoop. Killer and Floyd Jackson skyed, clawing at the ball, but Swoop arched it way over their outstretched hands, the ball falling gently as a snowflake, kissing the top of the tape before nestling into the twine.

Swoop pointed the rest of our guys downcourt to set up our socked-in zone as Maryville inbounded the ball. Then he turned to the baseline to harass their ballhandlers from end to end. Street flipped it in to Gates and Swoop jumped him, pinning him to the baseline with his quickness, swiping at the ball. Gates whipped it back to Street streaking upcourt, the ball barely clearing Swoop's hands, and Swoop snarled and gave chase. He caught him just past half-court where Street stopped, picked up his dribble and faked the pass high cross-court to Gates. Swoop bit and sprang in Street's face, but Street pulled it down and fired a side-arm bounce pass around Swoop's knee. When Swoop extended his leg in midair, kicking the ball downcourt, the ref called kick ball and Maryville had to take it out on the side.

Swoop was all over Street, leaping, threshing, flailing, and Street faked the pass low, then tried to fire it over Swoop's head. Stretching full-length in the air, Swoop got the side of his hand on the ball, deflecting it across half-court. He, Gates and Street all streaked for it with Swoop getting there first. He scooped it on the run and without a dribble flung himself at the rim. With Street and Gates running at his sides, Swoop threw it down from on high; landing, he crouched at the baseline, looking to steal it again.

"Get it in! Get it in!" Dance Wilkins paced the sideline, waving his big men upcourt to break Swoop's one-man press.

Killer Hayward hustled upcourt and Street drilled the inbounds pass so high over Swoop's head that even Killer skyed to haul it in. Landing just inside half-court, he fired it ahead to Jerome Handley in the offensive end. Swearing, Swoop fired upcourt in pursuit.

Though Swoop hounded their guards mercilessly the entire second half, Dance Wilkins had found the answer. He forbade, except as a last resort, his ballhandlers to dribble. Instead, the ball was to be passed, arcing high toward the ceiling, making their big men elevate and extend. They caught, landed, shot and crashed. Going airborne, with the ball rarely, if ever, touching the ground, Maryville could now simultaneously avoid Swoop's thieving paws and dominate our lead-footed front-court. Scoring on put-backs, alley-oops and turn-arounds, they forced Swoop to become an offensive machine, requiring him to score every time downcourt, just to keep us even. With the precious minutes of the second half draining away, Maryville inched inexorably ahead.

Late in the day, with them clinging to a one-point lead, Swoop brought it up, with Street and Gates swirling on him like flies.

"Now!" cried Dance Wilkins, and Handley charged up the lane, joining Street and Gates, attacking Swoop with a triple team, forcing him to give up the ball. Leaping high, Swoop whipped it to K'nada on the wing as Jackson and Killer dropped into the lane, protecting their exposed middle.

"Shoot!" we screamed from the bench, but the freshman hesitated. Sensing it, Swoop streaked toward him. "Ball!" he called, and just as the trio of defenders moved with him Swoop dropped back toward half-court. For a moment he was open, but as the five-seven guard raised the ball to loop it over the defenders Killer lunged from behind, getting all ball, deflecting it toward the sideline. The ball bounced toward our bench, with players racing for it from every angle. Handley got there first, stretching for it with both hands, but Swoop swept across his bows, a streak of blurred motion, snatched it, flung it backwards into our offensive end, then pitched headlong into the stands.

K'nada's speed ran it down just short of the baseline, where he grabbed it and knifed to the rim. As eighteen thousand spectators rose to watch him challenge Killer, few noticed Swoop emerge from the second row, a gash along his left forehead, blood oozing down his cheek. Killer soared into the rafters, thrashing arms and legs, and K'nada darted under him, came out the other side and rifled a backhand dart to Swoop closing on the right wing. Without a dribble, Swoop sprang and fired, a twenty-five-foot missile that homed on its target as if it were radar-guided. It splashed through the net as Swoop hit the ground, and our bench came to its feet. But one speck of blood dripped from Swoop's cheek, and K'nada had to wrap his arm around his waist and assist him downcourt.

Guys on our bench were up, signaling for time out, but Swoop waved them off. "We got the mo'!" he shouted, then hobbled to pick up Street at the circle.

But as Swoop limped after his man, determined to finish, events were hurtling toward a finish elsewhere, as well. In Hoppo Valley, virtually all residents were listening to the game. When Swoop thrust from the stands, blood dripping, to plunge a twenty-five foot dagger into Maryville's chest, fans who made up a standing room crowd at Bullock's shoved their fists upward and cheered louder than the radio. But when they looked back down, what arrested their attention was not the speakers rocking from the courtside fans' roar—nor the smiling faces of Society members—nor even the banner with the golden emblem flowing above. What pulled the lids of their eyes open wide were the five freshly-shaven young faces, led by a wiry six-six figure in front, staring at them fiercely from the sidewalk adjoining Bullock's lawn.

Janet McMenamin called the Police Department from Bullock's kitchen, but the phone rang several times before it was answered. By the time her message was delivered to Chief Sanders, the ex-basketball player and his cohorts had advanced, unopposed, into the crowd. As she ran out onto Bullock's lawn, they had just started to tear down the banner and to smash the lawyer's speakers.

At City Hall, the mayor had been interrupted just moments before. As he'd neared the end of a long list of terms under which he would refrain from prosecuting, the commotion outside the closed doors of his chambers was the breathless voice of a young woman.

"I don't care if the President of the United States is in there," she had said. "I'm going in."

When the girl—a tousled brunette too slender for her belted raincoat—entered and spoke to Bullock, informing him, "You were right, he wants the story," the mayor had only one question: "Who's she?" The lawyer's response had brought a hush to the room. "A young woman who's just spoken to an associate editor of *Newsweek's* Washington bureau. My assistant, that's who."

It was the insistent ringing of the telephone that distracted the mayor's attention. "Get that," he snapped. "*Newsweek?*" Observers were not sure, in the rush of events, if the color drained suddenly from Mayor Pedersson's cheeks. "What the he...What are you up to, Bullock?" "It's for Chief Sanders," said the mayor's aide, cradling the receiver, but for a moment no one paid him any attention. "It's simple, "Bullock said. "I have a friend—from years ago at Annapolis—works now at the Pentagon, Department of the Navy. Funny, the oath he took to uphold the Constitution must mean something to him. He knows several people at *Newsweek*."

The mayor didn't respond, but Chief Sanders strode across the room and took the proffered phone. "Trouble at your place, Dexter," he announced, and though the lawyer looked stunned, his assistant instantaneously reacted. "Get men there," she said." "We have two men on the way," the chief retorted. "You have more than that," Bullock replied, rousing quickly, motioning to his assistant. "Come on."

They were at the door before the mayor turned.

"Bad publicity from the national press will not intimidate us," he said quietly. "We are committed to what we know is right."

"I know it," Bullock nodded. "I'll see you in court."

"Mr. Bullock!" It was the Reverend Buttle making one last appeal to reach the ungodly. "There are higher courts than those created by man. Consider that your course leads away from Redemption. Christ died for your sins, as well."

Before the lawyer could respond, his assistant stepped back into the room. Her eyes blazed at the minister. "Some of us do not require redemption, Reverend," Patricia Boyle said. "Swoop lives for your virtues, as well."

Then they were gone. The only sound in the room was the muted volume of the radio as the announcer described the final minutes of the national championship game. Doug Smith cranked the volume as the members of the Heroes Society slowly filed out of City Hall—and the broadcaster's voice, tense with pressure, painted a picture: with two minutes and five seconds remaining in a tied game, Swoop brought the ball up the floor, his posture bent, his movements slow.

Maryville had just scored on a rousing two-fisted slam from Killer, precipitating a stomping, roaring chant from the thousands-strong Maryville contingent: "We the champs—Maryville! We the champs—Maryville!" As Swoop approached half-court, another chorus of voices could be heard, adding to the din. "Satan's child! Satan's child!" the evangelical choir cried.

Swoop didn't hear it. He leaned forward, sucking in air, trying to keep as much weight as possible on his left leg. Dance Wilkins, roaming the near sideline, bellowed: "Attack the ball!" Immediately, Street and Gates, who had played but twenty-eight minutes apiece, jumped Swoop, swiping mercilessly at the rock. With two fresh opponents drawing a noose around him, clawing in his face, Swoop didn't have the legs to slice through the trap. He whipped the ball over the heads of his crouching foes to K'nada right of the key. K'nada had the six-six Handley thrashing all over him, so he darted underneath, opening a passing alley to Dandy on the base-line. But Killer and Jackson, rested and ready, formed a defensive wall like the Maginot Line, blocking access to the lane. Dandy had to kick it back to K'nada, and our offense stalled. With a minute fifty-two remaining, thirty-six thousand eyes turned to Swoop.

He was hunched over the left sideline, in front of our bench. It wasn't primarily the hair pasted to his face or the eyes narrowed to slits that I noticed, but the weight balance poised on his flexed left knee, the right toes resting but lightly on the floor, heel up, right leg bent at the knee. As the ball swung around to him on the weak side, I only dimly sensed Kathryn Gately rise to her feet in the seats behind me. I saw nothing but the swollen knee on which he could put no weight.

Swoop jerked the ball from the air with his right hand even as he moved to the left. He took one dribble down the sideline as Street and Gates closed hard from the right. In the instant their momentum brought them to his side, as they still leaned forward, he cut back against the grain. Crouching underneath their swiping claws, he crossed over to his right and slid by the skidding defenders toward the circle. Only one foot touched the floor as he moved.

"He'll hop to the finish," I heard Kathy's wondering words above the sudden roar, as the crowd realized it, too. "He'll hop against the best team in the world." There was a gay quality, almost of relish in her voice, as she said it.

Jerome Handley relished it too, though perhaps for other reasons, as he hurtled toward the key, grinning, intent on slapping down the jumper surely coming. But Swoop thrust upward with head, eyes and shoulders, and when Handley bit, climbing toward the rafters, clawing vainly at the air, Swoop circled him to the right ánd was suddenly open at the line. The two giants held the lane, poised at either side of the paint, towering over the smaller men around them. But the look on each face was a question: would even Swoop challenge their swat unit on one leg?

The answer came immediately. Swoop thrust into the lane and pogo-sticked rimward. Killer got to the hoop first and elevated, with Jackson just a half-stride back. Both swung their mitts high over the iron, eager to cram any lame-duck attempt back down Swoop's throat. Swoop was tangled amidst their wingspan, unable to get sufficient height to jerk clear—but in mid-flight he leaned back at the waist, head and back almost parallel to the floor like an airborne limbo dancer, and squeezed off an arcing floater that spun softly into the sky, barely clearing the clawing fingertips of his foes. The ball kicked off the side of the rim to a hurtling Jerome Handley—and off-balance when he shot and landed, Swoop crashed in a pile, his right leg unable to take the impact. Handley flashed up the floor on a solo while Swoop struggled to his feet under our offensive basket. There was a minute-thirty left.

Handley streaked coast-to-coast for a slam that gave Maryville back a two-point lead. He slapped high-fives with his teammates, and the two thousand Maryville fans stood and chanted: "We the champs!" The evangelical battalion rose and pointed their Bibles at the fallen Swoop.

The attention of most spectators was torn between Maryville's celebration and the gesticulating cries of various factions in the stands, so it was only our players and Swoop's strongest supporters who, watching him rise painfully under the rim nearest the entrance, noticed the dark-suited, middle-aged figure striding purposefully from the doors toward the court. It was only Hoppo Valley residents who recognized that President MacPherson, flanked by two uniformed Kansas City police officers, had entered the auditorium. He clutched an official-looking document in his right fist.

"Hound him!" Dance Wilkins roared, jacket and tie flapping, gesticulating from the sideline.

Street and Gates were on Swoop instantaneously, pressuring the ball, looking to force the turnover that would break our back. Swoop panted, crouched low, straining to find an opening.

I rose from the bench. MacPherson was bellowing at the baseline, waving the legal document at the ref, struggling to make himself heard over the roar of the crowd. I started down the sideline toward him. Kathy barely noticed my movement at first. She stared at Swoop, her hands clenched in fists, as if bottled-up frustration was a threat to explode at any moment. I passed her as, behind me, Swoop faked right, then cut left, diving between the defenders toward the front court and a possible tying basket. Then MacPherson loomed in front of me.

He didn't see me as he screamed at the refs. Like a dispassionate bystander, I walked past him, then reached back with my right arm and hooked it around his throat. I had dragged him four feet away before the startled cops realized what was happening. They came for me with a bound. There was a minute-sixteen left.

Swoop was across half court, his left leg driving like a dynamo, his right barely functioning. Like a cat with only three legs, he was still sufficiently lithe to out-race any normal men. But these were not normal men. Street dived just inside the mid-court line, smacking chin, lips and teeth on the gym floor, extending the full length of his left arm, grazing Swoop's dribble with his fingertips. The ball rolled toward the left sideline, bouncing gently as it carried away the national title. Swoop fell to his knees, then pitched forward, clawing for the ball, as Gates hurtled toward him, jackknifed in a full layout dive. Gates rolled over Swoop, whom he pinned to the deck, and grabbed the rock. From his back near the sideline, he whipped it to Street, who had scrambled to his feet. Maryville's shock troops hurtled into the attack zone.

The cops were one step behind me. The president had twisted

to face me as I carted him off, and his mouth was a contorted snarl. Seeing who it was, he made no reference to administrative power but appealed only to a higher authority.

"God tolerates no interference from sinners," he hissed, his mouth but inches from my ear.

"Admirably exact," I said. "So butt out."

I pushed him to the deck and piled on top. The cops began raining blows on me with their nightsticks, so I hunched my shoulders and gripped him tighter.

The crowd's roar seemed dimmer as Street shoveled the ball to Handley, who exploded over our smaller men for a rim-rocking cram that put Maryville up by four. At the other end, Swoop was still stretched on the floor, unable to regain his footing. There were fifty-six seconds left.

Swoop staggered to his feet.

"Time out! Time out!" the reserves on our bench screamed. But even in pain, Swoop's alertness registered the commotion at the other end. Taking one look, he knew he was out of time. It had to be done now. He waved off the request for time, took the inbounds pass and fired it to K'nada.

"Stay with Swoop!" Dance Wilkins roared from the sidelines.

The defenders ignored K'nada, who raced the ball unimpeded into the front-court. They swarmed around Swoop, willing to let someone else shoot, seeking to deny Swoop a touch. Swoop came slowly upcourt, drawing breath after deep breath, ignoring our reserves on their knees before the bench, imploring him to hurry. He set up in the low post. Street and Gates, with their big men behind them, played in front of him. There were forty-two seconds remaining.

The cops' blows were having a cumulative effect, and I was losing consciousness. The blackness before me was not merely the fabric of MacPherson's jacket, and I could feel the president squirming out of my grasp. Then a blow that was heavier, and yet somehow softer, landed on my back, and I dimly heard a female voice cry, "You'll have to beat me, too!" The repetitive blows that had been driving me into darkness abruptly ceased, and when I realized that Kathryn Gately's body was lying atop mine, I pushed off the bottom of the abyss and slowly began to ascend. Daylight was just ahead of me.

The crowd's roar was growing loud again as K'nada, with a clear look, arced the ball high over the Maryville guards—and as Swoop, drawing a last deep breath, planted both legs beneath him and pushed himself into the sky. Later, he said the pain was so great that for one instant he blacked out, and the ball spinning toward him was a spherical chunk of coal—but all the crowd saw was Swoop shake his head in mid-flight, jerk the ball from the sky and, instead of assailing the giants, arch a shot high over Killer's outstretched reach, three feet over the rim, a gentle rainbow that softly fell, kissed off the tape and snuggled in the twine.

"You're under arrest, kid!" one of the cops roared, twisting both arms behind her back to cuff her. Kathy said nothing, but pressed each knee to my hips and clutched tight with her legs. Holding the president by the neck with one arm, I wrapped the other around her waist. The second cop shoved his nightstick between my arm and her hip and tried to pry her loose. But it would take more than cops to make me let her go. Feeling as if my arm would break, I closed my eyes and held on.

With the attention of the basketball fans riveted on the game, it was the evangelical battalion who first noticed the melee six feet beyond the far basket. Awaiting MacPherson's arrival, spotting the brawling swirl of confusion, they knew it was their cue. They rose as one, hundreds of worshipers, their faces solemn, hard, intent on performing their sacred duty. Clutching their Bibles to their chests, they marched out of the stands, slowly, purposefully, short on time but filled with the dignity of rectitude. They were children of an omnipotent father, and when Kathy grasped my hips with her knees, the leaders of the contingent were but three steps away.

"Get it in! Get it in!" Dance Wilkins screamed above the crowd. He too saw the turmoil, he knew the circumstances, and he feared a riot. He wanted this game done with and his troops safely out of the madhouse, clutching the championship trophy. He eschewed calling time and opted for immediate action.

Street scooped up the ball, stepped out of bounds just feet from where I lay embattled, and rifled it in to Gates. Swoop, at the threshold of a man's ability to withstand pain, chased him on two legs, fighting simultaneously to grab the ball and to hold on to consciousness. He angled Gates off, pinning him to the sideline just across half-court. K'nada darted in low, swiping at the ball, and when Gates tried to go up-top, the taller Swoop got the tips of his fingers on the pass attempt. K'nada, diving, got to the rock a nano-second before the streaking Street, and tipped it to Swoop; who, with blood on his mouth where he'd bitten through his lip, put it on the floor and raced the healthy Gates to our basket. There were nineteen seconds left.

A dozen of the raw-boned farmers shoved their Bibles into their belts, grabbed various limbs of Kathy and mine, and jerked us off MacPherson. They helped the wobbly president to his feet, gently took the court order from his hand, and turned to the police officers. "The anti-Christ must be stopped," one of the leaders said. His humble bearing was an open book of pained sincerity, but as he handed the paper to the closer cop, Kathy stretched her left to the limit of her reach and swiped it from his grasp.

"There are greater men than Christ," she said. "Worship them." Her hair waved as she threw her head back.

Her eyes gazed in the direction of the evangelical leader, but not at him, staring instead over his shoulder, at the hurtling, hobbling figure of Swoop who slashed to the rim just feet from where she stood.

Swoop couldn't elevate. When he pushed off, nothing happened, and he was but inches off the ground, beneath Gates's wingspan, when he transferred the rock from his right and shot it left-handed. He arced it high and soft, banking if off glass, gently to the iron, where it spun wildly in the vortex, then dropped into the net.

"Pressure the ball!" Swoop's words, intended as a rallying cry, came out as a croak, barely audible. Ding and K'nada raced into the back-court, hungry for a strip. Street stole a quick glance at his coach, expecting a signal for time-out, but found something else. Dance Wilkins had spotted a broken-nosed fire plug of a man, dressed in workboots and denim, followed by three hard-eyed companions, making his way toward the fracas under the Hoppo Valley basket. He didn't know Daniel Blaine or the members of the Kansas City Heroes Society—nor was he personally acquainted with the wind-burned dirt farmers involved in the fray—but he did know that if Swoop was banned, especially now, a full-scale riot would ensue. He held unwavering confidence in his men and unquestioning faith in his god.

"One shot!" he bawled, as powerfully as his aching lungs would allow.

Street picked up the rock and fired it toward Gates, who stalked the recesses of the back-court like some creature in a cage. Swoop and his comrades sprang for the ball. There were twelve ticks left on the clock.

A glassy-eyed president and two Kansas City cops just stared as Kathy shoved the paper into her panties under the waistband of her slacks. It was the leader of the evangelical faction who approached her hesitantly, licking his suddenly-dry lips. "I've never hit a woman," he said timidly. "How enlightened!" Kathy gushed. "Don't let me put an end to such a streak of chivalry." But the farmer knew he had no time. As gently as he could, he seized her wrist, and though her knees buckled, she made no move to retrieve the paper. Then Blaine stepped in. "I think you should let her go," he said, his voice soft but carrying clearly. The big farmer released her. "The will of God must be done," he said to Blaine. The union leader nodded. "It is being done. Don't oppose it."

As Ding and K'nada flailed at Gates, Swoop feinted and Gates bit. He fired cross-court to Street and when Swoop, back-pedaling, got his hand in the passing lane, the ball was suddenly loose.

Players swarmed like fliers in an air-raid drill. Ten men and thousands of spectators repudiated the existence of alien entities, seeing only a rotating, leather-covered sphere rolling loose toward our basket. Street got there first and dived. Dandy's body hurtled through the air and Killer was on his hands and knees. Street got his fingers on the skidding ball but it was jarred loose as Dandy crashed on his arm. It rolled to Ding, who scooped it and fired through traffic to Swoop on the sideline. There were four seconds left.

Swoop grabbed and pump-faked, twenty-five feet out on the left side. Defenders clawed from every angle, five maniacs forsaking all others, zeroing in on one target. With three swirling foes airborne, Swoop crouched and put it on the floor. He hurdled Killer, cut to the baseline and ran headlong into the shaven skull of Floyd Jackson. There was no time to maneuver. Braking, knee buckling, falling back, he launched a desperate, last-second heave rimward. Jackson, with a snarl, was on him, lunging fingertips flailing for the ball; then it was beyond him, sailing in slowed-time motion, arcing over his head and his straining reach, until there was nothing before it but the emptiness of space and a single iron cylinder. Eighteen thousand white-faced fans failed to notice Swoop drop to the floor as if he would never move again; they were oblivious to the crash of the final horn; they saw only the rock slide gentle as a kiss to the front of the rim, bound three feet into the sky, then plunge downward to splash like a raindrop in the twine. There was complete silence in the auditorium. Then it erupted like Vesuvius.

People said later that, for thirty seconds, the noise was deafening. They said that, outside on the street and for three blocks away, the crowd's roar could be distinctly heard. They said that when the cheering finally died, the spent crowd was as exhausted as the competitors, that they sank back into their seats, unable to move, and that nobody filed from the arena for a long time. I don't know. I sensed none of it. I neither saw nor heard the activities of the crowd, I didn't know where my teammates were, I didn't even see Swoop stretched unmoving on the floor, surrounded by crouching medical emergency staff. I saw only Kathryn Gately, who stared at me, something deeper, more primeval, in her eyes than the pain of Freddie's demise or the joy of victorious battle—and I knew that something far more important could be won than a national basketball championship for Hoppo Valley.

The police officers took several minutes to recover. When they did, they arrested both Kathy and myself. Cuffed, they dragged us to the station house and charged us with obstruction of justice and resisting arrest. "It's the biggest bust since the French Connection," Kathy murmured as they led us off. The last thing I saw as I was hustled out of the arena was Swoop lifted onto a stretcher, carried by medical personnel. The dark form assisting them, cradling Swoop's head, was the figure of Street.

We spent the night in jail and were released, on our own recognizance, in the morning. Swoop spent two days in the hospital, treated for dehydration, exhaustion and a badly bruised, swollen right knee. Classes continued at Hoppo Valley State College, and we had to get back. But we knew what to expect when we arrived in Hoppo Valley as national champions.

CHAPTER SIXTEEN
THE REDEMPTION

June third dawned with golden rays. The green of the country side lay still, as if avoiding exertion in the face of summer to come. It was two months to the day since our war with Maryville. It was also the day of the Heroes Society's return to the State Hospital.

Our first visit, a week after the title game, on Easter Sunday, had generated excitement across the Valley. Though Nick Bradlee had limited publicity to the hospital itself, word got out immediately and was blared to the general populace by both local radio and *The Independent*. When we arrived, there had been sixty people waiting outside, clamoring to get into the closed service. Swoop insisted that our observance be scheduled at the same time as the Easter service of the Campus March for Redemption. Before fifteen patients in the chapel, the Christians spoke of Christ's suffering and death on the cross. Before one hundred patients in the auditorium, the Heroes spoke of Swoop's triumph and achievement in the championship game. When we left, the hospital administrators gave us permission to replicate the service for the crowd outside in the parking lot. Ten days later, they invited us back. Swoop confronted me a week before our return.

"You've never been the featured speaker at a Heroes Society service."

"I know it."

"Don't you think it's time? Especially there."

I could feel my eyes glinting to match his.

"Yes," I said.

The kids were excited when we got there. Some were crippled, some had diseases, all were orphans. But they lit up like a nighttime skyline when Swoop strolled in.

"Swoop! Swoop! Swoop!" they chanted.

We met them in the gym. After our first visit, Swoop had taken thousands from his winnings and bought new sets of weights and exercise equipment for the hospital. But mostly he bought books—hundreds of copies from every era and culture on earth; they had only one theme in common: all were tales of individuals, male or female, pursuing some treasured goal in the teeth of daunting opposition. He had the hospital staff shelve the books in the gym.

"Is this the meaning of your life—helping others?" I had asked, only half joking.

"I like to help others," he answered simply. "But only when they want to help themselves."

Now, he read to them a scene from Dumas, in which Edmund Dantes, against staggering odds, escaped from the impregnable Chateau D'If. Then he, Bullock and I supervised through a short series of exercises, taking the time to work, not in groups but individually. Then Swoop ascended to the podium which had been mounted on risers at one end of the gym.

"I'll make this quick," he said. "Only one thing matters in the whole world: your life. I'm going to turn this over to the man who knows more on this subject—and who's done more—than anybody I've ever met. A man who, from dawn to dawn, works harder than anyone, and who is an inspiration to all who have the good fortune to know him. My comrade, colleague and dearest friend, Duggan Claveen."

As I walked, dazed, to the podium, with the children cheering, the only thought that filled my mind was that I had never before heard Swoop utter the name "Duggan." When I stood before the throng and saw Swoop take a seat in the last row, it hit me that I had no prepared text. But then, my whole life was preparation. The signs held by several children, reading, Hoppo Valley State College: National Champs, told only part of the story. I smiled at them, remembering the rest.

"To the victor goes the inwardness of his triumph," I said quietly to the prospective heroes stretched out before me. "To the loser goes a crown of thorns. And forlorn hopes of beatitude beyond the grave."

Coach had died in the hospital without regaining consciousness. He never knew that we were national champions.

"His soul knows," one of the attending ministers said to us in consolation as we left the graveside after the funeral. I looked straight ahead, and felt, rather than saw, Swoop stiffen. When he stopped, the clergyman had to halt and turn back.

"With due respect, Reverend, that was the problem. Coach only wanted what was gone—so he lost what was left."

In the silence that followed, I noticed that Swoop's hands were balled into fists. He was angry, the tense lines of his posture proclaimed it, but not at any individual, at something far more tenuous and elusive. He relaxed his hands slowly, as if on cue, and when he walked silently away, the rest of his teammates joined him, walking stiffly, with sad dignity. The minister watched our receding backs.

"Stand by the things you love!" I boomed from the podium, getting warmed up. "No matter who stands in the way."

The administration had expelled me on my return to Hoppo Valley. They'd brought assault charges against me and appealed the athletic association's ruling. They dropped the criminal case when the publicity evoked a firestorm of criticism from Swoop's supporters nationwide. But nobody could manhandle the president. They canned me.

I didn't protest. I had known the risks. I packed my bags and prepared to leave.

Kathryn Gately told the academic dean that he had to expel her too. When he refused, she quit. Several students joined her.

When Swoop called Westegaard, *The Independent* made it a cause celebre—and the campus paper followed. Parents of several dozen of my classmates flooded the switchboard with calls. Several local businesses, team backers, vowed to withdraw their support of the school. Zatechka now referred to "Dark Age U."

But it was the internal struggle that threatened to tear the institution apart. Several key administrators had walked out in protest of MacPherson's stand. While the president's office tried desperately to fill those positions, two of the disgruntled former administrators, in conjunction with both prominent members of the Heroes Society and several affluent and influential team boosters, exerted pressure equally desperate on the Board of Trustees to axe MacPherson and replace him with an educator more amenable to the new fervor sweeping the Valley.

Swoop didn't say a word.

He collected funds from the trust Jumbo held for him, purchased tickets and flew us both to the east coast. In a whirlwind we visited Princeton, Yale and Harvard in three days. Swoop gave them the full story and left out nothing. They pulled out my transcript and essays. They blinked. The admissions office of each school upheld my acceptance. We flew back to Hoppo Valley.

The athletic association denied the school's appeal. Coach's decision was upheld; Swoop's participation was allowed; the results stood. But MacPherson was uncompromising: the school would refuse the championship. The dissension in the ranks exploded into all-out war. More than twenty administrative support personnel went out on strike, effectively shutting down the university. Several key faculty members refused to teach, and dozens of alumni banded together, contacting the Board of Trustees with the non-negotiable message that not a penny more would they contribute until and unless sweeping changes were made. Kathryn Gately wrote scathing letters to every national news publication and *Time* printed one.

When reporters from *The New York Times* and the TV networks hit town, continuing their coverage of religious unrest in the national's vitals, some locals relished it and some cringed. When the national media lashed Hoppo Valley's archaic ethical teachings and made comparisons to Dayton, Tennessee and the Scopes trial, members of both the city council and even the state legislature panicked. They pressured the school to reconsider its stand and re-admit its finest student.

President MacPherson stood on his principles and refused to comply. Two members of the Board of Trustees—ardent supporters of our championship quest—protested bitterly. Acrimony reigned among the schools' leaders—debate raged in the city council—and Westegaard's editorials in *The Independent* called upon thinking citizens to align themselves with the members of the Hoppo Valley basketball team whose accomplishments remind us how much is possible.

Under increasing pressure to reverse his stand, President MacPherson took the only step possible: he resigned rather than knuckle under. He refused, he said, to be party to the spread of irreligious doctrines through the community he loved and served. One of his administrative assistants, the chaplain and the dean of student life joined him.

The Board of Trustees accepted their resignations and immediately appointed interim directors. Their first act was to re-admit me. Their second was to state publicly that Swoop was not suspended from the basketball team and that the national championship was ours. They placed under study the school policy prohibiting outside gambling.

I said nothing just as I had taken no part in protests or demonstrations. I had not interrupted my studies. I returned to class and crushed my final exams.

"A life of *purpose!*" I roared to the children in front of me. "Of passionately-held, relentlessly-pursued personal loves. This is the good life."

Swoop was already seeking another title. After our return from Kansas City, he had kept his word: we held midnight vigils before the school's trophy case, sitting in the darkened lobby, lighting candles, silent, staring at the championship statue. After we received our commemorative rings, some of the team's backers held a quiet, dignified dinner for us at the town's most exclusive restaurant. Swoop's finger was the only one bare. His ring was a thousand miles east, hanging around the neck of a slender brunette, and he sat through the affair with a smile lightening the corners of his eyes, sipping a glass of sparkling water.

He hadn't seen her. She had returned to her classes before his triumphant arrival in Hoppo Valley. But Bullock, eager for her continued assistance, had bought her a fax machine and a mobile phone, and she remained in his employ. Swoop didn't hear from her, except for one call in which she demanded the championship ring; which he shipped to her the next day. Nobody on the outside knew what it meant, but when Swoop sent the package, he addressed it to: Patricia Boyle—Crusader.

Two days after the dinner, he started us on our preparations to repeat. He got the entire squad to spend the summer in Hoppo Valley. The cases against Raif, Davy and Dandy had been resolved quickly. Charges against Dandy had been dropped when several witnesses swore that it had been self-defense. Raif had been convicted of buying for a minor and Davy of driving under the influence. Davy's license had been revoked, and both had been sentenced to perform sixty hours of community service. Such activities as Heroes Society services at the State Hospital counted. Several players would attend summer school, most would work, but all would be here to continue the brutal workouts that had made us champions.

In the early morning, before class or work, the players focused on upgrading individual skills. Under Swoop's supervision, Bobby worked on his left-hand dribbling, Dandy and Davy concentrated on their perimeter shooting, Raif toiled at getting inside rebounding position, and so on. In the evenings, they scrimmaged for hours, working as a team, perfecting their fast break and honing a pressure defense.

The entire team had attended my graduation.

"We must fill our lives with the things—and the ones—we love! Nothing has weight but these!"

The same faces were sprinkled through the audience now, gazing at me as raptly as they had a week earlier at commencement, several sitting as they had then, on their hands, to suppress the urge to applaud. I had graduated summa cum laude, as valedictorian, with my parents beaming in the front row of family members. Afterward, they had hugged and congratulated me, and I lapped it up hungrily. My father, as ever, had little to say, but the look of respect in his eyes was enough from this man whose work ethic I so admired. But still, after they had left, I remained with my real family, with the same pairs of hard eyes that glinted at me now.

"Whether it's wisdom or basketball, money or art, home or career, a man or a woman—or all of the above—we must fill our lives with the things we love!"

My muscles ached pleasantly from a pre-dawn workout with Swoop; I felt them ripple under my clothes with every movement. In an inner pocket, next to my chest, lay my acceptance letters from Princeton, Harvard, Yale. These things didn't stand out now, not because they didn't matter but because they were so much of my essence that I didn't have to be conscious of them.

"Never—not for anything or anyone—betray the things you love!"

Not every member of the team was present. Missing was Freddie's face, Coach's bulk. Not here to observe these holy days.

Freddie had returned only briefly to Hoppo Valley to withdraw from school. He attended Coach's funeral, dressed in black, accompanied by Judas Bittner. He didn't speak to Swoop or to me, and only briefly to Kathy. He had penance to do, he said. Then he dropped from sight. Word around town by late May was that he had joined the First Commandment Church's global mission and was on his way to the jungles of Guatemala. Determined to live, I bit my lip and pressed on. But honesty compelled me to acknowledge the pain. I missed them.

"Send the death peddlers packing!" I urged, tears stinging the corners of each eye. But I shed no tears for one other who was missing. Drew Doherty was paralyzed permanently from the nipple line down. He would spend the rest of his life in a wheelchair. In a drunken stupor after his excommunication from the team he had smashed his rented car into a semi at a Kansas City intersection. Shortly after his return to Hoppo Valley following his release from a Kansas City hospital, he had found God. Or rather God had found him. Judas Bittner had been waiting, ready for a soul screaming in its night of torment. The hardened heart of the sinner melted in the forgiveness of Christ. Doherty broke down in tears—he found the strength to hurl his wasted frame from the wheelchair—he writhed sobbing on the ground. "It's a sign," Bittner said. The members of the Mission clasped their hands. Doherty dropped out of school—he gave up criminal justice, his major—he devoted his life to the Mission. Late at night you could find him in the bars, broken and crumpled, crying his warning against the sinfulness of man. His mentor, garbed in a tattered monk's robe, pushed the wheelchair; a half-smile softened his mouth. Doherty avoided his former teammates.

"No one can tell a man of purpose that he's sinful or unfit!" I cried from the podium.

But the words were released as they were spoken, for negative truths could not animate me. Not when a tall redhead sat in the front row gazing at me, not like Beatrice at Dante, but like Penelope at the conquering Odysseus. Though I hadn't touched her, this relentless scholar looked at me with burning eyes torn not from a classroom, but from a less public, far more private room. Tonight, I knew, would be the first. Tonight. The sacredness of this could not be communicated to those clinging to sacrilegious creeds.

"Answer them loud and clear"—I trumpeted my theme—"that only one thing is moral: to live!"

More and more residents were deciding they wanted to. Funds had rolled in for the construction of a temple for the Heroes Society. Swoop shelled out a hefty amount, affluent members matched it, and others kicked in as best they could. People across the Valley dug deeper into their earnings, and a group of high school students even contributed a few dollars apiece, accompanied by a note stating, "A donation from heroes of all ages."

At the same time, chapters of the Society were formed at both the high school and the State Hospital. Gwen O'Neill, the founder at the hospital, was a fifteen-year-old orphan, who read voluminously, broke every rule of the institution, and, when not receiving rewards for academic excellence, was ceaselessly punished for willful disobedience. She had demanded more laboratory equipment—for by age thirteen she had already determined she would be a biologist—and raised holy hell when the hospital didn't provide it. "This girl's either a high achiever or a lawbreaker," the hospital administrator told Bullock. "Maybe she'll be both," the lawyer answered approvingly.

The fund-raising for the temple may have cut into Janet McMenamin's drive to generate money for the abortion clinic, but she had the solid support, not only of the area's medical community but, generally, of the town's most educated, affluent citizens. Her comrades in the Heroes Society lobbied for her in a ceaseless campaign that generated publicity as well as contributions. However, much to Dr. McMenamin's disappointment, the area's zealots, abashed somewhat by the Swoopian furor sweeping the town, left her alone. By late spring it appeared that, come fall, Hoppo Valley might be unrecognizable to people who were used to its traditional culture.

Mayor Pedersson, never one to back off regarding a matter of principle, continued to prosecute his case; but the "anti-hero resolution" had become increasingly unpopular among both members of the city council and the general populace. Bullock had no doubts regarding the outcome in court, and the mayor's stand against the new ideals sweeping the area would hurt him in November.

"The richness of a full life," I concluded to utter hush, "is the only sacred truth."

In the end, as at the beginning, he was there, an inescapable presence and anchor in my life. Two points in the crowd filled me, arcing me back and forth in an endless circle that completed my existence. One was the pair of eyes searing me from the back row; the other was my redheaded Penelope in front.

To say they were mine would have trivialized the truth by stating that which had no need to be stated. Given what they were, they had to be mine.

There is a law of gravitation in psychology as well as in physics. Those aching to climb set themselves apart in the striving, not by talent but by will. Truly, mankind is carried higher by a select few. Most let themselves be carried. Some try to cripple the carriers.

Clearly, I saw with whom I belonged, and knew the pride of Odysseus returning home. I, too, had the heart of a pagan.

THE AFTERLIFE

In the end, the shadow was dispelled from the Valley. Ignorance was supplanted and superstition lost its hold. The residents walked with straightened spine, and a heavy burden had been lifted.

A new structure was erected in the Valley, by a denomination more enlightened. The structure rose high in limitless aspiration, constructed solely of glass; it sat amidst the green grass, the hills and the lake outside of town, inviting the sun's rays to penetrate it, as if to possess a panting lover.

In the dawning day, the residents found the path they had lost. They needed neither shepherd nor flock for they had rediscovered a sacred truth: the internality of their own compass. They came together every week, on the sun's day, to celebrate the blessedness of this.

Boldness was the virtue most prized, and audacity the order of the day. Quenchless ambition reigned—and in their homes, on the walls overhead, as an anthem and a beacon, stood the words, "Swifter, Higher, Stronger." At the State Hospital, many gathered—to help the sickly get strong. The formerly-sick uttered the only words necessary—"Thank you"—then left behind those who had aided them.

Shrines were erected in each man's life, as he pursued his consecrated dreams. And though the messiah left in due time, he remained ceaselessly behind; the residents had no need of him, for they were become him.

And the Valley shined as an inspiration, for those who had eyes to see.

EPILOGUE

Some say there are no gods, that humankind exists in a vacuum, devoid of spirituality. Some say god hates man, abjures a being stained with sin. Many believe god loves this being, but favors the meek, the weak, the sick, the lame.

But some hold that god is not to be sought in another realm, or even high above. Some laugh at sin and deride the priests who spawn it. Some live the creed that their birth was free of moral taint. A few teach this truth to others. Some are born knowing to consecrate the best within themselves. Some endure the writhings of hell to learn it.

Some reject the gods. Others reject them in the act of embracing false ones. Many yearn for god without realizing their own hunger. Some search. Only a few know that the divine is not to be sought—that it is already theirs.

Printed in the United States
18844LVS00001B/198